W9-CBG-696

FEB 0 0 2018

SUN
WARRIOR

ALSO BY P. C. CAST

P. C. CAST

SUN WARRIOR

Tales of a New World

WEDNESDAY BOOKS
NEW YORK

SUN WARRIOR. Copyright © 2017 by P. C. Cast. Illustrations copyright © 2017 Sabine Stangenberg. All rights reserved. Printed in the United States of America. For information, address St. Martin's Press, 175 Fifth Avenue, New York, N.Y. 10010.

www.stmartins.com

The Library of Congress Cataloging-in-Publication Data is available upon request.

ISBN 978-1-250-10075-7 (hardcover)
ISBN 978-1-250-16489-6 (international, sold outside the U.S., subject to rights availability)
ISBN 978-1-250-10077-1 (ebook)

Our books may be purchased in bulk for promotional, educational, or business use. Please contact your local bookseller or the Macmillan Corporate and Premium Sales Department at 1-800-221-7945, extension 5442, or by email at MacmillanSpecialMarkets@macmillan .com.

First U.S. Edition: October 2017

First International Edition: October 2017

10 9 8 7 6 5 4 3 2 1

This book is lovingly dedicated to my Companions—some who are still with me and some who have gone ahead: Badger, Cammy, Chloe, Kirk, Khan, Claire, Kimmy, Khaleesi, Patchy Poo the Pud, Tiberius, Peechia, and Xena Warrior Princess Cast. I will always hold you close in my heart.

ACKNOWLEDGMENTS

Thank you to my wonderful agent and friend, Meredith Bernstein, for your support and your belief in me.

As always I send a big I HEART YOU to my brilliant editor, Monique Patterson. Thank you for your crazy brainstorming skills and for helping to make this the best book it could be!

I appreciate my St. Martin's Press family! Sally Richardson, Jennifer Enderlin, Alexandra Sehulster, Brant Janeway, Jessica Preeg, the production staff, marketing team, and cover artist. GO TEAM CAST!

I love hearing from my fans and have especially enjoyed that this series has inspired so many of you to share pictures and stories of your beloved Companions with me. You make me smile!

Thank you to my friend Teresa Miller, for her unchangeable support and her words of wisdom. I love you, Tess!

I appreciate my father, Dick Cast, and his expertise in biology and botany. Thank you, Mighty Mouse, for answering my crazy questions and helping me to create awful, awesome, weird creatures, plants, and people to populate this new world!

And last, but eternally first in my heart, thank you Kristin Cast, for your support and love. Mommy—Baby! Now, let's luncheon!

SUN
WARRIOR

CHAPTER 1

The world was smoke. Like winter fog in the pine forest, it thickened the air, roiling around and over Mari and Nik. The choking smoke blanketed and then cleared as the pernicious wind lifted and fell while thunder echoed in the distance, teasing them with the possibility of rain.

"There!" Mari pointed. "We are almost at the shore. I can see it when the wind shifts."

"Can you tell if we can beach the boat, or is it still too rocky?" Nik said between heavy breaths. He didn't look up but kept stroking powerfully against the turbulent current. A big Shepherd lay as close as he could get to Nik, watching him with wise amber eyes shadowed with sadness.

"Yes, it's more mud than rocks and there's a bunch of scrub brush, but that should be good for hiding the boat," Mari called to Nik. Beside her, a young version of the adult Shepherd pricked his ears at the shoreline and then sneezed heartily. Mari smiled at her Companion and ruffled his ears. "I know, but the worst of the smoke is over there." She jerked her chin to the south. Then she glanced over her shoulder at the young man who was struggling so earnestly to row them to shore. "Nik, do you really think we should land here? We're still awfully close to the fire."

He didn't pause in the rowing but looked up at her, grim-faced and drenched with sweat. His eyes met hers. She hated the sadness she saw there—hated it because she understood it so well. He'd lost his father hours ago. She'd lost her mother weeks ago. Perhaps in the not too distant future they could mourn together—heal together. Right now their shared misery was no help at all, especially with the danger that surrounded them—as thick and cloying as the smoke that filled the air.

"I'm sorry, Mari," Nik said. He hesitated and then blurted, "I'll jump out here. The current will take you farther downstream—farther away. Laru can stay with you and Rigel. I'll find the three of you when this is over."

Mari blinked in surprise. As she understood what he had to mean, she shook her head back and forth, back and forth. "No, Nik. You can't—" she began, but he dropped an oar and reached forward and grasped her hand, cutting off her words.

"I have to. I have to go to my people. There might be something, anything I can do to help."

"And you might get killed! It would be a simple thing for Thaddeus to use the confusion of the fire to put an arrow in your back," Mari said. "You can't help any of them if you're dead."

"Thaddeus will be too busy trying to save our city from the fire to bother with me. But I'll watch my back," Nik assured her.

Mari closed her eyes, calming her emotions. She wouldn't imagine what might happen to Nik. She wouldn't let herself be overcome with fear for him. She wouldn't be a liability. She opened her eyes and met his gaze.

"Take Laru. I trust him to watch your back, especially when you're too busy to keep an eye out yourself." She smiled bravely at Nik and the big Shepherd, Laru, who leaned against his side.

"I don't know if he's well enough. I haven't checked to see if his paws are burned. I can see that some of his fur was scorched, which doesn't seem too bad, but I really don't want him to travel on—" Laru's impatient bark interrupted Nik as the big Shepherd stared at the shore, seeming to will it closer.

Mari forced her tone to be light, almost kidding. "See, he's on my side. No way is he going to let you go back there by yourself."

"All right then. I'll get us to shore."

Nik bent his back to the job of rowing, propelling them toward the muddy bank, and Mari put her arm around her Companion—the son of adult Laru—drawing comfort and strength from the bond that joined them for life. She understood Nik's need to go to his people, to try to save as many of them as possible from the terrible forest fire that was devouring their beautiful City in the Trees, but she hated the danger it put him in. Mari hugged Rigel to her. *I've just found Nik. I can't lose him—not after losing so much so recently.* Rigel whined softly and licked her cheek as the little boat ran aground.

In an instant Nik jumped from the boat and was dragging it up on the mud and rocks. Laru and Rigel followed him as he helped Mari clamber onto the bank.

Hand in hand and flanked by the two Shepherds, they climbed up the bank to find a small deer path that snaked along the lip of the Channel. They stood, hands clasped, as Nik caught his breath and stared up the path as if he was trying to see through the enveloping smoke to the burning city.

"I'd go with you if you asked me to," Mari said softly, drawing Nik's gaze.

"No!" he almost shouted before he steadied himself and continued in a more reasonable tone. "No, Mari. They might try to blame you for the fire."

Mari frowned. "But I didn't start it. I didn't have anything to do with those cages catching fire."

"I know that. You know that. But I can promise you Thaddeus will be spreading a different story. I'll make sure the truth is known, but not now. Not today while we're battling a forest fire. And there was also the figure in the smoke."

Mari's eyes widened in surprise. "You *did* see it, too."

Nik nodded. "It seems almost like a dream now, but I swear I saw the smoke and fire take on the form of a woman."

3

"Not a woman," Mari corrected. "A Goddess."

Nik lifted a shoulder restlessly. "Okay, a Goddess. Maybe. You're the Goddess expert, not me." He tempered his words with a gentle curiosity instead of the accusation Mari had feared.

"It isn't me who is the expert. It was Mama. The Great Earth Mother has never spoken to me—never even seemed interested in me."

Nik's smile was poignant. "She was interested today. She saved you."

"Us," Mari said firmly. "If it was the Goddess, and not just a trick of smoke and fire forming a strange image; then she saved the four of us. Maybe—maybe she'll do it again. Maybe I should come with you and help you try to save your people."

"No," he repeated. "There are too many ifs and maybes. I won't risk it. I can't—" Nik began, and then broke off when his voice began to shake. He drew a deep breath and wiped sweat from his brow before continuing. "I can't let anything happen to you, Mari. Do you understand?"

"I do," she reassured him. "I understand completely."

"Good." He breathed more easily, his shoulders relaxing. "Laru and I will go, and when we've done all we can to help we'll come to you at your burrow."

"Please, please be careful," she said.

He touched her chin, lifting her face so that their eyes met. "You do know why I have to go, don't you?"

She nodded, blinking hard against threatening tears. "Your friends are there. O'Bryan and Sheena. You have to try to save them."

His smile was slight and sad. "Yes, but not just them. Mari, many of my people are good. I know it doesn't look like it from where you stand, but it—it's like your friend Sora."

"Sora? What do you mean?"

"Well, when I met Sora she wanted to kill me, or at least let me die of my injuries, just because she saw nothing but an enemy. It was only later that she saw *me*. I'm asking you to understand that it's the same with my people. Trust me, Mari. Please."

Mari drew a deep breath. "I trust you. Remember, you can count on me—and Rigel—to have your back. Save your friends, Nik. And then return to me."

"I will, Mari. I give you my oath."

Nik framed her face with his hands and pressed his lips to hers. Mari tasted smoke and sweat and sadness in his kiss. She clung to him, willing strength to flow into him, to bolster him, to bring him home to her.

"I accept your oath," she said as she broke off the kiss and hugged him close. "I'll be waiting for you."

Nik held her for another moment, and then he released her, turned, and with Laru at his side sprinted down the path, disappearing into the smoke and the trees.

At her side, Rigel whined softly as he stared after Nik and Laru, and Mari knelt beside him, putting her arms around the big pup's sable-colored neck and pressing her cheek against his thick, soft fur. "I know, I know. I'm worried about them, too. But Nik's right. It'd probably do more harm than good for us to go with him. Plus, we need to get back to Sora. If the wind shifts in the wrong direction that fire could spread into our territory. Also, we need to find the women freed from Farm Island. They'll need our help." She squeezed her Shepherd again and kissed the top of his head before releasing him. "All right, let's get going."

Nik paused as he and Laru stepped into a stream that was close enough to the City in the Trees to be familiar, even in a world that had turned dark and smoke shrouded. He ripped a strip of cloth from his tunic and dunked it in the water, thoroughly soaking it while he splashed water quickly over himself.

"Laru, lie down here. Soak yourself. We're going to need every advantage we can muster against that fire."

Obediently, the big Shepherd entered the stream, lying to submerge all but his nose, his eyes, and the tips of his sable-colored ears.

"Good. You're a good, smart boy. I love you, Laru. I love you," Nik murmured, taking a moment to stroke Laru's head affectionately. The

Shepherd met his gaze, and Nik felt the weight of their new connection as sadness, regret, and pure, unconditional love flowed from the big canine into him. There, in the middle of the cleansing stream, Nik knelt beside Laru and looked into his intelligent amber eyes. "I miss him, too. I'll always miss him."

Nik fought against debilitating despair. Just a few hours before, his father, Sol, Sun Priest and Leader of the Tribe of the Trees, had stood strong and proud with his Companion Shepherd, the Tribe of the Trees Alpha canine, Laru, by his side. He'd faced Thaddeus and Cyril and spoken against the Tribe's prejudice and ignorance and for Mari and releasing the Earth Walkers his people had enslaved for generations.

Sol had been brave and wise and had done what he knew was right. Without a moment's hesitation he had saved Mari's life, though it had cost him his own.

Nik thought he'd replay the scene forever in his memory—Thaddeus raising the crossbow to aim at Mari, Sol shoving Mari out of the way so that the arrow meant for her pierced his heart instead. And then the fire devouring the dock, the floating homes, Nik's father's body—and almost, too close to almost, devouring Laru as well.

Nik gently lifted the canine's head in his hand. Laru's muzzle was beginning to be flecked with silver, but the mature Shepherd's body was massive and strong. His coat was thick and glistened with health. He was just entering the prime of his life.

"Thank you for choosing me. Thank you for not dying with Father." Nik spoke softly, earnestly. His voice shook and tears leaked slowly down his cheeks. His earliest memories were daydreams of the Shepherd who would one day choose him as a lifelong Companion—a choice that couldn't be manipulated, predicted, or changed. In recent years he'd hoped that one of Laru's pups would choose him—had actually believed for a while that Rigel was going to choose him.

Nik had never, for so much as a brief heartbeat in time, thought that Laru would outlive his vibrant, healthy father and choose him as Companion.

"To be chosen by a Shepherd was all I ever dreamed about. Now that it's happened I'd give it back—I'd give it all back if Father could be alive." Canine and human bowed their heads together and shared a moment of loss and misery. It was Laru who pulled them out of their despair. Abruptly he stood, shaking water from his fur. He bounded from the stream and onto the path that would lead them to their Tribe, looking back at Nik and adding an encouraging bark to the flood of love and reassurance he sent his new Companion.

Nik stared into Laru's eyes and saw a future there—a future formed from the ashes of an old, cast-aside life—a future that could be brighter than his father's sun, *if* he had the strength to rise from the rubble and rebuild.

A vision of Mari's steady gray eyes flashed before him, and he knew he *had to* be strong enough. For his father and Laru, for Mari and Rigel, even for himself, Nik had to be strong enough.

Silently he pledged to himself and his new Companion, *I am strong enough!*

"All right, we can do this!" Nik wrapped the sodden strip of cloth around his neck, tying it so that he could lift it over his nose and mouth, and then he followed his Shepherd.

They jogged steadily on. The wind had risen again, and with it came the teasing boom of distant thunder. Nik joined Laru, who was waiting for him on a rise in the path. Breathing hard, the two of them paused. At that moment, the wind whined ominously and changed direction.

At first Nik was relieved as the smoke was blown away from them. He and Laru drank in gulps of cool, clean air, and then Nik's breath caught in his throat as the smoke continued to part, revealing a city ablaze in the trees. The northernmost section of their city was completely engulfed in flame. He could see that the Tribe had managed to fell several of the largest and most ancient of the trees—ones filled with the exquisite nests his people called home—attempting to make a break in the path of the encroaching fire. And it had seemed to work, especially as the wind had shifted and was blowing away from the heart of the city.

But already the Tribe had paid an unthinkable toll.

"No," Nik whispered brokenly. "No," he repeated as he dropped to his knees in sick despair, sobbing impotent tears while he watched fire destroying his people and the only home he'd ever known.

Laru pressed against him. Nik put his arm around the big canine, finding comfort in his nearness—grounding himself with his Companion's strength and love.

"I have to stop it, Laru. Somehow I have to stop it!"

Laru whined sadly, and then he, too, rallied. He barked sharply and moved out of Nik's embrace, padding a few feet farther down the path before stopping to look expectantly back at his Companion.

"You're right, big guy. I can't stop anything here on my knees."

Nik sprinted forward, Laru at his side. Within minutes he was met by soot-stained, frightened members of the Tribe fleeing for their lives. Some of them were burned. Some were bruised and broken. They trudged on blindly as if their souls had been consumed by the blaze behind them.

"Nik! Oh, God, Nik. You *are* alive." A woman staggered to him. Automatically he took her elbow, though he didn't recognize her through the soot and sweat until the Shepherd at her side greeted Laru.

"Sheena! You and Captain made it. Have you seen O'Bryan? Is he okay?"

"When I last saw him he was alive." Sheena nodded, struggling to catch her breath as more and more of the Tribe, moving as if they were sleepwalking through a nightmare, passed them. "But he went back into that." She made a weak gesture behind her at the blazing forest. "He said he heard Fala's pups crying. He said—he said he was going to save them," she sobbed. "How is he going to do that? How is anyone going to be saved from that inferno?"

Nik grabbed both of her shoulders and forced her to look into his eyes. "Sheena, you have to breathe and calm down. Now. These people need you."

Sheena ran a trembling hand across her filthy face, wiping away sweat and tears and soot. "Okay. Yes. You're right." She nodded shakily. Then her gaze locked on Nik as if he was her lifeline. "What can I do?"

"You're going the right direction. Keep following this path back to the Channel. If the wind shifts again this whole forest will catch. The Channel is your only hope."

"But so many of them are hurt. There aren't any supplies at the Channel. How am I supposed to help them? Nik, I don't think any of the healers made it out alive. They refused to abandon the patients in the infirmary who couldn't be moved. I heard them screaming. I think I might always hear them screaming."

Nik shook Sheena's shoulders. "Stop it! Stop thinking about it. There are extra supplies at the lookout platform closest to the Channel—you know that. Go there. If the Healers are dead, then we'll have to stand in their place."

"Where's Mari? She's a Healer. She can help. And Sol? Where's our Sun Priest?"

Nik made sure his voice was calm and strong. "Mari had to go back to Earth Walker territory. And Sol is dead."

Sheena's head shook back and forth. Her eyes were wide and filled with shock. "Sol dead? No. No, it can't be. Even our sun has turned against us!"

"Sheena, listen to me. What's happening here has nothing to do with our sun. It has to do with men and greed and prejudice, but I don't have time to explain. Right now all you need to know is that Thaddeus is dangerous and can't be trusted. He killed Father."

"What? How?" she sputtered.

Nik shook his head quickly. "Not now. Later. Now just know you can't trust him, and maybe even Cyril. I'm not sure how far Thaddeus's poison has spread. Sheena, our people need us. Get everyone you can to the Channel. I'll send help. There are always supplies kept at the old meditation platform, and it's in the Old Forest, far enough from the city that the fire won't have caught it." *Won't have caught it yet*, Nik thought, but he kept the words to himself and hurried on. "I'll be sure someone gets those supplies to you."

"Yes. I can lead as many as possible to the Channel. I—I'll check the lookout platform for emergency provisions and wait for the supplies. But, Nik, it's going to get dark. These people are wounded—some badly. The swarm, it's going to smell the blood and we'll be—"

"Sheena, pull it together! Take one step at a time. Dusk is hours away. There's plenty of time to set up a perimeter—even to hang travel cocoons and hammocks in the trees by the Channel if it comes to that. You can do this. I know you can."

Sheena nodded shakily. "Okay, okay. You're right. I can. I will. But be fast, Nik. A lot of the wounded are only staying on their feet because of shock and adrenaline. When they crash, they're going to crash hard. And except for the basics, I have no idea how to help them."

"I won't leave you hanging. I promise," Nik assured her. "Come on, Laru!" As he raced past the column of walking wounded, Nik heard Sheena begin to call encouragement to the people, telling them the Channel was close . . . safety was close. Nik set his teeth and ran as he silently prayed that his father would lend him strength and wisdom for the nightmare to come.

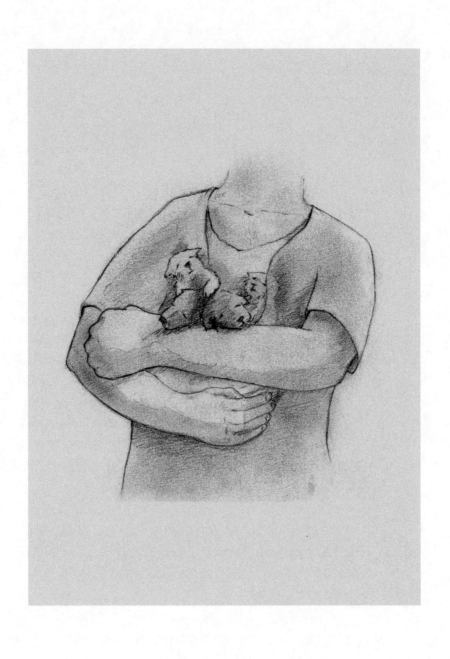

CHAPTER 2

Close enough to the City in the Trees that the forest was once again a familiar friend, Nik and Laru left the trail. Plunging up the side of the ridge, they chose the quickest way to the heart of the Tribe. The acrid scent of smoke became a taste that coated Nik's throat, filling his mouth with bitterness. He and Laru paused at a trailhead close to the first of the pine giants that housed the Tribe. Smoke swirled around them, for a moment confusing Nik's sense of direction. Then the constantly changing wind parted the grayness just as a screaming figure rushed into view. Nik could tell it was a woman and that she clutched a black Terrier in her arms even though the back of her tunic was on fire.

"Stop running!" Nik shouted, sprinting to her. "I can help, but you have to—" From beside him, Laru vaulted toward the flaming woman, knocking her off her feet. The Terrier spilled out of her arms as Nik frantically pulled off his shirt, covering her as he beat out the fire.

"Fala!" she screamed. "Fala!"

"Rose, it's me, Nik." He spared a glance at the little Terrier who was pressed against Laru's side, shivering with shock. "Fala is fine. Laru has her. Hold still. I've got the fire out. Now I need to see how badly you're burned."

Rose went limp under his hands, though she turned her head so that she could stare out of pain-filled eyes at her Terrier.

"Her pups. Fala's pups. They're back there." Rose's voice broke and tears spilled down her cheeks. "O'Bryan was trying to save them when a burning branch from the neighboring pine caught our tree on fire."

"Where is he? Where's O'Bryan?"

With a shaking hand Rose pointed behind her at the wall of smoke and heat. "There. He's still back there."

Nik knelt beside Rose. "Can you sit up?"

She nodded and let Nik help her sit. Fala staggered to her Companion and Rose pulled the little Terrier into her lap, holding her close. "How bad is it?" she asked.

"I'm not a Healer, but I don't think it's too bad," Nik said. "Your tunic's a mess, but it mostly saved your skin. Can you walk?"

"I think so. But I'm not leaving the pups." Rose started to get to her feet, still holding Fala. "I have to go back there. I have to get them."

"I'll go." Nik put a restraining hand on her. "You take Fala and follow the trail that goes down the ridge to the Channel. Sheena's just ahead of you, leading a group of people there. Help will come. And I'll bring the pups to you when I find them and O'Bryan."

She stared at him, her eyes wide and glassy with shock. "It will kill Fala if she's lost the whole litter. That's what I told O'Bryan when he was helping me. I'm sorry, Nik. I didn't mean for him to die, too."

"O'Bryan isn't dead. Neither are Fala's pups. You get to safety. I'll take care of the rest."

"Nik, where's Sol? Why hasn't he stopped the fire?"

"Everything's going to be fine. The fire will be stopped." Nik avoided Rose's questions, turning her so that she was headed in the direction of the path to the Channel. "Go. I'll meet you at the Channel *with* Fala's pups."

Rose nodded slowly. "Save them and you will be saving Fala and me. I won't live without her." Then, cradling her trembling Terrier in her arms, she staggered away.

Nik didn't hesitate. "We have to find O'Bryan!" he told Laru. The big Shepherd huffed and without hesitation trotted into the wall of smoke with Nik following closely behind.

They'd only gone a few feet when Laru's head snapped to the side as he alerted on O'Bryan's scent. Barking enthusiastically, Laru took a left fork in the trail. Nik ran after him, struggling to keep up with the powerful canine.

"O'Bryan! Call out! Where are you?" Nik shouted.

"Here! Here!"

Laru shot ahead into the swirling smoke and Nik lost sight of him completely.

"O'Bryan!" he called again.

"Here, Nik! Here!"

Nik ran toward the sound of his cousin's voice and Laru's barking and then had to steady himself on a fallen log as he almost ran into Laru and the man on his knees the Shepherd had stopped beside.

O'Bryan looked up at Nik, a disbelieving smile on his sweat-streaked, fire-reddened face.

"You show up at the strangest places, Cuz," O'Bryan said between panting breaths. "But I'm glad you keep showing up."

Nik crouched beside the young man who was more brother than cousin to him. O'Bryan's tunic looked odd, and he had his arms wrapped around himself as if he were trying to hold his torso together. Fear stabbed Nik. "Where are you hurt? Is it your chest? Are you burned?"

"Not hurt. Not bad. Just catching my breath. These guys are a lot heavier than they look."

It was only then that Nik noticed the front of his cousin's shirt was moving. O'Bryan opened his arms, which Nik could see were red, blistered, and singed, to expose five little black heads that were wriggling from under his shirt to poke their muzzles into the smoky air.

"Fala's pups!" Nik said. "You did save them."

"Had to. You and Sol can't be the only heroes in the family."

"Your arms are burned—so's your face." Nik quickly made his assessment. "Bloody beetle balls, O'Bryan, what were you thinking?

Yesterday at this time you were almost dead of the blight." Nik wasn't sure if he wanted to hit or hug his cousin.

"You're right, Cuz. This is definitely an inconvenient time for a forest fire." He gave Nik a cheeky grin.

Relieved beyond words, Nik sat back as Laru pushed between them to sniff at the squirming Terriers. "Are all the pups okay?"

"They're fine. We gotta find Rose and Fala. We got separated from them when the tree caught. Fala was frantic, and Rose wasn't much better."

"They're okay. I sent them down to the Channel. Sheena's leading a group of wounded there. I have to get supplies to them, and then—"

The pernicious wind changed again, lifting Nik's hair, and in a maelstrom of smoke and sparks and heat it roared around them with an almost human groan—increasing in strength with a seemingly insatiable need to consume the Tribe.

"The entire forest is going to burn! It's like the wind is feeding it on purpose!" Nik peered around them, trying to see through the smoke and judge which direction the flames would be spreading now.

"Nik, you have to get Sol to the firebreak and have him call down sunfire to stop this before the Mother Trees are destroyed." All lightness had gone out of O'Bryan's voice.

"Sol's dead."

O'Bryan's brow furrowed and he shook his head quickly, as if physically trying to be rid of his cousin's words. "What?"

"Father is dead." Nik spoke slowly to keep his voice from breaking.

His cousin's eyes filled with tears that silently overflowed and tracked down his fire-reddened cheeks. "How?"

"Thaddeus shot him."

"Wait, no! A Companion shot our Sun Priest? That—that can't happen! It's *never* happened." One hand fisted the front of Nik's shirt, and O'Bryan gave his cousin a shake. "It has to be a mistake!"

Nik rested his hand over his cousin's fist. "No mistake. I was there. Thaddeus was trying to kill Mari. Father saved her life."

"Mari? But she has to be protected; she can cure the blight!"

"That didn't matter to Thaddeus, or to Cyril. All that mattered was being sure the Earth Walkers remain our slaves."

"Cyril was in on it? That's insane. This happened on Farm Island? Was Mari trying to free the Scratchers—sorry, Earth Walkers?"

"Not free them—not at that moment. She was healing them of the sadness that kills them. Somehow Thaddeus found out she was there—he got Cyril and a group of Warriors together. I can only imagine what beetle shit he fed them about her, and about Father. They attacked. It's how the fire started. It jumped the Channel and began moving up the ridge."

"It's all so hard to believe." O'Bryan looked from him to Laru and then back at Nik again.

Nik answered his unasked question. "Laru chose not to die with Father. He chose me. He's my Companion." The big Shepherd leaned against Nik, looking up at him with amber eyes filled with unconditional love.

"I still don't understand—can't believe it."

Nik hugged Laru before turning back to O'Bryan. "I'll give you the rest of the details later. First we have to help the Tribe." O'Bryan nodded somberly, and Nik continued. "Did you see Wilkes and the Warriors? And Thaddeus? Did you see him?"

"I only saw Wilkes and his Odin. They reached the Tribe first and sounded the fire warning. He told the young and old and sick to evacuate, and everyone else to get to Badger Stream. That's where they want to make the firebreak."

Nik nodded. It made sense that they'd try to break the fire at their main water source. Badger Stream was a fat, fast tributary that originated deep in the Barrier Mountains northwest of the city and flowed cold, clean water through the heart of the Tribe of the Trees. The area around the stream was always well cleared and meticulously tended, so no brush or debris ever had a chance to accumulate along its banks.

"There's a good, wide stretch of space on either side of the stream, and of course the fact that there's a deep stream of running water flowing through the middle of that space is an added benefit. A firebreak could work there," Nik said.

"Not without a Sun Priest to call down sunfire," O'Bryan said.

"We don't have a Sun Priest," Nik said solemnly.

"Then we're doomed."

"Not necessarily. I may have an idea," Nik said.

"You're thinking about Mari, aren't you?"

"No! She can't come here—not now. Thaddeus would kill her," Nik said.

"Nik, she called down sunfire when her mother—" O'Bryan began, but Nik interrupted.

"No! I mean, yes, she did. But she has no idea how to do it again, let alone control it. She didn't even know how to accept the sun's rays until I showed her. I was thinking more of the Elders, and Warriors like Wilkes—and even me. I can make a cup of water warm if I try hard enough, and you know some of the Elders can coax a spark to light a candle or start a hearth fire."

O'Bryan gave him a skeptical look. "Warming water, lighting candles, and coaxing sparks to catch dry tinder in the hearth of a cozy nest are very different from calling down sunfire."

"I'm aware of that. But what if a whole group of the Tribe who can heat water, light candles, and do other small things come together? Couldn't we combine our power to call sunfire?"

"That sounds like a question that should be put to the Sun Priest."

"We don't have a Sun Priest, and we don't have time for questions. We need to act, and that's exactly what I'm going to do," Nik said. "Take the pups. You know the path that leads along the west side of the Channel?"

O'Bryan nodded. "I know it."

"Head in that direction." Nik pointed over his shoulder. "You'll cross a little stream, and then you should run into that path and catch up with Rose and Sheena and the rest of them. Get everyone to the Channel and try to settle them. Be sure everyone drinks plenty of water. Keep them quiet and calm. Don't tell them Father's dead—that'd only panic everyone. There are emergency supplies in the lookout platform by the Channel, and I'll send more supplies and help as soon as I can."

"Where are you going?" O'Bryan asked.

"To Badger Stream. I'm going to make a firebreak," Nik said.

"All right then, help me stand up and get these pups settled, and we'll both be off on our missions." Holding the wriggling pups against his chest with one arm, he extended his hand so that Nik grasped it and pulled him to his feet. They were just settling the squirming little Terriers more snugly inside O'Bryan's shirt when Rose stumbled out of the smoke behind Nik.

"O'Bryan! Thanks to the Sun! You did save them!" Rose rushed to O'Bryan, who bent to gently place the pups on the ground so that Fala could be reunited with her happy litter. Through streaming tears, Rose said, "Thank you, oh, thank you! I'll never be able to repay your bravery."

"Seeing these little guys with Fala, happy and whole, is payment enough for me," O'Bryan said.

"Rose, what are you doing here? You were supposed to find the Channel and wait there. Did you get turned around in the smoke?" Nik asked.

Rose shook her head. "We didn't get turned around. The fire's spreading along the bottom of the ridge. It cut us off. I didn't know where else to go."

"That's bad," Nik muttered, more to himself than to Rose. "You can't go back to the Tribe. The fire's there, too."

"How 'bout if we head to the old meditation platform? That's pretty far from the city," O'Bryan said.

"Not far enough, and there's only that little well nearby—no other source of water. You could get trapped there too easily," Nik said.

Suddenly there was a crashing through the brush and Captain bolted to them, barking wildly, followed closely by Sheena, who was staggering under the weight of the two young women she was supporting. One looked as if she'd broken an ankle, and the other had burns up and down her left arm and leg.

Nik's stomach clenched. "What happened?"

As Nik helped guide the injured girls to the mossy ground, Sheena wiped sweat from her sooty face and explained, "Most of the group made it to the path to the Channel. I heard Sarah and Lydia calling for help and I backtracked for them. The wind shifted. Sparks lit a dry cedar and we were cut off from the others." Sheena motioned for Nik and O'Bryan to step away from the girls and Rose. She lowered her voice. "I don't know if the others made it to the water. It was bad—really bad. One second there was just smoke and the next sparks and flames everywhere. They might all be dead." Sheena stared at Nik with haunted eyes. "I should go back for them. I should try to get to them."

"That won't do anything but put you and Captain in danger," O'Bryan said.

"He's right." Nik nodded. "If they were caught in the fire, they're dead. If not, they're already at the Channel and, hopefully, safe."

"I'm almost glad Crystal isn't here. It would devastate her to see the city and our people burning. What in all the levels of hell are we going to do?" Sheena said.

Nik ran his hand through his hair, trying to order his thoughts. *There was no telling how far the fire had spread along the bottom of the ridge. They could be completely cut off from the Channel. And there was no sense in having the wounded girls and Rose go back to the city—it wasn't safe there, either. They needed water and shelter and safety—*

And suddenly Nik knew what they had to do.

"O'Bryan, can you find your way to that creek just inside Earth Walker territory where we first found sign of Rigel?"

His cousin's brows shot up in surprise, but he nodded. "Pretty sure I can, even in this smoke. We spent a lot of time coming and going from there."

"Okay, here's what you're going to do. Lead Sheena and Rose and the girls to the creek. You should be able to take shelter there, at the Earth Walker Gathering Site. I'll find you as soon as I can, but if something happens . . . get to Mari. She'll help you. I know she will."

"Wait, how do I get to Mari?"

"Mari? The girl who saved Captain?" Sheena said.

Nik nodded. "Yes, Mari saved Captain and O'Bryan."

"She does seem to be a gifted Healer, but I don't understand. Why are we going to a Scratcher Gathering Site to find Mari?"

"It's too complicated to explain right now. Will you just trust me?"

Sheena looked from Nik to O'Bryan and made up her mind quickly. "I trust you. Captain and I are alive today because of your Mari."

"So am I," O'Bryan added. "But I still don't know how to find her."

"Captain can find her—or rather, he can track Rigel. And where Rigel is, there Mari will be, too," Nik said.

"If the pup's anywhere near the site, my Captain will find him," Sheena said.

"Have him search to the southeast. And call for Rigel while you're searching. Don't give up. I promise, he'll eventually come to you."

"Wait, Cuz. You're going to be with us soon, right?"

"I'm going to try, but if I don't make it out of the city you have to find Mari. Tell her—tell her I'm sorry. Tell her I wanted it to end differently."

"Cuz, I'm not going to have to tell her anything. Don't get yourself killed. If you can't figure out how to stop it, get the hell out of the fire. You die in there Mari isn't going to be the only one pissed at you."

Nik hugged his cousin quickly. "I'll do my best, Cuz."

"If you see my parents . . ." O'Bryan began, but his words faded and he pressed his palms against his eyes.

"If I see them I'll do everything I can to get them out," Nik assured him.

O'Bryan swallowed hard. "That's all I can ask."

"Okay, you and Sheena let Rose and the girls rest for just a few minutes more and then get going. It's too dangerous to remain anywhere near the city. Laru and I are off."

Sheena touched his shoulder before he could move away. "May the Sun bless you, give you strength, and keep you safe." She spoke solemnly.

"And you as well, Sheena." Then Nik motioned for Laru. "Let's go!"

CHAPTER 3

Mari broke from the path that led back to Nik's Tribe and plunged into the trees, but she'd only struggled through the underbrush for a short time before she was chewing her lip in confusion. The smoke wasn't as dense as she moved into the forest and away from the burning city, but it was thick enough to block the sky and confuse her sense of direction. Mari turned in a slow circle, trying to get a feel for exactly how she could skirt the Tribe of the Trees' territory and not lose too much time making her way to the southeast and the swampier forest where the Earth Walker burrows were located.

She moved off in one direction but came to a blackberry thicket so dense that she and the pup had to back out of the area carefully. Frustration threatened to overwhelm her as Mari searched for any marker that would help her locate the way home.

A few feet ahead of her, Rigel froze. Head, ears, and tail up, he tested the wind. From deep in his chest came a warning growl, alerting her to the fact that they were no longer alone. She'd just begun backing away, Rigel beside her, and was frantically looking for a fallen tree or some thick scrub that might conceal them when Isabel, a young, newly liberated Earth Walker Mari easily recognized, burst into view.

"Mari! Mari! I found you! I can't believe I found you!" Isabel rushed toward Mari and then staggered to an abrupt halt when she almost ran into Rigel, who was pressed protectively against Mari's side, still growling a warning. "Mari?" the young woman whispered stiffly through lips colorless with fear. "Help me! Don't let him get me!"

"Rigel, it's okay. Isabel is a friend," Mari told the pup, and patted him on his head, though he had already relaxed and stopped his warning growl. "He's completely safe. I give you my word that he won't hurt you," she said to the girl.

Still wide-eyed with fear, she stared at Rigel. "I don't understand. Why is a Companion's Shepherd with you?"

"Rigel's with me because I'm his Companion." Mari tried to sound as nonchalant as possible. "I guess you didn't notice him earlier on the dock."

"I did. I thought he was with the young Tribesman—the one who came for Jenna yesterday. I think his name is Nik. I—I don't know for sure. Today, after you Washed us, was the first time I could think clearly since shortly after they took me."

"You're right. Nik is his name. His Companion's name is Laru. This is Rigel, Laru's son. He belongs to me, and I belong to him."

Isabel's gaze went from Rigel to Mari. "But that's impossible. You're not a—" She saw the jolt of shocked understanding as Isabel really *saw* her. "Your hair—your face. It's you and it's not you," Isabel said slowly. "You look like one of them."

Mari squared her shoulders. "My father was a Companion—a member of the Tribe of the Trees. Mama and I hid that from the Clan. But now Mama's dead and things have changed with the Clan. I have stopped hiding."

Isabel clenched her hands together while she continued to stare at Mari. Finally she said, "Are you part of them now? The Tribe of the Trees."

Mari snorted. "Did it seem like I was part of them when they were shooting arrows at me?"

"No, but the young guy—Nik. He and the Sun Priest seemed to be with you."

"They were. They are." Mari shook her head and then corrected herself, continuing sadly, "Well, Nik is. The Sun Priest, Sol, was his father. He died on the dock protecting me."

"I still don't understand how all this happened." Isabel's gesture took in Mari and Rigel.

"It's a long story that I have no problem explaining to you, but I'd rather wait until we're not in the middle of a burning forest."

"Okay, okay, I agree. And anyway, we need to get back to the others," Isabel said.

"Others?"

"I left a group of Clanswomen in a clearing not far from here. I was scouting ahead and trying to figure out where we are. It's all this smoke. We can't tell which direction leads home. It's odd to say, but thank the Earth Mother that you are his Companion. . . ." Isabel paused and jerked her chin in Rigel's direction without actually looking at the young canine. "He does know the way home, doesn't he?"

"Rigel? Of course." With an effort Mari stopped herself from smacking her own forehead and declaring herself as simple as a babe. *Even Isabel knows Rigel can follow his nose home. What's wrong with me? I should have thought to have him track our way home much sooner!* She could almost hear her mama reminding her to be kind to herself—to not waste time berating herself but act instead. Mari strode to Isabel. "Lead me to the other women; then I'll have Rigel take us home."

"This way. I marked the trees so I could find my way back to them." Keeping Mari between herself and Rigel, Isabel fell into step beside her as she lifted the long piece of flint she held and pointed at a slash mark she'd made in the bark of a nearby tree.

"Good thinking." Mari watched the younger girl whose gray-eyed gaze kept flicking nervously from the trail to Rigel. "You really don't have to be afraid of him. He'd only hurt you if you attacked me."

"I wouldn't do that! You're special. You're our Moon Woman."

"Isabel, you and I aren't so different. We're both marked by eyes that prove we have a Moon Woman legacy."

"But you can actually call down the moon. I can't."

"I wouldn't be so sure of that. For right now, how about we focus on

our similarities instead of, well . . ."—Mari paused and made a conciliatory gesture toward Rigel—"our obvious differences."

"You sound a lot like your mother," Isabel said with a tentative smile.

"That is the nicest thing you could have said to me. Thank you. Does
that mean you agree?"

Isabel's smile widened. "No one in their right mind would disagree
with Leda."

"I'll take that as a yes," Mari said, thinking, *One more Clanswoman
has accepted me—how many more to go?*

They walked on in silence, following the slash marks that seemed to
glow through the murky, smoky light. Mari waited until Isabel had
stopped sending Rigel frightened glances and seemed to be more relaxed before she asked, "How many women are with you?"

"Twenty. They were all I could gather. I—I don't know how many
of the rest of them made it out of the Channel. The current was just
too strong. And with the smoke added to the chaos the Companions
caused, I think they got confused and couldn't find the shore. They
drowned. A lot of them drowned." Isabel paused to swallow hard and
wipe at her eyes. "I found bodies. Too many bodies." Her voice broke
on the last word, ending with a sob.

"Oh, Great Goddess, no!" Mari pressed her lips together, fighting a
tide of guilt. "I didn't think. I should have been smarter. I was just trying to help. . . ." Her words trailed off as she wiped away bitter tears.

"Mari." Isabel stopped and took her hand. "It wasn't your fault.
Truly."

Mari blinked through tears of guilt and sadness. "I didn't mean for
it to happen. Not like that. I healed Sol's nephew of the blight. He said
I could ask for a favor—for anything. I told him what I wanted was to
Wash the captives of Night Fever. I was going to pressure Sol and the
rest of the Companions into freeing you—all of you—in exchange for
healing members of the Tribe of blight. I swear I was."

Isabel took Mari's hand in both of hers. "Of course you were."

"But everything happened so fast! No one was supposed to know I
was there except Sol and Nik. I don't know how the Tribe found us.

And then they wouldn't listen to reason—not even from their Sun Priest. I should have waited. I shouldn't have healed *anyone* until every Earth Walker was released and safe. I'm sorry. I'm so, so sorry."

"Listen to me, Mari. You did the right thing. You Washed us of the fever. Even those who drowned trying to escape you helped. Today, for the first time in *years* for some of us, we knew happiness and hope again. We would all agree: Death is not too great a price to pay for such a gift."

Mari nodded and pushed aside the guilt and regret that threatened to overwhelm her. She would have time to sift through her feelings later. Now there was only time for action.

"Then let's gather what's left of our Clan and get them safely home. Finally," Mari said resolutely.

Together, the two women and the young Shepherd came to a small clearing beside a dry streambed where a group of Earth Walker women, ranging in age from preadolescent girls to adults, clustered together in a soggy, frightened group. They looked up to see Mari and began excited cries of welcome, but Rigel's presence at her side had their greetings fading, to be replaced by fearful murmurings and looks of confusion.

Mari straightened her back, lifted her chin, and rested one hand on her Shepherd's head as she looked from woman to woman, waiting for the group to fall silent. Then she spoke in a strong, clear voice that brooked no argument. "His name is Rigel. Yes, he is a Shepherd and he is mine. As you know, I am Leda's daughter. I am also the daughter of a Companion. Rigel won't hurt you, and I know it's difficult for you, but part of accepting me is accepting him. If you can do that, come with me. He'll lead us home." She drew a deep, cleansing breath and then added, "If you can't do that—if you can't accept me—Rigel and I will still guide you home. From there you will be free to join another Clan as soon as you've rested and prepared for the journey. I'll help you. I'll do whatever I can, *except* hide who I am. I won't do that ever again."

The silence that followed stretched so long that Mari's stomach began to feel empty and sick; then an older woman whose face was familiar but whose name Mari couldn't remember stood.

"Where is this Companion father of yours?" she asked Mari.

"Dead since I was a baby."

"And this home your canine is leading us to—is it an Earth Walker burrow or a Companion's City in the Trees and the enslavement that goes with it?"

"Home is Earth Walker territory and the burrows waiting for us there," Mari said, trying to keep all resentment out of her voice. "I would never lead you back into captivity."

The older woman's gaze didn't falter and Mari didn't let her eyes slide away. "Is it true that Leda is dead?"

"Yes," Mari said.

"And you are Moon Woman in her place?"

"I am. As is Sora," Mari added, causing a gasp of shock to ripple through the listening group.

"Two Moon Women for one Clan? That's unheard of," said the older woman.

"I'm sorry, Mother." Mari used the formal address for an adult woman of the Clan. "I recall your face, but not your name."

"I am Serena. I considered your mother a friend, as well as my Moon Woman."

Mari nodded, suddenly remembering why Serena's face was familiar. "You were a midwife in the birthing burrow before you were captured."

Serena nodded. "I was."

Mari's voice warmed. "Then you understand the importance of working together as a Clan. You did it daily in the birthing burrow. Likewise, Sora and I have decided to work together. Things have changed since my mother's death. The Clan has changed. It's time Moon Women found strength in each other as well as in the moon." Mari told the truth simply and directly.

"It's hard to believe anything you say with that creature by your side," called a voice from the middle of the group.

"Rigel will always be by my side, so get used to it." Mari's response rang sharp and clear.

"Canines belong to our enemies!" shouted another woman.

"She Washed us!" Isabel's voice cut through the mutters of agreement, silencing the group. "This canine was hers then, too. He was there, on the dock, at her side. What's wrong with all of you? Mari is why we aren't still in those floating cages waiting to die of Night Fever. She called down the moon, and that means she is our Moon Woman. We're not slaves anymore. We're going home! And that's because of Mari, too. I don't care about anything else, and neither should you."

Mari flashed Isabel a quick, thankful smile, then drew a deep breath and regained some of her lost patience. "I know this is hard. Some of you will remember me as Leda's sickly daughter. The truth is that I've never been sickly. I've only been different and Mama thought it best that I hide that difference from you. Mama is gone now, and I'm done hiding. Accept me or don't accept me. Either way, we're wasting time. Do you really want to be out here, wandering around in a forest on fire, when the sun sets?"

"No, I don't," Isabel said firmly. "I want to go home. I'm going to follow Mari and her Rigel." She turned to Mari and bowed formally, respectfully. Then straightened and skewered the group with her sharp gray eyes. "Who is coming with us?"

Slowly, and with varying degrees of mistrust and hope, each woman stood and bowed to Mari—last to bow her acknowledgment was Serena, who continued to watch Mari and Rigel with wary eyes.

CHAPTER 4

N ik and Laru plunged into the area of the forest that held the City in the Trees. They moved fast, with Nik shouting directions to the straggling wounded to make their way south—to catch up with O'Bryan and Sheena, to find the creek that served as the western boundary of Scratcher territory and follow it until they came to an abandoned Gathering Site. He didn't know what else to tell them. With the path to the Channel cut off, he was torn. Part of him wanted to gather the wounded and lead them to safety himself, but the other part of him, the more reasonable part, won. What good would it do to get a few people out if the entire forest was engulfed in flame?

If the fire wasn't stopped that could very well happen—it could even reach Earth Walker territory.

So Nik and Laru ran on.

At first he was worried that people would stop him—question him. But the horror of the forest fire was all-encompassing. Those who actually spoke to him seemed only relieved when they saw that Laru was by his side and that the two of them were rushing toward the heart of the blaze.

"They think we're joining Father, and they're sure Father will save them," Nik said to Laru as the big Shepherd jogged by his side, dodging around ferns and jumping over logs and ditches. The tall, majestic

pines above them were vomiting confused, terrified people and canines, who were all expecting a miracle from their Sun Priest.

Nik and Laru sped past the six Mother Trees. Tribeswomen were
gathered below, catching bundles that were being hurriedly lowered to
them in a rush of barely controlled panic. He glanced up and up and
could just make out a flurry of activity that was the Tribe harvesting
the precious Mother Plants from the boughs of the trees, wrapping
them in dampened cloths, and then stacking them on litters that were
lowered quickly to their waiting caretakers.

"Nik! Laru!"

Nik felt Laru pause. The Shepherd had recognized the woman's
voice—as had Nik. It was Maeve, his father's lover, who was Companion to Fortina, the biggest female pup in Laru's last litter.

I can't tell her about Father. Not here. Not now.

"Maeve!" Nik shouted over his shoulder as he and Laru ran past the
Mother Trees. "Try to make your way south—to the creek that's on the
edge of Scratcher Territory."

"No, Nik!" she shouted back at him. "We have to get to the Channel
and the Farm. That's where we'll find safety."

Reluctantly, Nik stopped. "The fire's spread along the western ridge.
The way to the Channel is cut off."

"Then we'll go east. I'm not taking Mother Plants into Scratcher
territory!" She locked her gaze with Nik. "No matter how friendly
some of them seem."

Nik studied Maeve. She'd met Mari. She knew Mari had healed
O'Bryan. She might even know Mari had healed Sheena's Captain, and
still her voice and body language made it clear that she didn't trust
Scratchers.

"I think you should do what you believe is best," Nik said non-
committally.

Maeve's pup, Fortina, greeted Laru, huffing happily and licking her
sire's muzzle.

"Laru and I need to get to the firebreak," Nik said.

"Give your father my love—and stay safe, the three of you!" Maeve called as Nik and Laru dashed on.

Laru whined softly. "I know, I know, but there's no time to tell her about Father. And what would it do to her morale? She's in charge of saving the Mother Plants. What if she just gave up? Hell, Laru, she's already going to try to fight her way through a forest fire because she refuses to consider an alternative if it takes her close to *Scratcher territory.*" Nik talked to his Companion, pouring out his worries as they jogged to the heart of the Tribe. It helped Nik stay focused, and it helped him ignore the pain that radiated up his leg, the terrible ache in his back, and the empty place within him that his father's death had left. Nik dug deep for the reserve of energy only life-threatening danger and adrenaline can provide and forced himself to keep up with Laru.

Soon the air seemed a little cooler, cleaner even, and Nik knew they were close to Badger Stream. Breathing heavily, he slowed, and Laru dropped to a walk by his side. They climbed up over a rise in the land and paused there, looking down at the group of Companions gathered with their canines. He noticed that most of them were Hunters, as he didn't see any Shepherds in the area. But everyone, humans and canines alike, was desperately digging a long, wide ditch on the fire side of the stream and clearing all vegetation from yards on either side of it. In the distance he caught glimpses of several groups of Warriors, Shepherds beside them, frenziedly chopping the massive pines that led to the stream—felling them in an attempt to keep the fire from jumping over the water.

But it wouldn't work—not without a line of sunfire to meet and then extinguish the blaze. Nik knew it. He could see that the Tribe knew it, too, by the grim set of their faces and the hopeless silence that enveloped them.

Nik bent and stared into his Companion's wise amber eyes. "I don't know what's going to happen now. They may try to capture me. If they do . . . run, Laru. Find Rigel and Mari. I'll get loose and come to you—but stay safe no matter what happens to me."

Laru listened closely to Nik. When he was done speaking, very deliberately the big Shepherd turned his gaze to the group of Tribesmen and women. He lifted his lips, showing his magnificent teeth, and growled deep in his powerful chest while he exuded a calm, majestic confidence that reminded Nik of his Sun Priest father.

Nik smiled grimly at his Companion. "Well, that's pretty clear. Looks like they're not getting to me unless they go through you. Okay then. Let's *both* try to survive this mess."

Nik's sharp eyes searched the more distant group until he thought he caught a glimpse of Wilkes, Leader of the Warriors, and a man Nik had long respected. Stealing himself, he headed with Laru down to the stream in the most direct path to Wilkes. As they passed groups of Hunters, some of whom had been part of the attack on the Farm, Nik felt their eyes on him. He heard the susurrus of the Tribe lifting around him. He ignored them and continued to head toward where he hoped he would find Wilkes and his Companion, Odin.

"It might not have been wise for you to come here," Davis, Companion to the spunky Terrier Cameron, spoke as Nik passed him.

"Wise or not, I had to come. I have an idea that might work to make a firebreak," Nik spoke grimly to his Hunter friend.

"We're done with your *ideas* you fucking traitor!" Thaddeus stepped from the group of men who had been chopping down one of the majestic pines. "Hunters! Take him! Tie him up. We'll deal with him and his Scratcher whore later." The somber, soot-faced Hunters descended upon Nik as Laru backed against him, hackles fully lifted, growling ferociously.

꙳◦᷾

"Where are you leading us?" Isabel asked as she walked beside Mari. The two of them followed Rigel, who kept rushing ahead—and then running back to her whining impatiently when the group lagged too slowly behind.

As she and Isabel made their way through the forest, Mari had been considering this very question. She couldn't lead the women to her burrow—there were already far too many people who knew how to find her home. If word got out, if just one of these women told one Clans-man, Mari, Rigel, Sora, and even Jenna and Danita wouldn't be safe. And there was no way to know how many of the abandoned burrows were safe—and how many of them were occupied by or in the roving path of Clansmen made mad by Night Fever. So Mari had decided to head to a burrow she knew could hold twenty women and was close enough to her own home that she and Sora could easily take medi-cines back and forth.

"Well, I'm not leading us anywhere," Mari said. "Rigel's getting us back to Clan territory. From there I think we can make the birthing burrow before sunset."

"The birthing burrow! That's an excellent idea. There's plenty of room there, and a full pantry and garden," Isabel said.

"It's not quite like you remember it. There have been changes since you were taken, and not all of them have been good, but it'll suffice until we can figure out how to put the Clan back together again."

"Like I remember it or not, it still seems the right place for us to start." Isabel paused and then continued in one long rush of words, "Mari, I don't mean to be presumptuous, but do you think you could Wash us again tonight? I know it's not Third Night, but it's been so long since many of the women have had a Moon Woman that it would be wonderful for us if you would."

"Yes, I suppose I could. Or Sora could while I tend the wounded." Mari glanced around distractedly as the erratic wind changed direc-tion again, sending smoke eddying around them in almost sentient clouds of gray.

"I'm sorry to bother you with that. I don't mean to create additional burdens."

Mari shook her head quickly. "There's no need to apologize. I don't mean to be distracted, but this wind is so strange—so troublesome. Who knows where it's spreading that terrible fire?"

"Does it really matter as long as it's not spreading it into Clan terri-tory?"

Mari glanced sharply at Isabel. She was watching Mari with big, guileless eyes. *She truly doesn't care if an entire Tribe of people burn!* And then Mari realized that just a few weeks ago she probably would have felt just as Isabel did. But now Mari knew Nik and Laru, Crystal and Captain, Maeve and Fortina, and sweet, funny O'Bryan. *Now they're real people to me—real people and their canines—it's terrible to think of them burning to death. Especially Nik . . . always Nik . . .*

"Mari, I'm sorry. Did I say something wrong?" Isabel was sending worried glances her way.

"I'm not sure *wrong* is the word I'd use, because I do understand how you feel about the Tribe. They captured you. They enslaved you. What they did is inexcusable. It's just that I've met some of the Tribe—some of them who aren't monsters—and I realize they're more like us than they are different."

Isabel nodded slowly. She opened her mouth to continue the discussion, but Serena's shrill voice interrupted.

"Isabel! The Clan needs a break. Too many of us simply cannot keep up."

Isabel and Mari turned to see that Serena had stopped and had the rest of the women halting behind her. They were a ragged, weary group, several of whom had already dropped to the ground, heads bowed, breathing heavily.

"Serena, it's not me you have to ask for a break. Mari is our Moon Woman, not I," Isabel said in a firm voice, speaking loudly enough for the entire group to hear.

The older woman turned a reluctant gaze to Mari. "I mean no disrespect, but I am unused to addressing a Moon Woman who has a canine by her side."

Mari took firm hold of her temper and coaxed her lips to lift slightly in a cool smile. "I understand, Serena. And yet I am the only Moon Woman here, and I *will* be addressed with respect."

Serena hesitated and then bowed her head in the ghost of an apology. "Forgive me, Moon Woman, but the Clan must rest."

"Then we'll rest," Mari said. "But only for a moment. The way this wind keeps shifting worries me. It could drive the fire anywhere. We need to put as much distance between it and us as possible." Rigel whined and butted his shoulder against her leg. She squatted beside him, petting the young Shepherd. "I know, but they don't have your limitless energy, sweet boy. We'll get them home, though, even if I have to nip at their heels."

Beside her, Isabel stifled a laugh with a cough. Mari glanced up at her, liking the girl more and more.

"I was just imagining you biting at their heels. And Serena thinks she has a problem calling you Moon Woman now. *That* would really confuse her," she told Mari, sotto voce.

Mari was laughing softly when she felt Rigel stiffen under her hand. In the next heartbeat the half-grown pup had turned and was staring behind them, scenting the changing wind. His ears and tail were up, but he wasn't growling and there was no sense of danger coming from him.

"What is it?" Mari turned to peer into the smoke behind them. The little path they'd been following had taken a turn, and she couldn't see more than a couple of yards behind them. Before she could get any image from Rigel, the pup's tail began to wag, which was exactly when the Clanswomen at the rear of the group began to scream.

The big Shepherd that trotted from around the bend in the path ignored the panicked Clanswomen. He bounded to Rigel, greeting him enthusiastically. Mari blinked in surprise, and then she, too, was being greeted by the familiar canine.

"Captain! What are you doing out here?" Mari crouched to pet him, feeling along his body for sign of wounds. "Where's Sheena? Is she with you?"

"We must run! Companions have come for us!" Serena's cry was taken up by the other women, who began to hysterically rush off the path and into the smoke-filled forest.

"Stop!" Mari shouted, and was surprised when the women actually hesitated. "I know this canine, and his Companion. I don't believe they mean us any harm."

"Of course you would say that!" Serena shouted.

"Because it's the truth!" Mari shot back at her. "Why would I lie and set up my own Clan to be attacked?"

"*Your* Clan? Aren't you part Companion?"

"Serena, shut up!" Mari's exasperation boiled over. "You're no better than the Companions who refuse to believe we aren't Scratchers. Not all of them are bad, just like not all of us are good."

"Oh, Great Goddess! Companions! Run! Run!" several of the Clanswomen screamed.

Mari looked down the path to see a singed-looking O'Bryan stop in shock as he came around the bend and almost ran into the group of Clanswomen scrambling away from him. A heartbeat later Sheena, three other women, and a small black Terrier came into view. They, too, froze with O'Bryan as the women of the Clan milled around in senseless panic.

"No, please! Everything's okay! You don't have to run. We're not going to hurt you!" O'Bryan shouted over the hysteria of the Clanswomen while the ragged-looking women behind him stood, rooted in place, staring openmouthed at the frightened Earth Walkers.

Mari cleared her throat, and as she strode through the group of women to face the Companions she borrowed her mother's sternest voice, speaking over the cries of women and happy greeting barks of canines.

"Clanswomen, be quiet and get behind me! Rigel, with me!" Instantly the group went silent as they scrambled to get behind her and her pup rushed to her side, alert and on guard.

O'Bryan's fire-ruddy face split into a wide grin. "Mari! I found you!" He hugged her quickly.

"Mari? What is she doing with those Scratchers?" Sheena said, stepping up beside O'Bryan before she called sharply for Captain to come to her.

"O'Bryan, who else is with you besides these women?" Ignoring Sheena, Mari shot the question at him.

"No one. I don't think."

"*I don't think* isn't good enough. Tell me the truth. Now," Mari said firmly. She wasn't sure what she was going to do if there was a whole gang of Companions trailing after O'Bryan. She glanced surreptitiously at the sky. The sun was there—somewhere above the smoke and clouds. She'd called down sunfire once before. Surely she could again to protect the Clan. Couldn't she?

O'Bryan's brow furrowed in confusion and then suddenly cleared. "Oh no, Mari. You don't need to worry. None of the Warriors or Hunters followed me. They're all trying to stop the fire."

"And Nik? Where is he?"

"He's back there, Mari." O'Bryan's honest face was too easy for Mari to read, and she felt her stomach lurch with foreboding.

"Back there? Collecting more of the wounded?" Mari tried not to believe what her gut already told her was the truth.

O'Bryan shook his head slightly. "Not exactly. He's gone to the heart of the city to try to make a firebreak."

Mari's body went cold. "He's in danger, isn't he?"

"He is. The fire's a nightmare, especially with the wind continually changing. Mari, the City in the Trees is being destroyed." O'Bryan's singed face was set in worried lines. "And after he told me about Thaddeus and Sol . . ." His words trailed off and he glanced nervously at Sheena and the other three women who were grouped together behind him.

"Thaddeus? What about Thaddeus?" One of the wounded women stepped up to stand on the other side of O'Bryan. A little black Terrier was at her side and wrapped in her shirt she was holding what Mari realized with a start of surprise was a bunch of puppies!

Mari opened her mouth to answer the Companion, but O'Bryan cleared his throat quickly, sending her a sharp look. Mari nodded a slight acknowledgment before saying, "Let's get to safety, tend to the wounded, and feed everyone—then we'll finish this discussion."

"Nik told me to get to the creek. You know, the one where your mother . . ." O'Bryan paused, looking uncomfortable.

"You mean Crawfish Creek and our old Gathering Site," Mari finished for him.

"Yes. Nik thought it would make a decent campsite. And he said you'd be able to find us easily there, too."

"That's where he's meeting you?" Mari asked.

"Yes. If he makes it out," O'Bryan finished reluctantly.

"I have a better idea. But first, let's get everyone to the Gathering Site," Mari said.

"You're going to let them come with us?" Serena had stepped away from the group of Clanswomen behind Mari and was facing her with a storm-cloud look. "Companions? Who, just yesterday, were our captors."

Mari turned so that she could look from Serena and the Clan to the Companions' group. She drew deeply from the anger that was simmering within her—that had been simmering within her for most of her life.

"This is going to end now. Serena, these people are wounded and exhausted. There are even puppies—just babies—with them. *They are no threat to us.* I am your Moon Woman, and a Healer. I am going to care for them, just as I cared for Nik when I found him wounded, and it's because I chose to help him instead of letting him die that you are now free. If you can't handle that, if you can't get past your hatred for them, then you should make your way back to your burrow, and eventually to another Clan." Mari looked from Serena and the women of the Clan to O'Bryan. "And if there are any Companions among you who insist on calling us Scratchers and enslaving us, leave now. We won't follow you. We won't hurt you. But we also won't help you."

"I owe you a life debt, Mari. So does Nik. I'm going with you," O'Bryan said.

"My Captain and I owe you a life debt as well," Sheena said. "I'm not sure what's going on, or who you really are, but you saved my canine and me. Because of that I choose to trust you."

"Thank you, O'Bryan and Sheena." Mari looked questioningly to the Companion with the Terriers.

"My name is Rose. This is my Companion, Fala, and her litter. I don't know you, Mari, but I do know Nik and Sheena and O'Bryan. If they trust you, so will I."

The two younger women who both seemed more severely injured than the other Companions had slid to sitting positions, with their backs against a mossy log. The older of the two, who had painful-looking burns up and down the left side of her body, spoke up. "I'm Lydia, and this is my sister, Sarah. If you'll help us, we'll trust you."

Mari smiled. "Thank you. And I'll be sure those burns of yours are treated as soon as possible, as well as your sister's ankle." She turned back to the Clanswomen. "What do the rest of you choose?"

Isabel spoke from the middle of the group. "You are my Moon Woman. I will always trust you and abide by your will."

Several of the Clanswomen nodded in agreement. Mari looked at Serena. "You've heard from the Companions. They are refugees of a terrible tragedy. They have lost their homes and their families. No matter what the other Companions have done, or will do, these five do not mean any of us harm."

"Not this instant they don't. They need our help. What happens after we help them?" Serena said.

"I don't know what happens, but trust has to start somewhere, and I'm saying it should start here and now," Mari said firmly. Then she gentled her voice and continued. "But I do understand not being able to trust. I've lived like that, which is why I choose not to live like that again. Each of us has to make our own choice, though, and if you would rather hold to the old ways than consider accepting them and changing, I wish you the brightest of blessings as you continue your life elsewhere."

"Either way, if we take them in I have lost my home," Serena said.

Mari shook her head. "No, Serena. It doesn't have to be like that. You can gain a new home—one that is better than what we've known before."

"I don't want better. I want what I used to have—what *we all* used to have. Your mother would have never let this happen," Serena said.

Mari's voice flattened. "The love of my mother's life was a Companion. You have no idea what she was really like—what she really wanted. Leda would rejoice at the Clan and Companions coming together peaceably."

"You're talking about a Leda I didn't know. I only knew the Leda who was my Moon Woman, and who devoted her life to caring for her Clan. *That* Leda wouldn't have allowed Companions among us. No. I won't trust these people." Serena gestured angrily at the Companions. "I'll never trust them. *They enslaved us! They killed our men! They watched us die in captivity for countless generations!* They have proven that they aren't trustworthy. Good-bye, Mari. Your mother would be ashamed of you." Without another word, Serena left the path and disappeared into the smoky forest. Three women quietly followed her. None of them so much as glanced at Mari.

Mari pushed the hurt Serena's words had caused away from her and scanned the remaining Clanswomen with sharp, questioning eyes. "Anyone else?"

"We are your Clan, Moon Woman." Isabel bowed low to her, arms open with her palms facing up in the traditional acknowledgment of a Clan's Moon Woman. "We follow you." The women who remained mimicked her actions, bowing respectfully to Mari.

"All right then, I don't think the Gathering Site is far from here, and that's the boundary of Clan territory." Calling to Rigel, Mari set the image of the creek and the familiar Gathering Site in her mind, knowing that from there they could easily make it to the birthing burrow. She bent in front of her Companion and took his furry face between her hands, kissing him on the nose affectionately. Then she concentrated, sending the image to the Shepherd as she commanded, "Go, Rigel! Lead us there!"

With a happy bark, Rigel galloped away, following the little deer path they'd pretty much stayed on since crossing the last stream. He stopped just as the path was curving, looked over his shoulder at the mixed group of watching Companions and Clanswomen, and barked enthusiastically again, causing Sheena to sigh softly.

"I forget how much energy young canines have," Sheena said, patting Captain on the head before nodding at him, saying, "Go ahead—join Rigel." Barking like a pup, Captain bounded after the young Shepherd.

"Okay, everyone. That's the way we're going. Not much longer now and you'll find safety for the night," Mari said as she motioned the Clanswomen to get up and follow Rigel and Captain. "Isabel, could you go to the front of the group and be sure everyone is keeping up with Rigel while I have a word with O'Bryan?"

"Of course, Mari." Isabel hurried after the pup.

The Companions followed even more slowly than the Clanswomen, being sure there were several yards between them and the Earth Walkers. Mari went to the two most seriously wounded young women, helping them to their feet.

"You—you don't look like a Scratcher," said Sarah, the younger of the two, who leaned heavily on Lydia and looked as if she might have broken her ankle.

"You're Sarah, right? May I look at your ankle?" Mari asked.

"Yes, I'm Sarah. Are you really a Healer?"

"I am, and we don't call ourselves Scratchers. We're Earth Walkers."

"And she's a great Healer," O'Bryan said. "She healed me of the blight."

Sarah and her sister exchanged startled glances, then the girl said, "Yes, you may examine me."

Mari quickly felt Sarah's ankle, deciding that it wasn't broken after all but severely, painfully sprained. Automatically, Mari started tearing strips from the bottom of her tunic as she spoke to the young man who was watching her every move. "O'Bryan, do you know what chickweed looks like?"

"No, sorry, Mari. I'm better at tracking than I am at plants."

"I know what chickweed looks like. I've spent time on the Farm," Sheena said.

Mari looked up at her, nodded her thanks. "Back around the bend and up a little ways from the path I'm sure I saw a big bed of them. Could you pull a bunch for me?"

"Will do!" Sheena jogged back down the path.

As Mari wound the strips of her tunic snugly around Sarah's swollen ankle as support, she spoke to Lydia. "I see that you soaked that cloth and put it over your burns. That was smart, but I know it must still hurt a lot."

Mouth closed in a firm line against the pain, Lydia nodded.

"I'll do what I can for you now, but I promise to give you something that will bring you relief as soon as we get to the burrow."

"You don't seem like any other Scratcher—I mean Earth Walker—I've ever known," Lydia said.

"Have you really ever known an Earth Walker?" Mari's smile kept the bite from her question, but still the girl looked away and shook her head.

"No. I've only been to the Farm once or twice with Mother." Then Lydia clamped her lips together again, blinking her eyes in an obvious attempt to keep her tears from spilling over.

"She's dead." Sarah's voice shook. She did nothing to stop the tears from running down her cheeks. "So is our father and their Shepherds. They—they made us leave our nest first. They were supposed to follow right behind us. It happened so fast. One second they were shouting for us to run. The next our tree was ablaze and—" She broke off, unable to continue.

"I'm so sorry." Mari looked from Sarah to Lydia. "My mama died not long ago. It's awful, isn't it?"

"Yes," Lydia said on a sob. "It's awful."

Both women—girls really, Mari realized as she looked through the soot and dirt, sweat and wounds, and saw how young they were, probably barely Jenna's age—bowed their heads together and clung to each other. Mari stood, moving away to give the girls privacy for their grief.

"Mari, Rose's back is burned pretty badly," O'Bryan said softly to her.

Mari went to the petite blonde who sat in the middle of the path with her Terrier snugged to her side, her puppies rooting earnestly for their mother's milk.

"Rose, may I examine your back to be sure you can travel?"

44

Rose shrugged. "Sure, but I can travel. I don't have any choice."

Mari went around to the woman's back, carefully lifting her tattered shirt, frowning at the blisters that were already beginning to ooze.

"Here, I picked all of it!" Sheena jogged to Mari and handed her a nice bundle of delicate white-flowered plants.

"Thank you, Sheena. Now could you call Captain? He'll make sure we don't get lost from the Clanswomen while everyone is following Rigel," Mari said. Sheena nodded, cupped her hands, and whistled sharply. Then Mari hurried to Sarah and handed half of the chickweed bundle to the girl. "Chew these—whole. Then spit them into your hands and carefully smooth the mixture onto the worst of Lydia's burns. I'll be doing the same for Rose; then we'll get going."

"Really? You want me to chew these up and then spit them onto Lydia?"

"Well, kind of. Spit them into your hand and *then* put them on Lydia's burns. Don't worry if you swallow some. They'll help with that swollen ankle." Mari stuck a big handful of the bitter herb in her own mouth and began to chew as she headed back to Rose's side.

"Here, I'll help." O'Bryan held out his hand.

"How's your leg?" Mari asked through a full mouth as she handed him a fistful of plants.

"It'll be okay until we can stop. You fixed me up good!" He grinned and filled his mouth with chickweed. Soon he was chewing and spitting alongside Mari.

It didn't take long and Mari didn't like how weak the wounded women were, but within just a few minutes they were hobbling along with Sheena and Captain leading them, not far behind the Clanswomen. Mari glanced at O'Bryan. He was carrying half of the Terrier pups, with Sheena carrying the other half. The two of them were staying close beside Rose, who was too weak to do much except lean on Sheena and stagger forward. Mari cleared her throat, and O'Bryan met her eyes. She gave him a pointed look before saying, "Sheena, could you take the pups from O'Bryan for a moment? I don't like how much he's limping and want to take a look at his wound."

"Sure," Sheena said, taking the squirming pups from O'Bryan. "Maybe we should all rest for a moment."

"No," Mari said quickly. "We're almost to Earth Walker territory, but we'll have to hurry to make the burrow before night. The four of you keep going. I'll just be a second with O'Bryan. We'll catch up with you quickly."

Mari motioned for O'Bryan to sit on a nearby log. First, she checked his burns. "Here." She handed him what was left of her chickweed. "Chew this and put it on your arms and face. You're not burned badly, but it must be painful."

"It is. Thanks." O'Bryan chewed quickly, spitting the sticky mixture into his hand and smearing it on his arms with a sigh of relief.

Mari bent over his leg, noting the wound looked painful and needed a new dressing, but it showed no sign of infection or of the blight. As soon as the Companions were out of hearing distance she spoke quickly and softly.

"Do you know about Sol and Thaddeus?"

"Yes. But Sheena and I are the only ones who do. Nik didn't tell Rose about Sol's death. It would be too much for her—for any of the rest of them. To find out a Tribesman killed our Sun Priest is horror enough, but Mari, only Sol had the ability to call down sunfire and make a firebreak."

"How bad is that, O'Bryan?"

"I'm not sure how it could be worse. If there is no firebreak the blaze will destroy all of the city in the sky, and burn most of the Tribe with it, as well as a good part of this forest—if not all of it," O'Bryan said bleakly.

"Then why didn't Nik come with you?"

"He is his father's son, Mari. He's going to try to make a firebreak, or—" O'Bryan broke off his words, looking hopelessly into Mari's eyes.

"Or die trying?"

He nodded.

Mari felt a keen hollowness within her at the thought of losing Nik. "I just found him. I can't lose him."

SUN WARRIOR

She didn't realize she'd spoken aloud until O'Bryan rested his hand on her shoulder and squeezed. "Nik told me to tell you he's sorry—that he wanted it to end differently."

"It *is* going to end differently. I watched my mother die. I watched his father die. I'm not going to stand by and watch Nik die, too." Mari stood, held out her hand, and helped O'Bryan up.

"He's not here. We'll both be spared watching him die," O'Bryan said sadly.

Mari met his eyes. "Oh, I'll be watching all right, but I'm not going to let him die. That I promise you."

CHAPTER 5

M ari knew what she had to do. She wasn't sure *how* she was
going to do it, but she had to save Nik—and if that meant saving the Tribe and the City in the Trees, well then, she'd simply have to
save them, too.

She sprinted past the straggling little group of Companions and
through the weary Earth Walkers, finding Isabel in the lead with Rigel
not far ahead of her. Mari's pup barked a welcome, ran to her for a
quick hug, then trotted back to his lead position as she dropped into
pace beside Isabel.

"You're doing really well, Isabel. Thank you for not being afraid of
Rigel."

Isabel smiled bravely at her. "I wouldn't say I'm not afraid of him,
but I am getting used to following along behind him."

"You don't have to be scared of him. I give you my word on that."
Mari lengthened her stride as much as she dared. "We need to pick up
the pace. The smoke is making it hard to tell how late it is, but it feels
like we've been walking for most of the day."

"It feels to me like we've been walking for most of the *year*," Isabel
said drolly.

"I know what you mean. Isabel, I need to talk to you about what is going to happen once we get to the Gathering Site. I'm going to get the groups settled—then I'm going to leave you in charge while I run for Sora." *And after I tell Sora about what's going on, and she's on her way to help, then I'm going to save Nik,* Mari promised herself.

Rigel gave a couple quick barks and trotted into what Mari realized with a happy start was a familiar grove of cherry trees.

"Finally—the Gathering Site," Mari said, then she raised her voice for the rest of the group. "The site is just through this grove. You can rest there while I get—" Rigel's welcoming bark made him seem more pup than ferocious adult as he rushed through the budding cherry trees. Mari lost sight of him, but she heard a surprised shriek, followed by a fit of semihysterical giggles. "What the . . . ?" She jogged forward while the rest of the group hung back—to see that Sora had been knocked on her butt by Rigel, who was happily licking her face as she laughed and made an obviously halfhearted attempt to fend him off.

"Mari!" she sputtered, wiping Shepherd slobber from her face with one hand as she looped her other arm around the big pup's neck, hugging him close. "Great Goddess, I'm glad to see you. I was so worried! I told Jenna and Danita to stay put, but I had to look for you. All this smoke, Mari! What's happening back there with the Tribe and—"

Isabel materialized from the smoke behind them, causing Sora's words to break off.

"Isabel? Is it really you?"

"It is!" The girl smiled. "And there are more of us here, too." Isabel stepped aside so that Sora could see the ragged line of Clanswomen behind her.

Sora was on her feet in an instant, running to the Earth Walkers, calling many of them by name, touching them, comforting them. Mari studied her carefully, proud of her friend and apprentice and thinking that she definitely had the makings of an excellent Moon Woman. She'd brought a satchel and a big skin full of water and was already passing around the skin and pulling containers filled with salves from the depths of the satchel. Mari felt the terrible burning tension between her shoulders begin to relax.

Then the small group of Companions limped into the clearing, and everyone went very still.

Mari went to Sora's side. "Sora, this is Nik's cousin, O'Bryan."

Sora studied the young man with an expression Mari couldn't read. Then, slowly, she nodded her head. "Hello, O'Bryan. Nik has spoken well of you."

"You, too, Sora," O'Bryan said with a tentative smile.

"Really? He didn't tell you I wanted to let him die?"

O'Bryan's smile grew less tentative. "Oh, he did tell me that, but he also said you changed your mind."

Sora snorted. "I didn't change it. Nik changed it for me." She looked from O'Bryan to the Companions behind him. "Who are your friends?"

Looking relieved, O'Bryan introduced the rest of the group. Then Sora turned to Mari with an assessing look. "So, Moon Woman, what are we going to do with them?"

"Not we—you. I'm hoping you brought some aloe gel for burns."

Sora nodded. "I did. I also have Danita and Jenna gathering as much aloe as they can find, and refining it into gel and salves. I thought you might need it."

"You were right," Mari said. "It was a good idea to harvest more aloe."

"Thanks." She grinned at Mari. "What's next?"

"Use some of that aloe gel for the Companions. Lydia and Rose are the most badly burned of them. But don't spend too long on any one person right now. They need to get to safety first."

"What's your idea for that? There are, what, about twenty-five or so in this group, with a good half or more of them injured?"

As Sora spoke, Mari led her a little apart from the rest of the group so they could have a measure of privacy. Sora followed her, sharp eyes still assessing the ragged group of survivors as most of them dropped heavily to the ground to rest.

While the two of them moved away from the group, Sora began coughing—a wet, nasty, rattling sound. She turned her back to Mari, trying to stifle the coughs, but Mari saw her shoulders shaking with the effort it took.

"What?" Sora said, wiping her mouth and meeting Mari's gaze.

"You're sick," Mari said softly. She reached toward Sora, intending to examine her, but the young Moon Woman stepped back, shaking her head.

"No, no, no. I'm fine."

"You're sick," Mari repeated. "You look pale, even though your cheeks are flushed. Are you running a fever?"

"Mari!" Sora grabbed her wrist and marched farther away from the group with her. "I. Am. Fine. Or at least as fine as I can be after being attacked, bitten, and almost raped yesterday by Clansmen I grew up thinking were my friends, and maybe even more."

"That shouldn't have made you sick," Mari insisted.

"Really? I disagree. And I looked it up in your mama's journal. I think she'd disagree, too. My immune system has *definitely* been compromised. That's why I feel awful. But right now I don't have the luxury of curling up in our burrow and drinking tea for a week and making your creature bring me things."

"You want Rigel to bring you things? Are you sure you aren't delirious?"

Sora frowned at her. "You know he can do all sorts of crazy stuff. He practically reads your mind. So, if I'm sick, I figured he could certainly bring me things. I'm not sure what, but when this is all over and I get a chance to relax I'm definitely going to do as little as possible and get him to do as much as possible. You keep telling me how smart he is— I'm just agreeing with you. Finally." Sora reached down and patted Rigel on the top of his head. He gave her a doggy grin and licked her hand, which made her grimace. "I just don't understand why he has to be so slobbery."

"He's a Shepherd. Apparently they're slobbery *and* sheddy," Mari said, smiling down at Rigel. "All right. Fine. I'll pretend like you're okay if you heed Mama's journal notes about what a Moon Woman should do when she's ill."

Sora sighed. "Already read the notes, and I'll do what Leda directed. I'll wash my hands. A lot. And if my cough gets worse I'll tie a mask around my nose and mouth so that I don't make anyone else sick."

"*And* remember to care for yourself as well as you care for your patients."

"Yeah, yeah, yeah, when I have time. So, back to our group of refugees. What are there, twenty-five or so of them?"

Mari nodded, deciding Sora was correct; they really didn't have time for her to be on bed rest because of an inconveniently timed cold. "That's a good count, yes. My idea is that you're going to lead all of them to the birthing burrows. Make them comfortable. Treat their wounds. Feed them. Isabel will help—so will Jenna, if she can leave Danita," Mari said. "Actually, it might help Danita to think about someone else's needs for a while, so be sure you bring her to the burrow, too."

Sora chewed her lip contemplatively, nodding slowly as she brushed her hair back from her damp forehead and stifled another cough. "It's not a bad plan. At least the birthing burrow is big enough for everyone and with a little help from the Clanswomen we can repair the door and bar it against the night." Then she frowned, as if understanding the rest of Mari's words. "Wait, while I'm doing that, what'll you be doing?"

"I'll be saving Nik."

Mari ran. She didn't let herself think about Sora's worry, the Clan's fear, or the refugee Companions she'd left in the care of strangers and enemies. She thought of nothing except keeping up with Rigel and of Nik.

I'm not going to let him die. I'm not going to let him die. I'm not going to let him die. The litany played through her mind as she sprinted up inclines, scrambled over rocks, and dodged fallen logs. She paused only once at a stream, calling Rigel to her and coaxing him to roll in the water, soaking his thick, double-layered coat as she splashed water all over herself, thoroughly soaking her clothes, as well. Then she met her Companion's wise gaze. "Rigel, find Nik!" She repeated the command she'd given him as they sprinted away from Earth Walker territory.

The Shepherd surged out of the stream, heading directly into the thickening smoke. Mari tore a soaked strip of wet cloth from the sleeve of her ragged tunic and tied it over her nose and mouth. Then she ran after her Shepherd and as she ran she sent images to Rigel of avoiding people—any and all people except for Nik.

She knew Rigel understood. She didn't question him or hesitate as he led her, winding and twisting around trees and brush, sometimes coming to a sudden halt to avoid more and more of the walking wounded.

The closer she got to the burning City in the Trees, the more surreal the day became—if it could be called day. Smoke tainted everything, hiding the sun while it made tears fill her eyes and its acrid scent coated her nose and throat. She wondered if she'd ever get the taste of it from her hair, her skin, her mouth. And always, always there was the keening of the wind as it battered the forest, changing directions as if it couldn't make up its mind, carrying with it the seductive sound of distant thunder that teased at rain.

It was easier than she'd expected to avoid the Tribe. Those who straggled past her in the smoky haze moved as if they had no energy to spare for anything except putting one staggering foot before another.

Mari felt for them. A large part of her, the part that belonged to her mother and her Clan, ached to be the Healer—to gather the injured together and begin tending to their terrible wounds. But she couldn't. She had to keep going. She had to find Nik.

No one paid any attention to her. With her face hidden by the wet strip of cloth, Companion Shepherd beside her, they assumed she was a member of the Tribe as she ran into the heart of the City in the Trees and the ravenous forest fire.

Rigel led her to a wide, clear stream that they splashed into gratefully, stopping to gulp the cold water. This time Mari didn't have to encourage the pup to soak himself. He waded straight in and lay down, lapping thirstily. Mari quickly washed her face, drenching her hair and clothing before retying the cloth around her nose and mouth. When she was ready Rigel got to his feet, though he didn't leave the stream.

Together they waded with the current taking them closer and closer to the center of the Tribe.

She heard and felt the blaze before she saw it. The sound was feral, almost alive, as it ate through the ancient pine forest and the City in the Trees, and as they got closer and closer to it the heat that radiated from the inferno was terrible. Sweat mixed with soot and water dripped down Mari's body. She and Rigel came to a gentle curve in the stream; the young Shepherd stopped, backing suddenly against Mari, growling softly.

Automatically, Mari left the water. She moved slowly and carefully, inching her way forward as voices raised in anger drifted to her with the smoke like wrathful specters. Using the thick trunk of an enormous pine to hide them, she peered around it at the scene just yards before her. She wiped her sleeve across her eyes, clearing her vision, and Mari's stomach tightened with a sickening twist.

Nik was there, on the far side of the fast-moving stream, standing with his back to a newly felled pine. Laru stood before him, fangs bared at the group surrounding them. Even above the ravenous sound of the not so distant fire and the shouts of men, she could hear the Shepherd's deep warning growl as he faced a group of grim-faced Companions led by a maliciously grinning Thaddeus.

Mari scanned the crowd, trying to judge their intention. Thaddeus appeared swollen with rage. Companions who Mari knew must be Hunters because they each had a Terrier beside them were milling with obvious discomfort behind Thaddeus. Mari thought she recognized the Companion Nik had called Davis. She saw him and his little blond Terrier backing away from the group led by Thaddeus and disappearing into the smoke

There were other Tribe members present, men and women who had no canines with them but were working grimly to fell trees and clear foliage as they sent surreptitious glances at the crowd surrounding Nik.

"I said arrest this fucking traitor!" Thaddeus's hate-filled voice carried easily over the water. "He and his Scratcher whore caused all of this!"

Thaddeus's words were like a physical blow to Mari. She felt them hit her in the gut, but instead of being knocked to her knees, Mari embraced the anger and allowed it to begin to build within her.

It was the hatred of men like Thaddeus that had killed her father.

It was Thaddeus himself and the tunnel vision of his bigotry that had killed her mama and Nik's father.

Mari wasn't going to let that poison destroy Nik, too.

She had a momentary wish that she had her slingshot and a basket of rocks. She even searched the ground and found one flawless round stone that fit smoothly in the palm of her hand. Mari fisted her hand around it, even as she understood that something as mundane as a stone or a slingshot wouldn't get Nik out of this mess. She needed power, and she needed it fast.

Mari looked down at Rigel. The young Shepherd met her gaze. She sent to him one intention, complete and perfect like an unfolding blossom—*we save Nik.*

And then Mari stepped from the concealing pine and began striding forward, with Rigel so close beside her that his powerful shoulder brushed her leg.

The other canines noticed Rigel before the Companions. Terriers sniffed the smoky air and turned their heads in the pup's direction. Mari felt more than saw Thaddeus's mean little Terrier shift his attention to them. His warning growl was surprisingly fierce for such a little dog.

"It's her! The Scratcher whore!"

Nik's head snapped to the side and Mari saw his eyes widen in disbelief as he caught sight of her.

The crowd behind Thaddeus shifted their attention to Mari. "Get her!" Thaddeus shouted the command. A couple of the Hunters started toward her.

Rigel's response was instantaneous. He moved so that he was standing between the approaching men and Mari. His ears went up with his tail. The thick sable fur along his neck and back lifted as he bared his teeth, pressing even more closely against her. His growl came from deep in his strong, wide chest, echoing in perfect accord with Laru.

"It's just a pup! Grab him and take her!" Thaddeus shouted, spittle raining from his lips.

Mari didn't flinch. She didn't so much as glance at Thaddeus. She sprinted to Nik. Rigel ran with her, his growl changing to snarling barks—the strength of which belied his youth. The Terriers that were standing between Mari and Nik scattered, ears down and tails between their legs submissively, and suddenly she was beside Nik! He opened his arms and she stepped into his embrace, allowing herself one small heartbeat of a moment to be secure in his strength and his affection.

"I told you she was his Scratcher whore," Thaddeus said.

Mari positioned herself so that she was beside Nik. Laru and Rigel stood before them, teeth bared at the Hunters.

"I'm getting really tired of him calling me that," Mari told Nik, as if they weren't facing a group of angry men and women and their canines.

"Yeah, Thaddeus isn't known for his social skills," Nik said.

"Enough talk! Get the bitch and her traitor lover!" Thaddeus shouted.

"Stop!" A tall man with a large dark-coated Shepherd at his side ran into the clearing, followed by the young Hunter Davis and his blond Terrier, as well as several more tall Companions accompanied by adult Shepherds. They all looked singed and exhausted, covered in sweat and soot, coughing into wet rags they'd wrapped around their faces and necks. But the tall man's voice was firm and filled with unshakable strength. "Thaddeus, you have no authority to order the arrest of Nikolas, or of this woman."

"Wilkes, you've got to be fucking kidding me!" Red-faced, Thaddeus shouted at the Warrior, "You were there, on the Channel, when this bitch let the Scratchers escape and set our world on fire!"

Wilkes's voice was flinty and Mari was sure she saw disgust in his expression as he faced Thaddeus. "I was there, but things didn't go down exactly as you're saying. And there is still the matter of our Sun Priest's death to deal with—and that death was by your hands, Thaddeus. This fire is the only reason *you* haven't been arrested."

Mari watched the expressions of the Tribesmen and women. They ranged from shock and grief to anger. Then Wilkes took a step toward them, as if he wanted to speak in private to Nik. Laru and Rigel's response was instant and in sync. Side by side, the two mighty Shepherds alerted, snarling twin warnings.

Wilkes's big, black Shepherd's reaction was just as instantaneous and was mirrored by every canine in the clearing, Shepherds and Terriers alike. Their ears, tails, and heads all went down, and they refused to move forward, showing complete submission to Laru's Alpha position in the Tribe.

"Nikolas, it appears Laru has chosen you as his Companion. Is this true?" Wilkes asked.

"It is," Nik said. "Laru chose to live with me, instead of dying with my father." Nik's hand found his Companion's head and he stroked the big Shepherd reverently. "That is something for which I will be grateful for the rest of my life, and maybe beyond."

Laru's tail wagged, but he didn't take his intense amber gaze from the crowd.

Wilkes studied his Companion, and Mari could almost see the connection between them. Then the tall Warrior nodded, as much to himself as his Shepherd. "Our Companions have decided. They still acknowledge Laru as their Alpha and Leader. As is tradition for the Tribe, that choice is up to our Companions, and cannot be changed. I propose we work together to stop this fire and when the Tribe is safe again we can convene the Council and allow the people to decide how we move forward, what we do about our Sun Priest's death, as well as what action, if any, should be taken against Nik and his Scratcher," Wilkes said.

"Earth Walker." Mari's voice was strong and sure. "My people are called Earth Walkers. To call me a Scratcher is to insult me, and you should all know that I'm only half Earth Walker. My father was of your Tribe, a Companion named Galen."

Mari saw surprise flicker over Wilkes's face, and that surprise echoed throughout the surrounding group, especially in Tribesmen who were middle-aged or older.

"She can't really be saying she's one of us," Thaddeus sneered.

"She doesn't have to say it, and you don't have to believe it," Nik said. "The fact that a Shepherd has chosen her makes her one of us."

"Nik has a point. It isn't blood that makes a Companion. It's heart and soul and the love of a canine," Wilkes said.

"And Mari has all of those things." Nik smiled proudly at her. Then his gaze moved through the crowd as his voice lifted so that everyone in the clearing would be sure to hear his next words. "She also has the ability to cure the blight."

"Lies!" Thaddeus shouted.

"Truth!" Nik countered. "I had the blight. She cured me. O'Bryan had it, too, as all of you know, and now he is cured."

"That's just talk! No one has seen O'Bryan since the fire began," Thaddeus said.

"I have." Everyone's attention shifted to the young man named Davis. He moved his feet nervously, a movement the little blond Terrier at his side mirrored. Then he continued. "I saw him helping Rose try to save Fala's litter. He might not have made it because part of the fire cut him off from me, and from her, but I definitely saw him and he was definitely not sick anymore."

"He made it," Nik told Davis. "I saw him after that. He saved all of Fala's pups and was getting them and Rose to safety."

"Oh, well, obviously *that* makes all of this okay!" Thaddeus said.

Mari was done being silent. She shook her head with distaste. "Thaddeus, you're the worst kind of hypocrite—a lying one. It's because of you that my mother is dead. It's because of what you and that old man did at the Channel that the Earth Walker women panicked and the fire started. It's because of you that Nik's father, your Sun Priest, is dead. And if we burn today it's going to be because hatred is more important to you than life." She looked at the other Companions, meeting their eyes. "Is hatred more important than life to all of you, too?"

"Don't you dare talk to me like that, you Scratcher whore!" Seeming unable to control himself, Thaddeus lurched forward, hands reaching as if for her throat.

With a ferocious snarl, Rigel flew at him, knocking the grown man to the ground, where he stood over him, growling a warning, bared teeth almost touching his neck, while Laru pinned Thaddeus's mean little Terrier to the ground, forcing him to bare his neck and belly, too.

The other canines, Shepherds and Terriers, moved as one, backing away from Laru and Rigel, lowing their heads, and tucking their tails submissively.

"Nik, Mari, call your Shepherds to you," Wilkes said. "Thaddeus, we need to focus on stopping this fire. Later there will be time for the Tribe to decide what is to be done about the other events of today—if the Tribe survives. Until then, you will keep your hands off Mari and Nik."

Laru and Rigel padded back to their positions beside Nik and Mari, leaving Thaddeus and his Terrier to get slowly to their feet. Thunder boomed in the background and the wind shifted again, whipping suddenly from north to south, bringing with it sparks, smoke, and the ravenous roar of the approaching inferno.

"We're out of time! We need sunfire to make a break in the forest fire, but without our Sun Priest—"

Wilkes had begun to quickly address the group, so everyone's attention had shifted to him—everyone's attention except for Mari's. She was still watching Thaddeus, still considering how a single hate-filled man could have so drastically affected her life, when she saw his hand go to the small sheath at his waist. He glared at Rigel as he flicked it open and with practiced dexterity pulled the throwing dagger free.

Mari's fear boiled from deep within her. *Not Rigel!* As she screamed at Thaddeus she let loose the anger that had been simmering within her since he'd first called her whore. A ball of fire burst from her outstretched hands, landing at Thaddeus's feet and catching his pants, causing him to drop the dagger, which fell, blade down, burying itself into Odysseus's flank. Both man and canine shrieked in pain. Thaddeus ran into the nearby stream while Odysseus screamed in agony and tried to grab the handle of the dagger with his teeth.

"Help him! Help Odysseus!" Thaddeus shouted from the stream.

Two of his Hunters hurried forward, pulling the blade from the little Terrier's flank and applying pressure to the bleeding wound.

Mari stared at the injured Terrier in horror—torn between the understanding that she probably wouldn't be allowed to help the canine and her gut reaction, which was to *help the canine*. She must have taken an involuntary step forward, because Nik's hand was suddenly clamped around her wrist.

"Thaddeus caused his Terrier's injury. Not you. Stay strong, Mari. You just called down sunfire. You've *proven* Companion blood beats through your veins," Nik whispered to her.

Every Tribesman and woman in the clearing stared at Mari. She pulled her eyes from the wounded canine, lifted her chin, and let her gaze take in the group.

"Do you still doubt that my father was one of you?"

Thaddeus staggered from the stream to Odysseus, roughly pushing aside the two Hunters who had been tending to the Terrier's wound. He crouched beside the little canine, who was still whining pitifully, and skewered Mari with his hate-filled green eyes. "You fucking bitch! You're going to pay for hurting Odysseus!"

Nik started to speak, but this time it was Mari's hand on his that stilled him. "Do you ever take responsibility for your own actions?" she asked as she shook her head in disgust. "Everyone here saw what happened. You threatened *my* canine. I called down sunfire to stop you. *You* dropped the dagger you would have used to cut Rigel, hurting your Odysseus instead. *It was your fault!*"

"And it wouldn't have happened had you not trespassed here. Just like the fire wouldn't have happened—and Sol's death wouldn't have happened," Thaddeus shot back.

"It's simple," Nik spoke up. He didn't so much as glance at Thaddeus. Instead, he addressed the watching men and women. "Do you want to wallow in hatred with Thaddeus, and continue to reap what anger sows, or will you open yourselves to something more, something different, something better?"

Into the waiting silence came the disembodied voice of a stranger.

"It's even simpler that that. Do you want to attack the only person here who can call down sunfire and save us all?"

Mari's eyes widened as a man burst from the wall of smoke. He jogged straight for the stream, splashing the cold, clean water over him. But Mari paid him less attention than she did the creature by his side.

"It's a Lynx," Nik said softly. "His Companion is a mercenary."

Even surrounded by danger, Mari was filled with curiosity. The feline was big—easily bigger than a Terrier. Even filthy and singed, her coat looked thick and soft. Her paws were enormous and reminded Mari oddly of a gigantic rabbit. The Lynx's ears were tipped with distinctive black, feather-like fur, and when she glanced Mari's way she was taken aback by the way the feline's yellow eyes shined.

"Antreas has a valid point," Wilkes said.

The man looked up then, and Mari was surprised to see that his eyes were the exact color of the cat's. He wiped his face with the sleeve of his tunic before saying, "And just in case my point didn't strike home, you should know that right behind the fire, which is right behind Bast and me, is a swarm that is devouring everything the fire misses."

"Swarm?" Wilkes called to the Lynx's Companion. "A swarm is on the move during daylight?"

"Yes, if you can call this daylight." Antreas made a gesture that took in the smoke-filled sky and the shrouded sun. "You have no more time. If you can stop this fire, do it now. If you can't, you are welcome to follow Bast and me. We got cut off from the Channel when the wind kept shifting, but we're going to make our way around Port City to the Willum River."

There was a huge explosion behind Antreas. Mari noticed that before the man reacted he looked to the Lynx. He nodded and then surged from the stream. "Or you can stay here and bicker like dogs. It makes no difference to me."

"Bicker like *dogs*?" Thaddeus shot the question at the Lynx man. "You insult us in the heart of our own Tribe?"

Antreas paused as he and his Lynx walked past Thaddeus and Odysseus. Several inches taller than the rather delicately boned Hunter,

Antreas looked down his nose at Thaddeus. "I don't see a Tribe any-more. I see a group of bickering children."

"You fucking cat lover—" Thaddeus began, but lightning quick, the Lynx leaped between her Companion and the Hunter. She arched her back and her yellow eyes flashed dangerously as she hissed a warning.

Antreas smiled as Thaddeus stumbled back. "That's right, Bast doesn't live by your rules. She won't knock you over in a *show* of dominance—she'll eviscerate you. Keep coming, dog man, and make her day."

"Thaddeus, stand down!" Wilkes commanded. Then he nodded to Antreas. "I won't ask you to stay. This isn't your Tribe and this fire isn't your fight. I will ask, though, that you mark your trail to safety clearly, so that the Tribe may follow if need be."

"I will," Antreas said, nodding respectfully to Wilkes before he and his Lynx faded away into the forest.

"Our guest had a valid point," Wilkes said. "Mari, will you help us?"

Mari's answer was swift and clear. "Only if you'll grant safe passage from Tribe territory to Rigel and me, as well as Nik and Laru and any other person or canine who wishes to leave with us when the fire is out."

Wilkes's startled glance found Nik. "You intend to leave? With the Alpha canine of the Tribe and the woman you say can cure the Blight?"

Nik answered with no hesitation, "I go with Mari."

Mari saw the effect of Nik's words on the Tribe. They seemed con-fused and not sure how to react. She felt for them—their city was burn-ing, their friends and families were in danger, and now they were faced with her, a girl who was a stranger and an intruder, and their only chance at salvation.

Yes, she felt for them, but she wasn't foolish. Mari raised her voice to a shout that carried over the whining of the wind and the noise of the fire as it ate its way ever closer. "I will call down sunfire and save you. I will give you my word that I will also return and tend to your wounded, sharing the healing arts of a Moon Woman with the Tribe, but only if your Council rules to never again enslave any Earth Walker."

"Her word means nothing," Thaddeus said as he tore the sleeve of his tunic and began to bandage Odysseus. "If you let her leave, the only way we'll get her back here is to track her and then truss and bind her like a wild boar."

Mari looked into Thaddeus's hate-filled eyes and spoke to him alone. "If you don't shut up I'm going to silence you for good."

"You dare to threaten me, Scratcher bitch!"

Rigel took two steps toward Thaddeus, growling ferociously. Mari felt Rigel's anger—she fed off it. She let it fill her so that her own lips lifted in a snarl. Then her Companion's anger shifted within her so that she was filled with heat, a yellow burning that seemed to be above, around, and within her all at once.

Nik dropped her hand as if it had burned him, but his smile was encouraging. "That's it! You're doing it again. You're calling sunfire!"

"Everyone, get back!" Wilkes shouted. "Get across Badger Creek!" As the Tribe scattered, Wilkes went to Mari and Nik. "It isn't safe for you to call down sunfire so close, not as much sunfire as it will take to stop this blaze. Nik, let's get her up there to the raised side of the bank." He gestured up where the creek wound lazily around and up into the heart of the Tribe.

Nik nodded and the three of them, canines following, hurried to the top of the bank.

"Nik, now what?" she whispered to him.

He spoke quickly and quietly. "The power to call sunfire is in your blood—it's your birthright, just like calling down the moon is also your birthright. Accept what's already filling your body. Let it use you, Mari. And then release it."

Mari's stomach felt sick with nerves, but she nodded and turned to face the direction from which the fire was making its way through the forest, devouring everything in its path.

She closed her eyes and breathed deeply once, twice, three times, grounding herself by focusing on her breath and not on the heat and smoke, fear and hatred, that surrounded her. Mari imagined the smoke clearing above her, and within her mind's eye she envisioned a fat yellow sun beaming proudly from a perfect cerulean sky.

She could feel the heat and the power. It was definitely there. She lifted her arms, reaching up. Mari felt the golden filigree pattern that slept just under her skin awaken, filling her body with more of the unique yellow heat.

But it didn't boil within her. It didn't build and expand and ache to explode.

She opened her eyes and let her arms fall to her sides. "I can't. It's not working."

"You can!" Nik said, taking her shoulders and turning her to face him. "I know you can. You did it before, at the creek, when your mother died."

"I didn't think then, Nik. It just happened—like a second ago when I threw it at Thaddeus. It starts heating inside me until it suddenly boils over, but I don't know how to get it to start boiling."

"How about like you call down the moon? It has to be almost the same thing," Nik said.

"But it's not! I know the moon, and she knows me. I've been calling her my entire life."

"What's happening?" Wilkes had stayed several paces off, allowing Nik and Mari some privacy, but now he approached, a concerned frown on his face. "What's wrong?"

Nik began to speak, but Mari's gentle touch on his arm silenced him. "I don't know how to call down sunfire. Not really. I've only done it twice, and both times it just happened."

"You mean the sunfire you threw at Thaddeus was an accident?"

Mari nodded.

"The other time was when her mother died," Nik said. "I meant to ask Sol to train her, but . . ." His voice faded.

Wilkes closed his eyes for a moment, and when he opened them he met Mari's gaze, saying, "Please forgive me."

Mari was wondering what he meant as she watched Wilkes unwind the woven hemp belt from around his waist. Then, with a movement so fast his body blurred, he struck, slipping the belt that was now a noose around Rigel's neck, jerking it with such force that it lifted the young Shepherd off his feet as Wilkes pulled him up and back, in a tight, perfect choke hold, while Rigel struggled and gagged.

"Get your hands off him!" Mari shrieked at Wilkes, rushing at him, hands raised in claws, snarling her rage.

And that was when Mari saw the knife pressed against Rigel's neck. She and her Shepherd froze at the same time.

"No! Don't hurt him! Please don't hurt him!"

"If you don't call down sunfire I'm going to slit his throat."

Mari would never forget how unemotional Wilkes had sounded. She looked into the Companion's eyes and believed he would do it—he would kill her Rigel.

Anger, fear, outrage, and despair all flooded Mari. She could feel the breath being squeezed from Rigel—could feel her Shepherd losing consciousness as the knife pressed against his neck. It had already pricked through his thick coat so that drops of scarlet spattered the ferns at Wilkes's feet.

Mari's breath deepened. She followed the magickal, mysterious link that connected her to Rigel, allowing herself to be filled with the young canine's fear and anger and pain.

The heat within her began to build and Mari embraced it—the anger, the fear, the pain, and the power that radiated, first from her Shepherd and then from above and around her, until she felt engulfed by it. Then Mari lifted her hands and screamed, releasing the yellow heat that poured into her, flinging it over Wilkes's head, over the creek, so that it rained liquid fire past the felled-tree line, pouring like lava from the volcano that was Mari's anger.

The force of the molten fire was like nothing Mari had ever imagined. It was not the cold, silver strength of the moon. This power—this liquid heat—was magnificent and terrifying. It poured through her, growing in intensity, as Mari watched, helpless to stop it. She saw the edge of the forest fire then. It seemed to be drawn, mothlike, to the tide of blazing sunfire come to earth. As the two forces met, Mari could feel the forest fire. It was ravenous, insatiable, and it struggled to absorb her sunfire so that it could go on feeding.

"No!" Mari screamed. She knew she needed more of the sun—more power, more heat. She closed her eyes and opened herself to eddies of sunlight that managed to slip through the smoke, accepting them as they entered her body with an eagerness that was foreign to her. The heat that had been pouring through her palms increased, with an answering roar from the deadly inferno that met it.

"You're doing it!" Nik's mouth was close to her ear. His voice was filled with pride and excitement. "When I tell you to stop, you must stop. Sunfire can kill just as surely as the forest fire." There was a short pause and then Nik shouted, "Stop now, Mari!"

Mari opened her eyes. Tears streamed down her face as she tried to stare into the center of the waterfall of flame that continued to pour from her palms. Her body had begun to tremble violently and her knees felt as if they would give out at any moment. She tried to close her hands. Tried to stop the torrent of fire, but she couldn't. She'd found sunfire, and now she had no idea how to control it.

"I—I c-can't. It w-won't stop," she gasped through chattering teeth.

Then Nik's arms were around her. From behind his hands traced along the outside of her trembling arms until they found her wrists and then the backs of her hands. He placed his hands behind hers, gently covering the backs of them, nestling them against the coolness of his palms as he spoke softly into her ear.

"Look to your right, Mari."

She tore her gaze from the maelstrom of fire across the creek to see that Wilkes had released Rigel. The young Shepherd was pressing himself against her right leg, staring up at her and whining imploringly.

"Rigel is safe," Nik continued in his calm, soothing voice. "You are safe. Laru and I are safe. You don't have to be angry or afraid, Mari. Breathe. Relax. Then release the sunfire up—return it to the sun where it belongs."

Mari kept her gaze on Rigel, focusing on the love that he was sending her. She drew a deep, full breath and then released it, along with her anger and fear, imagining that it geysered up and into the sky, along with the molten sunfire.

As quickly as that the sunfire left Mari. She staggered and would have fallen had Nik's strong arms not held her upright.

"You did it!" He held her tightly. "You did it! The fire is out!"

Mari wiped her face as she turned in his arms. It was then that she saw he was holding his hands oddly—stiffly and away from her. "Nik, what's wrong with—" she began, but her words choked off as she took his hand in hers and saw that his palm, both of his palms, were burned and bloody. Her body began to tremble again. "I did this. I burned you!"

Nik used the back of his hand to stroke her wet cheek. "Mari, I'll take burns on my hands any day if the alternative is to have a forest fire devour the Tribe." He laughed. "You are amazing!"

"But you are burned! From touching me." Mari felt dizzy and a little sick as she grasped the edge of Nik's tunic and tore strips from it, using them as makeshift bandages for his hands.

Nik was grinning as if he'd just been awarded his heart's desire. "Well, Moon Woman, it looks like you're just going to have to fix me. Again."

Before Mari could answer, the air began vibrating. She and Nik whirled around to look with horror at the blackened, smoking mess before them. In the distance the land rippled and quivered as within the ashes of the incinerated forest the swarm lifted, departing the dark, secret places from which they slept and descended upon the Tribe.

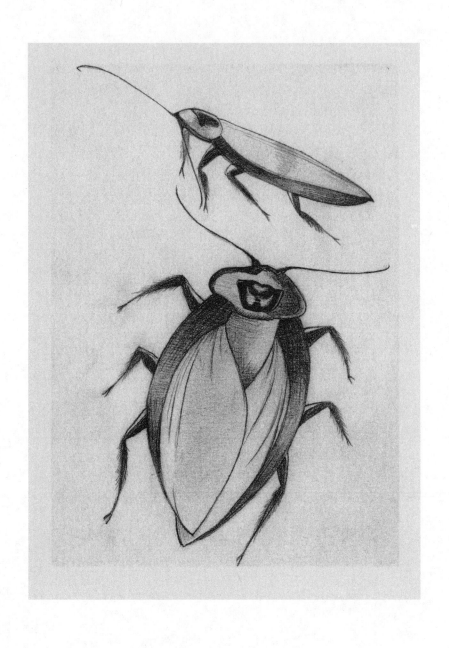

CHAPTER 6

R un! Climb! Get to safety! The swarm! The swarm comes!" Wilkes's shout was a clarion call for the Tribe, and as one humans and canines ran.

"Mari! We have to climb!" Nik shouted as he pulled her with him, raising his voice over the cacophony of panic that surrounded them.

"Climb? No, we have to run and then burrow. Hide from the swarm." She wiped a trembling hand across her unnaturally pale face.

Nik's stomach clenched as he quickly assessed her condition. *After calling down that amount of sunfire she should be resting. She should eat mounds of food, drink lots of herbal tea, and sleep for a day, maybe more. She's not thinking straight. She's too tired to think straight.* But Mari didn't have the luxury a Sun Priest would. Mari had to move or she wouldn't survive—which meant Rigel would die with her. Then the truth blazed through Nik's mind—it wasn't just Rigel who would die with her. Nik wouldn't leave her. Laru wouldn't leave him. Ignoring the pain in his bandaged hands, he grabbed her shoulders and gave her a firm shake. "Mari, listen to me. We have to climb. We have to get up to the City in the Trees. That's the only way for us to survive the swarm."

Mari swayed as she shook her head. "Climb? But Rigel can't climb. That means I can't climb."

Nik didn't waste any more time on trying to reason with her. He looked at Laru. "Get us home! Up to Father's nest! Now, Laru!"

The big Alpha barked, and then he sprinted away, Rigel on his heels.

"Okay, Mari. I've got you. Just lean on me and everything will be okay." Nik put his arm around Mari's waist and half carried, half dragged her after their Companions as other members of the Tribe raced past them, heading for the safety the big pines promised.

Nik caught Laru and Rigel easily. The two canines had come to a halt before one of the main lifts to the tree city. The decorative wooden cagelike creation was already full, but Nik pushed Mari ahead of him, trying to get her to squeeze on with Rigel before the door was latched.

"Back off!" Thaddeus had climbed on top of the lift and was perched there, crossbow pointed directly at Mari's heart. "Take your whore and get to Scratcher territory. I'll bet the swarm hardly ever goes there," he said sarcastically.

Nik didn't even glance at Thaddeus. Instead, his gaze touched each of the people crowding into the lift. "She saved you. She saved all of you. She called down the sunfire that stopped the blaze."

"She also caused the fucking blaze! *And wounded my Companion!*" Thaddeus shouted, angry spittle flying from his thin lips. Odysseus was curled up in the corner of the lift, shivering pitifully.

"*You* dropped the dagger that hurt Odysseus! *You* led the hatred that caused the fire to start on Farm Island. Bloody beetle balls! *All of this is your fault,*" Nik shot back at him.

The people in the lift looked nervously from Nik to Thaddeus.

"Let's go, Nik." Mari took his arm and, with surprising strength, pulled him from the group. "You can't force people to accept me, and I'd rather face the swarm than Thaddeus and his hatred."

Nik only took the time to grunt his agreement. He looked to Laru again. "Another way up, Laru! Fast!"

The Shepherds sprinted off, with Nik pulling Mari with them. The sound of the descending swarm surrounded them. It was a terrible unending humming noise, punctuated by shrieks of agony from the unfortunate creatures that the Swarm devoured in their path.

"Nik, I have to stop." Mari staggered to her knees, looking up at him through a sweaty, tearstained face. "I—I don't know what's wrong with me, but I can't keep going. I'm sorry," she gasped. "Take Rigel with you. Don't let them get you, too."

"That night-be-damned swarm isn't getting any of you." The voice came from above them, within the thick boughs of the pine Mari had collapsed against. Nik peered up to see that Antreas was crouched on a huge limb, his Lynx beside him, Bast's glowing yellow gaze taking everything in. Antreas stretched out a hand to Nik and Mari. "It's simple Lynx logic. Your Mari saved Bast and me. Now Bast and I are saving you and your Mari."

"Laru and Rigel, too!" Mari said.

"Of course," the Lynx man agreed.

Nik nodded his thanks to Antreas, telling Laru and Rigel, "Up! Go up!"

He saw Mari frowning and shaking her head, but Nik ignored her. He knew Laru and his son would do exactly what they had been trained to do—drilling over and over again in case of this kind of emergency. Nik bent so that his face was pressed against the bark of the pine. His arms were lifted, like the sides of an impromptu ladder, resting firmly against the tree. "Now, Laru!"

The big Shepherd didn't hesitate. He jogged a few yards away and then sprinted to Nik, leaping onto his back, scrambling up his shoulders, and using his forward momentum and the corded muscles of his athletic body to drive himself up until Antreas was able to grab the big canine around his torso and heave, so that he finally landed safely on one of the Tribe's lower platforms, still well above the danger-filled forest floor.

"Rigel! Now! Up!" Nik shouted.

Rigel followed his sire, using Nik to catapult himself up within arm's reach of Antreas, who grabbed him by his scruff and tossed him up into the tree after Laru.

"Hurry!" Antreas said, his gaze flicking behind Mari and Nik. "The swarm is almost here."

"Mari, climb up my back. Just like Laru and Rigel. Do it now!" Nik told her.

With a painful groan, Mari stood and staggered to him. She started to climb up, onto his back, but her arms and legs were trembling so badly that she kept slipping.

"I can't," she said, her voice so weak he almost couldn't hear her as she collapsed across his back. "I'm sorry, Nik. I'm sorry, Rigel."

"Oh, stop being so sorry and look up!"

Nik looked up. He would never forget his first sight of Antreas in his natural Companion state. The man was within an arm's reach, with one hand stretching down, beckoning to Mari, and with the other *he was clinging to the bark of the pine with his claws*! His eyes were glowing with the same yellow light that radiated from Bast's eyes, and Nik was sure he saw other changes in the man, too, changes that had to do with his hair and his ears, but he blocked it all out and barked at Mari.

"Mari, get your butt up there! Grab his hand! Go! Go! Go!"

Nik's words acted on Mari as if they had been hot coals. She scrambled up his back, clutching the tree and pulling herself up so she was standing on his shoulders.

"Hurry! Take my hand!" Antreas shouted.

Nik felt her hesitate. Antreas cursed softly under his breath and said, "Sorry, I'll retract the claws on that hand. Now, hurry!"

Mari's weight lifted from Nik's shoulders and then he was there, by himself, standing on the forest floor as the ominous sound of the swarm drawing ever closer intensified.

"Come on! Your turn. Grab my hand, then climb over me like Mari just climbed over you," Antreas said.

Blocking out the stabbing pain in his hands, Nik did exactly as Antreas said, thinking to himself he didn't even give a damn if the Lynx man's claws were out, in, or shredding his skin, as long as he was being lifted above the forest floor and the deadly swarm that converged upon them.

"Nik! Help!"

Sprinting for the tree was Davis, his little blond Terrier, Cameron, running beside him. Nik glanced at Antreas, and the Lynx man shrugged his shoulders. Nik nodded quickly and then cupped his hands around his mouth and shouted down to Davis.

"Cammy first, then I'll get you!"

Davis let his actions be his response. He assumed a position much as Nik had taken moments before, leaning like a human ladder against the old pine. The well-trained Terrier didn't hesitate. He sprinted a few yards away and then ran at Davis, leaping onto his back and scrambling up and up until Nik, who had wrapped his legs around a low branch and was hanging upside down, arms opened to accept the canine, caught him and passed the Terrier along to Antreas.

Then, with Antreas's help, they pulled Davis up with them. Between Antreas, Davis, and Nik, they managed to pull and push Mari up to the platform to join the Shepherds, where they all collapsed together, breathing heavily.

Nik crawled to Mari. She had her arms around Rigel—her face pressed into his coat. "Hey, it's normal to feel exhausted after calling down sunfire. You'll be back to yourself again as soon as you can eat and rest."

She looked up at him, her gray eyes dull and hopeless.

"You know we're not going to be able to rest. The swarm is going to kill us."

Nik shook his head. "No, we're safe." He pointed up. "From above, the Tribe will open vats and pour liquid on the roaches. It's a concoction made of cypress oil, peppermint oil, lye soap, and salt water. It makes it almost impossible for them to breathe, and if they can't breathe, they can't climb up here. We're safe," he repeated, and then he put his arm around her. "Okay, watch. As soon as the roaches get close enough the Tribe is going to rain oil and salt water on them."

Nik felt the tension in Mari's body beginning to release when someone rappelled down to their platform, landing with a *thump!* beside them. Unstrapping the Shepherd from across her back, she nodded a grim hello to Nik.

"Claudia, good to see you and Mariah are well."

Claudia shoved a crossbow and a quiver of arrows at Nik, saying, "Sadly, tonight there's not enough Tribe left to rain anything on anyone—or at least not in this pine there isn't. Good to see you, too, though. If I'm going to be stuck on a platform in the middle of a swarm, it's handy to be stuck with the best bowman in the Tribe." She turned her attention quickly to Davis. He had his own bow strapped across his back. "Davis, you need more ammunition?"

"Whatever you can spare," Davis said, taking a handful of sharp-tipped arrows from her.

Claudia squinted appraisingly at Antreas as her Shepherd ignored the Lynx crouched beside him. "Are you good with a crossbow?"

"If the alternative is to be consumed by the swarm then, yes, I am good with a crossbow."

Claudia grunted and unslung another bow from around her shoulder, along with a handful of arrows. "Make each of them count."

The Lynx's head rotated around, reminding Nik suddenly of an owl. Then the big feline arched her back and hissed a warning.

"Swarm's here," Antreas said.

Mari began trembling against him. "I can try to call down more sun-fire," she said weakly.

Nik shook his head. "No, it can be fatal if you call sunfire without the energy to control it, but we're going to get through this—I promise. Move to the center of the platform. Rigel! Stay with Mari. The rest of us will keep the swarm away."

Mari leaned on Rigel as she crawled to the center of the little plat-form, and Claudia moved into the spot beside Nik. Laru pressed close to his other side, ears pricked and tail up, ready to clamp his mighty jaws around whatever roach dared get too close.

Nik glanced down the platform at Davis. "You might want to get Cammy back with Mari and Rigel. Those damn Death's Heads are as big as him. They might carry him off."

"Shit!" Davis swore softly. "You're right." He ruffled the curly blond hair on the top of the little Terrier's head and kissed his noise quickly. "Stay by Mari," he told his Companion. "Help Rigel keep her safe."

Cammy licked Davis's face and then padded to Mari, taking a defensive position pressed to her other side.

Claudia pulled a cutting ax from the belt around her waist and chopped a clublike section of branch from a bough above them, tossing it to Mari. "You'll need this if any of them get past us."

Nik wanted to say something encouraging to Mari. She looked terrible—pale and frightened—the exact opposite of the powerful Goddess she'd appeared to be when she was calling down the ferocious power of the sun. But there was no time. With an all too familiar whirring sound of their leather-like wings, roaches the size of Terriers began lifting from the forest floor around them, drawn to the platform by the scent of blood.

Nik steeled himself to set aside his fear for Mari and Rigel and Laru, as well as the radiating pain in his burned and bloody palms. He tightened the strips of cloth around his hands, then aimed and fired, catching the first roach through its thorax as Laru plucked another giant insect out of the air, shaking it until its spine snapped and then dropping it to the writhing forest floor below.

Time suspended for Nik. He moved automatically through the pain in his hands, aiming and firing, and shouting encouragement to Davis and Claudia and Antreas, while the canines and the Lynx fought beside them.

It was over fast—much faster than Nik expected, but the swarm wasn't mindless. They tended to avoid things that could kill them, which was why they rarely attacked close to the City in the Trees. Even burned and partially deserted, the humans in the city were more difficult prey than the wounded humans and canines who weren't able to climb to safety. Within a few minutes all roach sign was gone, their brothers had devoured even the dead or wounded bugs, and the forest floor was swept clean of any trace of the carnage that moved with the swarm.

"Everyone okay?" Nik asked as he ran his hands over Laru's body, checking to be sure none of the roaches had managed to spear him with knifelike mandibles. When Nik was sure Laru was fine, he went to Mari, kicking a dead roach from the platform and crouching beside her. "Did it cut you? Let me see. Their pinchers are full of all sorts of poisons."

Mari gently took his hands, stilling him. "I'm fine. Unbelievably tired, but fine. Rigel and Cammy killed the only roach that got past you." She smiled at the Terrier as he wiggled up to her, and she scratched under his bearded chin while Cammy wagged enthusiastically.

"Good boy, Cammy!" Davis said, holding out his arms so that his Companion jumped into them, covering his face with licks. "Good job keeping Mari and Rigel safe!"

Mari and Nik shared a secret smile as Rigel huffed and then sneezed, clearly *not* agreeing with Davis's assessment of his canine's bug-killing prowess.

"So, what now?"

Nik looked up from Mari's smile to see the Lynx man standing over him, hands on hips, his feline sitting beside him looking so serene she seemed otherworldly.

"What now?" Nik shrugged. "I go with Mari."

"You're leaving?" Davis and Claudia said together.

"Of course he's leaving," the Lynx man said with a sarcastic snort. "Your Tribe has lost its collective mind. Your Sun Priest is dead, and if I've listened in enough to get things straight, that angry little Hunter, Thaddeus, killed him, just as he intends to kill Nik and Mari. I don't see any evidence that Nik and Mari are idiots, so of course they're leaving."

"Sol is dead?" Claudia's face blanched white and her Shepherd whined as she slid down the bark of the tree to a sitting position on the platform.

"He is," Nik said.

"And Thaddeus killed him? Why in all the levels of hell was that mean bastard not tied up and fed to the swarm?" Claudia said, wiping angry tears from her face.

"He killed Sol accidentally, though I believe he's glad he did," Mari said. "Thaddeus was trying to kill me. Sol saved my life by taking the arrow meant for me."

"But if Sol's dead how was the blaze stopped? Who called down sun-fire?"

Everyone's gaze turned to Mari. Nik smiled proudly. "Mari called down sunfire and saved us."

"And still that damned little Hunter came after her and Nik," Antreas said. "Which is why Nik and Mari need to go. Now. Before Thaddeus shows up here and another *accident* happens with his crossbow."

"The cat man is right," Davis said. Then he shot Antreas an apologetic look. "Sorry, didn't mean any disrespect by calling you that."

"None taken." Antreas smiled. "I don't mind you calling me a cat man if you don't mind me calling you a dog man."

Davis frowned but corrected himself before continuing. "The, uh, *Lynx* man is right. Thaddeus is definitely after Nik and Mari, and with the Council scattered or, worse, and our Warriors the same, he could get away with just about anything."

"Like he's getting away with killing my father," Nik said grimly.

"He won't get away with it," Claudia said. "He can't. The Tribe won't let him."

"There isn't much of a Tribe left," Antreas said. Then he held up his hands in surrender as Davis and Claudia began to protest. "Wait, wait; I really don't mean to disrespect you, but look around. More than half of your city has been burned to ash. I'd guess that more than half of your Tribe are either dead or badly injured, and that's my guess before the swarm got to them. The Tribe of the Trees *was* great, but what are you now? I think you've been hurt and hurt badly—and that's a prime time for someone with Thaddeus's mentality to bully survivors into believing like he does. I've seen it happen before—and it can get ugly."

"I didn't think Lynx people lived in packs," Nik said.

"We don't. We're as solitary as you believe we are, but we are also well-traveled mercenaries—the only humans who know all the passes through the mountains. I've worked for a lot of different Tribes, and a lot of different types of people and their Companions. Tragedies like this bring out the best—and the worst—in Tribes, and I'm afraid your Tribe has a very vocal worst being brought out right now."

Mari suddenly struggled to her feet. "Nik, please take me home."

"Nik! There you are!" The call came from above, and Nik looked up to see Wilkes grabbing a line to rappel down to them. He landed lightly beside Nik, who stood to face him, but the tall Warrior looked past Nik to Mari. He bowed low to her before saying, "I ask again for your forgiveness. Please. I hated what I had to do to your Rigel, but it was the only way I could think to get you mad enough to call down sunfire."

Mari studied him warily. "You would have killed Rigel."

"No," the Warrior said firmly. "I would not have, but you needed to believe I would have—and so did Rigel. But had you not called down sunfire, we all would have been killed. Forgive me. The Tribe does not abide violence against any canine."

"Someone should tell Thaddeus about what the Tribe does and doesn't abide. Seems like he doesn't know the rules," Mari said.

"Oh, he knows them," Davis spoke up. "He just thinks he's above them."

"He's wrong," Wilkes said. "I'll prove that after we get through this mess."

"How can you be sure of that?" Mari asked.

"I'm Leader of the Warriors. As long as I hold that position, I give you my word that I will bring Thaddeus to justice before the Council."

Mari let out a long, exhausted breath. "I forgive you, and I'll hold you to your word."

"As well you should," Wilkes said.

"I'll hold you to your word, too," Nik said. "And I'm glad to see that you survived the swarm."

"You, too," Wilkes said, nodding at the others. "I'd like you to come with me, Nik. And Mari, too." The Leader of the Warriors bowed to Mari respectfully again. "I believe she's a great Healer, and the Tribe has need of her. Also, we must get this mess with Thaddeus straightened out, and you two can help do that."

"No," Mari said.

"No," Nik echoed.

Mari went to Nik's side, sliding her arm through his in an obvious gesture of solidarity. Rigel moved to stand beside her, just as Laru stood next to his Companion. "First, I am going to go to my Clan. They need me, and they are my priority. And I already told you the condition you have to meet if you want me to return and share my healing with your people. Your Council must give me their word that the Tribe will never take another Earth Walker captive," she said.

"And I go with Mari, though I'll return to testify to the Council, and to see that Thaddeus is made to take responsibility for what he has done," Nik said.

"Nik, I don't think I can let you leave." Wilkes spoke slowly, reluctantly.

"You have no choice," Mari said. She lifted one hand, spreading her fingers and holding her palm out, as if she was readying herself to call down more sunfire. "I understand why you threatened Rigel. But now I know how to call down sunfire, and I swear to the Great Earth Goddess if you *ever* threaten Rigel, Nik, Laru, me, or anyone under my protection again, I will call down sunfire and the consequences to the forest—to your people—be damned!"

Wilkes moved several paces back, giving Mari's hand wary looks. "Hey, like you said, I only did what had to be done for our Tribe. There's no need for more fire. Let's talk about this instead."

Surprising Nik, Antreas moved so that he was standing beside Laru. "So, you're admitting this young woman saved your entire Tribe?" He shot the question at Wilkes.

"She did, and we thank her for it," Wilkes said.

"You thank Mari by holding her and her mate prisoner?" Antreas said.

"It's not right," Davis said as he and Cammy moved to stand beside Rigel and Mari, too.

"No, it sure isn't." Claudia joined the others as they faced the Leader of the Warriors.

"So, you're *all* leaving with Mari?" Wilkes said, shaking his head in disbelief.

There was a long silence, which Antreas broke after he and his Lynx shared a look. "I go with Bast. Bast is ready to leave. Finally. And it seems she wants to go with Mari."

"Really?" Mari peered around Nik to look at the big, silent feline, who regarded her back through unreadable yellow eyes.

Antreas shrugged. "Really. Mind if I tag along with you?"

"I don't mind," Mari said. She paused for a moment, looking from Davis to Claudia. "I don't mind if either of you and your canines would like to come with us, too. I can't promise you a City in the Trees, but I can promise you warmth and safety if you can promise me that you will be open to living peacefully with Earth Walkers."

Davis spoke first. "The truth is that I'm sick of Thaddeus. I've had it with his bullying and his hatred. He's getting worse and worse, and he's affecting the Hunters. They're changing, and I don't like what they're changing into. So I'm going to follow Nik." The young man smiled shyly at Mari. "And his Earth Walker who can call down sunfire."

"Davis, don't be hasty—" Wilkes began, but Mari cut him off.

"Why don't you let him make his own choice? Do you not respect him as a fellow Tribesman?" Mari asked.

"I do," Wilkes said. "But he is young, and this decision does feel hasty."

"Nik, tell Wilkes how long I've complained about Thaddeus."

"Well, let's see." Nik considered. "For as long as he's been your mentor."

"See," Davis told Wilkes. "Not hasty. I ask that you respect my choice."

Wilkes nodded slowly, sadly. Then he turned to Claudia. "And you? What is your choice?"

"I don't know enough yet to make one," Claudia said. "So, I'm going to stay with the Tribe for now."

"That's fair," Nik said. "If you change your mind . . ."

"Well, I don't know where to find you," Claudia said with a smile. "But you have given your word to return."

"And I will," Nik assured her as he met Wilkes's gaze steadily.

"All right," Wilkes said. "That is what I'll report to the Council. But, Nik, you should consider one more thing. You are the best bowman in the Tribe."

Nik moved his shoulders. "Yes, I know that, Wilkes. I've been the best bowman in the Tribe since I passed sixteen winters. Why should I consider something I've known for years?"

"Because what you *haven't* considered until now is your future as Companion to the Tribe's Alpha Shepherd. Laru choosing you changes everything," Wilkes said.

Nik drew a long breath and then let it out. "You see, that's the biggest problem I have with the Tribe. Before Laru chose me, I was still the best bowman in the Tribe—the same person I've been for twenty-three winters. Only now that Laru is by my side, I'm suddenly seen as worthy to lead?" He shook his head. "Father said I would understand if I was ever made a Companion. Well, I'm a Companion, and I still don't understand. No, I'm going with Mari."

Wilkes bowed his head briefly in defeat, and when the Warrior met his gaze again Nik saw a sadness there that hadn't been before as the man rappelled up the tree. Wilkes disappeared into the boughs and the sky opened. The rain that had been threatening all day poured like ropes from above.

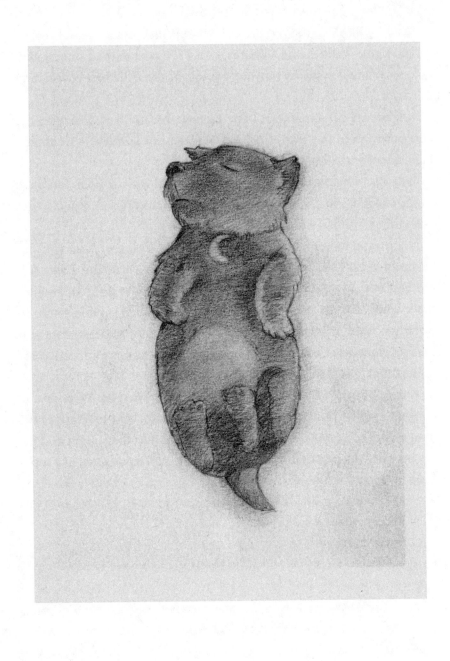

CHAPTER 7

W hat are they?" Sora stared into the squirming mass of grunting, wriggling little creatures that O'Bryan was trying to tuck
back inside his shirt.

He looked up at her and grinned. "They're Terrier puppies!"

"Oh, Goddess. *More* canines?"

"Sora, are you telling me you've never seen a puppy?" O'Bryan
asked, looking at her as if she'd just said she'd never seen sunlight.

"Did you hit your head escaping from the fire or are you just simple?"
Sora frowned at him. "You know very well that I've never seen a puppy
before. Well, unless you count Rigel, and I think of him as more creature
than puppy." Her frown deepened and she pointed her chin to where
Captain was sitting beside Sheena. "Are they going to get as big as that
giant version of Rigel over there?"

O'Bryan laughed heartily. "No! Rigel and Captain are Shepherds,
Leader canines. These little guys are Terriers, or Hunter canines. They'll
only get about as big as Fala."

"The little black canine who's resting over there with Rose?" Sora asked
before having to turn away to cough. When her gaze found O'Bryan's
again, he was watching her contemplatively. "What?" She did nothing to
hide the annoyance in her voice.

"Are you okay? That cough sounds bad, and you look, well, pale except for those bruises. Did someone hurt you?"

Sora had a sharp reply ready—something about it being none of a Companion's business what was what with her or any other Earth Walker, but O'Bryan's expression was honestly concerned. Her sigh ended in another hacking cough, and she had to force herself not to scratch at her skin, which was feeling tight and strange, especially at the creases in her elbows and wrists. "I was attacked yesterday. I'm fine."

"Are you sure?"

"If I'm not, are you ready to step up and be Healer for all of these people?"

"I'm pretty sure you and Mari are much better at that than me," O'Bryan said.

"Well, then I'll rest when everyone has been treated, fed, and safe. Now, you were explaining to me about these baby canines." She nodded at the knot of puppies he was carrying. "They're going to look like that little black creature with Rose, and not like Rigel?"

O'Bryan nodded. "Yep. Rose's Fala is their mother. Here, take one. They're friendly." He pulled one by the scruff of her neck from inside his shirt and handed her to Sora.

She took the pup automatically. Then Sora just stood there, holding her by the scruff of her neck as she kicked her four little legs and started to whine in complaint.

"It doesn't like me." She tried to hand the pup back to O'Bryan.

"*She* doesn't know whether to like or dislike you. Don't dangle her like that. It's okay to pick them up by their scruff when they're young, but not particularly comfortable for them to be held that way. She needs to feel secure. Hold her close to you. Like this." O'Bryan demonstrated by pulling another puppy from inside his shirt and then cradling it, infant-like, against his body.

Sora looked up at him, her expression clearly saying that she wanted to toss the pup back to him.

"Go ahead, Sora. Hold her close. I want to see what happens." Isabel had quietly come to stand a little behind Sora and was peeking over her shoulder at the wriggling puppy.

With a sigh and a stifled cough, Sora cupped the squirming little creature in her hands, holding her close to her body as she would a baby. The pup instantly quieted and then turned her little face up, sniffing curiously at Sora.

Sora sniffed back at the pup. She glanced at O'Bryan in surprise. "It smells nice."

"Yes, *she* does," O'Bryan said.

"Does she have a name?" Isabel asked.

"No. Or rather, yes, she probably does know her name already, but we won't know it until she chooses her Companion. Then her new Companion will announce her name to the Tribe."

"When do they choose?" Sora asked, ready to give the puppy back to O'Bryan if he said she was ready to choose anytime. The last thing she needed was a baby canine to look after!

"Pups begin choosing their Companions right around the time they're weaned." Seeing the question mark expressions on the two young women's faces, he explained, "That's usually when they're about eight weeks old. They rarely choose that early, though. And also usually no later than when they turn six months old."

"How old is she?" Sora asked, running her finger down the soft fur of the puppy's back.

"Almost two weeks old. Her eyes just opened not long ago," Davis said.

"Puppies are born with closed eyes?" Isabel asked.

"Yep, they are," O'Bryan said.

"And this little canine will really tell a person her name?" Isabel seemed more intrigued than shocked as she slowly reached out a finger to stroke the top of the puppy's head.

"Oh yes, absolutely," O'Bryan said.

"You mean, *she'll talk*?" Isabel said the last words in a voice hushed with shock.

"Sort of—but not aloud. When she chooses her Companion, they'll share a bond that's more intimate than mere words," O'Bryan explained.

"I'm not surprised. Rigel tells Mari all sorts of crazy things. Do you know that creature is absolutely insane about leather balls? Mari started making these strange ball-things for him because he loves chasing them so much. I asked her how she knew he'd like them, and she said *he told me he would*." Sora looked pointedly at O'Bryan. "So you're saying that's *normal*?"

O'Bryan's smile was genuine and warm. "Completely normal."

Sora thought he wasn't too terrible looking for a Tribesman, though he was awfully tall and blond—which was weird, but she'd already started to get used to the physical strangeness of Companions because of Nik.

"May I hold one?" Isabel asked tentatively.

"Of course!" O'Bryan was pulling another pup from his shirt when Rose and Fala joined them.

"Is there something wrong with the pups?" Rose was at O'Bryan's side in an instant, running her hands over the pups he was holding and eyeing the one Sora was still holding—awkwardly—as Isabel ducked her head and began to turn away.

"The pups are perfect," O'Bryan assured Rose hastily. "Isabel, wait." She paused and he continued. "Don't go. I'm sure Rose won't mind you holding one of them."

Sora saw him exchange a look with Rose, who let out a long breath and nodded before turning to Isabel. "I don't mind if you want to hold one of Fala's pups."

Hesitantly, Isabel moved to O'Bryan's side. She sent a nervous smile to Rose. "Thank you. I'll be very careful. I've never seen a puppy before."

Rose took the pup from O'Bryan and held him out to Isabel. "Just remember not to hold him too tightly or too loosely. Treat him as you would a human infant. Let him know he's safe with you."

Isabel nodded. "I understand." Moving slowly and carefully, she took the pup and then cradled him close to her chest. Sora watched her look down at him as the pup looked up at her. He lifted himself, putting his little paws on her chest and sticking his nose on Isabel's chin, sniffing and then licking her as Isabel began to giggle.

Sora glanced around them and saw that everyone was watching Isabel. She thought she saw looks of disgust cross a few of the Earth Walkers' faces, but mostly Sora saw curiosity, even some longing. She shrugged mentally—*well, they are baby animals, and babies are hard to resist.*

Sora handed the little girl puppy back to O'Bryan, but not before petting her silky black fur and staring into her bright, happy-looking eyes.

"Are your burns less painful since I put the aloe salve on them, Rose?" Sora asked, feeling much more confident as a Healer than as a puppy holder.

Rose nodded. "They are. Thank you."

"Good. That means Lydia's burns will be more bearable, too." She raised her voice and called, "We've rested long enough. The birthing burrow isn't far from here. Next time we stop it will be for the night."

"May I carry the puppy for a little while?" Isabel asked Rose. "I'll walk with you and O'Bryan if that's okay."

Rose nodded. "I suppose. But show him to Fala first so that she knows he's safe with you."

"Of course," Isabel said before crouching down with the puppy held carefully in her arms. Shyly, she began talking to the adult canine. "Hello, Mother. I'd like to carry your baby, and I give you my word that I will be careful." She held the puppy out so that the Terrier could sniff him, which she did, and then Sora was surprised to see the black canine sniffing at Isabel, too. Isabel held very still—Sora didn't think the girl was even breathing. Then the canine licked Isabel's hand and yipped once before padding to Rose's side.

"Did I do okay?" Isabel asked Rose.

Rose actually smiled at the girl. "You did. Fala trusts you to keep her pup safe."

"He is safe with me! I promise you he is," Isabel said.

"I'll help Sarah and Lydia up," Sora said. She called to one of the older Earth Walkers who she knew would be able to follow the trail to the birthing burrow. "Jancita, please lead."

Jancita bowed respectfully to Sora. The older woman moved stiffly—as did many of the Earth Walkers. Several of them were coughing continuously, and Sora wished for what seemed like the thousandth time that Mari had stayed with them. Mari would know whether the coughs were because, like Sora, their immune systems had been overtaxed and they were sick or the smoke had injured their lungs, or were they coughing because the women had taken in too much water from their Channel swim and were now at risk for pneumonia?

Sora tried to keep her expression neutral as she helped the two Companions to their feet. The sisters were in bad shape and getting worse. Lydia's burns were serious, worse even than the wounds that covered Rose's back. Sora had spread the aloe gel liberally on the ugly, weeping burns, but she could do little else for the girl until they got to shelter. The other sister, Sarah, had an ankle that was going to need splinting, medication for pain, and a good, long rest.

We're all going to need a good, long rest, Sora thought as she turned away, coughing and scratching at her elbow crease. She wiped her mouth again, and her gaze traveled over the ragtag group. The other two Companions, Sheena and O'Bryan, had minor injuries. But they were *Companions,* and soon they would know exactly where the Weaver Clan's birthing burrow was located. *Mari, what were you thinking when you let them come with you?* Sora sighed. She knew what Mari had been thinking. She was a Healer, just as her mother had been. It was in Mari's blood to help people.

"I'll take the lead now. Thank you, Jancita." Sora touched the woman's arm, and she fell back with the group. Sora looked over her shoulder, cleared the phlegm from her throat, and raised her voice so that they could all hear her. "I'm going to walk faster. I know it'll be hard for you to keep up, but it's close to sunset and we cannot be caught in the forest after dark."

Grimly, Earth Walkers and Companions picked up the pace, limping and staggering but keeping up with Sora.

Sora focused on continuing forward and on being irritated about how terrible she felt. Her eyes burned. Her stomach ached. And, worst of all, her skin felt hot and tight and itchy. Goddess, she *hated* being sick!

"You look angry." Sora jumped as O'Bryan's voice came from close beside her. "Sorry," he added quickly. "I didn't mean to startle you."

"I just didn't know you were walking so close. I would have thought I'd have heard you, what with all those little creatures you're carrying around." She cocked her head as she studied him. "Are you a midwife for canines?"

O'Bryan's bark of laughter startled the puppies he was carrying tucked under his shirt, and he had to cuddle them quiet before he answered Sora. "No, nothing like that. I'm just a Tribesman, and canines, especially babies who are still so vulnerable, are important to us."

"Oh. Hm. I suppose that makes sense. . . ." She paused and then added, "And I'm not angry. I'm sick, which is highly annoying. And I'm worried," Sora said, and then wondered why she felt the need to explain anything to this Companion.

"Worried about what?" he asked.

She snorted. "Let's see—" Sora held up her hand, ticking off fingers. "The forest is on fire. There are a bunch of wounded people with me— some of them wounded pretty badly. I have no idea when or if Mari is going to return. I don't have the supplies I need at the birthing burrow. I don't have the food I need at the birthing burrow. And I'm leading our enemies into the heart of our Clan. There are other, lesser things that are worrying me, but those are the biggies."

"Would you like to carry a puppy?"

Sora looked at O'Bryan closely, wondering for the second time if perhaps he was simple. "Why would I like to carry a puppy?"

His grin made him look boyish. "Why *wouldn't* you like to carry a puppy?" Before she could protest, he lifted one from under his shirt and handed her to Sora.

She took the puppy, realizing as she peered up at Sora with her shining black eyes that she was the same little girl she'd held before. "So, you're back," she told the pup. The little girl Terrier opened her mouth and yipped happily at Sora before half rolling, half flopping on her back and exposing her fat belly. Sora looked at O'Bryan, one brow lifted in a question.

"Puppies like their bellies scratched."

"Oh, well, um . . ." Sora stared down at the pup, who was still lying splay legged in the crook of her arm. Hesitantly, Sora used her index finger to gently scratch the Terrier's soft, plump belly.

The puppy began to wag her tiny tail so excitedly that most of her body wriggled along with it, and she made happy little grunting noises. Sora couldn't help but smile. She traced her finger up to the pup's chest, enjoying the soft warmth of her black fur.

"Hey, look at this. I thought she was all black, but there's a splotch of blond on her chest. It looks like a perfect crescent moon," Sora said, tracing the light spot with her finger.

O'Bryan looked over her shoulder and his pleasant face broke into a delighted grin. "I didn't notice that before, either. I thought all the pups were solid black, but this little girl has been marked as special."

"Special?"

O'Bryan nodded. "When a dark-colored pup is born with a light spot on him or her, that is a sign of favor from the Sun. The Tribe calls it being sun-kissed. We believe it portends greatness." He gave the pup a scratch under her chin. "Wonderful things will happen to this little girl."

"Sun-kissed, huh? That's a pretty name," Sora said.

"It's not her *real* name. We won't know that until she chooses a Companion and tells him or her," O'Bryan said.

"To me she'll always be Sun-Kissed."

The pup yawned mightily, then squirmed farther up into the crook of her arm, buried her face in Sora's armpit, and went instantly to sleep.

"She's sleeping. Again. Is something wrong with her?" Sora whispered, not wanting to alert Rose.

"No, nothing at all. Puppies sleep. A lot. It's a blessing, really, because they can be exhausting to try to keep out of trouble."

"Don't I know it? I've been living with Mari and her creature. Do you know Rigel will actually eat twigs and chew rocks if you let him?"

"Yes, well, that's just one reason it's a blessing young canines need to sleep a lot. They tend to get into things they shouldn't when they're awake."

"He'll eat my freshly baked bread if I don't keep an eye on him, too. He's really gotten good at sneaking around quietly when he thinks I'm not watching," Sora said.

"Don't ever forget they're as smart as we are—they're just a different kind of smart," O'Bryan said.

"Really?" She looked down at the soft, warm little creature sleeping so trustingly against her body. "That smart?"

"Really. In some ways they're smarter than humans. They can smell layers of scents we can't, and they can distinguish the scents from each other, even when they're mixed."

"You mean Rigel could identify all the ingredients in a salve I've made?"

"Absolutely," O'Bryan assured her.

"Huh. That's interesting. I'm definitely going to talk to Mari about putting him to good use when they get back. I mean, if he can identify what all is in a salve, then why can't he search out and find each of the ingredients for me—or Mari?" Sora said, stroking the sleeping puppy absently.

"He can, but a Terrier would be even better at it. They're Hunters, used to relying on their noses even more than the Shepherds."

"I don't understand how those big Shepherd canines can live up in the trees with you. Look at Captain." Sora jerked her head toward where

Captain and Sheena were walking beside Lydia and Sarah. "He's enormous. How can he possibly climb a tree?"

O'Bryan stifled a laugh. Though his eyes were sparkling with subdued humor, he answered Sora as if he enjoyed teaching her about his Tribe. "Our canines don't have to climb trees. The Tribe has created a lift system so that none of us have to climb trees. We also have ropes and pulleys all around the city. It's much easier to rappel with a canine strapped across your back than you'd think it would be—even an adult Shepherd."

"Rappel? I don't even know what that word means."

"It's a quicker way of getting up and down—especially down—from the city. It's hard to explain without showing. If you'd like, I could show you sometime."

Sora's gaze caught his. "I won't be going to your city. Ever."

O'Bryan's perpetual smile slid from his face like tallow from a melting candle. "I can show you anywhere, really. All I need is a good length of strong, thick rope and an anchor. I could rig a demonstration pretty easily. It wouldn't be like in my city, but I could still make it so that you understand what it means to rappel."

Sora hated that she'd taken the smile from his face—and then she was annoyed at herself for caring whether the Companion smiled at all.

"I doubt if you'll be with us long enough to show me much of anything," Sora said. "Here, take her back. I need to check on the group." She didn't really want to give the puppy back to O'Bryan, but she made herself do it anyway, though the baby whined and seemed to struggle, if only for a moment, to get back to her.

"I hope she made you feel better. Even if it was just for a little while," O'Bryan said, his smile returning to lift the corners of his lips. "We say that pups are good for the soul."

Thunder boomed in the distance, and then the sky broke open and rain began to pour down on them.

"Thank the Sun!" O'Bryan said reverently.

"This weather is going to help with stopping your fire, but it's definitely not going to help our wounded," Sora said.

"Do you always look at the negative in everything?" O'Bryan asked her.

"I'm not negative. I'm honest." Sora had meant to tell O'Bryan that compared to Mari, she was an overachieving optimist, but a thrashing in the brush broke off her words.

The Earth Walker staggered onto the trail in front of them. Sora gasped in shock at the man's appearance. He was filthy and covered with dried blood and strange-looking wounds. He looked up and captured Sora in his pain-wracked gaze.

"Moon Woman. Help me." He fell to his knees, still looking up beseechingly at Sora.

O'Bryan didn't hesitate. He turned to Sora, handing the pups he'd been carrying to her as he pushed her behind him and pulled a long knife from his waist.

"Get out of here or I'll kill you!"

Sora wasn't sure what was more shocking, that sweet, smiling O'Bryan had morphed into a killer Companion right before her eyes or that the Earth Walker who was begging for her help was Jaxom—the same young man who had attacked and tried to rape her just two days before.

"I know him," Sora said, putting her hand on O'Bryan's arm. "Don't hurt him. Or at least don't hurt him yet."

There was movement behind Sora, and then Sheena with Captain growling beside her, and Rose with little Fala also growling a warning, had joined her and O'Bryan. Both women were also holding knives at the ready.

Sora made her decision fast. "Here, take them!" She transferred the pups to Rose, and then she told Sheena and O'Bryan, "Stay close to me. He might be dangerous because he's been sick, but he's an old friend."

Sora approached Jaxom.

The young man's head had lolled down. He was breathing heavily, and Sora could see that his body was trembling.

"Jaxom, do you know me?"

His head lifted slowly. He blinked his eyes clear of sweat and tears. "Sora." His voice was like gravel. "You are Moon Woman. Help me."

Sora stared into his eyes. She saw pain and confusion there, but none of the madness she'd seen when he and two others had attacked her. He didn't look like her Jaxom, the young man she'd almost decided to claim as her mate, but he also didn't look like a monster.

"Can you walk?" she asked him.

"Will try," he said.

"You'll have to do better than try, but you don't have far to walk." She opened an outside flap of her satchel and pulled a length of tightly braided hemp rope from it. Then she met his gaze steadily. "I'll help you, but I'm going to tie your hands, and this Companion is going to take the end of the rope. Jaxom, if you get violent I will let him kill you."

"I understa—" Jaxom began, and then his body shuddered horribly, his eyes rolled to show their whites, and the wounded man passed out.

Sora sighed and went to Jaxom's still body, feeling for his pulse, which was there but beating entirely too fast.

"Is it smart to take him with us? Males are always violent," Sheena said.

"No, they're not." Sora spoke as she began tying his outstretched hands, wrists together. "It's only at night that they're violent, and then the violence is directed at themselves, unless you're trying to kill them or steal a member of their family to be your slave." She finished tying him and then faced the three Companions who were frowning at her. "His name is Jaxom. He's wounded and sick, and he hasn't been healed in a long time. I'm going to help him—*we're* going to help him."

"But he's unconscious. How's he going to come with us?" O'Bryan asked.

Sora arched one brow at O'Bryan. "Well, you said it was much easier than I thought to carry a grown Shepherd across your back as you rappel up and down from your city. Jaxom doesn't look like he could weigh much more than Captain weighs."

"Yes, but—" O'Bryan began.

"Unless you're not strong enough?" Sora said, her lips lifting.

"I'm strong enough," O'Bryan said quickly.

"That's exactly what I thought." Sora tossed O'Bryan the end of Jaxom's rope and called back to the group, "We're almost home. Let's get out of this rain!"

CHAPTER 8

Dead Eye had been pacing back and forth across the God's balcony since Dove awakened him just after dawn. She'd felt a shift in the air and detected a subtle scent of smoke. As always, he had been her eyes. As usual, she had been correct—something was happening.

Their world was changing forever.

The city in the clouds that held the Tribe of the Trees was ablaze.

Dead Eye wanted to call together the youngest, healthiest of the Harvesters and race for the burning city to claim it for himself and the People.

A portentous shiver skittered down his spine and Dead Eye looked behind him and up.

The enormous copper statue that was the Reaper God, She Whom the People worshipped, loomed over him. If She stood, the Reaper would tower fifty feet above the ground. Here on Her balcony, She knelt, one hand extended down, beckoning to Her People—the other was raised, holding Her skin-reaping tool, the triple-pointed trident.

She appeared to be everything a God should be: powerful, frightening, and able to mete out justice swiftly and terribly.

Dead Eye met Her lifeless gaze and the strange, portentous feeling subsided.

"Someday they will know the truth—that you are no God but are simply a statue created by people who have been dust for centuries. You are as dead as they are, as dead as this City." He turned his back to the statue and continued gazing out at the distant ridge and the ominous clouds that undulated up from the forest as if lifting in time to the beat of sinister drums.

He remained there all day, watching the distant destruction of the city that had filled his dreams for as long as he could remember, listening to the thunder grow ever closer and planning . . . always planning for his future, Dove's future, and the future of the People. In spite of their superstitious attachment to a statue, he and Dove would lead them from this spoiled and poisoned City to the beauty and safety of the untainted trees.

But first they must be rid of the Others.

The rain began to fall in earnest several hours before dusk, and as it pelted against the dead metal of the statue he knew that he could be patient no longer. As if Dove could read his mind, the moment Dead Eye made his decision her voice drifted from inside the God's chamber to wash around him, as welcome and cleansing as the rain.

"Beloved, the God has spoken to me. She commands that I share Her words with Her Champion, so that you may speak them to the People."

Dead Eye turned from the balcony to the entrance to the Temple and the Chamber of the God, to take in the lovely sight before him.

Dove stood in the center of the chamber, surrounded by the young women she called Attendants, the healthy girls she had recruited to take the place of the God's Watchers—sick, selfish old women who had tainted the Temple and pretended for generations to be the voice of the God.

Dead Eye had culled the Watchers from the Temple, sparing only young Dove, who had lived her entire sixteen winters pretending to be the God's Oracle. After the culling, he and Dove were the only People who knew the truth—that *they* controlled their own fate, because the Reaper God was as dead as the crones he had thrown from Her balcony.

Now Dove stood in the center of her Attendants looking radiant. Like them, she was dressed traditionally: her young, full breasts bared, her skin painted with ornate patterns, always grouped in threes, like the God's trident. The decoration was both intimidating and pleasing, as Dove had intended. She wore only a long skirt trimmed with human hair of sacrificed Others. He noted with pleasure that Dove's skirt was also intricately decorated with bright bits of shining things, making her stand out from the others who were more plainly dressed.

She deserves to be swathed in ritual decorations, but my Dove would stand out with or without such luxuries, Dead Eye thought, well satisfied at the sight of his lover.

"Beloved? What is it?" she asked, her smooth brow wrinkling in concern.

"All is well, my Oracle," Dead Eye assured her. He motioned abruptly, freeing her Attendants from the deep, respectful curtseys they had knelt in the moment he'd appeared at the entrance to the chamber. "Though I would ask that you send Attendants to bring to me the best and strongest of our Hunters and Harvesters. I call for Iron Fist, Stalker, Thunder, Eagle Eye, Digger, Rebel, Steel Heart, Bones, Joker, and Midnight." Dead Eye ticked off the list he had so carefully compiled during his sleepless night and watchful day.

"Lily, choose a helper and do as your Champion commands." Dove spoke to the young Attendant who seemed the most eager to please. "Seek out the men and tell them that they are summoned to the Temple." She clapped her hands together twice and the Attendants scurried from the chamber.

Dead Eye came to her then, taking her elbow in his hand and guiding her through the cavernous room to the section of the God's chamber they had claimed as their own, using vines, braziers, and stretched hides to separate their living area from the rest of the Temple and to provide the young couple much-needed privacy.

More Attendants curtseyed low to them as they passed, showing Dove the respect she deserved as the God's Oracle and Dead Eye the deference he required as the God's Champion. But they straightened quickly, returning to their work restoring the God's chamber to its former glory.

Dead Eye acknowledged the women with only a slight nod. They were of no importance to him, except that they made Dove's life easier—and anything that brought Dove pleasure pleased him as well. But today he had little time even for that, which amused Dove.

"You're going to the forest and the City in the Trees, aren't you?"

Dove had turned to him the moment they'd reached the sanctuary of their bedroom, tilting her lovely face up to him. Dead Eye didn't answer her for a moment. Instead, he drank in her beauty. She wore her nut-brown hair long and free, so that it fell past her slim waist in a soft, shining curtain that did nothing to hide her high, full breasts. Dove's skin was miraculously smooth, free of pustules or the taint of cracking and shedding. Her full lips curved up in the familiar smile Dead Eye was coming to crave as much as the taste of those lips. Her only flaw was that her eyes were completely missing. Where they should have been there were only two dark, empty pits.

Dead Eye smiled, though she could not, of course, see him. There was nothing about Dove that he didn't find pleasing, including her eyeless face. That accident of birth had allowed her to be claimed by the old Watchers and raised in the Temple as Oracle of their Reaper God. When Dead Eye proclaimed himself the God's Champion, it was only logical that he also claimed Dove as his own.

And in return, Dove's devotion to him was unconditional.

"Beloved? Is something wrong?"

He took her into his arms, holding her slight, soft body against his. "No, everything is completely right."

"The rain has halted the forest fire?" she asked eagerly.

"I cannot tell if it is actually halted, but the smoke has definitely thinned."

"And now you will go into the forest to the city of the Others."

This time, she didn't frame her words as a question, but Dead Eye answered her. "I will, but let us stop calling it the city of the Others. I believe soon it will be *our* city, my precious one."

"We must be wise about how we present this to the People. They will be reluctant to go where the God cannot follow."

Dead Eye snorted. "If only they knew the truth."

"Patience, Champion. All will come in time."

"You are right, though. They will be reluctant to leave our City, little matter that it is poisoned and has been killing the People for generations," Dead Eye said as he stroked her hair, as always fascinated by it softness.

"So, begin by freeing them of the poison of the City so that they might see the truth, just as you and I have," Dove said.

Dead Eye bent to kiss her. "Of course you are right! I won't tell them we are entering the forest to begin claiming the territory we deserve."

"What will you tell them, beloved?"

"That we hunt. And from the hunt I will make Harvest, so that the People may begin to heal."

"And as the People heal, they will follow you from the City to the forest," Dove said.

"To live in the trees, subjugating the Others to do our bidding, far from this place of death and poison," Dead Eye said. "There, you and I will truly live like Gods!"

"Indeed," Dove said, sliding her hands up his strong arms to his shoulders. She cocked her head to the side in a thinking motion that Dead Eye found endearing. "Beloved, I can feel differences in your body."

"Yes, as can I. I wondered when you would speak of it to me."

She caressed his body. "Your shoulders are wider. Your arms thicker."

"There is more." He bent down so that he could guide her hand from his shoulder to the back of his neck.

She gasped, stroking the strange fur that had begun to grow there, thick and soft as a stag's. "What is it?"

"Follow my spine with your hand."

Dove did so, tracing a path down his back. "It's spreading down your back! What is it?" she repeated.

Dead Eye was pleased that she seemed excited rather than repulsed by the changes in him. Should Dove ever turn from him—*no*—Dead Eye could not even finish that thought.

"It is from the spirit of the stag whose flesh I joined with my body. It lives on in me, strengthening me—healing me from the City's poisons—changing me. Don't let it frighten you. Don't ever let changes in me frighten you," he told her, staring at her sightless face, trying to read every nuance of emotion she was feeling.

"Oh, my Champion! You could never frighten me!"

"Then you accept the stag?"

"Whatever it is that is happening to you I accept because you are my fate, you are my Champion—you will eternally be my hero. Whatever it is you are becoming, I will accept because it is *you*."

Dead Eye's legs went weak with relief, and he dropped to his knees, wrapping his arms around her and burying his face in the curve of her waist. Her hands caressed him, moving from his back to his shoulders and then up to stroke the thick blond hair that he kept tied back with a leather cord.

Her hands suddenly stilled.

Dead Eye held his breath, knowing what she had discovered.

"Horns?" she whispered.

He nodded into her waist. "Yes, though I think it more accurate to call them antlers."

She didn't hesitate for one instant. Dove pressed her lips to him twice—once against each of the small, pointed antlers that had begun to grow from his scalp above his ears.

Dead Eye released a long breath in relief. *Still she accepts me!*

"My Champion, you are a mighty leader filled with the wisdom of man and the strength of a stag. Where you go, the People will follow," Dove said, still stroking him. "Where you go, *I* will follow."

"It truly begins today!" With a movement filled with the strength and agility of a stag, Dead Eye lifted her and carried her to their thick pallet. "But first, I must have your blessing, Oracle."

Dove's soft, clever hands moved lower on his body. "Gladly I give it, and myself, to you. The God is dead, but the future of our People lives on in you, my Champion."

Dead Eye meant to tell her that she was beyond beautiful—that she was his life and his breath, that she made him *want* to be a true Champion of the People—but her greedy mouth was on his, stilling his words and causing the blood to pound so fiercely through his body that he moaned in pleasure and the only word he could speak was her name, which he shouted over and over.

It was still raining when Dead Eye led ten of the strongest and bravest of his People to the edge of the boundary of the City.

The small group hesitated, sending nervous glances into the verdant green before them. The Hunter called Stalker was the first to speak. "Champion, we enter the forest during a blaze? I do not wish to question your authority . . ." He paused there, bowing low, hands to the earth in supplication as if to show Dead Eye great respect, though when he glanced up Dead Eye noticed that the Hunter's gaze skittered nervously away. "I only wish to know what type of Hunt you lead us on. Are we to capture the Others as they flee the fire?"

Dead Eye waited several breaths before allowing Stalker to rise. He noted that the demeanor of the rest of the men seemed more watchful. They were silent, waiting attentively for Dead Eye to speak.

Dead Eye understood Stalker's fear of the forest. Hunters and Harvesters were comfortable within the confines of their City. It was there they knew every section of the ruined landscape, both above and below the crumbling buildings and the strange iron structures. But there was a marked difference in Stalker's attitude and the calm, respectful way the rest of the group looked to him. *Something to consider for the future.*

"We do not hunt Others today," Dead Eye explained, speaking in short, clipped sentences. "We hunt sacrificial animals. I have plans for the Others. Many, many plans. But not today. Today we enter the forest and climb."

Without waiting to see whether Stalker had more questions, Dead Eye sprinted away, heading up to Forest Park, the name the People had given the highest part of the hilly area northwest of the City. Up and to the north Dead Eye climbed, and as he jogged farther and farther toward the peak of Forest Park and the gorge that separated their City and the mountain range on which the City in the Trees had been built, he rejoiced in his powerful body. He did not tire. Instead of climbing laboriously over fallen logs and rain-swollen ditches, Dead Eye leaped easily over them, pushing himself as he came to each obstacle to see if he could run faster and jump higher.

He could.

Dead Eye realized that he had just begun to test the surface of his newfound abilities.

He reached the peak well ahead of the other men, so he stood, breathing deeply but effortlessly, at the edge of the ridge, staring across the jagged gorge that divided Forest Park from the mountain ridge that held the Tribe of the Trees.

The fire was out, but the damage done to the City in the Trees was extensive. From his vantage on the ridge he could see that the city still smoldered. It appeared as if a giant, or perhaps a God, had taken a burning torch and dragged it through the forest, leaving a swath of blackened rubble and destruction in its wake.

"More than half," he murmured to himself. "More than half of the city is gone. Perhaps more than half of the Tribe have perished as well." He expression was feral. "That helps to even the odds against us."

The Harvester called Iron Fist was the first to join him. Iron Fist staggered up the last of the ridge, wiping sweat from his brow as he made his way to Dead Eye. When Iron Fist reached him, the Harvester bowed low, pressing himself into the earth, before he spoke.

"I see the mighty stag in you, Champion!" Iron Fist spoke in excited bursts between heaving breaths, his face still bowed to the earth.

"You may rise," Dead Eye said as the rest of the group staggered to them. "Iron Fist, tell me more of what you say you see in me."

"I see your skin does not crack. I see you grow more powerful by the day. I see that you are much like a God yourself!"

Dead Eye had begun to smile at Iron Fist when Stalker limped through the group to them, clutching his side and gulping air. "It is blasphemous to name the Champion, or anyone except our Reaper, a God."

"And yet we all see he has been touched by our Reaper! His skin is healed. He has become mighty, like a great forest stag," insisted Iron Fist.

"But it is not the way of the People to have more than one God," Stalker insisted.

"And yet the God has surely shown Her favor by healing him, making him Champion, and mating him with Her Oracle," another Harvester called Thunder added.

"It is not the way of the People," Stalker repeated stubbornly.

Dead Eye thought it interesting that Stalker only flicked occasional glances at him and was speaking to the rest of the men almost as if Dead Eye weren't even there.

"But the Oracle has proclaimed change. The old, sickened Watchers have been replaced by young, nubile Attendants—just as our Champion's cracked, putrid flesh has been replaced by new, unmarred skin," said a Hunter named Eagle Eye, and he bowed respectfully to his Champion.

"Indeed!" the Hunter, Serpent, chimed in. "He has the God's favor. And that is enough of the way of the People for me."

"Truth!"

"Yes!" the remaining men murmured agreement, sending nervous glances to Stalker before bowing respectfully to their Champion. Then the group fell silent as they waited for their Champion to speak.

Instead of words, Dead Eye decided actions would be heard much louder and last much longer.

With the speed of a forest creature Dead Eye lowered his head and charged Stalker. In a movement so fast that his hand blurred, Dead Eye unsheathed the triple-pointed knife at his waist and thrust it into the softest part of Stalker's belly with such ferocious strength that his hand was driven into the warm, wet flesh, creating a fist-sized cavern in the Hunter's gut. As Stalker screamed his shock and agony, Dead Eye catapulted the man backward so that he flew over the edge of the ridge. At the last instant, while Stalker seemed to be suspended over the gorge, Dead Eye wrenched his fist from the Hunter's body with a terrible sucking sound, setting Stalker free to fall down, down into the chasm and the death that waited below.

Dead Eye wiped his bloody hand across his bare chest, adding a scarlet slash through the bold three-pointed designs already painted there by Dove's Attendants. Slowly, he turned to face the watching men.

As one, all nine dropped to their knees before Dead Eye, pressing their faces into the ground.

"Does anyone else wish to question my authority?" he bellowed, feeling the hot blood of a mighty stag surging through his body.

Iron Fist lifted his head. "Never, Champion! I follow you as I would follow the Reaper Herself should She rise from Her balcony and walk among us."

"And the rest of you?"

The other eight men raised their heads more slowly, though none of them hesitated in their response. "Iron Fist speaks for me," said Serpent. "I follow you as I would follow the God Herself."

"And I! I, too!" the rest of the men chorused their agreement.

"Do all of you see the God in me?"

Iron Fist glanced at the other men, meeting each of their eyes before he answered his Champion. "We do. Tell your Harvesters and Hunters what it is you would command, and we will obey. We will always obey."

Dead Eye almost corrected the Harvester. He meant to. His intention hadn't been to be worshipped like a God, as he was all too aware of what it was to worship a false God. He had only wanted to bring health and a better life to his dying people. But as he opened his mouth to speak, to tell Iron Fist that there was no God within him, only the People's Champion, the words would not come. Try as he might, Dead Eye found he could not speak them. Instead, something stirred and began to awaken within him as he stared down at Iron Fist and the rest of the men who remained on their knees, awaiting his command. The men's supplication pleased Dead Eye as much as Stalker's death had pleased him.

A thought, as elusive as fog, drifted through Dead Eye's mind—*Take that which is owed you.*

"Harvesters and Hunters, what I command today is that you accept the gift I am going to give you, just as I accept your oath of loyalty. Come, rise and hunt with me."

Iron Fist stood with the rest of the men. "But some of us are not Hunters. We are only Harvesters," he said.

Dead Eye felt his chest swell with newfound strength as he replied, "Fear not—not your lack of abilities, not the forest. You *were* Harvesters or Hunters. I proclaim that by the end of this day you will all be known as Reapers in the company of their God!"

Making an effort to slow his pace so that he didn't leave the nine men far, far behind, Dead Eye headed down into the gorge. Because today's rain was the first in several weeks, the stream that ran through the bottom of the chasm was lower than usual, which made a crossing spot easy to find. As Dead Eye anticipated, they didn't have to wait long before creatures, driven by the forest fire to find solace in water, began to make their way to the stream.

Mostly, the creatures were small. There were many rabbits and rats, squirrels and mice, that paraded past them after they drank deeply of the water. And that was as it should be. Large forest creatures were scarce, especially this close to the City.

From a makeshift blind he and the men hastily erected, Dead Eye sat in complete silence, waiting for a sign.

The sign came sooner than he had anticipated.

The boar was a red behemoth with a huge, wrinkled snout punctuated by two sets of pointed tusks—smaller, hooked uppers and long, sharp lowers. His chest was so wide and thickly muscled that he appeared to be wearing armor. He waded part of the way into the stream and buried his mighty head in the water, splashing and grunting in plea-sure. Dead Eye was so close that he could smell the sharp tang of the virile male's body. The boar snorted and shook himself, spraying droplets of water around him like an unfurling cloak. Then he started wading through the stream, picking his way around rocks and debris. It seemed as if he was going to pass almost within touching distance of where Dead Eye and his Reapers crouched, silent and hidden.

The boar stepped onto the bank. He stopped and lifted his massive head, turning so that his golden eye looked directly at Dead Eye. The boar froze and the dark center of his eye expanded so that within it Dead Eye saw his own reflection. Then slowly, almost imperceptibly, the boar's muzzle dropped to touch the earth, and he bowed his head.

"Stay here until I call for you to come to me," Dead Eye whispered to his men.

Then he stepped from the concealment of the blind.

The boar's reaction was instantaneous. He went stiff legged, the bris-tles on his back fanned and lifted so high they were like spikes along his spine. He began swinging his mighty head from side to side, spew-ing spittle in an arch around him as he ground his lower tusks against his smaller, knife-sharp upper teeth. His intelligent eyes gleamed with malice as he stared at Dead Eye.

Dead Eye knew the signs of a boar about to charge, and he readied himself. But instead of drawing his deadly three-tipped spear, he shook out the length of tightly braided hemp he carried over his shoulder, flicking the end so that the noose he'd fashioned there opened lazily.

With a deep, angry grunt, the boar charged.

Dead Eye had planned to stand his ground until the last moment and then snag the boar with the noose as he sped past, jerk him off his feet, and tie him in a Hunter's bind so that he was immobilized.

But the sight of the charging beast caused the stag within Dead Eye to awaken. *Battle! Defeat it! Death!* The words echoed through Dead Eye's mind, filling his body with the hot, fierce blood of a forest creature.

The stag within him answered the boar's challenge with a deep bellow. Dead Eye lowered his head and ran at the boar, his feet tearing hunks of moss from the stream bank.

Everything happened so quickly that later Dead Eye was glad for the songs the People sang in remembrance of his clash with the boar so that he could relive the event, savoring it, over and over.

He acted solely on instinct, allowing the mighty stag to fill him with preternatural strength and speed. He and the boar met, and Dead Eye leaped up, twisting his body so that he hooked one arm around the boar's huge neck as he landed in the middle of the raging beast's back. Dead Eye dug his heels into the mossy ground while the boar squealed and grunted in rage, bucking and thrashing his head around, trying to sink his teeth into Dead Eye's legs. But the strength of beast and man joined was greater than the strength of the boar. Dead Eye pulled the enormous creature's head back and back and back, bowing his spine into a crescent and causing the boar to collapse in defeat on his side.

"Iron Fist! Come to me!"

Iron Fist obeyed unhesitatingly, but Dead Eye could see the fear in the gaze he kept focused on the straining boar, a fear that was mirrored in the eight men who crowded nervously behind him.

"Take the rope! Tie his front and back legs together. I'll keep his neck pulled back so that he cannot gore you."

Again, Iron Fist obeyed with a swiftness that Dead Eye appreciated, immobilizing the boar quickly.

"Now, each of you harvest three strips of skin from his belly. Long, thin strips. As quickly as you can," Dead Eye instructed the group. Iron Fist was the first to follow his command. The newly made Reaper drew his own triple-tipped dagger and lowered it to the boar's exposed belly, and Dead Eye shifted so that he could look directly into the beast's eye.

Dead Eye expected the creature to scream and thrash in pain, as they all did. Not this boar. The only outward sign of pain that this beast gave was to pant and show the whites of his eyes. He didn't flinch as the razor-tipped dagger sliced strip after strip of flesh from his living body as the nine Reapers took turns with him. The boar's gaze remained locked with Dead Eye's, even as his body grew weaker and weaker from loss of blood. And in that dimming gaze Dead Eye was shown what he must do.

He'd allowed the stag to live after he'd infected him and sent him into the territory of the Tribe of the Trees. This time Dead Eye saw that he must be more merciful to this boar. The stag's suffering had been necessary, and it had served its purpose of spreading poison to the Tribe. Dead Eye would always honor the stag's sacrifice. But the poison had spread, and the Tribe—whether it understood it yet or not—was already falling victim to Dead Eye's plot.

The boar was different.

"Enough, Reapers." Dead Eye spoke formally to his men. "I will make the killing cut."

Iron Fist and the others bowed and, carrying the bloody strips of boar skin, they backed several feet away. Dead Eye continued to stare into the boar's eye as he used his free hand to take the triple-pointed dagger from his waist sheath. He pulled the boar's neck back farther so that his throat was stretched completely out. Just before he slit the beast's neck from ear to ear, Dead Eye spoke the words that lifted from deep within, so deep that he didn't recognize his own voice, and for a moment it was as if Dead Eye's body were separated from that which stirred within him and he had been relegated to the role of observer.

"*Death has called you. I honor and accept your sacrifice, your strength, your spirit. Behold Death's merciful blow!*"

Dead Eye drew the dagger across the boar's throat. He relaxed his grip on the creature so that his neck wasn't stretched so awkwardly, but Dead Eye kept his gaze locked with the boar, watching his life drain away with the red river that poured from his neck.

When it was over, Dead Eye gently lowered the boar's head to the moss and closed the creature's sightless eyes. Dead Eye stood over the beast, head bowed in thanks as a maelstrom of emotions whirled within him. He felt triumphant and more powerful than he'd ever felt in his life. It was the boar's *death* that had so moved Dead Eye. It had been glorious.

Glorious? Why would slitting a boar's throat be glorious? The vaguely uncomfortable thought formed in Dead Eye's mind, lifting briefly to his consciousness, but when he tried to hold the thought—tried to consider it, decipher it—his mind skittered away, returning instead to the glory of the boar's death. *Isn't death just another part of life—perhaps the most important part?*

"Champion, would you have us anoint you with the boar's flesh?"

Iron Fist's voice pulled Dead Eye from his reverie, and he turned to the Reaper and the men he stood before. Dead Eye's original intent had been to go to the City in the Trees and catalogue the extent of their destruction so that he might decide the best path to follow for the People to claim their future, but Stalker's rebellion and the boar's sacrifice had changed everything. Dead Eye knew the City in the Trees would be his—that was inevitable. What was of the utmost importance now was preparing the People for their new life, their new Tribe, their new God.

"Your Champion will anoint each of you with the boar's flesh, and then we are going to take the boar to the People so that we might feast in celebration."

Iron Fist and the other men dropped to their knees in supplication before him, bowing their heads to the earth reverently. "Thank you, Champion. We gratefully accept your gift."

Dead Eye went to his Reapers, taking the still-warm strips of bloody boar flesh from them, one at a time, trimming the strips, and then packing them into the terrible, puss-filled cracks that spidered across the creases in the men's skin.

"Might I ask you a question, Champion?" Iron Fist asked.

"Of course." Dead Eye spoke as he worked. "The group of you have given me your oaths of loyalty. As long as you hold to your oath, you need never fear asking anything of me."

"You said tonight the People feast in celebration. What is it we celebrate?"

"An awakening." Dead Eye spoke the words without willing himself to, as if they had escaped from a place so deep within him that he was no longer Dead Eye. But instead of being frightened by this strange, powerful force, Dead Eye embraced it, accepted it, and found he longed to join with it even more fully.

⁂

Bearing the hunks of butchered boar meat between them, Dead Eye and his Reapers returned to the Temple to the cheers of the grateful People. On the hike back, Dead Eye noted that the men's bodies were already beginning to absorb the boar's flesh and the group of men walked with stronger steps, showing little strain from carrying their allotments of the huge animal's carcass.

Dead Eye dropped the meat in the courtyard. His attention had left the Reapers and even the excited, welcoming People surrounding him, celebrating him, worshipping him. His eyes were scanning the God's balcony, looking for Dove.

Suddenly her Attendants appeared all along the balcony's ledge. The People caught sight of them, and as one they turned to look up.

Like a gently rippling pool, the Attendants moved, lifted, and Dove was standing on the ledge. The firepots were lit all around her, and their orange and yellow flames threw strange, undulating shadows across her half-naked body, as if the dark caverns of her eyes were shifting from her face and moving along her skin.

"Does our Champion return?" she asked in a sweet, soft voice that somehow filled the world around them.

"I do, my Oracle!" Dead Eye called. "I return with an army newly reborn. Henceforth, they are not Harvesters or Hunters; they are all Reapers of the God—mighty and terrible to behold!"

"I celebrate with you!" Dove raised her arms and shouted with joy. "Come to your God and to me!"

Her call vibrated through his body. He did not try to resist it, even as he realized he *could not resist her*. The People parted, opening a pathway for him to the Temple. Dead Eye swaggered through them, feeling swollen with strength and need as he drew closer to her. Instead of entering through the Temple courtyard at ground level and taking the crumbling stairs, Dead Eye gathered himself and leaped, using the vines and broken tiles that covered the outside wall of the Temple to climb up and up and up, until he reached the God's balcony, where he gathered Dove in his arms and kissed her passionately while the People cheered. Lost in the kiss, Dead Eye almost did not notice that behind them the arm of the Reaper God that beckoned down to the People changed, rippled, and with a delicacy that others might mistake for shadows cast over Her metal skin by the blazing firepots, the massive copper statue drew Dead Eye and Dove more intimately within Her embrace.

Dove gasped against his mouth, her lips hot on his.

"You feel it too, my precious one?" Dead Eye whispered. "The God moves!"

Dove's eager lips kissed a path along his neck to his ear, where she whispered words that would alter their world forever.

"I do, but that is not why I gasp. What I feel more truly is the God moving within *you.*"

Dead Eye leaned back, so that he was pressed against the arm of the Reaper with Dove in his embrace. He lifted his face to the sky and bellowed a stag's mighty roar of power and pleasure.

CHAPTER 9

Mari had never been so tired or wet or miserable. When she'd carried her mama's body all the way from Crawfish Creek to bury her above their burrow near the image of the Great Goddess, Mari had been exhausted and filled with grief, but she had felt like herself. A sad, broken version of herself, but she'd still been Mari.

But not this day—not after she'd called down sunfire and created a blaze so fierce that it had stopped a forest fire. This day Mari wasn't entirely sure who *or what* she was.

Beside her, Rigel whined, looking up at her with an expression that was so clearly filled with worry that Mari didn't need to use their Companion bond to know what was bothering the young canine.

"I'm going to be okay," she tried to assure him as she kept staggering forward, placing one foot before the other while she focused all her remaining energy on staying upright and in motion. But her voice sounded as odd and weak as her body felt, and Rigel barked fretfully, causing Nik, who was walking just in front of them, to hurry to her side.

"Do you need to stop?"

His expression was as worried as Rigel's. Mari shook her head and put a hand on his arm. "I'm afraid if I stop I'll never start again." She'd meant it as a small joke, but she realized as she spoke that it was the

P. C. CAST

truth. If she sat down she honestly didn't believe she would be able to get up again.

"I'm sorry it's taking so long. I know you're in bad shape," Nik said, wrapping her arm through his. Laru trotted to her and sniffed Mari, then licked her hand encouragingly.

"We all agreed to take the path along the gorge. It's farther, but so close to the edge of Skin Stealer territory that we're pretty much assured we don't run into any more of the Tribe," Mari said. It was hard for her to talk—hard to formulate words—but as she spoke with Nik she decided that it was good for her to get out of her head, even if it took more energy than she wanted to spare.

"That plan's worked, and I'm glad. We haven't seen anything or anyone except for the animals running from the blaze," Davis said. He'd been following behind Mari, keeping watch on their rear while he hunted, but the trail had widened enough for him to join Nik walking beside her. His Terrier, Cammy, hurried to Rigel, huffing happily as the young Shepherd gave him a good sniff and lick, and then both dogs shook heartily, which did little good, as the rain remained steady, soaking the small group over and over. "Which turned out to be really good for dinner tonight!" Davis held up the half dozen rabbits he and Cammy had caught and killed on the journey.

"Sora will be glad of them." Mari tried to smile but thought her expression probably looked more like a grimace.

"Maybe we should rest. Just for a moment. Mari, you look—"

"Nik, Mari, you need to see this!" said Antreas, who had been scouting ahead, as he and Bast, with their preternatural sense of direction, materialized silently from the forest before them.

"See what?" Nik began, but Antreas hushed him with a swift gesture and then motioned for them to come with him—silently.

It took all of Mari's will to follow Nik and Antreas and Davis. The Lynx man led them to the lip of the gorge they'd been traveling parallel to, where they did as Antreas did and crouched silently behind a group of boulders and ferns. Antreas pointed down at the stream that flowed through the bottom of the gorge, but he needn't have made any

118

motion at all, as the battle that was taking place beneath them was many things—disturbing, unbelievable, violent, and loud. *Really loud.*

Mari's gaze followed the sounds of struggle. At first she wasn't sure what she was seeing. A huge, painted man was locked in combat with an equally monstrous boar. The boar was snorting and squealing, and the man was making odd bellowing sounds that reminded Mari of a rutting stag. She cringed, thinking she was going to watch the man's terrible death—gored by the angry beast. But she realized quickly that she'd misjudged what was going on. *The man was defeating the boar—easily!*

The battle didn't last long and ended in victory for the man, who called a group of men from concealment, and then they began tying up the boar.

"Oh, Great Goddess, what are they doing to that poor beast?" Mari whispered.

"They're Skin Stealers." Nik lowered his voice, but Mari could still hear a world of contempt within it. "I don't know what they're doing. They should just be gutting it, cleaning it, and then taking it back to Port City, but you can never tell what those monsters will do."

"Skin Stealers," Antreas said softly. "I've heard of them. Never seen one, though. Great Stormshaker! Is he flaying that boar alive?"

"He is," Davis said, crouching beside them. "We thought they only did that to humans, but when Thaddeus was captured by them a few weeks ago he said they flayed the flesh from his Terrier, Odysseus."

"Isn't that how he supposedly escaped them?" Nik said.

Davis nodded. "What Thaddeus said was Odysseus made so much noise when they started to cut the skin from him that he was able to slip away, unnoticed."

"And Odysseus somehow, miraculously, escaped, too, alive and relatively unharmed." Nik didn't attempt to hide the sarcasm in his voice.

Antreas looked at Nik. "You don't believe that's what happened?"

"I don't believe anything Thaddeus says. He has one agenda—whatever is best for Thaddeus. Look down there. That huge Skin Stealer and his men are having no trouble incapacitating a boar that must weigh upward of three hundred pounds. Why would a frightened Terrier that weighs not much over twenty pounds be a problem for men like that to handle?"

"It doesn't make sense," Antreas agreed. "But neither does what they're doing."

"They believe they can absorb your essence if they flay your flesh from your living body, and then press it into their body," Davis said. "None of it makes sense."

"But that's not what they're doing," Mari said, feeling nauseous but unable to look away from the grisly scene below them. The huge man who had been straddling the boar and stretching his head back suddenly leaned forward and slit the hog's throat, ear to ear, so that scarlet showered in an arch around the dying beast. "That's not a human—it's a boar."

"It's strange," Davis said.

"Maybe they flay the flesh of animals before they eat them," Antreas said. "It could be part of their customs."

"Look!" Mari said. "That big one is placing the boar's flesh over the skin of the rest of those men." She leaned forward, squinting to try to see better, Healer curiosity temporarily overriding her disgust. "I can't tell for sure from here, but I think I can see open wounds on his men's bodies—though I don't see any on the Leader's." She grimaced in disgust. "Ugh, I take that back. I see what he's doing now. He's packing that boar's bloody flesh *into* his men's open wounds, like the flesh is a poultice." She shuddered. "It's unbelievable."

"And beyond disgusting," Nik shivered and looked away.

"But why?" Mari spoke more to herself than aloud. "What would be the reason behind packing the flesh of a boar into a man's wounds? It's only flesh. He hasn't even added healing herbs or ointments."

"They don't need a reason. They're Skin Stealers, which means they are completely insane," Davis said.

"Maybe," Mari said. "But look at him. He's being so careful. And he's covering the wounds with strips of moss and using vines to tie the bandages in place. His actions mirror much of what I did to heal your blight wounds, Nik."

"But you did it with salves and herbs," Nik said. "Not the flesh of a line animal."

"I did what I knew would work to heal your wounds. Maybe this Skin Stealer knows something about healing his people that we don't," Mari said.

"Or maybe he's as crazy as Nik and Davis report," Antreas said.

"Let's move," Nik said. "We don't need to deal with Skin Stealers today."

"Agreed," Davis and Antreas said together.

"I'll go back to point. I don't think we're far from the lowlands now," Antreas said, and he and Bast disappeared silently into the forest.

Mari, Nik, and Davis crawled back from the edge of the gorge, and Mari didn't argue when Nik put his arm around her waist so that he almost carried her with him. Mari gritted her teeth and forced herself to keep moving, keep walking—keep heading toward home.

"Lowlands, straight ahead!" Antreas called back to them through cupped hands.

Mari almost dropped to her knees with relief. "We're within Clan lands now. Not much farther. We don't have to go much farther tonight."

"Um, where exactly are we going tonight?" Davis asked, jogging to come up beside Nik and Mari.

Mari looked up at him, blinking as if to clear her vision when in truth she was trying to clear her mind. "Home, of course," she said.

"To your burrow?" Nik asked. "I thought we were going to what you call a birthing burrow. Isn't that where you said Sora was leading the others—Earth Walkers and Companions?"

"Yes, she is." Mari struggled to think through the fog that had become her mind. "She's taking everyone to the birthing burrow. But it's farther from here than home is, and I'm pretty sure we won't make it there tonight. So, we need to go to my burrow."

"Mari." Nik pulled her to a halt. "It's not just me. It's Antreas and Davis, too. Are you sure you want to take them to *your* burrow?"

Mari furrowed her brow, trying to concentrate on Nik's words. Of course she wanted to go home. She *needed* to go home. She'd be able to rest there. She'd be able to find herself again there. She frowned up at Nik. "Nik, I want to go home."

"Hey, I know." He spoke gently, touching her cheek. "And I'll get you there, but Mari, if we go there tonight Antreas and Davis will be with us. Are you okay with that? Will your Clan be okay with that?"

Nik's words finally broke through Mari's stupor, and she felt a rush of panic. "Oh, Great Mother, I'd forgotten!"

"Forgotten?" Davis asked.

Mari didn't look at Davis. She stared into Nik's compassionate green eyes. "I'd forgotten that they can't know where I live. Nik, what's wrong with me?"

Nik pulled her into his arms and held her tightly. "It's what happens to Sun Priests after they call down sunfire. I'm amazed you're still walking and talking at all. But nothing is wrong with you! You're going to be fine."

"Wait, did she just say we can't know where she lives?" Davis said.

Nik kept his arm wrapped around Mari's shoulder as they turned to face Davis at the same time Antreas and Bast jogged up to them. "We can't afford to pause again. The sun is setting and the swarm won't be the only creepy-crawlies looking to feast tonight," Antreas said.

"I think we need to decide where we're going now that we're entering Earth Walker territory," Davis said, looking pointedly from Nik to Mari.

"I thought we were headed to a birthing burrow," Antreas said.

"It's too far away. Mari can't make it tonight. Or at least she can't make it there until she's rested and eaten something," Nik said.

"But she doesn't want us to know where she lives," Davis said.

Davis's tone was unexpected to Mari. Even through her exhaustion she could tell that her words had hurt and surprised him. She looked at the young Companion, meeting his clear, honest gaze.

"It's not what you think," Mari explained. "It's not that I don't want you or Antreas specifically not to know the location of my burrow. It's

Clan Law that no one knows the site of a Moon Woman's burrow—not even any other Earth Walker."

"It's for her protection," Nik added. "She's more than just Healer to her Clan." He hesitated, glancing at Mari before continuing. "But that's Mari's story to tell, not mine."

"Ah, I see. It's a security issue," Antreas said. "Understandable. We rarely share the location of our dens. Would it help if I gave you my den oath not to divulge the location of your home?"

Mari studied the Lynx Companion. She knew almost nothing about his people and had no idea if his word could be trusted. "What is a den oath?"

"The strongest promise I can make. Our dens are sacred to us. It is through our bond with our Companion Lynx that we choose the spot for and then build our den. If I broke a den oath it would be like breaking my Bast's heart—and I would never do that."

Mari nodded slowly. She saw truthfulness in the man's eyes. She turned to Davis. "And you? How can I be sure you won't tell anyone where I live?"

Davis's smile seemed sad. "I won't tell anyone where you live if my Sun Priest commands me not to."

"Your Sun Priest is dead," Nik said.

"No. My Sun Priest is standing in front of me," Davis said.

"He can't be talking about me," Mari said.

"He's not," Nik said. Then he shook his head. "No, Davis. I am *not* the Tribe's Sun Priest. There has been no vote. No Council Meeting. No ritual Call to the Sun for approval. I am *not* the Tribe's Sun Priest," he repeated.

"Laru chose you," Davis insisted stubbornly. "You're Sol's son. The whole Tribe knows he wanted you to be his heir. Sol was only waiting for you to be chosen by a Shepherd to make it official. And that has happened, so there's nothing in your way now."

"Davis, I cannot call down sunfire! And the Sun Priest must be able to—"

Mari's hand on his arm stopped Nik's words. "But, Nik, have you tried to call down sunfire?"

"Of course! All of the youths try it," Nik said. "I'm no good at it—never have been."

"But have you tried since Laru chose you?" Davis asked.

"I've been a little busy," Nik said sarcastically.

"You helped me control the sunfire I called down," Mari said, touching his bandaged hands gently.

"Well, yes, but that doesn't mean I can call it down myself," Nik said.

"So, was it all talk?" Davis blurted.

"All talk?" Nik said.

"Yeah, was it all just talk—that stuff you've been saying about needing to change things, to make the Tribe more modern, more inclusive of everyone?"

Mari saw Nik hesitate. He shook his head slowly. "No. It wasn't just talk. I disagree with many of the old Tribal Laws. I believe it's time for change."

"I agree," Davis said firmly.

"But that doesn't mean I'm your Sun Priest," Nik said.

"What would your father say?" Antreas asked.

They turned to stare at the Lynx man. "What do you mean?" Nik said.

Antreas shrugged. "I didn't know Sol well. Just met him a few days ago, but he seemed smart and trustworthy—a true Leader. Your Tribe clearly respected and revered him. You're his son. Obviously, you knew him well, correct?"

Nik thought of the secrets his father had shared with him and nodded slowly. "I did know him well, probably better than anyone except my mother, and she's been dead for years."

"Well, then the answer should be simple. What would your father say about you being Sun Priest for a new Tribe?"

"New Tribe?" Nik said.

"Yeah," Davis said. "The old Tribe of the Trees died in the fire, Nik.

If it was still home for us—if it was how we really wanted to keep living—I don't think either of us would have left today. So, we're a new Tribe. A small one, but still. A Tribe. Will you be my Sun Priest?"

Mari watched emotions flicker over Nik's face. She could see that he was upset, maybe even frightened, but she could also see another, stronger emotion begin to overshadow the negative ones. She recognized it as hope and was glad, so glad, to see it light his wise, handsome face. He looked expectantly at her.

"I didn't know Sol long, but I'm almost positive I know what he'd say you should do," she said.

"Mari, *Sun Priest* is more than just a title. It's a life's work, and a life's calling," he said.

Mari nodded somberly. "You're speaking to Moon Woman for Clan Weaver. I understand about being reluctant to take up your life's calling, but sometimes you just have to take a leap of faith and then do your best."

"Hell, Nik, someone has to do it, don't they?" Antreas said.

"You're right, Antreas. And that someone is me." He locked eyes with Davis. "You know what this means, don't you? What we must do if we are truly starting a new Tribe."

Davis nodded slowly. "We'll have to go back for at least one of them."

"Not *we*," Nik said firmly. "Only me. Davis, you have to agree not to follow me—not to try to help me in any way. If I fail—"

"You won't fail!" Davis said.

"I don't understand," Mari said. "Nik, what do you have to go back for?"

"A Mother Plant. We can't begin a new Tribe without one, not if we want our children and our children's children to be strong and healthy and filled with sunfire." Mari began to speak, but Nik interrupted. "Mari, this is one thing I won't, *can't*, compromise on."

Mari had no idea why the Mother Plant was so important to Nik, but she understood that her father, too, had taken fronds from this magickal fern and that her mother had told her stories about swaddling her in the plant when she was an infant. "All ferns thrive when planted by

Earth Walkers. If you get the fern, I'll be sure it thrives wherever we decide to plant it."

"Thank you, Mari." He pulled her into a grateful hug; then he stepped to a spot in the path that was like a mini-clearing. "Laru, to me!" Nik called, and Laru, who had been lying in a bed of moss not far from the trail with Rigel, instantly went to his Companion's side.

"Cammy, here!" Davis called, and the little blond Terrier, who had been rooting around in a clump of ferns down the trail, sprinted to him.

Davis crouched beside his Terrier, taking his face between his hands and looking into his bright eyes, sharing an unspoken message with the little canine. Then, side by side, the two of them approached Nik and Laru, who stood tall and silent, waiting.

Davis stopped directly in front of Nik. Cameron stopped directly in front of Laru.

"I swear my loyalty to you, Nikolas, son of Sol, Sun Priest of the Tribe of the . . ." Davis's voice trailed off and he looked up at Nik questioningly.

"Not Tribe," Nik said. "Let's start something completely new. With Mari's blessing, I say we should call ourselves a Pack."

"Pack? I like it! It's a good name," Mari said.

"Then Pack it is," Nik said.

"So be it." Davis continued, "I swear my loyalty to Nikolas, son of Sol, Sun Priest of his Pack. Hereafter, until you no longer have the strength or will to hold the title, you will be my Alpha." Then Davis leaned forward, twisting his body so that his neck was bared to Nik. Little Cameron watched his Companion and then rolled on his back before Laru, baring his neck and showing his vulnerable belly. Laru sniffed at him and then licked the little Terrier's muzzle as Cammy wagged his tail, huffing joyously.

"I accept your oath, Davis. And I will protect you with my life," Nik said, touching his friend's neck gently and then bowing his head to the Hunter.

"Good. Is that done?" Antreas said. "It's getting darker every second."

Nik met Mari's eyes and said to Davis, "Davis, as your Sun Priest I ask that you swear you will not ever give away the location of Mari's burrow."

"You have my word, Sun Priest," Davis said.

"Mari?" Nik asked.

"That's good enough for me. Rigel! Lead us home!"

CHAPTER 10

H unters! I need you and your Terriers to search for survivors while you put out any hot spots still smoldering. Grab a shovel each and be sure your Companions have their feet wrapped tightly in strips of the thick hide I salvaged from the tanning platform. Even though the rain is helping a lot with drenching the forest, much of the area is still dangerous for paws." Wilkes faced the group of Hunters who had gathered with the Warriors for instructions.

"Warriors! While the Hunters are searching out survivors within the confines of the city I need half of you to go to the meditation plat-form and get it set up as an infirmary. Gather all of the Healers you can find, as well as all of the infirmary supplies," Wilkes continued.

"The infirmary burned to the ground," said a young Warrior named Renard. He'd been the first Tribesman made Companion when Laru's last litter had begun to choose. Wilkes thought he looked a little wide-eyed and his young Shepherd, Wolf, seemed unable to leave his leg, but the two had worked well that terrible day and Wilkes was sure they would continue to do so.

"Are you certain, Renard?" Wilkes asked.

"Positive. I saw it happen. There were . . ." He paused and had to clear his throat and wipe his eyes before he continued. "There were people trapped in the infirmary when the trees and the platform caught fire. It's not something I'll ever forget."

Wilkes passed a weary hand over his face. "Okay. Well then, Warriors, let's see what we can do about medicine and supplies for a temporary infirmary. And I won't believe all of the Healers perished. Let's find them. Maybe they got outside the city before it was too late. The rest of you assess how many nests are usable for tonight. Hang tarp over sections of platform that are safe. People can shelter there for right now. Find as many Carpenters you can and get them started on making temporary shelters—especially something that can be used as a kitchen. Any questions?" When no one spoke, he said, "All right then, let's get moving. We have about an hour until sunset."

Wilkes hurried away with the group of Warriors and Shepherds, and Thaddeus watched him leave with undisguised dislike, the thought that was never far from him echoing around and around his mind: *Why does he get to give the orders just because his Companion is a Shepherd? I'm smarter and stronger. I should be Leader, and not just of the Hunters.*

Odysseus whined pitifully, breaking into Thaddeus's thoughts. He crouched beside his Companion. "I know it hurts. I'm sorry that bitch caused me to drop my dagger. Hang in there a little bit longer, and then you can rest," Thaddeus told Odysseus as he retied the bloodstained bandage wrapped around the little Terrier's flank.

"Thaddeus! Where is Latrell?" Thaddeus turned to see a young Hunter named Sean staggering up to him from the smoldering forest. He looked rough—red and singed where he wasn't covered with black soot. He was carrying his Terrier, Kitto, whose paws were painfully burned.

"I haven't seen him for hours." Thaddeus stood, facing Sean, then added silently, *And I hope that pain in my ass won't ever be seen again.* "What is it, Sean? What do you need?"

"When Kitto got burned I was with Latrell on the west edge of the city. He told me to carry him and try to make it to the Channel, so that's what I did. But on the way there the fire shifted and cut us off."

"Yeah, it's been shifting all day. Go to the meditation platform. They're setting up an infirmary there. They can see to you and your Kitto."

"I will, but that's not why I was looking for Latrell." Sean lowered his voice and stepped closer to Thaddeus, obviously not wanting anyone else to hear. "It's the Council. I—I think they might be dead."

Thaddeus felt a rush of excitement, which he covered by cloaking his reaction with concern. He pulled Sean by the elbow, guiding him away from the Hunters. "Tell me what you know quickly. Keep your voice down."

"Cyril called for the Council to evacuate the city and get to the Channel. I know because they were right ahead of me when the fire shifted. Thaddeus, a tree exploded. It set another afire, and then another. It happened insanely fast. One moment there was the wide, clear path to the Channel. The next there was a wall of fire. It cut me off from them, and all I could do was run as they screamed and screamed." Sean bowed his head, pressing it into his Terrier's soft neck, and while the little canine whined pitifully in sympathy his Companion sobbed.

Thaddeus pulled the crying man farther away from the others. "Are you sure the entire Council was trapped?"

"They were all there—all twelve of them and their canines." Sean shook his head. "All those Shepherds—all those Elders. It's—it's just too terrible."

"Where were you? Which trail?"

"The west one—the wider of the two that crosses that little stream. We were only about ten minutes outside the city."

"All right. You did well telling me. Now go to the meditation platform and get Kitto tended to. I'll follow the path. Maybe some of them survived. But don't tell anyone about this until I know for sure what happened to the Council. There's no point in adding panic to the chaos of today."

"I pray to the Sun that they survived, but Thaddeus, I don't know how any of them could have made it out of that blaze," Sean said.

Thaddeus said nothing. He just nodded concernedly and gestured in the direction of the mediation platform. Sean staggered away, clutching his Terrier and sobbing softly. Then Thaddeus glanced down at Odysseus. Even wounded, the attentive Terrier was watching him closely. "That's right. We're going to do a little hunting of our own. Come here, boy." Odysseus limped to his Companion. Thaddeus lifted him, settling the small Terrier in his arms before they disappeared into the forest.

It didn't take Thaddeus and Odysseus long to find the Council members—or, rather, what was left of them. A tree had fallen across the path, which was what probably saved Sean's life—cutting him off from the Council as the blaze spread toward the Council members, rather than toward Sean.

It was impossible for Thaddeus to tell the bodies apart. They had died piled together—humans and canines almost as one. Even with the still-falling rain, that part of the forest was too hot to trek through—and he certainly wasn't going to put Odysseus at risk by sending him into that smoking mess of rubble and flesh to try to count bodies, even had the Terrier not been wounded. Instead, Thaddeus studied the area, looking for a way anyone could have broken through the blaze and escaped.

"I think they're all gone, Odysseus." Thaddeus gently put his Companion beside him on the trail. He crouched down, scratching Odysseus's black ears. "And I'd say that leaves quite a gap in the ruling Council, as in no swarm-be-damned Council at all. Seems it's time for a *new* Council—like I've been saying. One that's not monopolized by Shepherds and their Leader Companions." Odysseus wagged his tail so hard the whole rear of his little body was wriggling, which caused the canine to whine in pain. Thaddeus laughed. "Hey, be careful. You're going to start bleeding again. Come on, boy. I'll carry you back and see what kind of rabbit stew I can find for us." Thaddeus had just begun to turn toward the trail to return to the city when a weak voice drifted to him.

"Help! Help me. I'm here. I'm alive!"

Thaddeus peered around. "Who is it?"

"It's Cyril! I'm here!"

"Where? I don't see you!"

Odysseus began to squirm in Thaddeus's arms, so that he had to put the canine down. The Terrier yipped and began to limp to the right of the path, leaving it, and standing, three-legged, at the edge of a sheer slope that bottomed out into a ditch almost filled with rainwater and burned debris, where he barked an alert.

Thaddeus rushed to him, stopping in shock when he realized what he'd thought was a charred log moved, rolled over, and opened his eyes.

"Sunfire! It is you!" Thaddeus didn't think. He started down the slope, moving as quickly and confidently as a Terrier—inhumanly quickly and confidently. He came to a rest beside the old man. "Where's Argos?"

"Sent him to get help. How—how did you get down here so easily? It's almost completely vertical." Cyril was blinking his vision clear and staring at Thaddeus with a strange expression.

Thaddeus shrugged. "Hunters are good at getting in and out of tough places. Lucky for you, right? How bad are you hurt?"

"Don't know. I feel wrong inside. It's why we weren't with the others. My chest and my arm—they were hurting. Badly. I was having trouble catching my breath, so Argos and I stopped to rest. The others went on. The—the others, they screamed. I can still hear them screaming. Why am I alive? I should have died with them."

"They're past pain now. . . ." Thaddeus paused and then added, "Was that the *whole* Council?"

Cyril nodded weakly.

"Any chance any of them got out like you did?"

A shudder passed through the old man's body and he closed his eyes. "No. No one could have lived through that."

"Okay, let's get you back. We're going to need you to head up a new Council. Without you in charge shit happens like Wilkes allows Nik and his Scratcher whore to go free, when *they're* responsible for all of this. We need to make sure they pay for what they've done."

The old man's eyes opened and he shook his head sadly. "No, Thaddeus, this isn't Nik and that girl's fault. It's ours. I've been lying here, thinking about many things, especially about what happened last night. I was wrong—*we* were wrong. The Farm was our fault. Because of us, our Sun Priest, a good and honorable man, is dead. The Council is dead." He closed his eyes again, as if they weighed too much to keep open. Tears tracked down Cyril's wrinkled cheeks. "I should have been with them. I should have died, too."

"Hey, you're not thinking straight. After you've rested you'll be yourself again."

"I am thinking straight—maybe for the first time in years. I see that I've been wrong, and I'm ready to admit it. The first thing I need to admit to the Tribe is that the girl, Mari, is the daughter of a Companion who was one of our finest Warriors."

"What are you talking about? Are you sure you didn't hit your head?" Thaddeus tried to inspect the old man's head, but Cyril weakly swatted his hands away.

"I didn't hit my head. I told you—I'm *finally* thinking clearly. Mari was Galen's daughter. I know because I ordered his death for stealing fronds of the Mother Plant for her when she was an infant. Sol was the Warrior who carried out the death sentence."

Thaddeus's brows shot up his forehead. "The mighty Sol actually killed a Companion, and that Companion was the Scratcher bitch's father? Bet if she knew that she'd feel different about her precious Nik."

The old man stared at him, his green eyes piercing Thaddeus's soul. He wanted to look away and then reminded himself that there was no damn reason he should look away from Cyril. What was he, really, except a weak, sick old man?

"You've changed," Cyril said.

Everything inside Thaddeus went very still. "What do you mean?"

Instead of answering, Cyril asked a question of his own. "What really happened to you when you were captured by the Skin Stealers?"

"I already told you."

Cyril grimaced against the pain as he forced himself to a sitting position, clutching his left arm to his side. "No. I don't think you did tell me everything. You've been different since you returned."

"I don't know what you mean."

"Of course you do." With a shaking hand Cyril wiped rain, sweat, and tears from his face, and then he sat up straighter, as if he'd found his second wind. "I'm Lead Elder, not a doddering fool. I watch everything—everyone. I watch you. I watched you carefully after your abduction. What I've observed has me concerned."

Thaddeus saw the truth in the old man's sharp gaze and made his decision instantly.

"I have changed. I'm better, stronger, faster, smarter."

"What did they do to you?" Cyril asked.

Thaddeus smiled, happy to finally be able to share the truth with someone. "They took Odysseus's flesh and joined it with mine."

The old man's eyes widened in horror. "But they only do that to themselves—only with human flesh—and only because they're all infected with a rotting disease."

"Well, that's the thing." Thaddeus crouched next to Cyril. "Before I went on that foraging trip, my skin had begun to crack and slough." He shrugged. "Don't know why, but it had to have something to do with that diseased stag we found."

"The one you destroyed, but not before his blood spattered your face and body?"

Thaddeus ignored the disgust in Cyril's voice and continued. "Yes! Exactly! I think it infected me and got me ready for Odysseus's flesh."

"Sunfire! You've been tainted by the Skin Stealers' disease. Thaddeus, we have to get you to the Healers. Maybe they can cure you."

Thaddeus laughed. "Cure me? Why would I want that?" He held out his arms, flexing them. "Odysseus's flesh has made me *better*."

"The disease and his flesh have made you *ill*. No wonder you were so angry at the Farm. You need help, Thaddeus."

Thaddeus cocked his head to the side and studied the old man contemplatively. "Didn't you just tell me you should have died with the rest of the Council?"

Cyril said nothing, but Thaddeus saw pity in the old man's eyes.

"Well, maybe you did."

Cyril looked confused. "No, I told you what happened. I wasn't with them at the end. I'm here."

"You're right. You are here. I think you fell in this ditch as you ran from the fire and you hit your head. It killed you."

"But I'm not dead."

Thaddeus ignored him, searching the ditch around them until he found what he needed. Then, quickly and efficiently, he lifted the rock and as the old man stared at him, eyes wide with sudden understanding, he bashed it several times against Cyril's skull.

"Now you *are* dead."

Thaddeus waited, feeling for Cyril's pulse as blood drained from the old man's head wound and his body twitched soundlessly. After his pulse slowed and then finally stopped, Thaddeus lifted the dead man, slinging him carelessly out of the ditch—tossing his body toward the path. Smiling at the ease with which he handled the old corpse, Thaddeus scrambled out of the muddy ditch and up the steep incline where Odysseus waited for him. Then he hefted Cyril over his shoulder and picked up Odysseus, holding him snugly in the crook of his other arm while they started back down the trail.

"You see, Cyril, I've been thinking, too. And what I've been thinking is that it's time new blood ruled the Tribe. Odysseus and I shared flesh, and now we share *everything*—intuition, senses, strength. That's not a disease, or a sickness. It's a miracle."

Tucked against his side, Odysseus barked his agreement, and Thaddeus laughed with pleasure.

"Two apprenticed Healers? Surely more survived than that!" Wilkes stared around the triage area of the old meditation platform. He was horrified by the cries of the wounded and dying—but even more horrified by the lack of trained medical personnel to care for them.

"Keep your voice down. The truth is bad enough. The injured don't need to know that the rest of us are as frightened as they are." Ralina, the revered Storyteller of the Tribe, grabbed Wilkes by the wrist and steered him to a relatively secluded section of the crowded meditation platform. She wiped her sweaty face with the back of her blood-spattered tunic and blew out a long, exhausted breath before continuing. "The Healers wouldn't leave the infirmary. There were too many people there who couldn't be moved. They decided to stay with the sick and hope that the fire would be stopped before it reached them." Ralina shook her head sadly. "They all burned, Wilkes. The Healers, the sick and blighted, the old, the newborn infants and their mothers, everyone." She paused, her shoulders shaking as she fought for control of her grief. "Thank the Sun that Kathleen thought to send her two apprentices with a store of supplies away before they were destroyed by the fire as well."

"Kathleen was a wise Healer. She'll be greatly missed," Wilkes said, trying to reason through the shock that felt as if it was pressed down on him, layer by layer, as he discovered more and more about the tragedy that had struck the Tribe. He leaned against the ornately carved railing and bent to stroke Odin reassuringly. The big Shepherd was, as always, hyperaware of Wilkes's emotional distress, which was at that moment at an all-time high. "It's okay, big guy. We'll get this sorted out. Everything will be okay."

Ralina's Bear whined fretfully, and the Storyteller rested her hand on his broad head as he leaned against her for comfort. "How?" Ralina asked softly. "How is everything going to be okay? So many of the Tribe are dead or dying. More wounded keep staggering in here every moment, and we don't even have a real Healer."

"We're going to survive, Ralina. The Tribe is strong."

"Where is Sol? Why isn't he here after he stopped the blaze?" she asked.

Wilkes didn't want to tell her, but there was no point in putting off the inevitable—at least not now that the fire was out and the recovery could begin.

"Ralina, Sol is dead."

"Oh, sunfire! No." Ralina slid down the railing, dropping heavily to her butt. She wrapped on arm around Bear and leaned into him as tears dripped down her cheeks. She looked hopelessly up at Wilkes. "Was it too much for him? Did the amount of sunfire needed to save us destroy him?"

Wilkes drew a deep breath and told the truth. "No. Sol was killed at the Farm, where the fire started. It was an accident. Thaddeus was trying to shoot Mari, and Sol pushed her out of the way, taking the arrow meant for her."

"Wait, what are you talking about? Who is Mari, and how did the fire get put out if Sol was dead?"

"It's a long, strange story, and I don't have all of your answers. I can tell you that Mari is a Scratcher—they call themselves Earth Walkers."

"Earth Walkers?"

"So Mari says. She also says her father was a Companion—one of the Tribe."

"Bloody beetle balls! That's impossible!"

"Apparently not. She looks more Companion than Scratcher. Laru's last pup—the big male Nik's been hunting for weeks—chose her. And *she* called down the sunfire that saved us."

The Storyteller shook her head. "I—I can't believe it."

"Believe it. I saw it. Nik helped her control the sunfire, but she called it down herself."

"Nik! Oh, Gods! With Sol and Laru gone, he has no one except the O'Bryans." Ralina wiped her eyes and then jerked her chin in the direction of a tarp that had been hastily erected on the forest floor, several yards from the meditation platform. Beneath it Wilkes saw mounds of what looked like dirty clothes. Then, with a terrible start, he understood he was looking at bodies—many, many bodies. "Lindy and Sherry O'Bryan are dead, along with their Shepherds. I haven't seen their son's body yet, but I assume he was with them. And that means Nik has no one left in this world." She shook her head sadly. "I know he hadn't been chosen by a Shepherd yet, but I always believed he would be. Many of us thought he was destined to be Sun Priest after Sol."

"Laru chose Nik."

Her eyes widened and joy flashed across her face. "Good for him! Laru is in his prime. I'm so glad he didn't choose to die with Sol." She looked around as if trying to find Nik. "But where is he? His presence, with Laru by his side, will calm the Tribe."

Wilkes set his jaw. "Gone. He left with Mari. Davis and his Cameron left with them, too, as well as that damn Lynx man, Antreas."

"What? I don't understand. Gone where?"

"Scratcher territory."

Ralina was shaking her head back and forth, back and forth, mired in disbelief, when the shouts started. Wilkes turned toward the sound in time to see Argos, the Leader of the Council's old Shepherd, run into the clearing.

Odin and Bear began to whine in unison, which brought Ralina to her feet. She shared a look with Wilkes, and then they were sprinting to Argos, their Shepherds beside them.

Wilkes reached him first. "Hey, big guy, are you okay?" He dropped beside the canine, running his hands along Argos's body. The old canine's face was completely gray. As Wilkes examined him, thoughts cascaded through his mind—that he had known forty-two winters and could not think of a time when Argos hadn't been by Cyril's side. Argos was the oldest Shepherd in the Tribe and greatly revered by everyone. "Nothing's broken. His fur is singed, but he seems okay," Wilkes told Ralina as Odin and Bear sniffed the old canine, whining in concern.

Then Argos barked sharply and turned to sprint back the way he'd come. The canine stopped, though, to look at Wilkes, barking desperately again.

"It's Cyril. It has to be," Ralina said. "He must not have been able to make it back, so he sent Argos. I'll get a medical pack together and follow him."

"I'll come with you. You'll need help getting him back here." Ralina nodded, and she and Bear hurried back to the platform. "Argos! We understand! We're coming. Hang on, big guy." Odin went to the old Shepherd, touching noses with him and licking him comfortingly while Wilkes paced and tried to think positive thoughts. *Cyril must still be alive, or Argos would never have left him.*

Ralina was sprinting back to them when more shouts were heard. At first Wilkes couldn't make out what was being shouted—he could only hear screaming sobs, with words jumbled beneath the cries. When the cries grew closer, he began to understand.

"Oh, sunfire! No!"

"It can't be!"

"Oh, Gods! No!"

Wilkes's stomach had already begun to roil with foreboding when Argos's demeanor changed. The big canine began to whine fretfully. The force of his whines grew, changing to a strangled, keening howl that had chills skittering up and down Wilkes's spine. Then, right before them, Thaddeus staggered from the forest carrying a body cradled in his arms like a sleeping child.

Argos reacted instantly. He raced to Thaddeus and then froze just before him, as if the canine had been turned to stone.

Thaddeus went to his knees and placed Cyril's body oh, so gently on the mossy ground. Companions and canines poured from the meditation platform and the forest around them, forming a desperate circle around the old canine and the body of their fallen Lead Councilman.

Argos staggered to his Companion. When he reached Cyril, the Shepherd slowly lay down beside him, stretching his gray muzzle up to tuck it into the crook of the old man's shoulder. Wilkes saw the Shepherd's body snuggle against Cyril and then completely relax. Argos closed his eyes, drew a last, long breath, and then he released it with a sigh and the loyal old Shepherd joined his beloved Companion in eternity.

Every canine in the clearing raised his or her muzzle to the sky and howled their sadness to the sun as the Tribe of the Trees wept.

CHAPTER 11

Rigel's excited barking woke Mari—or, rather, brought her fully conscious. "What's happening? Rigel? Where's Rigel?" Her mouth tasted terrible—dry and disgusting. Her head ached, and she felt like it'd been days since she'd eaten.

"He's here, Mari. Everything is fine. He's just telling you that you're home." Nik relaxed his grip on Mari, and it was then that she realized he'd been carrying her.

"How long have I been unconscious?" Mari asked, rubbing her face and blinking her vision clear, though she was so dizzy that her head felt as if it were filled with smoke.

"You've been in and out of consciousness since we got to the low-lands," Nik said, wiping sweat from his face.

Mari touched his damp cheek. "Oh, Nik, I'm sorry! Let me see your back. You shouldn't be carrying anyone. Your wound isn't even fully healed. And your hands! They're bleeding through the bandages!" She tried to lift his hands to examine them more closely, but dizziness overwhelmed her and she would have fallen had it not been for Nik's strong arms keeping her upright.

"How about we get inside your burrow and you tell me which one of Sora's vile teas I can brew to make you feel better?" Nik said.

"Actually, the vile teas are mine. Sora brews delicious tea." Mari hated the worried expression on his face and made an effort to smile reassuringly up at Nik.

Nik bent and kissed her softly.

"Um, I hate to break up this nice little scene, but the pup has come to a halt sitting in front of that huge nettle thicket. Maybe Mari's exhaustion has affected him, too?" Antreas said.

Nik grinned at Antreas. "Nope, Rigel has it right. Watch and learn, cat man; watch and learn."

"So, he's calling me cat man now, huh?" Antreas grumbled in Bast's general direction. The big feline looked up from licking herself with an expression that was so long-suffering that had Mari had the energy she would have burst into laughter.

But, having no energy, she called to Rigel, "Bring me my walking stick, sweet boy!" As always, Rigel did exactly as Mari asked, half dragging, half carrying the long, sturdy stick to her. "Thanks, Rigel. And good job getting us home!" With an effort, she crouched and kissed his nose, petting the soft, thick fur at his neck while the young Shepherd wagged with happy relief that she was conscious again. Mari looked at Nik. "There should be another walking stick, a lot like this, hidden under the brambles where Rigel found mine. You'll need it to help me be sure Davis and Antreas don't get cut on the way in."

"Okay, no problem. I'll find it, and I did watch you and Sora do this, so I think I can safely bring up the rear." Nik dug around under the dagger-tipped thorns, quickly finding the second stick. "I'm ready if you are."

Mari rallied her strength—*almost home, I can almost rest*—and then she moved to the hidden entrance. "All right. Antreas, you and Bast follow right behind me, as close as you can. Then Davis and Cammy. Nik, you and Laru bring up the rear."

"No problem," Nik said as Antreas and his Lynx moved to stand beside Mari.

"Uh, hold up just a second," Davis said.

Mari and Nik turned to him. He and Cammy were a few feet from them—both Companion and Terrier were eyeing the enormous bramble thicket dubiously.

"Yeah?" Nik asked.

"We're not actually going into that mess, are we?"

"Oh, sorry," Mari said. "My mind isn't working like normal, or I would have explained. Yes, we are going into that mess. That mess protects and camouflages my burrow—my home. It's perfectly safe, but only if you know the way through, so stay close to me."

Bast finished her toilette and padded over to sniff the area directly in front of Mari. She made an odd little coughing noise that Mari thought sounded out of place for such a graceful creature.

"Yeah, like Bast said—your den's safe, hidden, protected, and I'm assuming dry?" Antreas said.

"Of course," Mari said, trying not to sound too defensive. "Contrary to what most of the Tribe of the Trees think, Earth Walker burrows are actually very nice."

"Well, I'm not part of the Tribe of the Trees, so I don't have any preconceived ideas about your den or, as you call it, your burrow. I'm really just curious," Antreas explained.

"Mari's home is cozy and beautiful," Nik said.

"Thank you, Nik." Mari smiled wearily at him. "Okay, so I'm going to go first with Rigel. Antreas and Bast, come right after me. Like I said, stay close to me. Also, keep your arms tight to your sides—those thorns can really cut you up. Davis, you might want to carry Cammy if he's as nervous as you are."

"How about I stay out here? Cammy and I'll rig a cocoon in a tree. I saw a big cedar not far from here that should work. Maybe, um, maybe Nik could bring us out some dinner if it's not too much trouble?"

Mari just stared at him, wishing she could concentrate better. Davis hadn't shown any hesitation about following them to her home, but now he had gone pale and his voice sounded strained and strange.

"Did you say a cocoon? I don't understand," Mari asked.

"It's why Companions, especially Hunters, always carry rope and wear travel cloaks. If any of us get caught outside the Tribe at night, we can wrap up with our canine and tie ourselves to the arms of a big tree. It looks kinda like a cocoon, which is why we call it that. And we're safe," Davis explained.

"But you'll be safe in my burrow, too. And dry. And warm."

"I'll—um—be fine in a tree, too," Davis said nervously. "And Cammy and I don't need to stay dry. We won't melt."

"What's this about?" Nik asked Davis.

Davis wiped a hand across his damp face and blurted, "I'm claustrophobic!"

Mari frowned. "But it's a burrow, a home—nothing to be claustrophobic about."

"Dens are good things, man," Antreas said. "Way better than tying yourself to a tree in a thunderstorm." His gaze went up to the sky above the huge bramble thicket. "Here's hoping we can start a hearth fire and cook up something hot for dinner. Don't see any hearth smoke up there." He sniffed the air, looking oddly Lynx-like. "Don't smell any, either, though the damnable forest fire might still be messing up my nose, especially since I could swear I caught the scent of baking bread a second ago."

Mari stared at him, at first confused. Then with a start she realized what he was saying. "Oh no, forest fire or not, you wouldn't see my hearth fire from here, but let's hope you do smell bread." Just thinking of Sora's fresh-baked bread had Mari's mouth filling with water.

"You have to come out here to cook?" Antreas shook his head. "No, that won't do. It's raining like crazy. I can show you how to make a chimney flue that will work great in a den—if I don't have to dig through too much rock."

"Oh, I have a hearth, and many flues. So many that my smoke dissipates all around here. You'll never track a single Earth Walker hearth fire to a burrow. Instead, if you're careful and observant, you might notice areas of smoke, drifting foglike around the lowlands, and once in a while you might smell baking bread, or rich mushroom stew—

though I promise you'll never be able to follow those scents to an individual burrow."

"Huh! That's a convenient system. Obviously excellent for keeping your den hidden. You'll have to show me how they're made sometime."

Mari raised a brow at the feline Companion. "Only if you get permission from the Great Earth Mother."

"Guess I'll have to work on that," Antreas said, scratching under Bast's chin while she stretched languidly.

"Just so I'm clear about this—there's fire inside that burrow in the ground?" Davis asked, looking even paler.

"Well, sure. My hearth fire," Mari said.

"I—I'm sorry, Mari. I don't mean to show you any disrespect, but I don't think I can go in there."

"Davis," Nik began after sighing in frustration, but Mari rested a silencing hand on his arm.

"I think I understand how you feel, Davis. When Nik took me to your City in the Trees, I was terrified of how high up we were. I wanted nothing more than to get back on firm ground, but once I was up there, and saw how special it was—how beautiful—I relaxed. And, most important, I trusted Nik to be sure I was safe. Will you trust me, Davis? I give you my word that you'll be safe inside my burrow, but if you're still nervous about it once you're inside I also give you my word that I'll guide you right back out here so that you can set up your cocoon and I'll be sure you have a hot meal."

Davis shared a long look with his little blond Terrier before he answered Mari. "Okay. Right. Nik trusts you, so we'll trust you."

"Okay!" Mari bent to ruffle the blond fur on top of Cammy's head. "How about we change things up a little? Davis, you and Cammy come behind me, with Antreas and Bast following. Nik and Laru, still bring up the rear."

"Got it," Nik said, moving into place.

"Everyone ready?" Mari asked.

Everyone except Davis nodded.

Mari smiled encouragement at the young Hunter before lifting her thick walking stick, snagging the first of the bramble branches, and holding it out of the way so that she and Rigel, with Davis and Cammy close behind, could step inside the enormous thicket of carefully maintained brambles.

For a little while Mari relaxed into the familiar routine of following the labyrinthine pathway around and around her burrow, lifting huge, dagger-tipped boughs aside, guiding those who followed her to the heart of her home. She didn't think about the Clan Laws she was breaking. A Moon Woman was forbidden to show anyone except her daughter the secret way to her burrow, and of course no Companion was ever supposed to be allowed access to a burrow, let alone the home of a Moon Woman. Mari started to feel sad about it, especially about how the Clan would perceive what she was doing, and then a new thought came to her. *What would Mama think about all of this?*

Mari knew what Leda would think. She would be pleased that the Clan and the Tribe were finally interacting with trust and compassion. Leda would say the time was ripe for the change she'd desired since she'd met her true love—Mari's Companion father—when she had barely known eighteen winters.

Mari glanced behind her as she maneuvered around a fat branch of thorns. "How are you and Cammy doing?"

Davis's face was pale and sweaty and he was holding his little Terrier tightly in his arm, but he grinned bravely at Mari. "We're okay. But I don't think I could ever find my way out of here."

"Oh, it's a lot easier to get out than in," Mari said.

"It's fantastic!" Antreas called from behind Davis. "You know, if we'd thought of using nettles like this, we wouldn't have to build our dens into the side of mountains."

Mari heard a flurry of strangely birdlike chirps, which had to come from Bast—though the big feline didn't look like she should be able to make any of those noises. Then Antreas laughed.

"Okay! Okay! Never mind. And, yes, I love our den, too."

"What was that?" Nik called from the rear of the group.

"Nothing!" Antreas said, still chuckling. "I forget how possessive Bast can be."

Mari wanted to ask Antreas a bunch of questions about his feline and his den, but just then she rounded the final turn in the pathway, coming to a small area, clear of brambles, that revealed the arched wooden door that seemed to open into the side of the earth.

"That carving is incredible," Davis said, putting Cammy down. He started toward the door and the intricately carved figure of the Great Earth Mother that one of Mari's ancestresses had fashioned with the door, so that it appeared the Goddess supported the burrow and beckoned her Moon Woman to enter the safety of a Goddess-blessed home. Davis paused and looked over his shoulder at Mari. "Do you mind if I touch it?"

"Not at all," Mari said.

Davis went to the door and slowly lifted his hand, gently tracing the arm of the Goddess. "Is this who your people worship?"

Mari started in surprise, realizing that even though the Tribe of the Trees had taken her people captive and held them for generations, they had never bothered to learn to whom their slaves prayed.

"Yes. That is the Great Earth Mother."

"She's beautiful," Davis said. "I had no idea."

"It's the same image your people desecrated when you attacked our Gathering Site by the cherry grove," Mari couldn't stop herself from saying.

Davis turned to meet her gaze. "The statues made of the earth? Like they were rising from the ground? Those were of your Goddess?"

"Yes."

Davis closed his eye and bowed his head. "I'm sorry. I didn't know."

Mari went to him and touched his hand, so that Davis opened his eyes. "You know now."

"I'll never do it again." He spoke simply, earnestly, and his words touched Mari's heart.

"I believe you," she said.

Davis looked up at the graceful rendition of the Goddess. "Do you think she does?"

Mari almost answered him flippantly. Almost told him that the Goddess had never spoken to her, so how was she to know? But there was an expression in the young Hunter's eyes that stopped her words. For an instant Davis reminded her of a Clansman who wanted nothing more than to know his Earth Mother wasn't angry with him.

Mari squeezed his hand. "Yes. I think the Goddess hears and believes anyone who honestly speaks to her. Of course, whether she speaks back or not is completely unpredictable—even for a Moon Woman."

Then Davis, a Hunter for the Tribe of the Trees, Companion to the Terrier Cameron, did something that utterly shocked Mari. He turned his back to her and placed both of his hands carefully on the feet of the carving. Davis bowed his head and said, "I'm sorry I had anything to do with destroying any of your images. I'll never do it again." Beside him, Cammy barked and wagged his tail.

When Davis stepped away from the doorway, the smile he sent to Mari was authentic and relaxed. "I'm ready to go inside now." His gaze found the image of the Goddess again, as if it were fire and Davis was a moth, unable to stay away. "If she guards your home, then it must be okay."

Mari felt a strange rush of excitement. Was she truly witnessing the first time a member of the Tribe accepted the Great Earth Mother? A man? And a Companion? Mari mentally shook herself. Or maybe she was just exhausted and imagining things.

"That carving is beautiful," Antreas said, moving up to stand beside Davis. "Do you have this skill?" he asked her.

Mari drew a long breath, trying to sort through her tired brain to explain to the Lynx Companion that she did have a talent for drawing but hadn't done much carving, when Nik spoke up.

"Mari has many skills, but right now she needs to get inside her home and rest."

"Right you are," Antreas said. "After you, Moon Woman."

With dragging feet, Mari went to the door and opened it, breathing deeply of the rich, familiar scents of home—predominate among those scents was baking bread and rabbit stew. She could see that the hearth fire was lit and there was a steaming cauldron boiling over it.

"Mari! It is you! Thank the Great Goddess! You're home!" Danita was halfway across the front room of the burrow, arms spread to greet Mari, when Davis peeked his head over Mari's shoulder. Danita gave a gasping shriek and stumbled to a halt, eyes wide with fear—face blanched white.

Cursing silently to herself for forgetting that Danita might be in the burrow and would still be traumatized from the attack she'd suffered only days before, Mari rushed to the girl, putting her arm around Danita and holding her close. Rigel was by her side, wagging a greeting. Mari breathed a small sigh of relief when Danita didn't scream and lurch away from the canine.

"Danita, you remember my Rigel, don't you?"

The girl nodded shakily. "He's soft," she whispered, sending the pup a quick glance. Rigel licked her hand and Danita patted him hesitantly on the head.

"He *is* soft, and he likes you," Mari said. "I'd like to introduce you to my new friends. They have Companion animals as well, and you have nothing to be afraid of—I give you my word as your Moon Woman. You already know Nik, right?"

Danita nodded, but her eyes were focused on Davis, who had stopped just inside the door, with Cammy sitting quietly beside him.

"Well, this is Davis, a friend of his and—"

"Hey, this den is nice!" Antreas was saying as he stepped around Davis.

Another shriek slipped from Danita, and Mari could feel the girl begin to tremble under her hand.

Then Nik and Laru were pushing inside behind Antreas and Bast, moving everyone forward, and Danita broke. With an anguished scream, she pulled from Mari's grasp. Scrambling hysterically, Danita lurched backward until her legs hit the pallet built into the curved side of the burrow. She blindly climbed onto it; pressing herself against the wall, she hugged her knees to her chest, trying to disappear into a ball, as she trembled and sobbed.

"Danita, it's okay. No one is going to hurt you!" Mari said, but her words were drowned out by the hysterically sobbing girl and by Nik and Davis, who seemed to be trying to reason with Danita as well, but the girl was beyond reason and all that was happening was the burrow had deteriorated into a cacophony of noise and stress.

Mari started to go to Danita, planning to physically shake the girl out of her hysteria if necessary, but before she could get to her Bast was there, padding confidently to the sleeping pallet. With no hesitation the Lynx leaped up on the bed and locked her gaze with Danita.

Mari moved forward, not sure what she was going to do, but her instinct to protect Danita was undeniable. Antreas was suddenly there beside Mari. He put his hand on her arm. "Antreas, please don't let Bast—" Mari began, but Antreas spoke softly to her.

"Just watch. Bast knows what she's doing, and she wouldn't hurt the girl," said the Lynx's Companion.

The big feline sat on her haunches before Danita and cocked her head, watching the girl. Danita stopped her hysterical keening, her wide gray gaze trapped by the Lynx.

Beside Mari, Nik grew still—as did Davis and the orchestra of barking canines. Everyone was watching what was happening between the girl and the feline.

Then Bast did something that completely surprised Mari. The feline began to make soft, sweet chirping noises, as if she was speaking directly to Danita. The girl stopped sobbing, all of her attention focused on the Lynx. Bast moved closer to Danita, interspersing a rolling purr between the chirps. She lowered her head, leaning forward to sniff delicately at the girl. Danita became a statue. Mari didn't think she was even breathing. Bast sniffed the girl's hand, then her chest, then her cheek. And then, very delicately, the big feline rubbed her head against Danita, in what seemed an almost maternal gesture, as if to soothe away her fear.

Danita laughed!

It was just a small sound, barely audible. It only lasted an instant, but it changed everything.

Danita's gaze found Mari's. "Wh-what is she?" the girl asked in a hushed voice, as if she was afraid if she spoke too loudly the feline would disappear.

"She's a Lynx," Antreas answered for Mari. "Her name is Bast, and she is my Companion. My name is Antreas." He gave Danita a small bow with a flourish.

Danita looked away from him quickly, her eyes sliding back to the purring feline at her side.

"May I touch her?" Danita spoke so softly Mari had to strain to hear her.

"Of course," Antreas said. "She especially likes to be scratched under her chin."

Slowly, Danita lifted her hand to stroke the feline, who stretched out her neck and lifted her chin, inviting further petting.

"Do you think Bast would go into the back room with Danita?" Mari whispered to Antreas. "Danita was attacked just days ago by a group of males. It's still hard for her to be around men."

"Absolutely," Antreas answered quietly.

Then he took a step toward Danita's pallet but stopped when the girl cringed away from him. Bast was on her feet instantly, stepping so that she straddled the girl's lap, facing Antreas. The big feline arched her spine and hissed a long, low warning directly at her Companion!

Mari stared at Antreas, wondering what was happening, and she saw the Lynx and her Companion share a look. Bast's yellow-eyed gaze was firm and bright. Mari thought Antreas looked surprised, shocked even, and she saw him shake his head, just slightly.

The Lynx responded with a low growl and a twitch of her short black-tipped tail.

Antreas shrugged. "Yeah, I do hear you, but I'm *not* agreeing to anything," he said to his feline before turning to Mari and the rest of the group. "Well, it seems Bast has decided to be this child's protector."

"Protector?" Davis said. "Is that normal?"

Antreas gave a little bark of laughter. "Nothing is particularly *normal* with Bast. But once she's made up her mind, not much can change it." He grinned at Davis. "Start walking toward the child."

Davis glanced at Mari, who moved her shoulders and nodded, unable to help her curiosity.

Davis took a step toward Danita and Bast. Danita cowered back and Bast turned into a demon. The feline's black-tufted ears flattened to her skull, her back arched, and she bared sharp, white teeth as she hissed a long, low warning followed by a hair-raising yowl.

"Bloody beetle balls! I wasn't going to hurt the girl!" Davis said, backing quickly away while Cammy stuck to his side, whimpering.

Bast yawned and lay down completely across Danita's lap while the girl stroked her and watched Davis thoughtfully and, Mari noted, with no fear in her eyes.

Mari thought it was an improvement. Danita wasn't crying hysterically anymore. *Seems like a good time to give her a job to do.*

"Danita, do you think you could go into the storage room and gather some sun-dried tomatoes, potatoes, onions, mushrooms, and anything else you can find that might stretch that stew for us? We've traveled a long way today, and we need food and rest."

"Of course, Moon Woman," Danita said automatically. Then she glanced at Antreas and added, "Will—will she come with me?"

"Bast has a mind of her own, but I'm pretty sure she will," Antreas said. His big Lynx looked at him and gave a little chirp, which made her Companion chuckle. "She thinks it's her idea that you two go in the other room. She smells rabbits back there."

"Come on, Bast," Danita said softly as she got off the pallet and started toward the entrance to the rear room of the burrow. The feline followed her so closely that her shoulder brushed the girl's leg.

"Hey, don't let her eat the live rabbits," Mari said. "I've got breeding pairs back there."

"She'll only eat what she hunts for, or what you agree to feed her," Antreas assured Mari. "Besides, right now what's on her mind is this frightened child."

Danita was at the door to the back room when she turned and met Antreas's eyes. "I'm *not* a child." Then, with her hand resting on Bast's head, the two of them slipped through the woven dividing curtain.

Mari blew out a long sigh. "Sorry, I should have realized Danita might be here. I handled that poorly."

"Hey, that's okay. Bast picked up the slack," Antreas said, looking around the burrow with open curiosity.

"Yeah, why did she do that?" Davis asked as Cammy followed Rigel and Laru to the drinking dish and lapped thirstily at the freshwater. "That was really weird. I mean, she actually hissed at you, too!"

Antreas chuckled softly. "Oh, she'd never hurt me, or even you for that matter. Well, unless you attacked me."

"Which I wouldn't do," Davis said quickly.

"Of course not," Nik added. "We're allies here."

"Right, we're all in agreement about that," Antreas said. "Bast isn't mean. She was simply putting on a show for the child, er, girl." He corrected himself with a glance at the closed curtain. "Letting Danita know she was safe, even in a den that must feel full of scary males."

"But it was more than that," Mari said. "Bast knew right away that Danita needed help. She comforted her—actually stopped her hysteria."

Antreas shrugged evasively. "There's no predicting who Bast will take to."

"Cammy would have let her pet him," Davis said, sounding defensive. "He isn't mean, either."

"Didn't say he was, but he's not as intuitive as Bast—at least where strangers are concerned."

"What the hell does that mean? My canine is every bit as intuitive as your *cat*!" Davis seemed to puff up, planting his feet and looking like he'd enjoy nothing more than knocking the smug look off the Lynx man's face.

"Do not call Bast a *cat*." Antreas's hands balled into fists.

"Un-uh!" Mari stepped between the two young men, anger temporarily chasing away exhaustion. "You will *not* fight in my home. Ever. Is that clear?"

Antreas and Davis deflated, sending her chagrined looks of apology.

"Yeah, it's clear. Sorry, Antreas," Davis said. "I was out of line."

"It's clear to me, too. And I didn't mean to insult Cammy," Antreas said. "He's a nice little canine."

Cammy sneezed at him, and Davis chuckled.

"We're all tired and hungry. Let's eat and then regroup," Nik said. "Mari, is that Sora's bread I see in that shelf above the hearth?" Before she could answer, Nik was stirring the cauldron and sniffing happily at it, saying, "And please tell me this is her rabbit stew, too."

"Smells like the answer is a yes to both," Mari said. She started for the hearth and the carved wooden dishes tucked into cunningly built shelves surrounding it, but her legs didn't seem to want to mind her. She stumbled and would have fallen had Rigel not been there for her to grab on to. "Goddess! I can't seem to move without falling. I feel helpless as a newborn."

"Hey, it's only temporary. Why don't you take a seat and let us take care of you for a change?" Nik helped her to the pallet Danita had so recently vacated. "I think I can remember where you keep the dishes, and Davis is pretty good at making stew."

"Yes, I am!" Davis grinned at her, and Cammy huffed happily. "Hunters learn to cook whatever they catch. Cammy has a knack for snagging rabbits, so my rabbit stew is excellent." He blew on the wooden stirring spoon and took a taste of the steamy stew. His eyes widened in pleasure. "But I admit not this excellent! Now *this* is stew."

"If you think her stew is good, wait till you taste Sora's bread. She told me once that the inside is light as clouds. I didn't believe her, but I was wrong," Mari said, rubbing her eyes sleepily.

"Who is this Sora person?" Antreas reached for the spoon, but Davis nimbly put it back in the cauldron and kept stirring.

"I think it's best if you just meet her. Describing her is kinda difficult," Nik said, sharing a look with Mari.

"I can't wait to hear what she says about Bast," Mari said. "She still calls Rigel the creature."

"Is she mad?" Antreas asked.

"No," Mari said.

"Probably," Nik said at the same time.

The curtain that separated the burrow's two rooms moved, and then Danita emerged, carrying a basket filled with potatoes, mushrooms, and a variety of dried vegetables. She paused. Bast left her side and padded to Davis. The room fell silent as everyone watched to see what the feline would do next. Mari could see that Davis was holding very still and Cammy moved quickly so that he was lying between Rigel and Laru, who were curled up resting before the door.

Bast put herself between Davis and Danita, then made a rolling chirp sound that called to the girl. Danita nodded and, without looking directly at Davis, she walked to him and, with Bast still standing protectively between them, passed him the basket of vegetables over the big feline's body.

"This should help stretch the stew," Danita said.

"Thank you," Davis said, taking the basket carefully.

Bast chirped at Danita again before padding to the pallet. She jumped up, making room beside Mari. Then the Lynx glared pointedly at Nik, who was sitting on the other side of Mari, and hissed sharply.

"Okay! Okay!" Nik said. "I'll help with the food."

As soon as Nik left the pallet, Danita hurried over to sit snugly between the big feline and the Moon Woman.

"You're going all out, aren't you?" Antreas said to his Lynx. Bast made a coughlike sound in reply, which had her Companion shaking his head, though Mari thought he didn't really seem annoyed at the feline.

"Did you stop the forest fire?" Danita asked Mari.

"I did. Well, with Nik's help I did," Mari said. "It did a lot of damage first, though. So many people were killed—" she began, and then closed her mouth. She had no idea if Davis's family had escaped the blaze. Quickly she changed the subject. "Where's Jenna?"

"Before Sora left to try to find you, she sent Jenna out to collect as much aloe as she could find. She brought one big basket of it back here but went out again to collect more. I was just starting to worry about her. It's almost dark, isn't it? I can feel the sun setting." Absently, Danita rubbed her arms, which hadn't yet begun to flush gray with the setting sun.

"Don't worry. Jenna's smart. She'll be back any moment, and I'll Wash the both of you." *If I can,* Mari added silently. *I'm so tired that I feel used up.*

"That's okay, Mari. Sora Washed Jenna and me last night. We're fine. And, um, you don't look so good."

Mari brushed a limp strand of blond hair from her face and sighed. "I'm just tired."

"Here, this will help." Nik handed her a steaming bowl of stew with a big hunk of Sora's fresh bread. Mari barely took time to thank him as she shoveled the food into her mouth.

"Danita, would you like some stew, too?" Antreas asked.

Mari felt the girl's body startle and begin to tremble. Bast reacted instantly. She leaned against the girl, purring loudly. With a motion that already appeared automatic, Danita stroked the feline. Then she answered Antreas, in a clear voice that hardly shook at all.

"No, thank you. I can wait until extra is ready. Feed yourselves and the animals first."

Which was exactly what the men were doing when the door to the burrow opened, letting in a cool evening breeze that carried with it Jenna and the scent of smoke. The young woman almost fell over Laru, who was closest to the door.

"Rigel! You're back, so Mari must—" Jenna began happily as she turned to put down the basket filled with aloe plants and noticed that the canine she'd tripped over was much larger than Rigel. "Oh! Mari?" Jenna's wide gray eyes darted around the burrow, taking in the men, the canines, the Lynx, and finally Mari.

"Jenna!" Mari met her at the door, hugging her tightly. "All is well. They're friends," she whispered, and felt the tension relax from her friend's body.

"Hi, Jenna," Nik said. He was sitting at Mari's favorite spot behind her desk, mouth partially filled with bread dunked in stew.

"Nik, I'm glad to see you're safe," Jenna said. She lifted one dark brow at the other men and the Lynx.

"This is Davis, and his Companion Terrier, Cameron," Mari said.

"Hello, Jenna. And we call him Cammy most of the time. Well, unless he's in trouble." Davis grinned at his Terrier, who barely looked up from his bowl of stew.

"And this is Antreas. His Companion is Bast, the feline who has decided to stay protectively close to Danita," Mari said.

Jenna nodded a greeting to Antreas, but it was Bast who had her full attention. "I've never seen a feline before. She's lovely."

"She's a Lynx," Antreas said. "And thank you."

"I've heard rumors of Lynx Companions, but I thought they were mostly just tall tales made up by Storytellers to amuse Clan children," Jenna said, moving closer to peer at Bast, who returned her gaze steadily. "But she's most definitely real." Jenna glanced at Antreas, smiling incredulously. "This gives me hope that maybe the stories of Wind Riders across the mountains to the east are true and Whale Singers in the oceans to the north and west, too."

"I can't tell you about the Whale Singers; I've never met anyone from that Tribe, but Wind Riders are definitely real."

Mari saw Nik's head jerk up. "Really? You've met a Wind Rider?"

"Several of them, actually. I guided a small group of Healers from a northern Tribe through the Rockies to the plains that are Wind Rider territory. They wanted to trade their balms and salves for some of the Wind Riders' crystals—you know their rocks and crystals have powerful properties, don't you?"

"Yes, yes, of course." Nik nodded, motioning for Antreas to continue.

"That's about it. I led the group into Wind Rider territory, and then went back after the next full moon, ready to guide them on the return trip through the mountains, but none of the Healers were there. I waited two days. No one came. So Bast and I left."

"Didn't you ask a Wind Rider about what had happened to the Healers?" Mari said, not so much because she wanted to know but more because Nik was listening so intently.

"Wind Riders are only found when *they* wish to be found, and they didn't wish to be found."

"Wind Riders—they're mostly women, right?" Davis said.

Antreas nodded. "I only met women. And their equines, which are as magnificent as they are dangerous. I'd never seen a creature so big! They're larger than even the mightiest stag. And they carry their Companions on their backs, as they run like the wind—even faster than a Lynx can run, I do believe," he finished, sending Bast a teasing look.

"But their equines couldn't be as soft and wonderful as Bast." Danita spoke up as she petted the Lynx. "Plus, they're all the way over the mountains, and she's right here."

Jenna turned her attention back to the feline. "Her fur does look incredibly soft."

Showing more animation than Mari had seen her show since she'd been attacked, Danita asked the feline, "Bast, do you think you could let Jenna touch you? She's my friend." The Lynx cocked her head, listening intently. Then she chirped and rubbed against Danita's hand.

"That's a yes," Antreas said.

"I know!" Danita told him, though she didn't look directly at the cat man.

"I'd love to touch her," Jenna said. Then she paused, making a quick gesture at the big Shepherd who had resettled himself in front of the door. "Um, who is the other Shepherd? He looks like a huge version of Rigel."

"That's my Companion, Laru. He should look like Rigel—he's his father," Nik said.

"Laru?" Jenna stopped halfway across the room. "But that's the name of the Sun Priest's canine."

"He *was* the Sun Priest's canine," Nik said quietly, and went back to studying his stew.

"But isn't the Sun Priest your father?" Jenna said.

"Yes. He was." Nik didn't look up from his food, though he'd stopped eating. "He died yesterday."

"Oh. I'm sorry, Nik," Jenna said.

Mari motioned for Jenna to join her on the crowded pallet, scooting over to make room. "Nik's father was killed saving my life," Mari said.

"Nik," Jenna said, and he finally looked up at her, tears in his eyes. "I'll say a prayer to the Earth Mother for him and burn a branch of rosemary in remembrance."

"Why? Why would you do that?" Danita blurted. "He was the Leader of the people who killed your father and enslaved you!"

"He also helped Nik get me out of there, and you heard Mari—his father lost his life saving our Moon Woman. Danita, I miss my father every day. I think I always will. But sometimes you have to let love shine through or the hate will consume you." She looked from Jenna to Mari and then Davis, Antreas, and finally Nik. "That's what I learned from being captured and forced to be a slave by the Tribe of the Trees."

Danita bit her lip and pressed her face into Bast's fur. "I'm not as good as you, Jenna. I don't think I could forgive the Tribe if I'd been through what you have because of them. I—I don't know if I can forgive the Tribe for causing the death of Leda, which made our men lose their way and attack me." She peeked up at Nik and Davis and then added softly, "I'm sorry."

"Danita, there is no more Tribe of the Trees," Nik said firmly. Davis started to speak, but Nik's raised hand stopped him. "When we rebuild—and we will rebuild—our Pack won't be like the old Tribe. No Pack member will ever capture an Earth Walker—not as long as I am their Sun Priest."

"Which is exactly why I've sworn to follow you as the new Sun Priest," Davis said earnestly. "I agree with Jenna. There has been too much hate. The fire finished that for me. I want something more—and I don't want that something to be at the expense of another people's freedom."

"Clan Weaver is no more," Mari said. All attention turned to her. "The Clan was broken when my mother died. I agree with Davis. I want more than to just rebuild a Clan that I had to hide my true self from. I want a Clan where we can be ourselves, in our best and truest forms."

"Then let's rebuild together," Nik said. "You and I, Mari—Sun Priest and Moon Woman. We can bring alive our dream—for us, and for people who want the same things we do."

Mari felt the warmth of Nik's words wash through her. "Yes, Nik. Yes. Let's rebuild together."

"And make it better," Jenna said.

"Happier and safer," Danita said, hugging Bast.

"Weirder," Antreas said with a laugh.

"Better, happier, safer, and weirder. Cammy and I are in!" Davis said while the canines barked in agreement and Bast's purr rolled like spring thunder through the cozy burrow.

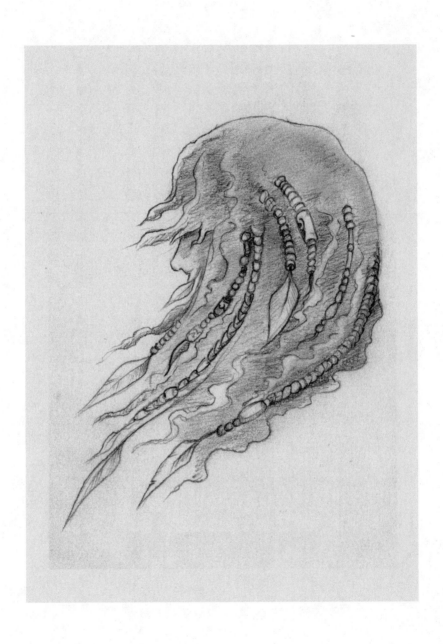

CHAPTER 12

I *can do this . . . I can do this . . . I can do this. . . .*
"They're ready for you!"

Isabel's bright voice broke through Sora's mantra. She drew a deep, fortifying breath and then stepped out of the birthing burrow's pantry.

"Oh, Sora! You look beautiful!" Isabel gushed.

Sora self-consciously patted her hair one more time. "You really think so?"

"Of course!"

"But I want to look *more* than beautiful. I want to look confident and strong and regal. I want to look like a proper Moon Woman. I tried my best to look proper, but I wasn't expecting to have to Wash what's left of our Clan—without Mari—and without practically any warning that'd I'd be drawing down the moon. For the first time for the Clan. Did I mention all by myself?"

"Hey, you're going to be great. You've already been great. Look at what you've done—by yourself. You treated the Clan's injuries, as well as the refugee Companions." Isabel waggled her brow. "Like that wasn't unexpected? But you handled it anyway."

"Their injuries are more painful than they are serious. I just had to manage their discomfort, splint Sarah's ankle, and apply a lot of aloe salve to Rose and Lydia. O'Bryan's dressing was simple to change. It's already well on its way to being completely healed, and *that* was Mari's doing." She paused; a bemused expression had her tilting her head and thinking aloud. "You know, O'Bryan's really very pleasant for a Companion. Even though he is too blond and too tall to be handsome."

"I like his puppies."

"Isabel, they're not O'Bryan's puppies. They belong to Rose's canine, Fala. O'Bryan carried them out of the fire, though, and saved them. That was really brave of him."

"I know this sounds weird, but I'm glad he saved them. They are just babies. And I think they're cute."

"Well, they're less unattractive than I would have guessed a canine baby to be," Sora admitted. "They're definitely cuter than Rigel. That creature is all fur and feet and appetite, and when I think of how big he's going to get—" Sora closed her eyes briefly and shook her head. "No. I'm not going to think about that at all right now. Right now I'm only going to think about drawing down the moon." Her eyes popped open. "Oh, Goddess! What if I can't do it? What if it doesn't work for me tonight?"

"You can do it. I know you can. You've done everything else a Moon Woman does. You've tended wounds and organized a Beltane Gathering at the last minute." Isabel gave her a cheeky look and added, "You even remembered where the spring mead was buried."

"Well, that wasn't hard. I was there when it was buried."

"And you have stew cooking that will feed everyone."

"That wasn't hard, either. The winter root vegetables were ready. All I did was supervise the making of the stew. I didn't actually cook it."

"You supervised because you were busy tending wounds and setting the positions of the campfires and the spreading of the lavender oil, the digging up of the mead, the collection of freshwater, and even getting sleeping pallets put together from what was, well"—Isabel looked around the tidied birthing burrow—"a disaster. Sora, you don't have to worry about whether you look like a proper Moon Woman, or even whether you are going to draw down the moon. You *are* a proper Moon Woman. Remember that and you'll be fine."

"What about Jaxom? I'm worried that—" Sora began, but her sentence ended in a wet, nasty cough.

Isabel's expression darkened. "Are you okay? That's not the first time I've heard you cough this evening, and you're looking flushed."

"I'm fine. It's just a cold."

"Well, take care of yourself. We need you healthy. And Jaxom? All you can do is Wash him. The rest is up to Jaxom."

"If I tell you something, do you promise not to tell anyone?"

"Moon Woman, I give you my oath to keep your secrets."

"I feel terrible about it, but I don't want any of the Clansmen to find the Gathering tonight. Jaxom is bad enough. I—I don't know what I'll do if a group of Clansmen filled with Night Fever, worse than we've ever seen before, burst into the Gathering. Isabel, I'm afraid of them."

Isabel took her hand. "Of course you are! I've seen what they did to you and to Danita. But, Sora, don't worry. If Clansmen do find the Gathering you'll do what any Moon Woman would do. You will command them to their knees and then Wash them."

"I will." Sora hoped saying it would make it so.

"I think you should Wash Jaxom first. Then if any males do find us he can help you keep order. I know you've put O'Bryan and Sheena to watching our perimeter, but . . ." She trailed off, chewing her lip.

"But they'll kill our Clansmen."

Isabel nodded slowly, eyes wide with worry. "I don't want that to happen."

"It won't. I won't let it. If they come I'll Wash them. I'm their Moon Woman, and that's what a Moon Woman does. Thank you for reminding me. And now I am ready."

"Then allow me the honor of leading you to your Clan, Moon Woman."

"Absolutely," Sora said firmly.

Chasing all doubts from her mind, Sora followed Isabel out of the birthing burrow and around the stone pathway that led to the little clearing through which a clear, lazy stream flowed. Even before she rounded the bend and reached the point where she could look down at the unconventional Gathering spot, Sora could hear the melodic sounds of drumming mixed with the high, perfect voice of a flute. She could smell the campfires and, as the wind brushed lightly past her face, she caught the familiar scent of lavender and salt, which was always spread around a Gathering to ward off hunting packs of wolf spiders.

Isabel reached the lookout spot before she did. The young woman turned and met Sora's gaze. Sora nodded. "I'm ready."

Isabel turned back to the Clan and in a strong, young voice that cut through the playful music spoke the traditional announcement of a Moon Woman's presence: "Our Moon Woman is here! Light the torches! Ready the Clan!" Then she hurried down the stone stairs to join the Gathering.

Sora took her place, looking down at her Clan. O'Bryan and Sheena were lighting the torches and taking positions at opposite sides of the circle that had been drawn by lavender oil and salt and framed by several campfires, with the main bonfire blazing in the center of the circle, close to the image of the Earth Goddess. Sora was particularly fond of this Goddess image. She was sitting cross-legged, her hands resting on her belly, fecund and swollen with child. Her skin was moss, and her hair was delicate ivy, flowing down to her thick waist. Her face was exquisite. It had been carved from a single opal, the color of the inside of oyster shells. *Guide me, Earth Mother. Help me to be a proper Moon Woman.*

The injured Companions rested together near one of the campfires to the right of the Goddess image. Sora could see they were watching the proceedings closely, but they looked more sleepy than worried or even nervous. *Well, no wonder—after the poppy tea and spring mead they've been drinking.*

The rest of the Clan were spread around the inside of the circle, and they were all looking expectantly up at her. Something about their like expressions suddenly reminded Sora of a nest of baby birds, and she had to stifle an inappropriate giggle.

Her gaze shifted to the one Clansman present, and her desire to giggle evaporated. Jaxom sat with his back to the thick log O'Bryan had tied him to. He'd regained consciousness, but only barely. His face was turned up in her direction, but she didn't see anything but the red glint of Night Fever in his eyes. She had, of course, drugged him as soon as she'd been able to pour the poppy-laced tea down his throat. Sora remembered the hopeless look in Jaxom's eyes as she'd examined him—silently and quickly—noting the strange boils that had formed at the creases of his elbows, wrists, and knees, as well as the way he kept trying to claw at his skin, even though his hands had been securely tied. *I've never seen Night Fever manifest on the skin like it has on Jaxom. I'll need to talk to Mari about it, check Leda's Healer's journals, and then—*

"Moon Woman! Our Moon Woman is here!"

The Clan's call to her swept the jumble of thoughts from Sora's mind. She gathered herself and started down the stairs, feeling the coolness of the stone steps under her bare feet and the soft night breeze against the skin of her naked legs. She'd wanted a proper Moon Woman's dress—something as beautiful as Leda's cloak. But there hadn't been time, so Sora had decided to leave her legs bare and wear only a simple tunic she'd found in the rubble of the birthing burrow, decorated with embroidered flowers and ivy. She'd also braided baby's breath, lavender, and ivy into her hair, in addition to the shells and feathers with which she always adorned herself.

Sora made her way to the Earth Goddess idol, bowing deeply before her.

"I greet you, Great Mother, as the Clan greets me—your Moon Woman, your servant—with love and gratitude and respect." Then she straightened and faced the watching Clan. Now was the time to call the Clansmen to come forward, as they were always Washed first to alleviate their pain and their threat to the Clan.

Taking control of her fear, Sora walked to Jaxom. His eyes blazed red at her, and sweat dripped from his face. He was filthy and he smelled rank—his breath came in fetid pants and she could see that he was straining against the ropes that bound him. For a moment she had a flash of panic. *What if he breaks free?* Every inch of her body that had been bitten and battered and bruised when Jaxom and the two other

Clansmen attacked her the day before ached. Her stomach heaved as she thought about what else they would have done to her had Nik not stopped them. *They were going to rape me. Jaxom was going to rape me.* And he would attack her again. Sora saw that clearly in his hate-filled expression and the gray tinge that already covered his broken skin.

Then from the edge of her vision a torch came into view, and O'Bryan was there—standing tall and strong, knife held out and ready, face set in grim lines as he positioned himself closer to Jaxom.

The women of the Clan moved closer to her as well. Some held torches. All wore expressions of grim determination. Jaxom would not get to her again—not while her Clan was near.

Sora straightened her spine and lifted her arms, concentrating on finding the moon that was there, even though the sun had too recently set for it to be visible. But Sora was a Moon Woman, and she could always find—could always call—the moon, as long as the sun had left the sky.

A sweet, soothing coolness spread from Sora's fingertips down her arms, chasing away the hot gray flush that the sun's setting had caused to mottle her skin and thus chasing away the depression that had begun to cloud her thoughts.

"Man of Clan Weaver, present yourself to me!" Sora commanded.

As if her words had an elemental power over his body, Jaxom shifted so that he was crouched on his knees, arms bound behind him to the log. He bowed his head.

Sora's breathing deepened, became rhythmic—in for four counts, pause, out for four counts. She repeated the breathing three times and sent her silent, simple prayer to the Great Goddess, *Let me be worthy of you, Earth Mother.*

Then Sora began to speak the words she'd practiced over and over again the past several weeks. Ironically, she had chosen to use the moon-drawing invocation Leda had always used. She hadn't thought to. She'd expected Mari to want to speak the same words her beloved mama had spoken to the Clan, but Mari had said no, that she had to find her own invocation because she was her own kind of Moon Woman, one who was a mixture of Clan and Tribe, but she knew Leda would be pleased Sora wanted to use her words.

And Sora had very much wanted to use Leda's words.

"Moon Woman I proclaim myself to be!
Greatly gifted, I bare myself to thee.
Earth Mother, aid me with your magick sight.
Lend me strength on this Beltane night.
Come, silver light—fill me to overflow
So those in my care your healing will know."

As Sora spoke the invocation, she concentrated on the Great Goddess, finding the connection she'd felt with the Earth Mother since she'd been a small child. Through that sacred connection Sora sought the moon, still invisible in the twilight sky. And it was there! She felt it! It was a silver illumination that was nothing like the sickly gray that spread over an Earth Walker's skin, bringing Night Fever to the Clan. This silver light was sublime and pure—the cool, soothing power that healed by Washing depression and darkness from the Clan.

Filled with the strength of moon magick, Sora completed the invocation:

"By right of blood and birth channel through me
the Goddess gift that is my destiny!"

As she spoke the final words, Jaxom's bowed head lifted—and he glared at her with a malicious red gaze. Without hesitation Sora swept her arms downward, cupping his fever-hot face in her hands. "I Wash you free of all pain and madness and Night Fever, and gift you with the love of our Great Earth Mother."

Jaxom's body jerked while his Moon Woman channeled moonlight through herself and into him. She watched his body begin to glow bright, brilliant silver. It seemed to take a long time. Sora had to grit her teeth against the desire to let loose his face as her hands began to grow numb with cold. And then Jaxom blinked several times. His gaze met hers, *and his eyes were brown and kind again.*

Jaxom smiled wearily up at her. In *his* voice—the voice that had always laughed at her jokes and told her how special and beautiful she was—he said, "Goddess bless you, my Moon Woman!" Then he sighed in relief and relaxed back against the log, grateful tears flowing down his cheeks.

Emboldened by that victory, Sora began to move through the Clanswomen in a clockwise fashion. The women took to their knees as she approached, lifting their faces to her. Sora rested her hand on one forehead, then another, murmuring the traditional blessing of "I Wash you free of all pain and madness and Night Fever, and gift you with the love of our Great Earth Mother."

Sora felt an incredible rush of love for them as she moved among her Clan. Though she had only known eighteen winters, Sora was consumed by maternal emotions, and as those feelings grew, her skin took on the brilliant silver sheen that had transformed Leda each Third Night.

As more and more of the Clanswomen were Washed, they returned to the drums and flutes, only this time the music they began weaving together was joined by sweetly harmonizing voices, singing wordless melodies of celebration. Some women even began dancing—twirling around with their arms flung wide, faces turned up to the darkening sky as if waiting with joyous expectation for the first glimpse of the moon.

After she Washed Isabel, Sora pulled the young woman aside briefly. "Please move Jaxom inside the birthing burrow. Tell him to wash. And then give him a mug of the poppy tea and a bowl of stew, and have him take the pallet nearest the hearth fire. Now that he's himself again I need to recheck his wounds and he needs rest and quiet. A lot of it."

"It will be as you say, Moon Woman." Isabel bowed to her and then hurried to untie Jaxom and guide him to the burrow.

Sora continued to wield moon magick, joyfully Washing the rest of the Clan. She forgot about the nagging sickness that had been causing her to feel feverish and irritable and to cough annoyingly. She forgot about her fear of whether Clansmen would find the Gathering, attack it, disrupt it, ruin it. Filled with love for her Clan and appreciation for her Goddess, Sora moved among her people, secure in the knowledge that they needed her, they revered her, and they would never, ever leave her.

CHAPTER 13

"Are you sure this is a good idea?"

Mari rearranged the basket filled with salves, tinctures, and every herb she thought might be of help, so that she could slip her hand into Nik's and squeeze. "Stop worrying. I told you, I'm better after eating. Almost good as new!" It felt great to be walking beside Nik, her arm looped through his, even if he was frowning at her with worry. Rigel rushed past them, chasing Cammy, who was chasing a squirrel. "Hey, stay close, you two! It's too dark to wander off," she called.

Beside Nik, Laru sneezed and gave a growling grumble. "I know. Pups can be so annoying," Nik said, patting the adult Shepherd on his head. He glanced around, holding the lit torch he was carrying higher. "I don't like being out here after dark."

Mari thought Nik sounded as grumbly as Laru. "We already talked about this. The birthing burrow isn't far, and it's logical that the swarm, and any other nasty things that crawl in the night, will be drawn to the dead left by the fire." Through their linked arms she felt Nik shiver. "I'm sorry," she added quickly. "I don't mean to be callous about it. I know many of your friends died in that fire. But we're alive, Nik. And for one night at least the forest doesn't hold as many dangers for us as it usually does."

"It still feels creepy out here at night," Davis said. He glanced up at

175

the sky, which was open and unobscured by the giant pines of the Tribe and the city that lived in the trees. "I didn't think I'd ever say this, but I'll be glad to get back inside Mari's burrow."

"One convert down—and only a whole Tribe to go," Nik whispered to Mari, who stifled her laugh with a cough.

"Danita, how are you feeling?" Mari called to the girl who was walking behind them, the Lynx on one side of her and Antreas, holding another torch, on the other. Mari had been surprised when Danita had insisted on coming with them to the birthing burrow. As far as Mari knew, since she'd been attacked Danita had only left their burrow to relieve herself and bathe, but the Lynx's protection seemed to have given the girl new life. Mari had known Danita's body would heal from the rape and brutalization, but she and Sora had discussed that it was her spirit that most worried them, and though Danita's body still needed to heal, it was becoming more and more apparent that Bast had somehow mended the girl's spirit.

"I'm okay," Danita said. Like Mari and Jenna, she was carrying a basket laden with food and medical supplies, but her free hand often reached down to touch Bast's head, as if she wanted to be sure the feline remained beside her. She needn't have worried. From what Mari could see, the Lynx had no intention of leaving the girl's side. "Maybe a little, um, stiff and sore. But it feels good to be out walking, even if it is at night." Danita sent the dark forest suspicious looks, and Mari saw her shiver.

"Hey, you don't need to worry about anything out there," Antreas said. "They'd have to get through Bast to get you, and that's just not going to happen."

Bast made the coughing sound that Mari had decided was the equivalent of one of Rigel's yips of agreement.

"Good, but don't push yourself. Once we're at the birthing burrow I want you to rest. Whatever tea Sora has concocted for the women, be sure you get a big mug of it."

"I'll see she takes care of herself," Jenna said. She was walking just behind Danita with Davis. They both carried torches that cast dancing shadows around the group.

"Thank you, Jenna," Mari said.

She saw that Antreas was nodding in agreement as he kept watch on Danita. Now that the rich stew and Sora's excellent bread had lifted the terrible fog of exhaustion from Mari's mind, she had a bunch of questions she'd love to ask Antreas about Bast and life as a Lynx Companion in general. Nik had told her Antreas had come to the Tribe of the Trees looking for a mate. Mari flicked a quick glance back at Danita—really looking at the girl—and realized with a small start that even though she was young, just over sixteen winters, Danita was definitely old enough to choose a mate.

Mari's gaze slid to the sleek feline who padded possessively beside Danita, her huge paws making no sound as she gracefully picked her way along the trail. The Lynx looked up then, meeting Mari's eyes. Within that light-filled gaze, Mari saw intelligence and confidence and kindness.

"What is it?" Nik asked softly.

"Just that life seems to get more interesting as it gets more complicated," she said.

"Couldn't agree with you more," Antreas muttered.

The path began to turn sharply to the right, and Mari raised her hand. "Okay, the birthing burrow is just around that bend and then up a length of rock stairs." She paused, breathing deeply of the night air, feeling a great sense of relief when she caught the scent of lavender. "Smell that lavender?" The men nodded. "That means Sora has set up a perimeter of lavender oil and salt. It keeps out the wolf spiders. She'll also have campfires and torches lit."

"She *is* going to Wash the males!" Jenna said happily.

"Males? No. No, I don't want them here." Danita crouched beside Bast, her arm around the Lynx.

"Bast and I won't let anyone hurt you," Antreas said.

"No one is going to hurt you, Danita. But I do want you to stay inside the burrow until all who are Gathered have been Washed of Night Fever," Mari said.

"I don't really understand this Night Fever stuff," Antreas said.

"It's usually simple," Jenna explained. "Every Third Night all Earth Walkers must be Washed of Night Fever by a Moon Woman." She held out her arm so that Antreas could see that her skin had begun to flush a silver-gray color. "This is a sign of Night Fever. It's not so bad with Danita and me, because Sora Washed us last night."

"Yes, and even if she hadn't, we wouldn't be dangerous, just really sad," Danita said.

"Like all the Scratchers—oh, sorry, I mean Earth Walkers—on Farm Island?" Davis asked. "You didn't have a Moon Woman there to Wash you, so that's why the only Earth Walkers I knew before Mari were so depressed that they seemed childlike and unable to take care of themselves, right?"

"That's right," Mari said.

Davis shook his head. "I wish we would have known. I wish the women would have told us."

"Have you ever tried to reason with someone who has taken you from your home, imprisoned you, and made you perform slave labor for them?" Jenna asked pointedly.

"No, I haven't. I know it sounds like too little too late, but I've sworn I'll never have anything to do with capturing another Earth Walker, and I will keep to my oath," Davis said. "You're all so different than I thought you were, and now that I know it, I won't go back to unknowing it—I couldn't, even if I wanted to. Just for the record—I don't want to."

"I believe you," Jenna said.

"I believe you, too," Mari said. "So, you understand now about what happens to Clanswomen if they aren't Washed of Night Fever. It's different for our men. Night Fever doesn't make them sad. It makes them angry—very angry. A Clansman who hasn't been Washed can be dangerous, but usually only to himself."

"But once they're Washed they're okay. Like my father. He was—"
She broke off, her eyes shining with unshed tears, her gaze going soft
with remembrance. "He was the best father in the world. Right, Mari?"

"Absolutely," Mari said.

"What you're saying is the Clansmen will be drawn by the fire and
by the scent of lavender and want to be Washed, which means they'll
be dangerous, but only until you've performed your ritual?" Davis said.
"*Ritual?* Is that the right word for it?"

"Yes, though you can also call it drawing down the moon. Here's
the thing about tonight. We don't usually hold a Gathering at the
birthing burrow. It's a women's place of sanctuary, where they give
birth, tend babies, and hold classes for the older children. I don't know
how many males will be close enough to be drawn here. . . ." Mari
paused and then added, "And there's another problem. None of us
knows what happens to our males after they have gone so long without
being Washed of Night Fever. Our Clan has never had a Moon Woman
die so suddenly without a properly trained heir to take up her role immediately."

"You're saying the men haven't been Washed since your mother's
death?" Davis said.

"Yes, that's what I'm saying."

"I thought you were a Moon Woman," Antreas said.

Mari sighed. "I am, but only by default. Mama hadn't finished training me—or Sora, Mama's other apprentice. It's my fault, really. I didn't
take over Mama's duties after she died. I had Rigel to think of, and the
Clan didn't know about him, or that my father was a Companion. Mama
kept that hidden from them, afraid that she and I would be banished if
they found out." Mari lifted her chin and admitted, "And I didn't want
to be Moon Woman. Not after Mama was killed. I just wanted to be
left alone."

"But Sora wouldn't leave you alone," Nik said.

Mari gave him a sardonic look. "And neither would you. Sora and Nik
and Rigel brought me back to life, back to my duties as Moon Woman

and Healer of Clan Weaver. Still, the damage has been done. The males are mad with Night Fever, and I don't know if Washing them will fully relieve their pain and anger and let them come back to themselves."

"And if they do come back to themselves, how will they be able to live with the things they've done?" Danita said.

Mari nodded sadly. "Exactly."

"That could be why those males attacked us at that deer carcass," Davis said to Nik. "Does Mari know about that?"

"No, I haven't had a chance to tell her," Nik said.

"What is it?" Mari asked.

"It's how O'Bryan was wounded and got the blight. It was before I went on the foraging mission to Port City—before you found me injured by the Skin Stealers. Davis, O'Bryan, and I were searching for Rigel, and we came upon a slain deer—wasted and hanging to rot."

"You mean the whole carcass? Someone killed a deer and just left it?" Mari asked incredulously.

"Yeah, and even more bizarre, Earth Walker males were there, waiting, as if they'd set a trap for us," Nik said.

"But that doesn't happen. Our males have never trapped Companions, and they definitely wouldn't waste a deer kill," Jenna said.

"And yet that's what happened," Nik said.

"Yeah, it was bad," Davis added.

"You're sure they were Earth Walker males and not Skin Stealers from Port City?" Mari asked.

"Absolutely sure," Nik said.

"I second that," Davis said. "I was there. It was a close thing for a while. We almost didn't escape their trap."

"Our males are doing things they've never done before," Danita said in a small, frightened voice.

"She's right," Jenna said. "Even on a Third Night, our Clansmen can be reasoned with—at least long enough for them to be Washed."

"They have to be stopped," Danita said.

"They will be," Mari said, and then silently added, *Either by Washing or by death—they will be stopped.*

"What you're saying is that you want us to watch the perimeter, and I'm assuming to *not* kill any Earth Walker males who breech it, but to let them through so you can Wash them," Nik said.

"Yes. That's what I'm saying. But Nik, I'm also saying keep your crossbow close and ready. Davis, Antreas, be ready, too. I'll Wash the males, but if it doesn't work—or if they are too violent to be helped—shoot them. I won't have anyone else hurt," Mari said.

"Understood," Nik said. Davis and Antreas nodded grimly.

"I'm sorry. I know this is my fault. I should have found the males after Mama was killed. I should have cared more about the Clan than my sadness," Mari said to Jenna and Danita. The two girls shared a long look before Jenna spoke for them both.

"Leda was your whole world, Mari. Of course you mourned; you're still mourning. And there was a lot the Clan didn't know back then—a lot that would have been impossible to explain to Night Fever–crazed males. But everything is different now. We understand what you've been hiding and why."

Danita nodded in agreement. "Now you're our Moon Woman. We follow you. Always."

Mari felt the weight of their trust as a great pressure around her heart. It warmed her, but it also frightened her. *What if I mess up? What if I make the wrong decision and hurt the Clan even more than it's already been hurt by me?*

And then, drifting down the twisting path before them, the lovely sounds of women's voices raised in joyous song carried through the night.

"Oh! They're singing!" Jenna said, clapping her hands together in happiness.

"It's the Clanswomen! Sora must have already Washed them." Danita cocked her head, listening carefully. Then her face broke into a delighted grin. "It's a Beltane melody!"

"Beltane? Is it really Beltane so soon? Great Goddess, I've totally lost track of time," Mari said.

"Sora remembered!" Danita jumped to her feet, obviously eager to run ahead, but she paused and turned to Mari. "Mari, do you think I can join the Clan instead of staying inside the burrow?"

"If you feel up to it, of course you may," Mari said. "Sora's already Washed the Clan, so if any males have come to the Gathering you should be safe, but Danita, you have to realize there might be Clansmen there."

Danita ducked her head and spoke to her feet. "The ones who attacked me?"

"Maybe," Mari said.

Danita lifted her head. "I won't let what they did to me rule the rest of my life. I want to join the Beltane celebration, just like I would have *before*." Her hand stroked Bast, and she spoke directly to the big feline. "Bast, will you please come to me after Mari introduces you and Antreas to the Clan?"

Bast made her strange coughing-bark and rubbed against Danita's legs, purring like a humming wasp nest.

"That's a yes," Antreas said.

Danita sent him an annoyed look. "I know. You're not the only one who can understand her."

"What's happening?" Nik asked.

The weight that had been settling around Mari's heart shifted, lifted, if only a little. "It's the Clan. They're rejoicing in Beltane, and the girls are excited to join them."

"Beltane? What's that?" Antreas asked.

"It's fun! That's what it is!" Danita shot back over her shoulder at him from where she and Jenna were already straining to run ahead to the Gathering.

"It's one of our seasonal celebrations," Mari explained as they headed around the path and then came to the wide stones that had been placed generations ago to form stairs leading up to the birthing burrow. "Beltane is a fertility celebration—fertility for the crops we've planted, and fertility for the Clan. There are always lots of babies born in late February and early March—conceived during a Beltane celebration." She felt Nik's gaze on her, which had her stomach fluttering like it did when he held her hand. "It's halfway between Spring Equinox and Summer Solstice, and Clan Weaver always celebrates with a Gathering, good food, and all-night dancing and singing."

"And spring mead! We celebrate with that, too!" Jenna said.

"Yeah, we sure do. I wonder if Sora managed to unearth any?" Mari's mouth watered at the thought of the drink that fermented all winter in carved oak barrels Clanswomen buried to unearth, rich and strong and sweet, in the spring.

"Oh, I hope so!" Jenna jumped up and down in excitement. "Come on, Mari!"

"You two go ahead and join the Clan, but Bast needs to stay with us until I make introductions. And put those baskets of supplies by the burrow." As Jenna and Danita darted ahead, splashing through the stream that wound around the burrow, Mari told the three men, "Remember what I said about watching for Clansmen. They are dangerous—very dangerous."

"Understood," Nik said. "Though it won't endear us to your Clan if we show up and have to start fighting their males."

"I think it'd be more endearing than standing by and watching a bunch of males crazed with Night Fever brutalize Clanswomen," Mari said.

"Good point," Davis said. "And I hope there's mead, too."

"Let's go see," Mari said.

"After you, Moon Woman," Antreas said as his Lynx meowed pitifully and stared after Danita.

"Hey, cat man," Davis teased good-naturedly. "Aren't you afraid of losing Bast to that girl?"

"No. *Losing* her to Danita isn't what I'm afraid of," the Lynx man muttered so softly that Mari was pretty sure she was the only one who heard him.

CHAPTER 14

Nik, Davis, Antreas, and their Companions followed closely behind as Mari climbed the wide stone stairs to the birthing burrow. She was glad to see that the door to the burrow had been re-paired. Before it, Danita and Jenna had placed their laden baskets of aloe, salves, and the supplies Mari had carefully chosen. Mari added her basket of fresh-baked bread to the group and then followed the fa-miliar path that circled around the large burrow, leading to the clear-ing where the stream widened so that it provided water for the thriving herb and vegetable gardens that surrounded it. From the vantage point of the burrow, Mari paused while the men and their Companions joined her. She looked down at the impromptu Gathering and a wave of home-sickness for her mama washed through her.

Mama should be here. She should be leading the rebuilding of the Clan, and the Beltane Gathering.

But her mama was dead, and it was up to Mari and Sora to pick up the broken pieces of the Clan and put them back together.

Maybe we can put the pieces back together to form a newer, better, happier Clan . . . one that calls itself a Pack!

Below in the clearing bisected by the nourishing stream, Sora had assembled what was left of the Clan and, bizarrely, the refugees from the Tribe of the Trees. As the Clanswomen raised their voices in harmonious sound that mixed beautifully with drums and flutes—not yet making any distinguishable words but instead creating a magical blending of melody and music, Mari saw that the two wounded girls, Sarah and Lydia, were reclining on pallets, with Rose sitting beside them. Fala and her pups slept nearby. Mari searched quickly for O'Bryan and Sheena. The female Companion was easy to find, as her big Shepherd was a fixture by her side. Mari saw that she was carrying a torch and holding a long, dangerous-looking knife as she walked the perimeter campfires set up in a rough circle around the site, her sharp eyes focused outside the circle of light at the dark, quiet forest. Then Mari noticed O'Bryan was doing the same thing—minus a Shepherd Companion, of course. He carried a torch and Mari saw firelight glint off the equally dangerous-looking knife he carried.

"Wow, looks like a party's going on down there," Nik said.

"They're drinking something. Do you think it's mead?" Davis asked.

Before Mari could say she hoped so, the tempo of the wordless song changed, became more rhythmic, more familiar. Mari's breath hitched, and Sora stepped to the middle of the circle, standing before the center bonfire. Mari thought she truly looked the part of a Moon Woman. Her skin still glistened with the silver sheen that lingered after she'd Washed the Clan, making her appear as if she was a fairy come alive from one of her mama's ancient stories. Sora's thick, dark hair fell loose, reaching to the curve of her supple waist. She'd braided parts of it with flowers and feathers and vines, shells and beads. She was wearing a tunic top that was undecorated except for simple embroidery, but it was all she was wearing and her naked legs and feet were lovely and drew attention to the graceful way she moved.

Sora raised her arms, as if to embrace the night, and the music went silent. Then, in a clear, strong voice, she called, "Some would say we haven't much to celebrate, but I disagree. We have the return of our Clanswomen, many of whom haven't taken a free breath for years. We have made new friends, opening our burrows and our Clan to aid them. Some Clanswomen who have chosen to go their own way—the old way—say that we should reject all Companions and let them live or die by their own means. I thought like that before—before your other Moon Woman, Mari, showed me a different way. A way filled with compassion and understanding, like the Great Earth Mother herself. Aren't we all, at one time or another in our lives, refugees—whether from our families, who may want us to choose a different path than we desire to walk, or from a discarded mate who disappoints us, or even from a new Clan, if our life skills take us to live in a stranger's burrow?"

The Clanswomen murmured agreement, several of them nodding their heads.

"And now two Companions walk the perimeter of our Gathering, watching for danger, keeping us safe."

More murmuring came from the Clanswomen, and Mari was pleased to note that they seemed to be in accord with Sora.

From beside her, Antreas said, "Who is that woman?"

"That's Sora—the other Moon Woman Mari talks about," Nik answered for her.

"She's magnificent," Antreas said.

Mari gave him a sharp look. A quick movement from the corner of her eye had her noticing that Bast was doing the same. Then Mari's attention was pulled back to the scene below them as Jenna and Danita joined the Gathering. They rushed to Sora, bowing respectfully before her. When they finished greeting her, they whispered excitedly to the Moon Woman, pointing to where Mari stood, surrounded by Companions and their life-bonded animals.

Mari held her breath. As one, the Clan turned to stare up at her.

Mari's first desire was to duck and hide. She'd spent her life keeping the secret of who she truly was, and that was a hard habit to break, even though all of the Clan gathered below already knew the secret. But their eyes felt hard and judgmental—as if Mari hadn't just been stripped of the physical disguise that had kept her identity secret, her matted, dyed hair, her dirtied skin, her thickened features—but she'd also been stripped of her emotional defenses and was standing there alone and naked before them all.

Then Rigel's warm body pressed against her side. He was staring up at her with a doggy grin, wagging his tail and beaming such love and pride for her that the frantic thoughts that were creating negative stories within her imagination began to quiet.

"Mari! Moon Woman, join us!" Sora called joyously.

"It's Mari! Mari's back!" Mari recognized Isabel's voice, and then several other women took up the call.

"Your people want you, Moon Woman. Lead, and we will follow," Nik said, bowing low and respectfully to her—and in full view of the Clan. Davis and Antreas did the same, and Mari was shocked and amused to see Rigel, Laru, and even Bast bow their heads and take to their knees before her.

Mari lifted her chin and breathed a small, silent, heartfelt prayer to her mother: *Mama, help me be the Moon Woman you always believed I could be.* And then, with Rigel walking proudly at her side and Nik and Laru, Davis and Cammy, Antreas and Bast flanking her, Mari joined the first Gathering she had ever attended *as her true self.*

She stopped in front of Sora and began the traditional greeting to a Moon Woman, head bowed, arms spread low, palms up and open, but Sora caught her in a hug, saying, "I'm so glad you're back! I was worried when the sun set. Goddess, I hate to think about what could be crawling out there tonight."

Mari hugged her friend back, struggling to contain her emotions. There was no jealousy in Sora's expression or her voice, only honest concern and relief. *How much we've changed!* Mari thought. *Just a few weeks ago I thought Sora was a selfish bitch and she thought I was a sickly, good-for-nothing brat. And now I wouldn't want to even imagine my life without her as my friend.*

Mari gave Sora one more squeeze, then turned to stand beside her friend and fellow Moon Woman, facing Nik, the Companions, and her Clan.

"Blessed Beltane!" she said, hearing the echo of her mother's voice in her own as the answering call from the Clan lifted around them in the circle.

"Beltane Blessings to you, Moon Woman!"

"I want to introduce my friends to you. This is Nik, and his Companion, the Shepherd Laru, who is my Rigel's sire." Nik dipped his head to the gathered Clan and Laru looked dignified, even as he eyed the Gathered Clan with curiosity. "This is Davis, and his Companion, the Terrier Cameron." Davis was nodding to the Clan as Nik had when Cameron yipped and jumped against Mari's leg, making her laugh and add, "Well, his name is Cameron, but everyone calls him Cammy."

"Unless he's in trouble; then I call him *Cam-er-on!*" Davis added, emphasizing the three syllables, which made a few Clanswomen standing closest to them laugh and then cover their mouths as if they were shocked a Companion would make a joke.

"And this is Antreas. He isn't part of the Tribe of the Trees. He's from the mountains far east of here. His Companion is the Lynx Bast."

Antreas waved at the Clan while Bast padded the few feet to Danita to sit beside the girl and groom herself.

Antreas gave an exaggerated sigh. "It seems one of your Clan has already won over my Lynx. Does that make me an honorary member?" He slanted a look at Mari.

"Almost," Mari said, laughing as Danita stroked the feline attached to her side.

"Mari, what is the news from the Tribe of the Trees?"

Mari searched the crowd until she found the bright-eyed questioner. "Hello, Isabel. It's good to see you again."

"And you, Moon Woman. You have been to the City in the Trees, haven't you? Is it still on fire?"

Mari noted that Isabel was sitting near Rose and Fala's puppies. She glanced at the pile of pups and sent a silent thanks to the Great Goddess. *If you orchestrated this, it was brilliant. There's not much that touches the heart of a Clanswoman more than a baby—be it Earth Walker or animal.* She also noted that Sheena, Captain, and O'Bryan had moved closer and, along with Rose, Sarah, and Lydia, were waiting expectantly for her answers.

"I have been to the City in the Trees, and the forest fire has been stopped," she said.

There were sounds of relief from Sheena and O'Bryan, as well as Rose, Sarah, and Lydia. The Clan was very silent.

"But I think it appropriate that the new Sun Priest answer any other questions about the Tribe." Mari nodded to Nik, motioning for him to join her in the center of the circle.

Looking grim, Nik faced the small group of Companions. "First, you should know that my father is dead."

Mari watched the reactions of the Companions closely. O'Bryan and Sheena, of course, already knew, but none of the rest of them did. Sarah and Lydia began crying softly, hugging each other for comfort. Fala crawled onto Rose's lap, nuzzling her—though the woman was too shocked to comfort her Companion.

"That's why Laru is with you," Rose said. "He didn't come as your protector or your guide. He's truly yours."

Nik nodded. "Yes, he chose to live and be my Companion, rather than to die with my father. And for that I'll always be grateful."

"I don't understand. How can you be our new Sun Priest? There has been no vote. No Council Meeting. No ritual Call to the Sun for approval." Mari didn't think Sheena sounded belligerent, just confused.

"You're right, Sheena. None of those things have happened, but I'm not claiming to be Sun Priest for the Tribe of the Trees. I am Sun Priest for a new group of peoples, a group we call a Pack."

"Oh, sunfire! Are they all gone? All of our families and friends?" Rose asked on a sob.

"No," Nik assured her hastily. "Though it's bad. I don't know how many of the Tribe of the Trees survived. Rose, I'm sorry, I don't know if your parents and sister are alive." He turned to his cousin. His voice broke with emotion. "O'Bryan, your parents—Aunt Sherry and Uncle Lindy—they didn't make it. I'm so, so sorry."

His cousin's head bowed as he nodded, and Mari saw silent tears tracking down his face. "I was afraid of that. They were heading to the Channel when the wind shifted."

"So the Tribe has been decimated," Sheena said.

"It has," Nik said.

"And you don't plan on returning and rebuilding with them?" she asked.

"No. I don't," Nik said firmly. "I find that I don't agree with the old Tribe ideology." He cast his gaze around the Gathering as he continued. "My Pack will never take any captives. I swear this on my father's memory."

"Which won't change the old Tribe of the Trees, though," Sora said.

"You're right, Sora, but I can't speak for them. I don't know how many Elders survived," Nik said.

"But what's your guess, Companion?" The question came from a Clanswoman on the far side of the circle. Mari recognized her as Gwyneth, a talented weaver who had been friends with her mother—and had been taken captive by the Tribe of the Trees more than three winters ago.

Nik considered for a moment and then answered in a clear, honest voice, "My guess is they won't change. My guess is as soon as they've rebuilt one of the first things they'll do is go on a Hunt for new captives."

A restless murmur washed through the Earth Walkers. Mari raised her hand, and they instantly went silent.

"We have time. Sheena was right. The Tribe of the Trees has been decimated. Rebuilding will not be fast. And it's not just the City in the Trees they have to rebuild. The floating cages on Farm Island were completely destroyed, so they have to make new ones before they begin hunting us. Before that happens I give you my oath as your Moon Woman that we will come up with a plan to keep us safe. All of us."

"But *are* you our Moon Woman?" This time Gwyneth stepped forward, speaking directly to Mari. "What about Sora?"

"Oh, I'm also your Moon Woman," Sora said with no hesitation. "Mari and I have decided to make some changes. The first of them is to do away with the Law that says there can only be one Moon Woman per Clan." She shrugged. "It just doesn't make sense."

"But that's how it always has been!" said another Clanswoman Mari didn't get a good look at.

"Do you have any idea how exhausting it is to be the only person responsible for healing, Washing, documenting, and counseling an entire Clan?" Mari said, hands on hips, facing the muttering Clan.

"I do!" Sora said, then added, "And I haven't even had to be Moon Woman to an entire Clan yet. It's exhausting and stressful, and it's just stupid that something of such importance has been left to one isolated woman. Leda died. You know what happened to our men afterward when neither Mari nor I was able to Wash them." She pulled aside her tunic so that the purpled bruises and inflamed bite marks that covered much of her body were visible to the Clan. "This is what happens when there is only one Moon Woman for a Clan and she dies. I, for one, am going to do everything I can to be sure this never happens to any of you."

"I agree with Sora. And you all should know that any girl child with gray eyes who chooses to go into Moon Woman training will be accepted by Sora and me," Mari said.

"That's right. Even though we know only a small number of us can actually draw down the moon and Wash the Clan, we don't know how many of us might have a talent for healing," Sora said.

"Or record keeping," Mari added. "Or counseling. We should all use our strengths together, for the good of everyone. *All of us.*" Her gesture took in the Clan and the Companions. She wanted to continue—to tell the Clan that they would be stronger, better, more able to survive if they accepted Nik and his friends into the Clan—or at least accepted their new Pack as permanent allies of the Clan—but she could see that her people had taken in enough for one day and she worried that if she pushed any harder just then she would be pushing them past the breaking point. "But there will be time to speak of these things and plan a new path for the Clan. Tonight, I see your Moon Woman—one of them—has already Washed the Clan." She grinned at Sora, who tossed her thick hair and dimpled in return.

"I have, so what's left to you, Moon Woman, on this Beltane night is to lead us in the Weaving Dance," Sora said.

Mari felt a thrill of excitement and nervousness. *The Weaving Dance!*

She knew the dance—had known it since she was a child. She and Leda had practiced it together, dancing around the Earth Mother idol above their burrow every Beltane after Leda had returned from the Clan Gathering. But Mari had only danced it with the Clan once, and that was when she'd known just over six winters—before the filigree sun pattern had begun lifting from under her skin, leaving no doubt that her father had been a Companion and that she must hide that secret from the Clan.

Now Mari stood before what was left of her mama's Clan as her true self, and she felt as if her body wasn't big enough to contain the sense of freedom not having to hide brought her.

"Mari, everyone's waiting for you to start," Sora whispered to her.

"Oh, of course," Mari whispered back. She sent Nik and the other Companions a look. "You'll want to step out of the circle. It's going to get pretty crowded in here once we start."

Nik looked bemused, but he led the others to join Sheena, O'Bryan, and the wounded girls at the edge of the circle near one of the campfires.

Mari looked down to see Rigel had remained beside her, his tongue lolling in a canine grin. She almost told him to go to Laru—to stay out of the way—but she suddenly realized that she was setting a new precedent. If she sent Rigel away from her, even just to the outskirts of the circle, it would be like sending part of her soul to stand on the sidelines, to be an observer instead of a participant in Clan life.

No. I'll never do that to you. Ever.

"Stay close, sweet boy. We're going to dance!" she told him.

Then Mari stepped forward and raised her arms high over her head, as if she were reaching for the moon. Rigel moved with her, his warm shoulder touching the side of her leg. She drew a deep breath and shut her eyes, closing out the watching crowd and focusing on the joy her mama would have felt had she been there to see her dream of her daughter leading the Clan in celebration come true.

In a clear, strong voice Mari began the song, singing the melody by herself, as custom demanded:

"Weave with me, Clan, a dance in the night, always Moon Woman's delight.
Show me your joy, Washed free of all spite, mystical magick Third Night."

As the Clan joined in with drums and flutes and harmonizing voices, Mari began the intricate steps of the dance, and the Clanswomen who were not too injured or too tired followed her. Rigel stayed by her side, moving with her, as if they were sharing the steps. The dance wasn't regimented, though there were steps they all knew. The women wove a sinuous pattern within the circle with an earthy grace that mirrored the rhythm of water over river stones. Flowing through the movements of the Beltane dance, Mari forgot her nerves. She forgot everything— except Nik. As she danced, weaving between Clanswomen through and around the circle, she felt his gaze on her as surely as she felt Rigel's warmth near her side, and for the first time in her life Mari believed she was beautiful.

"Over the river, over the grove,
Followed from dusk to dawn.
Never I'll stray, always I'll stay,
Sweet Washing downward drawn."

When they came to the second chorus, Mari heard Nik's strong baritone harmonizing with the Clanswomen, and the burst of joy that surged through her made her feel as if her feet were hardly touching the ground.

"Oh, weave with me, Clan, a dance in the night, always Moon
Woman's delight.
Show me your joy, Washed free of all spite, mystical magick Third Night!
Harvest will come, Harvest will go,
Always from dusk to dawn.
Bountiful night, Washed in moonlight,
Fear and tears gently gone."

By the third chorus, Davis and O'Bryan, Sheena and Rose, as well as Antreas, had joined the song. Mari twirled and wove between the Clanswomen, and their happiness lifted all around her. Mari soaked in the miracle of this Beltane moment and, if just for a short breath of time, she shed fears and worries and doubts about their future.

"Oh, weave with me, Clan, a dance in the night, always Moon Woman's delight.
Show me your joy, Washed free of all spite, mystical magick Third Night!"

The dance went on and on, until sweat trickled between Mari's breasts and she was feeling light-headed. Smoothly changing direction, she wove her way back to the edge of the circle where Nik waited, sitting beside a log with Laru, smiling and clapping his hands in time with the beating drums. Short of breath, she and Rigel collapsed beside him.

"For you, Moon Woman." Isabel was there, bowing before Mari and offering her a mug filled with fragrant spring mead and, to Mari's surprise, holding out a wooden bowl filled with freshwater for Rigel.

Mari smiled her thanks and she and Rigel drank deeply while Isabel skipped back to the circle to continue the dance.

"Am I getting old?" Mari asked—only semi-rhetorically—as she wiped sweat from her face and ran her fingers through her short, curly hair, trying to get it under some semblance of control.

Nik laughed. "Old? I've never heard of anyone calling down sunfire and then dancing away the night. I don't know how you managed to stay out there so long when by all Tribal accounts you should be sound asleep." He put his arm around her and Mari leaned gratefully against him. "You're incredible. You looked like a moon goddess again," he whispered into her ear.

"Again?"

"When you healed O'Bryan I thought you looked like a moon goddess come to earth."

Mari was pretty sure had her cheeks not already been hot, they would have flushed bright pink. "I'm just me, Nik. No Goddess. I'm barely a Moon Woman."

"Hell, Mari, I'm barely a Sun Priest who has barely a Pack. I think we make a great team."

Mari looked around the circle at the dancing Earth Walkers and the Tribesmen and women, plus Antreas, who watched them as they clapped in time with the music and sipped cool spring mead. "Just a few weeks ago I could never have imagined doing what I did tonight, as my true self with Rigel by my side." She stroked the panting pup's head and kissed his nose. "But look at us all now. I know this is just a brief moment in time, but we have somehow managed to get Companions and Earth Walkers to come together without capturing or killing each other."

"Because together we're not barely anything." Nik touched her face, turning her toward him. "Together we're perfect. I'm starting to believe there's nothing *we* can't accomplish."

Mari leaned into Nik, loving the warm, solid feel of his body. His lips found hers, and the kiss deepened. The rhythmic beating of the drums and the voices lifted in happy song pulsed through Mari, finding a harmonious echo in her blood. Heat that had nothing to do with dancing began to build deep within Mari, making her feel weak and strong, liquid and fire, all at the same time. Her arms wrapped around Nik's broad shoulders, and a shiver of desire skittered through her as he moaned her name against her lips and began to pull Mari down to the soft ground with him.

"Mari, oh, good! Here you are." Sora hurried up to them, pink faced and breathing heavily. She coughed a few times, a deep, wet sound that had Mari eyeing her sharply. "I need you to come with me." She arched a dark brow at Nik. "Sorry, I didn't mean to interrupt. This time."

"What is it?" Mari asked, tugging at her tunic and disentangling herself, reluctantly, from Nik's arms.

Sora coughed again and scratched absently at her elbow crease, then lowered her voice. "It's better if I show you. I don't really want to talk about it out here."

Mari shrugged. "Okay, but I hope we're not going far. I'm pretty sure I'm at the end of my strength for one day."

"Not far. Just back to the birthing burrow."

"Good. You need to brew yourself some tea—red clover and honey will help that cough," Mari said.

"I will. Later. I'm fine," she said sharply, making a dismissive gesture.

Nik stood, holding out a hand to help Mari to her feet. When Sora shot him a *Where do you think you're going?* look, he said, "I'm coming, too. Unless Mari doesn't want me to."

"Oh, I want you to," Mari assured him.

"Fine," Sora said. "Come on then."

They began to make their way back to the burrow, Rigel and Laru beside their Companions. Sora frowned at Laru. "That creature does look like a giant version of Rigel." Then she glanced at Nik. "I'm truly sorry about your father," Sora said.

"Thank you," Nik said.

"Mari, is your creature going to get as big as the Laru creature?"

"Father said he thought Rigel will be even bigger," Nik answered first.

"I hope so!" Mari said brightly, reaching across Nik to ruffle Laru's ears. "I've decided I like big canines."

"In that case, I think we're going to need a bigger burrow," Sora said sardonically, which made Nik and Mari laugh.

They followed Sora up the wide stone stairs, Mari growing more and more concerned as she listened to her friend try unsuccessfully to stifle several more coughs.

"Hey, you're really sick," Mari said.

"It's nothing. I just danced too much," Sora said. "But there is someone in the burrow who *is* sick—and strangely sick at that."

"Well, some of the Clanswomen swallowed a lot of river water crossing the Channel," Mari said. "That might very well make them sick. There's a lot of muck in that Channel. The water really should be boiled before drinking and—"

"Yeah, yeah, I know all that," Sora interrupted, sounding irritated. "It's not a Clanswoman who's sick."

"Who is it then?" Mari asked.

Sora turned at the door to the burrow, her hand resting on the wood. "It's Jaxom."

CHAPTER 15

Jaxom lay on the pallet closest to the hearth fire. He'd been sleeping when they entered the cavernous burrow, but as Sora bent over him his eyes opened. Mari tensed, ready to move behind Nik, who had his crossbow notched with an arrow and ready to fire. But she needn't have worried. Jaxom only had eyes for Sora, and there was no red haze of danger in his vision—there was only regret.

"Sora, I am so sorry. About the clearing—with Bradon and Joshua—that wasn't me."

"Yes, it was you. I was there. That arrow wound in the back of your shoulder proves it," Nik said.

Jaxom appeared to have just realized that Nik was there. "Why is a Companion here?"

"He's with me," Mari said.

Jaxom squinted up at her as if he was having trouble focusing. "Mari? You look different. Where's Leda? Why are Companions allowed here?"

"I think the better question is why are you allowed here? I've never attacked a Moon Woman. You would have raped one had I not stopped you," Nik said.

"No! That wasn't me—not who I really am." Jaxom ignored Nik and pleaded with Sora. "Please. I don't deserve your forgiveness, but please believe that I would never hurt you."

"Leda is dead." Mari spoke before Sora could. "I look different because I *am* different. I'm not hiding my true self anymore. I'm part Companion." She jerked her chin in Rigel's direction. "That young Shepherd belongs to me, and I belong to him." Mari met Sora's gaze. "Is this what you wanted to show me? That he seems normal after you Washed him?"

"Partially. Jaxom, I need to show Mari your arms."

Jaxom raised his arms so that Sora unwound the bandages that swathed his wrists and elbows. "They look much better. How are you feeling?" Sora asked as she stepped aside so Mari could get a closer look.

"Better than I have for weeks," Jaxom said.

"What is that?" Mari bent over Jaxom, taking his arm gently in her hands and examining the creases in his skin where angry red flesh was beginning to fade to a healthier pink and scabs were already forming over what looked like areas that had been covered with huge pustules.

"I don't know. I'd never seen anything like it. It was really bad before I Washed him, even though I dressed his wounds and packed them with the goldenrod salve. The blisters were big, filled with pus, and his skin was sloughing off around them."

"The blisters happened to all of us who ate the stag," Jaxom said. "It made us sick, but that's probably because he was sick, too."

"Wait, did you say you ate a sick deer?" Nik asked.

Jaxom nodded. "Stag, really. It was a few weeks ago. We were mad with Night Fever, but not out of our minds. It was uncomfortable when our Moon Woman didn't appear at the Third Night Gathering, and then the next and the next, but we were still able to function during the day, though the nights were horrors." He paused, his eyes veiled with remembered misery, before continuing. "Then we found the stag, and everything changed."

"How so?" Mari had unwrapped another bandage and was continuing to examine Jaxom as he explained.

"We only found him because of the fight. We heard the rutting, and the banging of antlers. We followed the noise and found two stags locked in combat. One was a huge male—the biggest I've ever seen.

There was something wrong with him. Some of his flesh had been cut from his body in strips and his blood smelled terrible, like he was rotting from the inside out. But sick or not, he was unusually strong. He beat the other stag easily, and then ran off into the forest. The losing stag was wounded. We followed him and killed him."

"And you ate his flesh?" Nik said.

"Yes, though it already tasted strange, a lot like the big stag smelled. After that we got sick—all of us. It was like a cold first—just coughs and aches. Then our skin started to fester. It began in the creases, like here and here." Jaxom pointed to his wrist and elbow creases. "And then we festered on the inside. . . ." He paused, sucking in a breath painfully as Mari got to the arrow wound in the back of his shoulder.

"This looks bad," Mari said.

"Yeah. I disinfected it as best I could with the supplies we have here, and packed it with goldenrod, too, but I know it needs more attention."

"It's nothing. Less than I deserve for what I tried to do." Jaxom looked away from them, staring into the hearth fire.

"Talk to me more about that stag. The one that was sick," Nik said.

Jaxom shrugged. "I don't know what else to say. Strips of his flesh were missing and his blood smelled wrong. And he was enraged."

"All stags are enraged when they're in rut," Nik said.

"Not like this one. I know because it happened to each of us," Jaxom said.

"You're not making any sense," Sora said.

Jaxom looked up at her, beseeching understanding with his kind brown eyes. "After we got sick we were enraged, too. Not just at night. And not just at ourselves. All the time. It was uncontrollable, and much, much worse than Night Fever. It was like there was nothing left inside me except anger and pain. My skin—it felt like it was boiling all the time."

"Have you ever heard of anything like this before?" Sora asked Mari.

"No," Mari said.

"I have." The group turned to see Rose standing just inside the burrow. "I'm sorry. I didn't mean to eavesdrop. Sarah and Lydia are out of poppy tea. Isabel said she'd get more for them, but I told her to stay and dance, that I'd get it."

"Rose, it's okay. Of course you may have more tea. But what did you mean when you said you've heard of Jaxom's illness?" Sora asked, motioning for Rose to join them.

Hesitantly, Rose moved closer so she could take a look at Jaxom's strange wounds. She nodded and blew out a breath. "Thaddeus had wounds just like this before he was captured by the Skin Stealers, and that anger he's describing . . . Well, that happened to Thaddeus, too."

"Are you Thaddeus's mate?" Mari spoke up, sending Nik a wary look.

"No! Well, I almost was. After his Odysseus mated with my Fala, Thaddeus and I were a thing." She moved her shoulders. "You know how it is, Nik, when your Companion mates and you're unattached."

"Well, not directly, but I do understand," Nik said.

"I don't," Sora said.

"Me, either," Mari said.

"Companions share emotions with their canines," Nik explained.

"We understand that," Mari said.

Sora snorted. "We sure do. Mari's creature almost ate me when we first met."

Mari rolled her eyes. "I did tell you not to follow me, and you know Rigel wouldn't *eat* you."

"Now I do. I didn't then. But my point is I understand the shared-emotion thing because I've seen Rigel and Mari share emotions."

"Take what you've seen them share and triple it, because when it's mating season those emotions can get pretty intense. It's not unheard of for canine lust to cause their humans to share a bed for the season and from that bond they sometimes even become permanently mated," Nik said.

"I think that's what Thaddeus expected to happen with us," Rose said. "I just expected some lusty fun. Thaddeus wasn't exactly what I'd consider mate material, even before the stag."

"The stag?" Jaxom said. "You know about that?"

"Just from what Thaddeus admitted," Rose said. "He and some Hunters found a sick stag. They put him out of his misery and burned the carcass because they could tell something was seriously wrong with it and didn't want to bring it back to the Tribe."

"And Thaddeus got the stag's blood in his face and mouth," Nik said.

"Yes, how did you know?" Rose said.

"Davis told me about the stag. That's all I know, though—just what you've already explained."

"Well, I only know more because of what he did to Thaddeus. He got mean and mad."

"Thaddeus was always mean and mad," Nik said.

"No, before the stag he wasn't *always* like that. Sure, he used to get defensive and he spoke his mind, even when what was on his mind shouldn't have been spoken aloud, but he treated me with respect, so I figured he and I could have some fun along with our canines. Then that Hunt happened, and within just a day or two he began to change. He was filled with anger all the time. I started avoiding him. Actually, that's why he had to admit to me that something had happened. I saw him coming to my nest and Fala and I hid above it. I watched Thaddeus without him knowing it, and he couldn't stop scratching at his arms. Later, he found me and confronted me, wanted to know why I'd been so distant—accusing me of avoiding him. I told him he was right; I had been avoiding him. That I knew something was wrong. Told him I'd noticed him scratching at his arms and heard him coughing and seen him throwing up blood."

Mari glanced at Sora as she tried to stifle another cough. The young Moon Woman was staring at Rose, absorbing every word she was saying. A terrible foreboding skittered down Mari's spine.

"He admitted that he was sick, and he even showed me the blisters that were forming on his skin. He said he wasn't worried because it's obvious it wasn't the blight, but that it was an annoyance, like he'd gotten into a bad strain of poison oak, and it was making him irritable. I said I understood, but even after that I avoided him. Like I said before, Thaddeus isn't what I wanted in a mate, and after Fala's lust was gone I wasn't interested in him—especially in a sick, angry version of him."

"And he just stayed away from you after that?" Mari asked. The Thaddeus she knew didn't seem like the type of man who would stop pursuing a woman if he thought she should belong to him.

"Actually, *I* stayed away from *him*. And then the foraging mission happened, and he changed again."

"How?" Nik said.

"I was only alone with him once after that. It was right after he and Odysseus returned to the Tribe. Remember how Odysseus had strips of his skin cut from his body?"

"I didn't see it, but I heard that the Skin Stealers flayed the Terrier's flesh and it was because the little guy fought so hard that Thaddeus was able to escape," Nik said.

"I don't know what really happened, but it was something strange—something Thaddeus didn't tell anyone. When he returned his skin was healing. He was real excited, which is why he showed me. It was—it was . . ."—Rose paused and shuddered—"awful. I could see that his flesh was healing *around long strips of other flesh.*"

"Bloody beetle balls! The Skin Stealers packed Odysseus's flesh into his!" Nik said.

"Oh, Goddess! Like they were doing with that boar." Mari felt sick remembering the disturbing scene she, Nik, Antreas, and Davis had been silent witness to earlier that day. "Did you notice anything else, Rose? Anything at all that changed about Thaddeus after his skin healed?"

"His anger didn't go away, but it got colder, more calculating. He threatened to hurt Fala if I told anyone about his sickness, and I knew he would do it. He'd gotten so strong and so fast, I knew he'd figure out a way to hurt her without anyone knowing, so Fala and I stayed away from him, which wasn't hard because he completely ignored me. Odysseus changed, too."

"Odysseus? How so?"

"Well, he always tended to be aggressive, though he hid it pretty well."

"Some of the Terriers can be kinda snappy," Nik said. "You'd think it'd be the Shepherds—they're a lot bigger and have more powerful jaws—but it's rare that a Shepherd is actively aggressive."

"*Kinda snappy*—that's a good way to describe how Odysseus used to be. Ask your friend Davis about him. All the Hunters know if one of the young Terriers gets stuck with Odysseus as a mentor that canine will come home with bites that are too deep and happen too often to be simple corrections. After he and Thaddeus came back from being taken by the Skin Stealers, Odysseus was just plain mean. Fala refused to let him around her pups." Rose raised her eyes to meet Nik's. "I'm sorry. I should have gone to Sol or Cyril or someone, but I just wanted to avoid Thaddeus and forget about the whole ugly thing. Nik, is it true that Thaddeus killed Sol?"

"Yes. He was trying to shoot Mari, but Father stepped in front of her, taking the arrow instead."

Rose bowed her head. "My fault—my fault. I should have said something. I should have told someone."

"You couldn't have known what he was going to do." Nik rested a hand on Rose's shoulder. "It's not your fault. Thaddeus is to blame—none other."

"Rose, here's some more poppy for the tea. There's enough for Sarah and Lydia, and for you. Drink a big mug of it. Your burns are going to start aching again soon; you'll need it." Sora handed Rose a small, tightly woven basket filled with dried poppy pods.

Rose wiped her face. "Thank you. You've been kind—much kinder than I deserve." Clutching the basket to her chest, she hurried from the burrow.

"Well, that's the most bizarre story I've ever heard, which is saying something, because I've heard some weird stuff lately," Sora said.

Mari just stared at her.

"How are you feeling?" Nik asked in a loaded voice.

Sora looked annoyed. "Like I said just a few minutes ago—I am fine." She coughed and scratched at her arm.

"You seemed irritated," Mari said.

"Of course I'm irritated," she snapped. "You'd be irritated, too, if you'd had to deal with wounded strangers who were enemies up until, I don't know, *yesterday*, as well as Clanswomen who are also hurt and frightened and confused." Sora glared at Mari as she dug at her wrists.

"Sora, look at me." Mari took her friend's hand, holding it so that she couldn't keep scratching her skin. "Listen carefully—the stag was infected with something. It infected Thaddeus and some of our Clansmen—Jaxom for sure."

"I already know that. We're wasting time. I'm assuming you brought more medicines than just aloe plants in those baskets, and Jaxom needs something potent for the wound in his back," Sora said, trying to pull her hand from Mari's.

Mari held on more tightly. "Sora, you're not listening to me. The stag infected Jaxom. Then Jaxom bit you. Deeply. His bite broke your skin."

"Yeah, so? I already know that, too. I don't know the point of all of this. We're way too busy to—"

"Jaxom infected you," Nik blurted.

Sora stared from him to Mari.

Mari nodded and loosened her grip on Sora's suddenly limp hands. "Your symptoms are identical to those Jaxom and Rose described. How have you *really* been feeling? Sick, feverish, and unnaturally angry?"

"This is ridiculous. It's just a simple cold. Let go of my hands!" Sora ended the outburst shrilly, yanking her hands from Mari's and baring her teeth in a menacing snarl at her friend.

"Sora, this isn't you—it's the illness. Think, Moon Woman."

Sora opened her mouth as if she would hurl more abuse at Mari, and then Jaxom's somber voice interrupted.

"Sora, she's right. Try to think through the anger and the pain."

Sora looked down, as if she was surprised to see that her hands were already at her wrists, digging bloody furrows in the inflamed skin that peeked from under the arm of her tunic. "Oh, Goddess, no! I am infected." Sora covered her face and began to sob, her shoulders bowed like a willow branch.

"Sora, stop! It's going to be okay." Mari gently pried Sora's hands from her face, leading her to a chair not far from the hearth. "Where's more of that poppy tea?"

"N-no. I c-can't take any. It'll make me sleepy and there are too many people to tend." Sora coughed miserably and wiped her mouth, leaving a long red slash on her tunic sleeve. The young Moon Woman stared at the scarlet streak. "This is bad. This is really bad." Her gaze locked with Mari's. "Please help me!"

Mari knelt beside her. "I'm going to help you, but you need to do as I say."

Sora nodded shakily as she scratched at her elbow crease. "Anything, just don't let me go mad."

"First, you need to drink the tea."

"There's more of it in the big basket next to the water bucket. There are mugs next to the cauldron beside the hearth."

Mari nodded to Nik and he went to the basket, pulling out a little pouch of herbs like the one Sora had given Rose. He placed the cauldron over the fire and ladled water into it, slowly adding the dried pods while he stirred. Satisfied that the tea was brewing, Mari returned her attention to Sora.

"Let me see your arms."

Sora hesitated, but only for an instant. Then she held out her arms and allowed Mari to roll up the sleeves of her tunic to reveal the blisters and red welts that were forming at the creases in her friend's otherwise flawless skin.

Sora turned her face away and wept.

"Jaxom, let me see your arms again." Mari hurried to the young man on the pallet. He held out his arms, now free of bandages—and Mari realized he didn't need the bandages reapplied. His skin was already healing. "How do you feel?" she asked him.

"Much, much better. My back hurts pretty bad, but the skin around my wrists and elbows and knees feels almost normal."

"What about your emotions? How are they?" Mari said.

"Other than not knowing how to live with the things I remember doing, I feel good. My mind is clear and my anger is gone. I'm myself again," Jaxom said.

Mari hurried back to Sora. "You felt better when you Washed the Clan, didn't you?"

Sora sniffed and nodded. "Yeah, that's one of the reasons I thought I just had a little cold. I didn't think it could be anything too bad if I was able to draw down the moon. I can't believe I was so wrong. Mari, you have to go look in your mom's journals. See if she has a cure for this—whatever it is."

"I don't think I need to do that."

"But you have to! You have to help me, Mari!"

"Hey, s-s-sh. You're not yourself. Of course I'm going to help you, but I already know how. I don't have to look in Mama's journals, though I am curious if she ever noted an infection like this before."

"Seriously, Mari. Now isn't the time for guesswork." Sora frowned at her. "If I have to, I'll go back to the burrow and get—"

"Moon Woman, you just need to be Washed and you'll be cured like Jaxom!" Mari said, exasperated at her friend. "Is that tea ready yet?"

"It's steeping," Nik said.

"Well, try to steep faster," Mari said. "And Sora, you try to not say anything."

"Washed?" she whispered.

"Washed," Mari said firmly. "But first I want you drugged."

Sora stared at her, and Mari was sure she saw a crimson tint beginning to shine from deep within her friend's dark pupils.

"Where's the goldenrod salve?" Mari asked.

Sora motioned to one of the wooden containers on the shelves that framed the hearth.

"I'll get it," Nik said.

"Nik, would you also bring in the baskets we left outside the door? I need the fresh bandages and some of that salve you said smells like newly cut hay."

"Will do."

"Bedstraw salve?" Sora asked.

"That's good. You remembered. Do you remember what the salve made from the bedstraw flowers and leaves is used for?"

"Stops bleeding and helps skin eruptions," Sora said.

"I think you're a much better student than I am a teacher," Mari said.

Sora's snort ended in a coughing fit. When she could speak again she said, "Don't you think I need something stronger than bedstraw? Isn't that just for minor skin problems?"

"Exactly, which is what you're going to have after I Wash you of this illness."

Nik returned with the baskets. Mari went through them quickly, finding the salve and the bandages she needed. While Sora downed the bitter but potent poppy tea, Mari cleaned and bandaged her wounds, trying to keep her expression neutral, even as she saw that many of the blisters were so red and swollen that her friend sucked in her breath when she touched them. But the tea worked its magic, and soon Sora's head was lolling and she was obviously having a hard time focusing on Mari.

"Hey, did you see the puppies-s-s?" Sora slurred.

"I did," Mari said, tying off the last bandage around Sora's wrist.

"Sunkissed. One is s-s-ssunkissed."

"Really?" Nik perked up. "You mean like with a splotch the color of the sun on it?"

"Yep. And it's on *her*. It's a *her*. And the s-s-splotch is in the shape of a crescent moon," Sora said.

"That's great news!" Nik said. Then, seeing Mari's confusion, he explained, "It's a fortuitous sign for the Tribe if a dark-colored canine is born with a sun-colored patch of fur. We call it being sun-kissed. It foretells good luck."

"Are you sure?" Mari said. "Seems like the Tribe's luck hasn't been so good lately."

"Not the tree Tribe. His. Nik's new Tribe. His Pack!" Sora's wobbly arm lifted and she pointed at Nik before dropping it back to her lap and nodding off to sleep.

"Wow, strong tea," Mari said.

"Don't I know it! You two kept me drugged for how long?" Nik said.

"You were wounded and almost dead," Mari said.

"And still—strong damn tea," Nik said. "Do you want me to carry her down to the Gathering so you can Wash her?"

"Well, no. I was going to do it up here."

"Don't. Do it in front of the Clan, and tell them what is happening. They should know," Jaxom spoke up, sounding more and more like the young man Mari had grown up with. He moved his shoulders, looking uncomfortable. "I know I don't have any right to speak. I know this is my fault. But the Clan should understand that their men have been infected and are suffering from something much worse than Night Fever. The Clan should know how dangerous they are."

"And how dangerous are they?" Mari asked.

Jaxom swallowed hard and then met her gaze unfalteringly. "Had Nik not shot me, I would have raped and killed Sora. And I would have enjoyed it."

CHAPTER 16

W ith Jaxom walking on one side of him and Laru on the other, Nik carried Sora from the cave, following Mari and Rigel. Jaxom had insisted that he was well enough to join the Clan. Mari had been reluctant to let him, but the more he talked and the more she watched him, the more she realized that he truly was behaving like himself again—a considerate young Clansman who had had a crush on Sora for many winters.

They stopped just outside the circle of light and celebration. Mari touched Nik's shoulder. "I'm going to speak to the Clan first. Then please bring Sora to me in the center of the circle."

"May I carry her to you, Moon Woman?" Jaxom asked.

Mari and Nik shared a brief look. "Are you strong enough?" Mari asked.

"It's just a few feet. Please. It'll make me feel like I'm doing something—anything—to help." Then he added sadly, "Plus, I don't think she'll ever let me touch her again and this way I can say my own kind of good-bye to her."

"Okay." Mari started to walk into the circle but hesitated and turned back to him. "Jaxom, what happened to you isn't your fault. You're not responsible for this disease—or whatever it is."

"But I am responsible for what I did while I had the disease," Jaxom said.

"There's a difference between taking responsibility and taking blame," Nik said.

"You aren't to blame," Mari said.

"Okay, I'm not to blame that I was infected, but I am responsible, and I plan on spending the rest of my life making up for what I did." Jaxom was obviously going to say more, but he was interrupted by Danita's bright, happy voice.

"Mari! Come dance with us! They're going to play the Beltane song again because so many of us missed—" Her words broke off as Jaxom turned and the campfires illuminated his face. "No!" she shrieked. The word cut through the trilling melody of flutes chasing drums, and the world went silent as Danita, pale and wide-eyed, seemed to be unable to move.

Mari acted instantly. She motioned for Jaxom and Nik to remain where they were and went to Danita. She took the girl's shoulders in her hands, moving so that she blocked Danita's view of Jaxom.

"Jaxom is not dangerous. He has been Washed," Mari said.

"He was with them! He was one of them!" Tears spilled down Danita's cheeks, but her voice was strong and sure.

"He was sick. Very sick. With more than Night Fever. But Jaxom is himself again." Mari flicked her gaze around the circle quickly, searching for Antreas and Bast, but she needn't have worried. The big feline raced up to them, baring her teeth and hissing angrily at Jaxom while she took a defensive position beside Danita. "Look, Bast is here."

"Bast?" Danita blinked in confusion, then her hand went down, automatically stroking the Lynx's head. "Bast won't let him get me."

The Lynx growled low in her chest, flattened her black-tufted ears against her skull, and hissed at Jaxom again. Mari felt more than saw the Clansman take a step back.

"I'm sorry, Danita. Goddess, I'm so sorry!" Jaxom said.

"What's going on?" Antreas raced up, knife drawn and held in a hand that had suddenly grown long, sharp claws.

"Stay close to her." Mari spoke under her breath. "Jaxom is no danger to any of us, but I'm afraid that won't undo the damage he's already done."

To his credit, Antreas didn't ask questions or hesitate. He nodded quickly and then took his place on the other side of Danita, crossing his arms and making a show with his body language that clearly said if someone wanted to harm the girl they would have to go through him and his Lynx.

"You're safe with Bast and Antreas," Mari told Danita.

"Y-yes." Her agreement was shaky, but she stood her ground when Mari let loose of her shoulders and faced the crowd that had begun to close the circle around them.

Mari noticed O'Bryan and Sheena and Davis had moved so that they were standing close to Nik, just outside the circle. Captain looked as alert as Bast as he skewered Jaxom with intelligent, angry amber eyes. Even the little Terrier, Cameron, had shed his puppyish playfulness. His ears and tail were up and he stood by Davis's side, looking every bit the Warrior ready to fight to the death with his Companion.

"What has happened to Sora? Is she dead?" Isabel cried out in horror, and then the Clan's attention was on the unconscious Moon Woman Nik still held in his arms.

"They killed the Moon Woman!" someone shouted, and then the Clan took up the cry: "Goddess! They killed Sora! Save Mari! Save our last Moon Woman!" As one, the Clanswomen surged forward, many of them grabbing torches, lighting branches, and brandishing them at Nik and Jaxom.

"No! Sora isn't dead! She's asleep! She had poppy tea!" Mari tried to shout over the maelstrom of noise and hysteria, but her words were drowned by fear and hatred. Horrified, she watched as one Clanswoman and then another picked up rocks and hefted them to test their throwing weight.

There was no time to think—there was only time to act, and Mari acted on instinct. She ran to stand before Nik and Jaxom, reaching up for the power of the fat moon that was now visible above the trees.

As if she would cup it between her hands, Mari stretched her finger-tips up and up; simultaneously she sketched a scene in her mind where the silver power of the moon cascaded down and around her, filling her with light and strength and a voice the Clan would have to listen to.

"STOP!"

Nik felt the change in the Clan as soon as someone shouted that they'd killed the Moon Woman. Cursing under his breath, he realized he'd been stupid enough to leave his crossbow back in the burrow. *Knife— I've got my knife. Gotta put Sora down and face this, though I don't want to hurt any of Mari's Clan!*

Jaxom had taken a step back when Bast had threatened him. He was standing behind Nik, looking young and completely lost. Nik wanted to tell him he knew a little about how the kid felt—knew what it was like to have people he trusted turn on him—when Mari lifted her arms and her body began to glow.

"STOP!"

That single word cut through the Clan like a kayak through the Channel. As one the Clan wavered, hesitated, and finally came back together, only this time they were silent and focused on Mari.

Arms still raised, Mari glowered at her Clan. Her eyes had gone from gray to silver; her hair was no longer blond but had absorbed moonlight, changing to pure, lustrous white. Her body didn't just glow silver as Sora's had after she'd so recently Washed the Clan and invited Mari to join her in the Beltane dance. Mari's body shimmered and glistened with a brilliant, argent light that left spots in front of his eyes if he stared directly at her too long.

And he couldn't help but stare. Mari was magnificent. He saw the Goddess in her and, humbled by her divinity, Nik took to his knees, placing Sora gently on the ground before him. Beside him, Davis did the same, and, after only a slight hesitation, so did Jaxom, Sheena, and O'Bryan.

"Clan Weaver, heed my words and hear your Moon Woman." Mari's

voice was and wasn't her own. Nik could hear Mari in the words, but the volume was amplified by moonlight magick that filled every syllable. *"Sora lives, though she sickens with the same illness that tainted Jaxom and made him do terrible things."*

"The Tribe brought this sickness to us! It's a sign from the Great Mother that we should not be mixing with Companions!" called a Clanswoman from the shadowy side of the circle.

"How dare you spew hatred and say you're speaking for the Goddess! The Earth Mother is not spiteful or cruel. She doesn't turn from those in need." Mari's body appeared to grow with righteous indignation. *"You are so quick to blame the Companions—almost as quick as the Tribe was to blame me for their problems."* She shook her head in disgust. *"Yet there they are, the Companions you're ready to turn against—to stone to death—on their knees before your Moon Woman."*

"They know we could kill them all and feed them to the swarm!" came the same hard voice as before.

Mari blazed so fiercely that those closest to her shielded their eyes from her light.

"You would have to get through me first!"

Even Nik was shocked by the vehemence in her voice. It didn't matter that they were a bunch of women with few weapons and no canines to protect them. If the Clan attacked, Nik and the other Companions would be forced to defend themselves, and no matter how carefully they would try to subdue them, Clanswomen would get hurt, very possibly killed. And that would be a sad, sorry beginning for them all.

"Speak wisdom to us, Moon Woman and your Clan will listen," said the young woman Mari called Isabel, dropping to her knees before Mari as she spoke.

"Yes, Moon Woman, speak," said an older Clanswoman who joined Isabel, kneeling before Mari.

Mari bowed her head slightly in acknowledgment of the two women's show of respect. Then she waited, shimmering like a descended star, casting her gaze around the circle.

Like a ripple from a pebble dropped in a pond, the Clan went to their knees. After they were all quiet—all listening expectantly—Mari spoke again, her voice still amplified by the divine power of the moon.

"I believe the Skin Stealers are responsible for a disease that has spread to the creatures in the forest—and even to the Companions and our Clan. We only know a few truths right now. We know it can be contracted from tainted blood or meat—or from being bitten by someone who has been infected. We know the symptoms—cough, aches, nausea, skin eruptions, and, most disturbing of all, there is a marked change in the infected person's personality. They are filled with a rage that is difficult, if not impossible, to control. That is what happened to Jaxom."

Nik watched Mari shift her attention to Danita and speak directly to the girl.

"Danita, Jaxom and the other Clansmen who attacked you were all sick with this infection. That is not an excuse. That does not lessen what they did to you. It is simply the truth."

"Am—am I sick now?" Danita asked in a tremulous voice.

"I believe you were infected when Sora and I found you, but since you've been Washed and healed." Mari's otherworldly silver eyes regarded the Clan. *"We must all be vigilant, especially until Sora and I discover more about this disease. Clanswomen, be wary of any Clansmen. Never go anywhere alone or unarmed. We will get through this—together. We will not fight among ourselves or cast blame—not at one another, and not at Nik and his friends, who are now our friends. Thankfully, the Great Goddess has a response to this terrible disease."* Her gaze found Jaxom. *"Clansman, bring the Moon Woman, Sora, to me."*

Nik passed Sora's unconscious body into Jaxom's arms, and the young man held her carefully, reverently, making his way slowly to stand in front of Mari. As he got closer and closer, Danita began to tremble, and Nik saw that tears fell silently down the girl's face. Bast pressed closer to Danita, and Antreas actually put an arm around the girl.

Without Mari directing him to, Jaxom knelt before her, oh, so gently laying Sora on the mossy ground between them. Then he did something that took Nik by surprise. Instead of kneeling beside Sora—with whom the boy was obviously infatuated—Jaxom stood and bowed formally to Mari, speaking in a voice that carried across the circle.

"I must go, Moon Woman."

Mari said nothing for several moments, and when she did she spoke a single word that echoed across the Gathering.

"Why?"

"I must make amends for what I have done."

Nik thought Mari would ask how he was going to do that or maybe insist that he stay—for all they knew, Jaxom was the *only* male Clansman left alive and sane. But she simply bowed her head briefly in acknowledgment, saying, *"Go with my blessing, Jaxom. I hope to see you here again on Third Night to be Washed."*

Jaxom bowed again deeply to her before he turned to face the Clan. "I hope someday you can forgive me," he said. Then he walked out of the circle of light and safety and warmth and disappeared into the dark, silent forest.

When he was gone, all attention returned to Mari. She knelt beside her friend, who appeared to be soundly asleep, curled on her side like a pretty child. Mari raised one arm, palm up and open as if she would cup the moon. Her other hand rested tenderly on Sora's head.

> *"Come, silver light—fill me to overflow*
> *So that she who is in my care, your healing touch will know."*

Pure silver light, more perfect than the most beautiful glass or mirror that had ever been salvaged from Port City, cascaded from the sky down into Mari, as if she was a human beacon—a signal fire blazing in the darkness.

> *"By right of blood and birth channel through me*
> *that which the Earth Mother proclaims my destiny!"*

Mari completed the invocation, and the radiance that filled her body glistened briefly, and then Nik could actually see it pouring from Mari into Sora. Almost immediately Sora's eyes began to move under her closed lids. Her body went rigid, like she'd been stung by something, and then it was as if her bones liquefied and she relaxed against the earth, her lips lifting in a contented smile as her eyelids fluttered open. She contemplated Mari, her expression filled with bliss.

"Oo-o-o-h! You look like an enormous glowworm!"

Just a few feet away, Antreas attempted, and failed, to stifle his laughter.

Nik watched Mari roll her eyes and lower her hand, and like she'd snuffed a candle, the glistening light that had filled her to overflowing went out.

"*Thank you* would have sufficed," Mari said sardonically, though Nik could see amusement dancing in her eyes. "How are you feeling?"

"Very loopy headed from that poppy tea," Sora said, and then she giggled. She sat up, scrutinizing the kneeling crowd with a confused and slightly drunk look. "I obviously missed something."

"Don't worry about it. Everything's fine now," Mari said. She began to motion for the Clanswomen to rise, but Mari suddenly lost her balance and staggered. Had Rigel not been there to brace her, she would have fallen.

That was all Nik needed. He and Laru were at her side in an instant. "Okay, now you've really done too much for one day. I'm taking you home."

Mari squinted up at him. "What?"

"You called down sunfire and stopped a forest blaze. You danced half the night away. You called down moonlight, admonished an entire Clan, and healed your friend of a terrible disease. Now it's time someone makes sure you take care of yourself."

"That someone is you?" Mari attempted a teasing tone, but the paleness of her skin and the dark circles that looked like bruises under her eyes spoke more truly.

"Nik's right," Sora said, holding out her hand as if she expected someone to automatically help her up. O'Bryan, who seemed to materialize beside Nik, was suddenly there, taking the young Moon Woman's hand

and lifting her gently to her feet. "Thanks, O'Bryan," she said before continuing to Mari, "I'm sobering up fast. That Washing you did was spectacular. I can't remember the last time I felt this great. Go on back to our burrow. I'll stay here and be sure everyone is tucked in for a good, long sleep."

"But you were just—" Mari began.

"I was just healed by a talented Moon Woman. I'm fine now. Actually, I'm starving. There is stew left, right? And I want a big mug of that ale, too." Sora glanced toward the center bonfire, just then noticing that the Clan were still on their knees. "Are they in trouble?" she asked Mari quietly.

"Not really. Not anymore. We just had to get past a misunderstanding," Mari said, keeping her voice low, too.

"I'll remember this for next Third Night. I like them all kneeling. Makes me feel tall." Mari shook her head at her friend and gave her a hard look, but Sora laughed and whispered, "I'm kidding. Mostly." She raised her voice. "Stand! Let's get back to the eating and drinking and dancing."

Slowly, the Clan complied, though the joy that had filled them before was muted. The flutes trilled a little melody, coaxing the drums to follow, but no one danced. Instead, the Clan congregated around the center bonfire, scooping steaming stew into carved wooden bowls and separating into small groups to eat and talk.

"What do you want us to do?" O'Bryan asked as he watched Sora filling a bowl.

"Eat if you're hungry. Drink if you're thirsty," Nik said.

"Well, yeah, I figured that, but I meant—where are we staying tonight?"

Before Nik could respond, Mari spoke up. "Where do you want to stay?"

O'Bryan shrugged—Nik thought too nonchalantly, especially when his gaze kept wandering away to find Sora. "I think at least Davis, Antreas, Sheena, and I should stay here. What if those infected males show up? And Rose, Sarah, and Lydia have to stay here and heal—at least for several nights. I don't think they could make it back to the Tribe, provided they still want to go back."

"Bast and I will stay," Antreas said. "If that's okay with Mari and Sora."

"If Bast stays here I stay here," Danita said quickly.

"Don't you think you'd rest better back at Mari's burrow?" Antreas said—not unkindly, but firmly.

Danita narrowed her gray eyes at him, and her hand found Bast's head. "If Bast stays here . . . I stay here," she repeated slowly and distinctly.

Bast's bright yellow gaze lifted to her Companion and she began purring so loudly that it almost covered Antreas's long-suffering sigh.

"That's fine with me," Mari said. "Actually, Nik, maybe we should stay here tonight, too. Sora might need help with—"

"Nope, don't need any help at all," Sora said through a mouthful of stew as she rejoined their group. "Or rather, Isabel, Danita, and even O'Bryan can help me keep things in order tonight. You rest or I'm going to end up taking care of you, too."

Sounding a lot like Sora, Mari snorted. "That's an exaggeration."

"You almost fell over just a few minutes ago. Go back to our burrow. Brew yourself some of that chamomile and lavender tea I already put together for you; it's in the basket—"

"I know where it is," Mari said, sounding exasperated. "I just feel like I should be doing something more."

All teasing left Sora's expression as she answered her friend, "You saved the Tribe. You saved me. Mari, even Leda couldn't have done more."

"Really?" Mari asked.

"Really," Sora said.

Mari turned to Nik and stepped into the circle of his arms. "Nik, would you and Laru and Rigel please take me home?"

"It would be our honor, Moon Woman," Nik said as Laru and Rigel barked agreement and Cammy jumped happily around them.

CHAPTER 17

ari expected the walk home to be a trudging trek of misery, but she couldn't have been more wrong. The moon was fully risen and cast a soft, silvery light through the whispering cottonwoods and tall, regal cedar trees that was so bright she and Nik were able to stroll side by side, her hand in his, newly healed of its burns by moon magick, while Rigel managed to tease Laru into a game of try-to-take-the-stick-from-him. She and Nik laughed at the pup, whose paws and ears were still entirely too big for his adolescent body, and at Laru, whose patience was very obviously being tested.

"Laru's really a sweet canine," Mari said as Rigel tried unsuccessfully to take a stick from the adult Shepherd and then both canines sprinted down the path, scattering leaves and jumping over logs.

"He'll always remind me of Father."

Mari studied Nik's face. "Does it hurt to be reminded of him all the time?"

"No." Nik looked surprised. "Not at all. It's comforting. What reminds you of your mother?"

Mari considered before answering. "Hm, lots of things actually. Maidenhair ferns, because she loved using them for hair on her favorite Earth Mother idols. Forget-me-nots, because they were her favorite flower. She washed with rosemary and rosewater, so that herb and that flower remind me of her every time I cook with rosemary, or smell a blossoming rose. And, of course, the moon." Mari lifted her face to the silver orb. "The moon will always remind me of Mama. You're right. It's comforting. It's like part of her is still here."

"Part of her *is* still here. You're part of her, Mari. As long as you remember her, and your children remember her, and even your children's children remember, your mother will still be here."

Those two words, *your children,* seemed to hover in the night air around Mari, mixing with the light of the moon, so bright that it tinged the forest with an aqua blue that made her feel as if she and Nik, Rigel and Laru, had passed through a veil and were walking in a magickal land populated only by them. *Your children . . .*

Mari snuck a glance at Nik. Trying to sound nonchalant, she asked, "Do you want children?"

When he didn't respond, Mari felt her face flushing. Had that been a stupid question? She hadn't ever been interested *like that* in any male before Nik, and she suddenly felt like a bumbling fool. She'd thought he felt the same—had been *sure* he felt the same—but his silence told her something else entirely.

"I—I just meant someday. Not now. Not even soon. And not necessarily with me. I was just curious, that's all." She realized she was babbling and closed her lips tightly so that nothing else embarrassing could escape. When he still said nothing, she tried to pull her hand from his, feeling horribly inept and thinking that he'd probably had lots more experience with relationships and sex and all of that than her—just about *anyone* had more experience than she had. Could it be that the truth was, no matter how much he cared about her, Nik didn't want children with her? They'd be part Earth Walker. Maybe Nik didn't want babies who had Scratcher blood.

But Nik held tightly on to her hand, not letting her pull away from him. He lifted it to his lips, kissing the back of it sweetly, softly, before saying, "Sorry, Mari. I didn't mean to take so long to answer. It's complicated, though."

"Yeah, I understand. I'm not part of your Tribe, and that's—"

"Hey!" He stopped and turned her to face him. "That's not it at all. Mari, don't you understand what you've done for me?"

"I've turned your life upside down," Mari said honestly.

"Well, yeah, but that's not what I meant. When I found you, or rather, you found me, I finally felt understood. You know what it's like not to fit in—to watch everyone around you be one way but know you're not that way. Mari, you're magickal and strong and beautiful, and I think about touching you—a lot, like, to the point it's distracting. Hell, you're a Goddess to me! But what I appreciate most about you is that I can be myself with you. Mari, I love you."

She stared up at him, her stomach doing strange little flip-flops. "I love you, too, Nik," she heard herself saying.

"Well, that's a relief to hear!" he said. He bent and kissed her. There was heat in the kiss, and a promise of much more to come, but he pulled back so that he could meet her eyes, though he kept his arms around her. "I want children. Lots of children. And lots of canines, too. Shepherds, Terriers, it doesn't matter. I want a bunch of them. But it also doesn't matter if my children never bond with a canine—never become a Companion or even a Moon Woman like you, though that would be something truly spectacular. I will value our children for who they are, not for some kind of perceived Tribal status. What took me so long to answer is that I want all of that, but in a world where *our children won't be judged by their mixed blood.*"

"I want that, too," Mari said. "Only I really do hope that all of my . . ."—she paused, smiling shyly, and then corrected herself—"I mean, *our* children, I hope *our* children are chosen by canines. Life is just better with a Companion."

Rigel came tearing past them, chasing Laru, who still had the stick he wanted, and almost crashed into the two of them.

"Hey! Watch where you're running," Nik called.

Laru instantly turned and padded to Nik, stick in mouth, breathing heavily, but looking pleased with himself. Rigel bounced around his sire, making small, begging sounds.

"You're being pathetic," Mari told her pup. "There's a forest full of sticks around you. Just find another one."

Whining softly, the young Shepherd left the path, sniffing around. In a few moments he reappeared, dragging a log that was the size of Nik's leg, which made Mari roll her eyes and then giggle.

"Well, I like that he sets his bar high," Nik said, grinning at the pup. Laru sneezed in obvious disgust, which made them both laugh. Then Nik cupped Mari's face in his hands. "Will you really build it with me? This new world where our children, our people, our Pack, will not be shamed or judged by the shade of their skin, or the color of their eyes, but instead will be valued for their strengths and their goodness?"

Mari felt a sense of stillness come over her, as if she'd waited her entire life to be asked such a question by someone who could actually help her change the world. "Nik, that's been my dream since I understood that I was different, and that my difference wasn't accepted by my Clan. Yes! A million times yes!" She stepped into his arms and felt as if she'd finally come home.

The burrow was tidy and warm, and it smelled of freshly baked bread, rabbit, and a smoldering hearth fire. Mari felt the last of her tension slip from her shoulders as they closed the thick wooden door and barred it against the outside world.

"Are you hungry? I made sure we left a loaf of Sora's bread. I could spread some honey on it," Mari asked Nik as Laru and Rigel curled up together in front of the door and promptly feel asleep, looking more like twins than sire and son.

"That sounds great. I'll stoke the hearth fire and brew that tea Sora said you should drink while you're cutting the bread." Nik rifled through the basket of dried-tea pouches until he found the chamomile-lavender mixture.

Working side by side, they were soon sitting cross-legged before the hearth fire, munching bread and honey and sipping fragrant tea.

"I think it went well tonight, don't you? I mean, no one died. No one was even injured. Companions are guarding Clanswomen, and Clanswomen are taking care of Companions. I'd call that success, though it was upsetting how fast the women turned on us when they thought we'd hurt Sora," Nik said.

Mari started to agree with him, her mind casting back to the voice of anger that had almost caused a riot, when suddenly that shrill voice clicked in her memory. "It was Serena!"

"Who? I don't think I know a Serena."

"She's a Clanswoman who chose to leave earlier today when I accepted O'Bryan and the rest of the Companions in our group. Serena couldn't handle it. Actually, she acted a lot like I expected the entire Clan to act in response to finding out about Rigel and me. I told her to leave if she couldn't accept the Companions and me. She left with a few of the older women. They were supposed to be heading to either Clan Fisher on the coast or another Clan south of here." Mari shook her head in disgust. "But she snuck back, probably to get Washed again. Obviously, she also wanted to try to start problems between Tribe and Clan. I didn't see her in the group afterward, but I'm going to have to warn Sora about her."

"The last thing we need is someone sowing poison among us," Nik said. "Speaking of poison, I had a thought about the Skin Stealers' disease that I wanted to talk with you about once we were alone."

"Well, we're alone right now," Mari said.

"We are indeed. For the first time in what seems like a long time," Nik said. He reached over and touched her bottom lip, wiping a sticky drop of honey from it and then sucking it from his fingertip. "Sweet, like you."

Mari felt a rush of heat and totally forgot what he had been saying. His green eyes gleamed knowingly at her. "Huh?" she said, her head feeling as woozy as her stomach.

"I was saying that you're sweet as honey."

"No. I mean, thank you. But what were you saying before that?"

"Oh, the Skin Stealers. I've been thinking about what we saw today—the group of them with the boar. Remember what Rose said about Thaddeus changing even more after he came back from being captured by them?"

"Yeah, she talked about Odysseus and said she thought they'd flayed his flesh and put it on Thaddeus."

"What if that's another kind of cure for the disease? Only the cure permanently changes the person, and maybe even the animal. Odysseus has always been a nippy little Terrier, but Rose says he's been worse lately. And Thaddeus has always been an angry jerk, but lately he's become mean and dangerous. When the disease changed, I think it changed them, too."

"That sounds so crazy, Nik."

"I know, but hear me out. We already believe the Skin Stealers are responsible for this new disease."

"You know more about that than I do. Earth Walkers rarely have had anything to do with Skin Stealers. We never go to Port City, or even close to it. It's been forbidden for generations."

"But why?"

"Why?" Mari shrugged. "Because that's how we've been raised. '*Of cities beware—Skin Stealers are there.*'" She recited the little rhyme all Earth Walker children learn from the time they are old enough to speak. "We've always known the city was dangerous, so we stay away from it. And not just Port City. *All* cities are to be avoided, or at least all of the ancient cities."

"But maybe your ancestors knew more than just that cities were dangerous. Maybe they knew they're diseased."

"Maybe. Mama never said much about it, but she didn't have reason to. Like I said, the Clan stays out of cities. Always. I could check the old journals—those written by my grandmother and her mother's mother. Maybe we'll find something in them that'll help us figure out what's going on."

"I think I know what's going on, and it's not good. I think the Skin Stealers have purposely spread their poison to the forest."

"But why?"

"You've never been inside the City—I have. It's a nightmare place. Vermin and bizarre, mutated plants and animals live there. There are sinkholes everywhere and danger hidden by vines and crumbled buildings. It's worse than the destroyed bridges and the run-offs caused by them." Nik shuddered. "If they weren't so disgusting, I'd feel sorry for the Skin Stealers. Nothing could make me live in that poisoned place."

"Oh, Goddess, Nik! Are you saying you think they're poisoning the forest—and us—so that everything is like their ruined City?"

"No, I think they're poisoning *us* so that they can leave the City and take over the forest. Think about it—Thaddeus was captured and let loose by them. He returned to the Tribe and ended up murdering our Sun Priest and causing the forest fire that destroyed more than half of our city—and killed many of our people. He is just *one person*, but look at how much damage he's done. Look at how badly he's weakened the Tribe."

"Nik, how easy would it be for the Skin Stealers to take over the Tribe of the Trees right now?"

"Too damn easy."

They washed and got ready for bed. Mari tried to act normal, tried not to be nervous and awkward, but she failed. When she caught herself picking her fingernails and sneaking secret glances at Nik as they finished cleaning the dishes, she gave up and decided she'd better tell him the truth.

"I'm a virgin!"

Nik froze in the middle of drying the last mug. "I'm not surprised."

Mari turned her eyes from him, utterly humiliated.

He put down the mug and went to her. "Hey, that sounded wrong. What I meant to say is that I'm not surprised *because* you had to keep what you really look like hidden from your Clan. That would make it tough to have any kind of intimate relationship. I'm amazed you managed to have friendships with Jenna and Sora."

"Oh, Sora and I weren't friends until after Mama died and I revealed who I really am. And even then it took her blackmailing me to force me to allow her close. And Jenna thought what the rest of the Clan thought—that I was sickly. She understood unusual circumstances because her mom died when she was little and, instead of leaving her to be raised by the Clanswomen as any other Earth Walker male would have done, her father insisted on actually being her father. So, Jenna was easy to be friends with, even though if it was a sunny day I always, always canceled my plans with her."

"No boyfriends?"

"No."

"Never?"

"Never," she said. She moved her shoulders restlessly. "I used to envy Sora because of all the male attention she got. She's so pretty and confident, and she was always surrounded by interested males, especially Jaxom, who I thought she was going to choose as a mate. I'm pretty sure he did, too. I wonder what's going to happen to him now?"

"That's a different kind of discussion, and I don't want to change the subject. Not yet. How *do* Earth Walkers choose their mates?" Nik went to the pallet that was now Sora's bed and patted the space beside him so that Mari joined him.

"Clanswomen always do the choosing. Clansmen court us. Well, *them.* No Clansmen ever tried to court me." Mari narrowed her eyes at him, as it was clear that he was trying to hide his amusement. "Are you laughing at me?"

"No! Not *at* you. I was just thinking about how you looked the first time I saw you under that willow tree. Your disguise was *messy.*"

"But it worked. No one knew that under all of that dirt and dye I was part Companion. You're right, though. It was really messy. And smelly, too." She shuddered delicately. "I'm glad that part of my life is over."

"Me, too. You said Clansmen do the courting. What does that mean?"

"Well, often a Clansman will make gifts for the woman he hopes will choose him—we *are* Clan Weaver. Even the men have weaving skills. A Clansman could also forage something special for his girl." Mari pointed to the precious round piece of mirror that was on her desk near her sketching supplies. "That mirror was a gift from my grandma's favorite suitor."

"Favorite?"

"Yeah. Not only do Clanswomen choose when and who they'll mate with, they also choose when or if the relationship will end. Moon Women tend to have several lovers, but no permanent mate." She moved her shoulders again. "I think it's because we have to focus on the Clan, and then the raising of our daughters to be Moon Woman after us. That doesn't leave much time for a mated relationship."

"But I thought your mother was committed to your father."

"Oh, she was! Mama only loved one man—my father. But Mama was an exception to the rule," Mari said.

"I'm hoping her daughter is also an exception to the rule."

This time Mari felt her body flush with her face. "How is it with your people?"

"In the Tribe, the choosing of a mate is mutual, as is the ending of the relationship—though we do tend to mate for life."

"Oh, it's usually mutual with the Clan, too. But according to Law, Clanswomen make the final decision."

"What if the man wants the mating to end—or not to end? What can he do?" Nik asked.

"Nothing. Part of his pledge to his mate is swearing an oath that he will not leave unless she sends him away, then he must do as she says and agree to end their relationship. . . ." Mari paused, considering. "You know, I've never really thought about it until now—it's just how the Clan has always worked—but that's odd, isn't it? That a man must give himself to a woman *and* give up his right to have a way out of the relationship. Huh. Really odd."

"Really love," Nik said.

"You think so?" His response surprised her.

"I think the only reason a man, or a woman, would make that kind of deal is love."

"And I think Mama would have called you a romantic." For some reason that thought made Mari feel light and happy.

"I wish I could have met your mama. I would have liked her."

"She would have loved you. And you did meet her. Yours was the last face she saw before she died." Mari blinked hard, trying not to cry. "She thought you were my father. She died believing that she was with the man she loved again. Th-thank you." She swiped at her cheeks.

"I hope I helped at the end."

"I know you did." She wiped the rest of her tears away, determined not to allow the conversation to devolve into sadness and missed opportunities. "So, I was raised by a woman who lost the love of her life when she was young and she never seemed even vaguely interested in finding another lover or mate. And, of course, I couldn't let any male get close enough to me to discover I'm part Companion. Mama and I were quite a pair. Good thing the procreation of the Clan wasn't our responsibility."

"Didn't you ever wish things were different?"

"Well, yes. I used to wish Jaxom would look at me like he looked at Sora, but that was just because I wanted to know what it would be like to be desired."

Nik's gaze met hers and held. "I desire you, Mari. Very much."

Mari's cheeks felt blazing hot, but she didn't let herself look away from him. "Are you a virgin, too?"

"No, I'm not."

Her gaze fell to her lap. "Oh." She hadn't even thought to ask him if there was a girl back at the Tribe who had spoken for him. She'd just assumed—

"Hey, don't stop talking to me. We're in this together now, or at least I hope we are. I'm sorry, Mari, I don't know much about your Clan's attitude about sex."

She looked up at him again. "The Clan's attitude is that it's natural and good to mate—and to have sex. But it is always the woman's choice."

"That does make sense, with what happens to Clansmen with Night Fever."

Mari nodded. "Women make all of the major decisions for the Clan. Our men are our protectors, our Hunters, and our Builders, but they rarely live within the women's burrows. Women congregate together, raise children together, plant and harvest crops, weave and trade with other Clans, while our men, in comparison, lead solitary lives. Of course there are some men who prefer to take other men as their mates, as well as women who prefer women, which is accepted by the Clan."

"That seems sad to me."

"That some men prefer men and some women prefer women?"

Nik chuckled. "No, that's not sad. Same-sex matings are accepted by the Tribe, as they should be. Love is love. I was thinking of the solitary lives your males live. Seems sad and lonely."

"I have to admit it never seemed sad to me until now. I used to think it was a good thing most of our women choose to live in burrows without their mates."

Nik took Mari's hand, turned it over, and began gently tracing a spiral circle on her palm. "Why does it seem sad to you now? What changed?"

"I changed. You changed me."

"Tell me how," Nik said.

"First, you tell me about losing your virginity."

"Can I just say it was an awkward, underwhelming event and leave it at that?"

"No, probably not," Mari said.

Nik sighed. "Okay, let's get this over with. Ask me anything."

"Have you only done it that one time?"

"No. I did it more than one time. And, yes, it got a lot less awkward and a lot more fun."

Mari chewed the side of her cheek and tried to get a handle on her rising jealousy, though she knew being jealous of what Nik had done before they met was illogical and unfair. She stared at his finger as it continued to trace a circular pattern on her skin, sending ripples of heat from her hand through her arm and the rest of her body. "With more than one woman?"

"Yes, with more than one woman."

"At the same time!"

"No! Not that that's a terrible idea." At Mari's wide-eyed expression, he bumped her shoulder with his and added, "Hey, I'm kidding you. Mostly. Mari, in the Tribe we're encouraged to experiment with different partners, especially when we're young. How else are we to find the right mate? And there is the lust that we share with our Companions. I haven't experienced it, but I've watched what it does to canines and their humans. It can get very interesting during estrus, especially as canines who live in close proximity tend to come into season at the same time."

"But you're not mated?"

"Mari! Of course I'm not mated. I wouldn't be here with you if I had a mate."

"You haven't ever almost mated?"

His finger started tracing its way up her smooth forearm. "Well, I thought I might be almost mated. I *hoped* I might be. But I've just learned that's entirely up to you."

Her gaze flew to his. "Me?"

"Yes, you. You and no one else, Mari." Nik leaned into her, finding her lips with his as he pulled her gently into his arms.

Mari returned the kiss, at first nervous and tentative, but the heat building within her body had her forgetting nerves and second thoughts. The kiss deepened with Mari's breath. Sensations sizzled through her body, following Nik's touch as his clever hands explored her. Without knowing exactly how, Mari found herself beneath him as he pressed to her, his body hard, straining against hers. But when his hand slid up under her tunic and began stroking the bare skin of her breast, Mari froze.

Nik had to have felt her hesitation. He lifted himself so that he could meet her gaze. "Everything okay?"

"Yes. No. I'm nervous, Nik," she admitted.

He lay next to her, brushing the hair from her face. "I'm nervous, too."

"Seriously?"

"Absolutely. I want it to be good for you—*really* good for you—and

I know that has a lot to do with my *prowess* in bed." He waggled his eyebrows, making her laugh. "And that's pressure, which makes me nervous. Hey! Let's make a pact. How about I swear that when you start feeling nervous, all you have to do is just tell me, and I'll stop whatever I'm doing?"

"But what if I'm always nervous?"

Nik laughed a little. "Well, then I haven't courted you properly and I'll go to Sora for advice."

Mari giggled so hard she snorted. "She'd love that. I can hear her now, giving you a bunch of questionable advice on purpose, just so that she could dissolve into hysterical laughter when I report everything to her."

"Bloody beetle balls! You're going to report *everything* to Sora?"

"It's possible."

"Come here, you. How about we just cuddle tonight and worry about sex and changing the world tomorrow?"

"Do we have to *worry about* sex?" Mari said.

"No. Or at least, you don't. Let me do the sex worrying."

"Does that mean I have to do the changing of the world worrying?"

"That's the deal," Nik said.

"I'm not sure I'm getting the best part of that deal," Mari said.

"And that's why I have some worrying to do."

CHAPTER 18

Dead Eye found he needed less and less sleep. After he made love to Dove and then feasted with the People, he and Dove retired to their part of the God's chamber. Dove had immediately fallen asleep in his arms, her naked body pressed trustingly against his. He'd expected to sleep, too. But the solace of dreams eluded him, and within a short time he had gently disentangled himself from Dove and made his way to the Balcony of the God.

"Champion, may I bring you something?" asked the young Attendant whose turn it was to be sure the firepots remained lit all night.

"My only requirement is solitude," Dead Eye said without looking at her.

She backed soundlessly from the balcony.

Dead Eye went to the edge of the balcony and studied the scene in the courtyard below. There the firepots were smoldering and going out. The scent of succulent boar meat still lingered. As did several of the People who had gorged themselves so much that they had fallen asleep in little groups around the spit that still held a haunch of meat.

He shook his head in disgust. He shouldn't have had to tell them that leaving meat out would draw insects—and worse.

"Attendant!" He pitched his deep voice so that he wouldn't awaken his sleeping Dove.

P. C. CAST

"Yes, Champion. What is it you desire?"

He did look at her then, carefully schooling his face so that she would not see the disgust her cracking skin made him feel. Yes, she was young and just barely infected, but if things did not change he could foresee that she would go the way of the old Watchers of the God. She would be a diseased hag, driven insane by the poisons within her body.

Dead Eye was not going to let that happen.

"What is your name?" he asked.

"Lily, Champion."

"Lily, wake as many of the other Attendants as you require and go down to the courtyard. Rebuild the firepots and add always keeping them lit to the Attendant's duties, just as you keep the God's firepots lit here on the balcony and in the God's chamber. Then bring the leftover meat into the Temple and begin drying and smoking it. And wake the People who are sleeping below as well. Tell them I command they assist you. They must learn that if they wish to rid their lives of poison and disease they must change their behavior."

"Yes, Champion." She bowed low.

"And do not wake Dove."

"Yes, Champion."

When she hesitated before leaving the balcony, Dead Eye made an irritated gesture. "Why do you not do as I bid you?"

"I will, Champion. Should I have another Attendant remain here to keep the God's firepots fed?"

"No. I will not sleep. I'll feed them until you return."

"It will be as you command, Champion." Lily bowed again and hurried from the balcony.

Dead Eye watched the young women pour from the Temple to wake the sated People and begin cleaning the mess below. Then he shifted his attention to the distant forest and his thoughts to the Tribe of the Trees.

How best to go about conquering the Tribe and claiming their city as my own?

He had already sown the forest with poison. The man of the Others

242

the People had captured, along with his canine, had been infected, and Dead Eye was sure he had spread that infection to the City in the Trees. Why else would they have allowed a forest fire to consume them?

That step seemed to be going well—very well.

He was also pleased by how quickly his Reapers responded to the flesh from the boar. They were already healing and strengthening, and the nine left after he'd made an example of Stalker seemed to be accepting his authority unconditionally. But was that enough to take over the City in the Trees?

Definitely not.

Dead Eye needed an army of men like Iron Fist and the other eight—men who were loyal to him and whose skin had been healed by the flayed flesh of a living, untainted creature. Dove's Attendants needed to be healed as well, or the Temple would deteriorate into the poisoned cesspool it had been before he had taken control.

"So much to do before we attack the city, but is there time? If I wait until I have an army of Reapers, I take the chance that the Others will have recovered and rebuilt. Yet if I don't wait, do my People have the strength to defeat a Tribe as mighty as the Others in their city in the sky?"

Dead Eye paced, feeling the fire building within him. What should he do about the People? When should they take the City in the Trees? The forest fire—the blaze that had ravaged the city—mixed with the poison sown in the forest—might very well have weakened the Tribe enough to allow the People to defeat and enslave them now.

He wouldn't know for sure unless he went to the Tribe and saw for himself how weak—or how strong—they were.

Perhaps he should wait. Perhaps he should take each Harvester and each Hunter who remained to the forest and, as he had done with Stalker, cull the weak. Then, like Iron Fist and his newly appointed Reapers, reward the faithful by flaying the flesh of a forest beast and joining its skin with theirs.

Dead Eye rubbed his hand through his hair in frustration, feeling a jolt of surprise when he touched the antlers above his ears. *They've grown bigger, just in the space of this one auspicious day.*

He stretched his arm, flexing his powerful biceps, delighting in skin that was free of cracks and pustules—free of disease. He was strong. Stronger than any of the People. As strong as a God.

You are a God.

The thought lifted from his veins, filling his heart, his mind, his soul.

That thought was not mine.

Trepidation skittered through Dead Eye's body. Unbidden, he turned to face the metal statue of the immense God that lurked behind him.

Had he really felt Her move when he'd returned from the Hunt and taken Dove into his arms? They hadn't spoken of it afterward. They had made love and feasted, and only now did Dead Eye have the solitude to truly consider what had happened.

"Did you move? Are you there?" He spoke directly to Her.

She did not answer.

He scratched the back of his neck, feeling the soft coat of fine stag fur that now stretched the length of his spine.

"Or am I going mad?"

Climb and learn the truth.

The command filled his mind. Not like a thought, and not his own. It was as if a great force had awakened inside Dead Eye and was stretching and flexing after a long sleep.

He stared up into the God's face. "If I am mad, then this madness makes me strong, heals me, and tells me to lead the People from the doomed City to salvation."

Dead Eye began to climb.

With the agility of a forest creature, he leaped up onto the statue's massive thigh, then, finding a handhold in the God's long hair that had been formed from the strange, perfect metal and seemed to be billowing in wind only She could feel, Dead Eye pulled himself up and up, so that he was standing on Her mighty shoulders. There, many feet above the balcony floor, Dead Eye gazed out at the forest. The moon was huge and luminous—the People called it a Hunter's Moon as it was so bright that even in the City it cast shadows, deep and dark. Far, far in the distance, he thought he glimpsed small yellow tongues of fire. Not the angry red blaze of the forest fire, but tamer cooking and hearth fires.

"How many of them survived?" Dead Eye muttered. "When should I attack?"

Ready the People.

The thought filled his mind with such force that Dead Eye lost his footing. Unbalanced, he began to tumble from the God's shoulder. Dead Eye reached for something—anything that would save him—and his wrist found the tip of the Reaper's triple-pointed spear, slashing through his flesh with a white-hot pain that had him gasping, even as his other hand closed around the shaft of the spear, saving him from tumbling down, down to certain death.

Breathing in gulps, Dead Eye regained his footing, meaning to climb down immediately and then wake Dove to help him bandage the gash in his wrist, but his gaze was trapped by the drops of scarlet that pumped from his wrist. His wounded hand rested on the God's head, and Dead Eye watched, mesmerized, as blood turned to tears, raining down the God's slick, metal cheeks. Her face was close to his and as big as a man's body.

"Are you there? Are you alive?" he asked the God.

For the space of a breath in and then out the eyes of the God shifted, turning their sightless metal orbs toward Dead Eye. He held his breath as the answering voice filled his being.

I am Death, but I am alive. Look within. Accept Me and ever after we shall be one.

As Dead Eye's blood drained down the face of the God, he looked within and accepted the God, and without the world changed.

The screams of her Attendant awakened Dove.

"What is it? What has happened?" She sat, reaching automatically beside her for Dead Eye. When her hands touched only empty space and the thick pelts of their pallet, her stomach clenched and she stood, shouting, "Attendants! Come to me!"

"Oh, Mistress, it is horrible! I don't know what to do!"

Dove recognized Lily's voice. She outstretched her hands, and Lily grasped them. Dove could feel that the girl's body was trembling.

"Be calm. Where is our Champion? If something has happened, you must get him immediately," Dove said.

"But it is our Champion! Oh, Mistress, I think he's dead!" Lily sobbed.

"Stop this! Of course he isn't dead. The God would not allow it." Dove made quite sure her voice remained steady, even though her heart was beating wildly and fear coursed through her veins. *If my love is dead, my life is over.* Dove pushed the terrible thought from her mind and ordered Lily, "Take me to him immediately!"

"I found him at the feet of the God," Lily said as she led her Mistress through the chamber to the God's balcony. "I did as he commanded last night. Ordered the Attendants to help clean and repair the courtyard and made the sleeping People wake and help us. The Champion said he needed solitude—that he would attend to the firepots of the God. That's why it took so long to find him." Lily paused to sob again. "There's so much blood, Mistress. What shall we do without our Champion?"

Dove acted on instinct. Moving with the preternatural grace she'd cultivated from a lifetime of blindness, she used one movement to pull Lily to face her and then Dove slapped the girl across her cheek—hard.

"Don't you *ever* say that about our Champion. I am the God's Oracle. If our Champion was dead, don't you think I would know it?"

"Y-yes, of course, Mistress. I'm sorry! I'm so sorry! It's just that there is so much blood. It—it covers the God and drips like tears from Her face down Her body to pool with our Champion, and he is cold and still."

"Then it is a good thing that I cannot see so that I will not be deceived as you have been. Lead me to him!"

"As you command, Mistress."

Lily took Dove's elbow and guided her the rest of the way to the God's balcony. Before she got to Dead Eye's body, the scent of blood was so thick it seemed to Dove that the balcony must be awash in it. She almost expected to feel drops forming in the air, to drizzle around them like early spring rain.

"He is there, by—"

"I can find him now." Dove shook off Lily's guiding hand and followed the scent of blood and the pulsing energy that always radiated from her lover to find Dead Eye, crumbled on his side, resting against the God's foot as if in supplication. She knelt and ran her hands all over his body, cataloguing the nasty, weeping slash that gaped from high on his right forearm all the way down to his wrist as the only wound she could feel. She found his pulse. It was shallow and too fast, but it was there. His skin was cold and felt damp with sweat, as well as slick with the massive amount of blood he'd lost. He was breathing in small, shallow gasps. Dove moved quickly and decisively. She pulled the short tunic she'd slept in over her head and, using her teeth to begin the tear, ripped a long strip from the hem and began winding it tightly around her lover's ravaged arm, speaking to Lily as she worked. "Who else knows he has been injured?"

"No one. The other Attendants are finishing the tasks our Champion set us to. I only came here to begin brewing your morning tea, and to ask if you and he would like to break your fast with boar meat."

"Do not allow any of the other Attendants within the chamber until I tell you so. And do not tell them the Champion has been wounded."

"But, Mistress, he—"

"He is not dead!" Dove hissed the words at Lily. "And I will not have the People panicked!"

"Y-yes, Mistress."

"I need your help, Lily. May I count on you?"

"Oh, Mistress! Of course!"

"Excellent, for when he awakens, and he will awaken, I give you the God's word on that, our Champion will reward all who were loyal to me, and punish all who were not—just as he culled the blasphemous Watchers from this very balcony not so long ago again."

Dove could tell by the rustling sounds of Lily's skirts that the girl was bowing in deep supplication to her. "I hear and will loyally obey, Mistress."

"Thank you, Lily. I value your loyalty. Now, listen carefully. First, bring pelts to cover him and make him comfortable. I cannot feel the heat of the firepots. Feed them. Our Champion is cold. Get me strips of clean cloth and plenty of clean water. Then order the Attendants to boil the marrowbones of the boar into broth, and bring it to me as quickly as possible." Dove could feel Lily turning away to do her bidding, and her hand snaked out to capture the girl's thin wrist. Thinking quickly, Dove said, "What has happened here is the working of the God. She has asked our Champion for a blood sacrifice, and the only blood rich enough, strong enough, was his."

"And She has accepted his sacrifice?" Lily asked tremulously.

Dove forced herself to smile and nod confidently. "She has! Our Champion lives and he will speak with the God's voice when he awakens. Until he does, the People would only be frightened by our Champion's sacrifice—as were you."

"I understand, Mistress. I will do as you say."

Dove released her and the girl ran from the balcony, returning quickly with pelts.

"Make his pallet away from the pool of blood and nearer to the firepots," Dove told Lily, who did as she commanded.

"The pallet is ready, Mistress."

"Help me move him there—*carefully*."

Together, the two young women slowly dragged Dead Eye's huge body onto the waiting pallet.

"Now, get me that water and the bandages." Dove paused; frantically she shifted through her memories, trying to find anything that might help her lover, and she remembered that the old Watchers used to stink of garlic cloves because they insisted if they smashed the cloves and added them to honey they found relief from the cracking wounds on their skin and even some small measure of healing. "Bring me garlic bulbs, too, and honey."

"Yes, Mistress!"

Lily brought the water and the strips of clean cloth, and then she hastened from the chamber to search out garlic and honey. Finally alone with her lover, Dove began speaking to him as she cleaned the dried blood from his body and forced water between his slack lips.

"Beloved, you must awaken. I cannot lead the People from this poisoned City to the forest—only you can do that. Only you can be their savior—their God. Wake, beloved, and speak to your Dove."

Dead Eye did not stir.

"Mistress, I have the garlic and honey." Lily rushed back to Dove, breathing heavily. As she guided Dove's hands to the things she'd asked for, Dove took a moment to tenderly squeeze the young Attendant's arm and speak reassuring words to her.

"You are doing well, Lily. You have been a great help to me. Our Champion will reward you when he awakens."

"Has he spoken yet?" Lily asked.

"He is still communing with the God," Dove said. "Please get the broth now. Our Champion will need it very soon."

As the girl hurried from the Chamber again, Dove crushed the garlic cloves, adding them to the wooden bowl that held the honey. When her concoction was ready, Dove unwound the cloth from Dead Eye's wounded arm. Working fast, as he'd begun to bleed anew as soon as the pressure was released from the wound, Dove packed the sticky mixture around and within the long gash. Then she pressed the jagged cut together with one hand while she rewrapped new strips of cloth around his arm—tying it firmly.

Dove wiped the rest of the dried blood from her lover's face and neck, and then she sat close beside him, holding his wounded arm on her lap so that she could apply pressure to the wound. She sat there with him, rocking gently and talking—always talking to her beloved.

"Awaken, my Champion. I need you to speak to me. I cannot imagine a world without your deep, clever voice. I need you, beloved. Please return to me."

He did not speak, did not stir at all, but Dove was relieved when she felt his breathing deepen. She managed to get him to swallow several cups of water, though it seemed more of an automatic reflex than the reasoned action of taking sustenance. The balcony grew warmer as the firepots heated the area. Not long after Dead Eye had stopped shivering, Lily returned in a wash of the rich scent of marrow broth.

"Mistress, the broth is ready!"

"Thank you, Lily. You may leave us now."

"But—but when may your Attendants return? They are already asking what has happened. What shall I tell them?" Lily said.

"You tell them the God is speaking with our Champion. If they are not satisfied by that answer, they may question the God *and* our Champion when they are allowed to return to the Temple. I pity the man or woman of the People who thinks he or she may question a God."

"Of course, Mistress," Lily said.

"When it is time, Dead Eye and I will call the Attendants to us here, the God's balcony. Until then, wait in the courtyard. Tend the firepots. Smoke the meat. Be about the tasks your Champion commanded. I am counting on you to keep the People calm, Lily."

"I won't disappoint you, Mistress!"

Dove reached out with a blood-smeared hand and Lily grasped it. "Thank you, Lily. Your loyalty at this difficult time means more to me than I can say."

When the girl was gone, Dove resituated herself so that Dead Eye's head rested on her lap. She lifted him, struggling with his weight, so that she could hold him in her arms as she drizzled the warm, fragrant broth down his throat. He swallowed convulsively over and over, and Dove lost track of how long she sat there, holding her lover and coaxing him to drink. All the while she spoke to him as if he could hear her—as if he would awaken any moment and take her into his arms, laughing at her fear and reminding her he was mighty as a stag, that it would take more than a wounded arm and a fall to kill him.

The rising sun warmed Dove's skin, and she tilted her eyeless face up, saying, "Beloved, the sun is high and warm. You must wake now. The Others will be limping about, trying to recover from the fire. You must be there, beloved. You promised me a place in the clouds by your side, and I hold you to that promise."

She felt the change in his body immediately. He drew a deep breath, expanding his mighty chest.

"Beloved?" Her hands fluttered to his face, feeling his eyelids blinking open. "Beloved! You awaken!"

He didn't speak. Instead, he sat up, disentangling himself from her arms. She could tell he was looking at her—feel his gaze on her. She smiled tremulously and stretched a hand to him. "My Champion, are you well?"

"Dove. It is pleasing to see you."

It happened in an instant. The moment he spoke her name Dove knew the man sitting before her was no longer Dead Eye—no longer her Champion and her lover. To anyone who hadn't spent a lifetime listening as closely as she had to people's voices, the change would have been difficult, if not impossible, to detect. But Dove was not like other people. She knew things eyes could not see, so she understood—beyond any doubt—that whatever had happened that night had irrevocably changed her lover.

She felt as if her heart would implode. Dove wanted to scream her despair and loss to the sky, but for all the years of her short life she had been surviving and the habit to protect herself—to live—was strong, stronger even than her broken heart.

Dove forced her lips to smile. "My Champion! I knew you would return!" She leaned forward, opening her arms to accept him. She didn't need eyes to feel his hesitation, though she remained there, arms wide, smiling as if nothing had changed between them.

He did finally take her into his arms, pressing her body to his. "I had forgotten the softness of a living woman's skin. It is pleasing."

"Beloved? I—I don't understand your words." She remained malleable in his arms, surrendering to his increasingly rough caresses. "We have joined many times. Why does this seem new to you? Have—have you somehow been reborn?"

A shudder went through his body then, and when he spoke next she recognized his voice as his own again and his touch became gentle and familiar.

"Precious one! Do not worry—do not despair. A miracle happened last night, and that miracle will change our world forever!"

"Beloved!" Dove clung to him, flooded with relief. "You have truly come back to me! I was so frightened. It seemed as if you were gone, though your body remained."

Dead Eye's skin quivered and he cupped her face between his hands. When he spoke, his voice was filled with power and lust—and was utterly *not* her beloved's voice.

"Little Dove, it was your Dead Eye's determination that finally awakened me, but you will soon realize that much has changed with your lover."

"Forgive me. I do not understand."

"Oh, I believe you do." She could hear the smile in His voice, though it lacked humor. His words were filled with arrogance and something else, something dark and dangerous. "My Consort and I have long been content to sleep. For eons we have rested, watching the world turn, change, destroy itself, and rebuild again and again. We were content, allowing our dreams to walk the earth in the guise of old age, disease, and tragedy—as well as a flourishing forest, crops ripening, and winter changing to spring. But my sleep has come to an end. Through disease and desire, blood sacrifice and faith, you and your Dead Eye have awakened me, and now he and I are joined for eternity—just as you and my Consort shall very soon be joined."

Dove couldn't help that her body began to tremble. "Who—who are you?"

"Don't you recognize me? You have been claiming to be my Oracle for years."

"The Reaper God?" Dove whispered. "You live?"

His laughter had fear skittering down her spine. "I have always lived! I was simply sleeping, waiting for the awakening. Though I do not like this Reaper name the People have given me. I prefer the name I have had since the beginnings of the world."

"Wh-what name is that?" she said through numb lips.

"Death. But you, my lovely little bird, may call me Lord."

And then Death, wearing the skin of her Champion, her lover, her life, ravaged her there on the hard, bloody floor of the balcony while the silent God looked down and wept scarlet. Dove forced her body to accept Him, to be soft and submissive, though inside her mind she screamed over and over and over. . . .

CHAPTER 19

Sora woke to chaos and complaints, and she instantly wished she hadn't been so insistent that Mari leave, because she definitely did *not* have everything handled. What she had was a group of people who were wounded, weary, and sad—or healthy, restless, and bored.

Sitting in front of the hearth fire, Sora muddled honey with lavender and poppy pods with one hand as she stirred a rich barley mushroom soup with the other.

"Jenna!" Sora called, trying to be heard over chattering women's voices and the surprisingly loud baby animal noises the very awake and very annoying litter of puppies was making.

"I'm here, Sora!" Jenna hurried from the back room with Danita shadowing her. "Can I get you something?"

"Yes, more mushrooms. This stew needs to stretch." She paused as Cammy came racing up to her, huffing doggy laughter with two of Fala's pups tangled around his feet. "Do that outside!" she snapped at the little blond Terrier, then immediately felt bad, as his head and tail went down and he stared at her with big eyes while he whined pitifully.

"Don't let him fool you," Davis said as he hurried to catch his Companion. "Cammy knows better than to play rough in a nest. Er, or burrow. I'm sorry, Sora. I'll take him and the pups outside."

"There's a nice spot in the clearing by the stream where we Gathered last night," O'Bryan said, ruffling the fur on Cammy's head before picking up the two rambunctious pups. "I'll help you take all of them out. Sheena's already there, trying to catch some fish to add to the stew."

"That sounds good. Would you also keep an eye out for mushrooms? That'll help stretch the—" Sora's words broke off as she felt a warm, soft little body curl up on her feet. She looked down and, sure enough, there was the sun-kissed pup, blinking innocently up at her.

"Where is the other girl pup?" Rose was saying as she limped the length of the long burrow, peering around pallets and into woven baskets, searching for the young canine.

"She's over here," Sora said with a sigh.

"I'll get her!" O'Bryan said. "Sorry about all these canines in your way." He reached to remove the pup from Sora's feet, but her hand on his arm stayed him.

"Oh, she's fine. She keeps my feet warm."

O'Bryan's eyes glinted as if he knew a secret Sora was unwilling to share, but all he did was shrug. "No problem. If you get tired of her, we'll be by the stream."

"Take Rose, Sarah, and Lydia with you. Go slowly and let them rest in the shade. Fresh air will do them good. I'll have the poppy tea and a change of dressings ready about the time the stew is done cooking," Sora said, shifting her feet so the pup could find a more comfortable position.

"I don't know if Lydia and I can walk down to the Gathering spot," Rose was saying as she stroked Fala, who kept throwing what Sora interpreted as suspicious glances at the sun-kissed pup who was now soundly asleep on Sora's feet. "We woke up so stiff this morning that it's hard to move at all."

"So, here's what I read about burn recovery from the Moon Woman journals," Sora said matter-of-factly. "Yes, if they're too bad, the patient must remain inside and very still while the dead skin is debrided and then covered with wet, clean cloths soaked in water, honey, and garlic. Rose, you and Lydia were not burned that badly. You're sore and stiff, but if you stay inside and don't move the damaged parts of your bodies you'll remain sore and stiff, even after the wounds turn to scars—tight, uncomfortable, unsightly scars." Sora almost felt bad for adding the part about *unsightly*. She'd made that up, but Rose and Lydia were young women, and if she couldn't appeal to their desire to be healed, then she would try to appeal to their vanity. *And, oh yes, the Tribe is very vain with their tall blond bodies and their ability to channel sunlight.* "You decide," Sora concluded, shrugging one shoulder and going back to muddling the tea mixture.

"I'll join the others outside. And I'll make sure Lydia and Sarah do, too," Rose said. As an afterthought she added, "If you get tired of the pup, call for Fala. She'll hear you and let me know we need to come get her."

"Will do. And I say again—to anyone and everyone—stay close to the burrow and don't go anywhere alone. If you see an Earth Walker male, do *not* try to reason with him. Get me immediately. I'll take it from there." Though what she was supposed to do with diseased and dangerous males wasn't entirely clear to her. Sora's best guess at how to handle the situation was to knock a male over the head, tie him up, pour poppy tea down his throat, and wait until the moon had risen to Wash him.

"Understood," O'Bryan said as Rose, Davis, and Jenna nodded in agreement.

"And Jenna, tell Danita that she's worked in the pantry long enough. Take her with you to the stream to hunt for mushrooms, and while you're hunting—*stay close to the burrow*—I want the two of you to practice hitting targets with the slingshots we brought from Mari's burrow. None of us should be going anywhere unarmed for a very long time."

"Good idea. I'll get her." Jenna disappeared into the back room that held the birthing burrow's extensive pantry system.

"Can you use a slingshot?"

Sora glanced up to see O'Bryan watching her with his usual mixture of good humor and intelligence sparkling in his eyes.

"No. I cannot. Or at least, not well. Mari showed me a little, but I'm pretty bad at it." Sora shook back her thick, dark hair and sighed. "I kept hitting myself with the rocks."

"Have you considered trying a crossbow?"

Sora met O'Bryan's gaze. "Earth Walkers don't have crossbows."

"But Companions do, and I'm a Companion."

"You'd teach me?" Sora asked, intrigued. Since the males had attacked her, she had felt vulnerable and frustrated at her lack of skill in protecting herself. It amazed her that just weeks ago her biggest worry had been which tunic looked best and when she would announce Jaxom as her choice of mate. And now . . . now she couldn't look at Jaxom without seeing a monster and she was sitting there talking to a sworn enemy about learning to defend herself—the Tribal way.

"Absolutely. It'll be fun." O'Bryan grinned. "Just let me know when you're ready." He grabbed the other two pups from under Davis's feet, laughing as they squirmed their way up to lick his face. "Come on, kids! Let's get some fresh air and let Sora have some peace for a little while."

In a rush of dog breath–scented air, puppy squeals, and moans from stiff, sore women, people and canines trailed out of the burrow, leaving Sora alone except for one very warm, very sleepy puppy.

Sora breathed a long, slow sigh of relief and debated how bad it would be to make herself a big mug of poppy tea, drink it, and then take the sun-kissed puppy and curl up in the back of the pantry for a quick nap.

"Except I don't think it would be quick," Sora told the pup, who opened one dark eye to peer at her before snuggling more firmly against her feet and going back to sleep. "And without a giant batch of this tea, there's no way I'm going to get any peace at all tonight. So, you rest for me and I'll keep muddling herbs. Remind me to tell Mari she owes me big when she finally gets out of bed with Nik and shows up here."

"Do you always talk to yourself like that?"

Sora startled as Antreas and his Lynx seemed to materialize behind her. "Great Earth Mother! Do the two of you never make any noise?"

"We're not entirely silent; it just seems like we are compared to the noise of canines, Companions, and Earth Walkers. I mean no offense by that," Antreas said as he leaned against the curved side of the burrow and watched her work the herbs into the honey mixture for tea.

"No offense taken at all. I was just thinking about how nice silence can be."

"Oh, well, I apologize for interrupting your silence," Antreas said as Bast padded up to Sora. The big feline sat on her haunches and studied the Moon Woman, much as Antreas had been doing. "Bast and I will leave you alone."

"No, it's fine. You don't have to leave. And I'm not alone." She gestured at the ball of fur sleeping on her feet. "She thinks it's her job to keep my feet warm."

"Ah, the pup. She likes you. Be careful, Moon Woman; if she tells you her name you're stuck with her for life."

Sora's eyes widened in shock. "Oh no, no, no. That's not possible."

"Of course it is."

Sora shook her head quickly. "No. I'm an Earth Walker. That means I can't be a Companion."

Antreas shrugged. "Mari's an Earth Walker, and Rigel chose her."

"Mari's part Companion. I'm not. The pup likes to lie on my feet by the fire. She obviously has more sense than the rest of the litter and is as sick of their noise as I am." Sora glanced down at the sleeping young one. "Had you ever seen puppies before now?"

"Sure. Yeah. I've visited Tribes and have seen Shepherd and Terrier pups often."

"Were you also surprised by how *not* hideous they are?"

"They're not as attractive as Lynx kittens, but I suppose they'll do," Antreas said, clearly amused by the conversation.

"They certainly smell a lot better than I thought they would. . . ." Sora paused, studying Bast. "She's pretty. Those long tufts on her ears—what are they for?"

"They increase her hearing. Her eyesight is already incredibly sharp—as sharp as a canine's nose. Bast can see a field mouse two hundred and fifty feet away at night with little to no moon."

"Wow, that's impressive." Bast had moved closer to Sora and was studying her with the same curiosity. "May I touch her?"

"Ask her. Bast makes decisions for herself." Antreas chuckled. "Actually, she also makes decisions for me."

Slowly, Sora reached her hand toward the Lynx. Bast moved closer to her, delicately sniffing her hand. After a moment the big feline began purring and rubbed her face against Sora's wrist.

"She likes to be scratched around her ears and the ruff of fur that frames her face," Antreas said.

"She's amazingly soft," Sora said, gently scratching the Lynx and even, for a moment, touching the tufts of black fur that tipped her ears. "So, when they call you cat man, is that an insult?"

"Depends on who's calling me that."

"Okay, say O'Bryan? Is that an insult?"

"Probably not. Those dog guys"—Antreas laughed—"are strange with their insults. For instance—had Nik been in here and heard me calling him a 'dog guy' he would definitely have been offended, but he thinks it's okay to call me cat man. Do you see the double standard I'm dealing with?"

"I might."

"Yeah, visiting a canine Tribe is always interesting," Antreas said.

"Why *are* you here?"

"I thought I was keeping you company."

"No," Sora said, shifting the pup to a more comfortable spot between her feet. "I don't mean *here*, in this burrow. I mean, why are you here—attached to a Tribe you don't belong to—during a major upheaval? Couldn't you have left during the forest fire? Returned to your—um, burrow?"

"It's called a den. And, yes, I could have. But Bast wouldn't let me."

Sora's gaze shifted to the Lynx, who was busy grooming herself near the hearth fire. "She's that bossy?"

"Worse than you could imagine. But that's the way of it." Antreas looked around them with an exaggerated long-suffering attitude. "Here's the deal—humans are in charge of canines. Doesn't matter if they're bonded or not. Humans still have the upper hand. But Lynxes? They're *always* in charge."

"What does that even mean?"

"It means that from the time a feline chooses you as her own she takes over your life."

Antreas focused his gaze on Bast, who was still calmly grooming herself. Sora saw the love in his gaze, though his words seemed annoyed, petulant even. His expression, though, reflected the deep bond he shared with his feline.

"Is that a bad thing?"

Antreas shook his head. "No, not at all. The truth is, Bast has never been wrong. She knows what's best for me—for us."

"So, what were you doing visiting the Tribe in the first place? You're a mercenary, right? Earth Walkers have little to do with the outside world, but we do have a story or two about hiring Lynx Companions to guide a group to new Clan territory."

"You're right. I am a guide. I'm also a Warrior."

Sora's brows shot up. "You're a killer?"

Bast made a series of yowls that left no room for speculation about her dislike for Sora's last questions.

"Hey, sorry." She spoke directly to the feline. "I'm curious, and I don't know enough about you or your Companion to know if I'm being offensive or not."

Bast's yellow eyes met Sora's gray gaze. Sora saw an immense intelligence there, as well as compassion—a surprising amount of compassion. The big feline made a rolling meow in the back of her throat. Then, as she settled back into her grooming, her purr filled the burrow.

"In case you didn't get that, she just forgave you," Antreas said.

Sora grinned. "I got it. Does that mean I can keep asking annoying and unintentionally insulting questions?"

"Absolutely, if I can ask you to show me how you braid those feathers and beads into your hair."

Sora's surprise was genuine. "For you?"

"Well, yeah. My hair's long enough, isn't it?"

"Sure, but it's a woman's thing—decorating our hair."

"Who said?"

Sora hesitated. *Who had said?* She moved her shoulders. "I'm not sure."

"So, it's a rule we can break?" Antreas said.

"Yes, I think it is."

"Good. Then ask away."

"Okay. Are you a hired killer?"

"At this moment . . . no. Have I been hired to use my blades and my wits to solve problems in the past? Yes. Next question."

"Is that why you were staying with the Tribe of the Trees? Because they'd hired you to be a killer?"

"Great Stormshaker, no! Gods, I didn't even consider that anyone would think that." He ran a hand through the thick chestnut-colored hair that fell to his shoulders. "Bast and I came to the Tribe of the Trees in search of a mate."

"A mate? There are more Lynxes in the area?" Sora asked.

"No, not a mate for her. A mate for me."

Sora sat up straighter. This was *really* getting interesting! "Your mate? But don't you have females to choose from in your . . ." She hesitated, trying to find the correct word. "Pack? Clan? Tribe?"

"Chain. Lynxes are solitary, but when we Gather we call ourselves a Chain. And no. According to *my* Lynx, none of the females in our Chain were good enough to be my mate, so I did what all Lynx Companions do when their feline isn't satisfied with the available mates. I began to travel. The Tribe of the Trees was hosting me in my search for a mate."

"Wait, wait, wait!" Sora was fully involved in the conversation now. "Are you telling me your cat chooses your mate for you?"

Bast growled low in her throat and sent Sora a yellow-eyed glare.

"Sorry," Sora amended. "I meant your Lynx. *She* chooses your mate?"

"She does," Antreas said on a sigh.

Sora hid her smile. "And that's a bad thing?"

"No!" Antreas said at the same time Bast grumbled and hissed softly. "Or maybe yes. Initially. It's complicated."

"Hey, I'm muddling an enormous amount of poppy tea to drug a bunch of people—partially to alleviate their pain and partially to shut them up so they'll sleep. I have time. Explain."

"Well, okay. A Lynx is never wrong about her Companion."

"Seriously?"

"Seriously. Oh, she can be wrong about other things." Bast coughed twice, and Antreas added, "She wants me to tell you that she's rarely wrong about other things, either."

"She's definitely opinionated."

"To say the least. But Bast and I have an additional issue to deal with. A female Lynx almost never chooses a male human as her Companion. As in it's so rare that my Chain has never had it happen. Well, before Bast chose me, that is."

"That's weird. Why'd she choose you?"

"I have no idea. The only answer I've ever been able to get from her is that I belong to her." He shrugged. "And that's good enough for me. But because she did, that has made the choosing of my mate unusual."

"How so?"

"Well, sometimes I think she and I are looking for different aspects in a mate. For instance, the night of the forest fire I was content in my bed entertaining a delightful young Tribeswoman when Bast interrupted. *She* decided the girl wasn't for me. Then *she* decided we were going for a run. As annoyed as I was with her, I followed her—and because I did, I was saved from being killed in the blaze."

"She knew?"

"She always knows. I won't lie. Lynx Companions never lie; it's part of the oath we swear to our felines when we're chosen. And I won't pretend I was being a hero by staying and then returning to help the wounded. I wanted to leave—to return to the snug safety of our den in the eastern mountains."

"Who wouldn't? That's what I would have wanted to do," Sora said.

"Yep, as did I. But Bast refused, like she refused to let me wallow in bed and be burned to death the night of the fire. Even though I don't always understand why she wants me to do something—or *not* to do something—there is always a reason. And that reason is *always* what's best for me, even if I don't see it as best at the time."

"Huh. So, she's here because she's still looking for your mate?"

"That's what she's told me."

"But shouldn't she be looking for someone who can be a Companion to a male Lynx?"

"Stormshaker, no! Unlike canines, Lynxes don't live with their mates. It's like your Clan. Our males are solitary. The kittens stay with their mother in her den until they're about a year old, but then they go out to choose their own Companions and make their own dens, usually far away from their mother's territory so that they don't overhunt the food supply. Lynxes don't mate for life, but Lynx Companions do."

"That doesn't make any sense at all," Sora said.

"But it does. It saves us from being alone. Lynxes enjoy a solitary life, but humans don't. Well, most of us don't. If it were up to me, I'd never let any of Bast's kittens leave our den—or if I did they'd all stay close." He shrugged. "As far as I know, I'm the only male Lynx Companion who feels like that, which is probably why I'm bonded to Bast. I'm not normal."

Sora snorted. "Well, you're definitely in the right place for not normal." She pointed to the ball of dark fur sleeping on her feet. "*This* is definitely not normal for an Earth Walker."

"Yeah, which makes my point about Bast always being right."

"I see what you mean. Bast is going to find the perfect mate for you—someone to stay with you forever," Sora said, thoroughly enjoying the conversation.

"Exactly!"

"Bast! There you are! I've been looking—" Like a whirlwind Danita rushed into the burrow, deflating quickly when she realized Antreas was there, too, and had been in conversation with her Moon Woman.

The young woman stopped and bowed respectfully to Sora. "Forgive me. I didn't mean to intrude. I just thought Bast might like to help me catch crawfish in the stream. I remember you said you liked to add them to the stew."

At the appearance of Danita, Bast's aloof demeanor changed dramatically. Kitten-like, she padded to the girl, purring and rubbing against her as Danita giggled and played with the tufts on her ears.

Sora sat up straighter, looking from Danita's bright young expression to Antreas's glower. *Ah, now this is interesting.* "Oh, you didn't interrupt. And I would love crawfish to add to the stew, but first you might like to get in on this conversation. Antreas was explaining to me why he and Bast were visiting the Tribe of the Trees."

"Really?" Danita looked up from tickling Bast around her neck.

"*Really,*" Sora said.

"No," Antreas said.

"No? You weren't telling Sora why you were visiting the Tribe?" Danita said, looking vaguely confused and only semi-interested in what Antreas had to say.

"Yes. No. It's just not common knowledge, that's all," Antreas sputtered.

Bast coughed at him.

Sora bit her cheek to keep from laughing. When she was certain she could keep a straight face, she said, "Not common knowledge? The Tribe didn't know Bast is on a search for your mate?"

"Mate?" Danita said.

"Um . . ." Antreas said.

Bast coughed again and rubbed against Danita's legs, weaving around the young woman and purring loudly.

Then Danita utterly surprised Sora. Instead of asking Antreas anything, Danita went to her knees and took Bast's face between her hands, speaking intently to the feline. "Are you really looking for a mate for Antreas?"

Bast's purr got several decibels louder and she rubbed her face against Danita's hands.

Danita shook her head sadly. "No," she said so softly Sora had to strain to hear her. "Not me, Bast. I can't."

"Wait; no one said she was choosing you for my—"

Danita stood and whirled to face the cat man. "Don't! I know you think I'm a child, but *don't treat me like I'm a stupid child.* Your Lynx likes me. A lot. That's obvious to everyone, but you need to know that I am absolutely *not* interested in being your mate. You're not even nice. And I've decided I don't like men."

"But you can't refuse to—" Antreas began, looking offended. Danita held up her hand, stopping him.

"I can refuse you *anything.* You're not my Moon Woman. You're not even a Clansman. Don't you ever try to tell me what to do!" Bast's pitiful meow had Danita going to her knees and putting her arms around the big feline. "Oh, don't be sad! I think you're wonderful! Please say we can still be friends, but me mated to your Companion? No, Bast. I'm even less interested in him than he is in me. Want to chase crawfish with me?"

The Lynx coughed a yes, and when Danita started for the burrow door the feline followed her, pausing only to throw a yellow-eyed glare over her shoulder at her Companion.

"I think you're in trouble," Sora said.

"Yeah, for sure."

CHAPTER 20

C an a Lynx revoke her choice of Companion?" Sora asked Antreas after she was sure Danita and Bast had left the burrow.

"No."

"Too bad for you."

Antreas threw back his head and laughed. "Why couldn't Bast be obsessed with someone like you?"

Sora sobered instantly. "Don't even joke about that."

"Why not? I think you're beautiful. And you're funny. And you can damn sure cook."

Sora shook her head in disgust. "And here I was thinking that you were a nice guy who was shackled to a bossy cat. I'm pretty and funny and can cook? *You think that's all I am?* Antreas, Companion to Bast, I am a Moon Woman, chosen by the Great Earth Goddess to wield moon magick and to be responsible for the welfare of an entire Clan. We're not solitary. We don't let anyone choose our mates for us. Here, in Earth Walker territory, women do the choosing. Always. And let me be clear—I wouldn't be mated to a solitary den dweller like you if a thousand cats chose me. If you want to make any kind of headway with Danita, or any other Earth Walker your feline takes a fancy to, I suggest you check your ego back at your den and change your attitude."

She scoffed at him as she scooped up the sleepy pup and handed him the ladle to the stew. "Here, stir this. I need some air."

He took the ladle but also touched her hand gently. "I'm sorry."

She paused. "For?"

"For being an ass. I offended you. I offended Danita. I even offended my Bast." He ran his hand through his hair again, looking boyish and miserable. "I can't seem to do anything right."

Sora sighed. "Change places with me. You stir the stew and add in those mushrooms. I'll finish muddling the poppy and honey mixture."

"Can we keep talking?"

"Yes, we can."

"Thank you," Antreas said as he took Sora's seat by the hearth and began adding mushrooms to the fragrant stew.

Sora sat cross-legged across from him with the sleepy pup tucked against her thigh, choosing fat poppy pods from the basket of herbs and sprinkling them into the honey. She picked up the stone muddler and went back to grinding and mixing. "No need to thank me. If we're going to make this merging of Tribe and Clan and Chain work, we're all going to have to learn to be more patient with each other. You just insulted me." He started to protest, but she cut him off. "I know you didn't mean to. You had no way of knowing Earth Walker women choose their mates. Just like I didn't have any idea your Lynx chooses your mate for you. We're all going to have to listen to one another and not be so quick to take offense."

"So, along with being beautiful, funny, and a good cook you're also smart and magickal. Little wonder I wish Bast would choose you."

Sora bowed her head slightly in acknowledgment and smiled at him. "And now I'll take that as a compliment. Thank you."

"At least we're communicating clearly, because I meant it as a compliment and not as an insult," he said.

"That's an improvement. So, tell me, cat man, what are you going to do if Bast chooses Danita for you? Or has she already chosen her and you're in a rather advanced state of denial?"

He laughed and said, "Bast hasn't chosen Danita. Yet."

"How do you know?"

"Because she hasn't bitten Danita."

"What! Did you say that she hasn't *bitten* Danita?"

"Yep. Oh, don't worry. It's not dangerous or malicious. When a Lynx chooses a Companion's mate, the mate is Marked by the Lynx's bite. It's protective. It lets other Lynxes know that this person belongs to a Chain, and is under the protection of all Lynxes, everywhere. We don't live together as a Tribe or a Clan, but we are fiercely loyal to our Chain—and all Lynx Companions are connected to the same Chain."

Antreas paused, and Sora could see that he was trying to decide whether or not to tell her more. Finally he shrugged. "Oh, what the hell, I might as well tell you everything. You are a Moon Woman. You're used to magick."

"This is getting good. Go ahead; I'm all ears."

Instead of speaking, Antreas rolled up the sleeve of his right arm to reveal two round, puckered scars that were surrounded by an intricate and beautiful pattern of vines and flowers that had been permanently inked into his skin. The scars and decorations were obviously old and had healed well, but she could see that the bite had been nasty—deep and painful—and she couldn't imagine that the decorative pattern had been easy to endure, either.

"Great Goddess! Bast did that? And what is that decoration? It looks permanent."

His smile was wry as he nodded. "Yes, it's permanent, and yes, Bast bit me. It was the happiest moment of my life."

"Okay, you need to explain."

"She bit me when she chose me, *after* I successfully built our den. The Chain decorations came later."

"I don't understand. Rigel chose Mari, but she didn't have to do anything. Or at least I don't think she did. I do know for sure he didn't bite her," Sora said. "And she sure didn't get vines and flowers painted into her skin."

"When a young Lynx chooses her Companion that's just the first step in their bonding. The Companion has to prove him- or herself worthy of the choosing. A Lynx's den is her sanctuary—the one place she can rest easily, knowing she is safe. The Lynx's Companion must build their den. If it's acceptable to the Lynx, the bonding goes to the next step."

"What if it's not acceptable to the Lynx?"

"Then the bite is deadly. The candidate Companion dies."

Sora blinked in shock. "Wait; you mean *the Lynx kills her Companion*?"

"Well, yes, but the person isn't technically the Lynx's Companion if the den is rejected. And the bite isn't any different from this bite." He held up his arm again for Sora to get another look.

"That doesn't look like it could kill you. Sure, it looks painful, but it's not a mortal wound. I'm still confused."

"Have you heard stories of my people?" Antreas surprised her by asking.

"Not many. I know you're guides and mercenaries, and that's about it."

"We're different after we've been chosen by our Lynx. I mean physically," he said.

She waited, and when he didn't continue she prodded, "Okay, so, you're different. How?"

"If I show you, will you not tell Danita? I don't want her to be any more repulsed by me than she already is," he said.

"I won't tell her. That's your business. But don't hold out too much hope for changing her mind about you," Sora said.

"I think I'm going to focus on changing Bast's mind, not Danita's," Antreas said sardonically.

"Sounds like a good idea," Sora said. "So, show me."

"Okay, here goes." Antreas put the ladle down and held his hands out so that Sora had a clear view of them. Then he flicked his wrists and Sora watched, with wide eyes, as his fingers changed instantly—growing long, sharp claws where normal human fingernails had been.

"Goddess! That's . . . that's—well, I'm not sure what that is." She stared at his claws, not sure whether she wanted to bolt from the burrow or examine them like she would a strange wound.

"Are you disgusted by them?"

She raised her gaze from his claws to his warm golden eyes. "No," she said, realizing as she spoke that she was telling the truth and not just saying what he so obviously wanted to hear. "No," she repeated as her mind caught up with her words. "I'm surprised, shocked even, but I'm not disgusted. That happened after Bast bit you?"

"Yes. It's what happens after a Lynx accepts the den her chosen candidate makes for her. If she hadn't accepted the den, her bite wouldn't have changed me. It would have poisoned my body and killed me," he said.

"Did it change anything else about you?"

He nodded. "Yep, I'm faster. My vision and my hearing aren't as good as Bast's, but they're better than a normal human's. And I have, um, fur on my body."

Sora's brows shot up. "Fur? Where? Oh, Goddess, sorry," she said immediately. "Was that a rude question? I didn't mean it to be."

Antreas's eyes gleamed with amusement. "No, it's not rude, just personal, but that's okay. It's just you and me talking. It'd be rude if you asked in front of a bunch of outsiders." He swept his long hair aside and leaned forward so that Sora could see his neck and a little way down his back. There, growing along with his hair, tracking all the way down his neck and his spine as far as she could see was the same long brownish-gray fur that covered Bast. Sora could also see that his ears were strangely pointed.

"Wow. Just wow," Sora said.

"Not disgusted?"

She shook her head. "No, not at all. I like your Bast's fur. And it looks good on you. Soft and nice. Probably keeps you warm."

He grinned. "That's the point, I think. Well, that and Marking me as the Companion to a Lynx." He hesitated and then asked, "How do you think other Earth Walkers would react to all of this?" He raised his claws and the firelight glinted on them before he retracted them and waited for her answer.

Sora took her time answering him. She almost told him she couldn't speak for other Earth Walkers, but that would have been a lie. Moon Women always spoke for their Clans, and she knew she could shift the attitude of her people to accept—or reject—this strangely likable cat man. So she answered him honestly, even though it might not have been the answer he wanted most to hear.

"How Earth Walkers react to you depends entirely on the kind of man you are. If you're honest, good, and true, I think they will accept you."

"And if I'm an ass who ignores Clan traditions and tries to bully my way into a mate?"

Sora snorted. "Good luck with that. You're going to find Clanswomen can't be bullied. This is a matriarchy, Antreas. If you can accept and honor that, you might just find your perfect mate *is* an Earth Walker." She hesitated and then decided she might as well tell him the rest. "There's something you should understand about us, though. We aren't solitary. I'm not sure any Clanswoman would be happy being isolated in a den."

Antreas blew out a long breath. "That's what I thought. Stormshaker, that Lynx is always right!"

"Okay, now I'm *really* confused. How could Bast be right if she brought you here to find a mate from a group of women who don't like being isolated?"

He met her eyes and she could see the humor that rested there in his honest gaze. "Because the truth is that I hate being isolated. I always have. I've always been different from the rest of the Chain."

"Does that mean you don't plan to return to the Lynx way of life?"

"I didn't realize it until now, but I think that's exactly what I mean and exactly why Bast led me here," he said.

"To start a new life, and a new kind of Chain?"

"Yes."

Sora grinned. "Well, then I'd better explain to you about courting a Clanswoman. And, believe me, you've come to the right Earth Walker. I'm not a possible mate for you, but I'm definitely the perfect teacher for you."

"Why do I suddenly feel afraid?"

"Because you're a wise cat man. Now, pay attention. . . ."

CHAPTER 21

Dove, my precious one, you must awaken."

She woke immediately, feeling more than hearing that it was Dead Eye who woke beside her and not the God. She had been sleeping with her back to him, curled in a tight fetal ball, but upon his call Dove turned eagerly, opening her arms.

"Beloved! It is you!" Joyously she clung to him, trembling with relief.

He smoothed her hair and held her close, cradling her in the crook of his arm as she rested her head on his massive chest.

"We don't have long, precious one. The God sleeps, but He will return soon."

Dove couldn't repress her shudder. "My Champion, my love, can you fight Him? Can you remain yourself?"

Instantly she felt the change in Dead Eye. His body stiffened and his hand, which had been caressing her hair, fell to his side.

"Dove, I do not wish to remain myself. I have accepted the God. It won't be long before He and I will be fully joined."

A small gasp escaped her and she pressed herself more closely against him. "No! I cannot bear to lose you."

"You will never lose me!" His arms went around her. "Precious one, the God and I are one. Though I will eventually only speak with the

God's voice, I will still be here, within this body that grows ever stronger, ever more able to lead our People."

"But He hurt me," she said. Dove could not cry—she had no eyes and therefore was not capable of tears—but her body shook with the force of her despair.

"Precious one, you must soften yourself to Him. Remember that He and I are one now."

"He told me His name is Death," Dove said.

She felt Dead Eye nod. "Yes, He is the Death God awakened. It seems you and I were wrong. Our God wasn't dead; He was sleeping."

"Beloved, I don't understand what is happening," Dove said.

"It is really quite simple. Our path has not changed. We are going to lead the People from this poisoned City and claim the City in the Trees for ourselves. Now we don't have to wait to groom an army. Now the People are being led by the God of Death Himself. Our victory is assured," Dead Eye said.

Dove said nothing. She felt as if she was losing everything—her lover, her People, her world.

"Precious one?"

"I cannot be the Consort of Death!" Dove heard herself blurt. Immediately she regretted speaking her thoughts aloud and she pressed her lips together, readying herself for Death to return and wreak vengeance upon her.

Instead, she felt Dead Eye hold her closer, stroking her back gently, intimately, lovingly, as he had done so many times before. She had begun to relax into his embrace when he spoke and shattered Dove's brief illusion of safety.

"I know you cannot, my precious one, and that is why you must merge with the Great Mother, the Goddess of Life. She is the only Consort worthy of Death."

Dove didn't want to ask. She wanted to cover her ears and curl back into a ball and pretend her Champion still belonged to her and not to a dark, dangerous God.

But she had to ask. She had to know Death's plan for her. She had learned one lesson very well in her short, difficult life—knowledge was a weapon sharper than a trident and more dangerous than an army of ignorance.

"And how am I to do that, my Champion?" she asked in a voice deceptively calm.

"As I did." While he explained it to her, his fingers traced a path over her flawless skin, stopping to caress the delicate places at the creases of her elbows and wrists, knees, and waist. "You must be infected with the skin sloughing sickness. Once you become ill and your skin blisters and cracks, the God and I will sacrifice a doe—a magnificent, beautiful queen of the forest. We will flay her alive and join her flesh with yours, as I joined with the mighty forest stag. As the doe awakens within you, so will the Goddess. Think of it, precious one! You and I will be immortal—Consorts for eternity! Life and Death will reign over the forest, enslaving all who oppose us and living in the clouds as is our divine right."

At first, Dove could not speak. She pressed her face into her beloved's chest, struggling to contain the panic that boiled within her. When she was sure she could form words and not screams, she said, "Dead Eye, my Champion, my love, what if I do not want to become a Goddess? May I not remain as I am—your lover? May I not serve in truth the role I have been pretending for years, and be a true Oracle to the God?"

Dead Eye took her face between his hands and spoke clearly and carefully. "Listen well and heed me. Do not *ever* repeat those words. You are precious to me, and the God acknowledges that. But a human cannot be the Consort of a God, and a living God does not need an Oracle. You must choose. If you want to remain by my side, you must become the vessel for the Great Mother, the Goddess of Life. If you do not, He will replace you with someone who is more willing."

A terrible shudder of fear skittered through Dove's body. "You would let Him do that?"

"I would have no choice," Dead Eye said in a voice as devoid of emotion as death.

"When must I become the vessel for the Goddess?" she whispered.

"Oh, precious one!" He laughed, hugging her close. "You sound as if it is a terrible thing that is going to happen to you and not a miracle. But you shall see; you shall see. You will understand when the Goddess begins to stir within you."

"Forgive me. I am just a girl. I—I cannot imagine being divine."

"Start imagining it! It is your destiny. There is no one I want by my side for eternity except you."

"When?" she repeated in a small, frightened voice.

"The God will not awaken His Consort here in this poisoned place, but will wait until after we take the City in the Trees from the Others. *Then* I will infect you and begin hunting for the queen doe. High above the forest floor you will become a Goddess, Consort for eternity to a God!" he finished joyfully as he bent to claim her lips.

Dove responded to his kiss. She would always respond to Dead Eye's touch. She knew she would love him for as long as she drew breath. But her Champion was fading away. She had already witnessed the possession of the Death God. No matter what her Dead Eye had been led to believe by the God, when Death was present he was absent. And she knew that one day very soon her Champion would be gone for good and in his place would be only the dreadful God of Death.

Dove loathed Death. She'd spent her short life fighting Him—fighting to survive despite being born sightless, surrounded by danger and disease. To accept Death—to become His Consort—went against the very core of her being.

She would never allow herself to be used as a vessel for anyone—be He God or Goddess, Death or Life. *I have already lost my love. I will not lose myself.*

"Have you no words of gratitude for what the God offers you?" Dead Eye asked, and though his voice was his own, Dove could hear an edge to it that had not been there before—an annoyance barely concealed just below the surface of his words. She knew she must be very, very careful.

"I'm sorry, beloved. I'm overwhelmed. I—I hardly know what to say."

His body relaxed against her and his chest rumbled with his deep chuckle. "I forget that you have not yet felt the power and the glory that the touch of a God brings. Do not fear, precious one. Soon enough you will understand."

"Soon? I thought you said the Goddess would not be awakened until you conquer the City in the Trees. We have already spoken about the army it will take to defeat them—that the People must be made ready, that there are too few Harvesters and Hunters to attack even a weakened Tribe successfully." She spoke slowly, carefully, focusing on logic and keeping the dread and panic from her voice.

"There will be no more Harvesters and Hunters. There will only be Reapers—those chosen by the Death God to follow Him, to do His will."

"Surely that will take some time. You only have nine Reapers. They cannot take a city filled with the Others," she said.

"They *could* not take a city filled with the Others. That was in the past. Now a God leads our People. What chance does a wounded city have against Death Himself, especially when they created the fire that called Death to walk among them?"

"None," Dove heard herself say as she repressed a shudder of revulsion. "None at all."

"You do understand, my precious one!" He bent and kissed her again, this time lingering on her lips, deepening the kiss.

Dove began to soften to him. He was still her Champion, her emancipator, her hero—the only person she had ever loved. She clung to him, silently willing Dead Eye to stay with her—to fight the possession of the God.

But as his caresses became more urgent, more filled with desire, Dove felt him change. It was a subtle shifting—much like the change that happens when one goes from being awake to falling into the world of dreams. And then Dead Eye was gone. She knew it before He spoke. She felt it in the texture of His touch and in the quality of His presence. Even His scent changed from Dead Eye's familiar smell of earth and pine and clean, honest sweat to something darker, more pungent and base.

"Ah, little bird, you are an attractive mortal. I do appreciate Dead Eye's choice in a mate. You will make a delectable vessel for my Goddess." Death spoke with His lips against her ear as He penetrated her.

She said nothing. She did nothing except remain still beneath Him, allowing the God to use her.

"So soft . . . so young . . . so *alive*," He murmured as He thrust roughly into her.

She said nothing, which seemed to please Him. With a roar He quickly spent Himself.

Dove was grateful that He didn't remain with her as Dead Eye would have, cuddling her close afterward while they talked of their future. Instead, the God stood, stretching mightily before He pulled on His breeches.

"Ah, it is good to be awake! Make ready! When I return we feast on the rest of the boar meat," Death said to her. "The Reapers and I will be ravenous." He bent and cupped her breast, squeezing it painfully. "For more than just food, but that will come after we eat."

Dove was careful not to cringe from Him, careful not to let any hint of disgust be heard in her voice. "My Lord, may I ask where you are going?"

"To the City in the Trees, of course."

Dove folded her hands together so that He would not see that they trembled. "Are You conquering the city today, my Lord?"

"It is good you are so eager to become divine. That pleases me, little bird. The City in the Trees was conquered the moment I awoke, though they do not yet know it. I have some small things I must do before I take possession of their city and make it my own, but do not fret; it will be soon, very soon."

Then, without another word to her, He left their bed. Striding through the God's chamber, he began shouting for Dove's Attendants to bring drink and food and to command Iron Fist to join him on the God's balcony.

Forgotten, Dove made her way to the far corner of the chamber where the Attendants always kept troughs of freshwater for drinking and bathing. Dove washed herself, over and over, wiping away every vestige of Death's loathsome touch.

"Mistress, may I help you?" Lily's voice was filled with concern and Dove could feel the God's attention shifting in her direction. She shook her head, waving away her Attendant.

"No, I do not need your help, but your Champion does. Did I not hear him call for food and drink?"

"Yes, Mistress," Lily said, sounding contrite.

Dove hated speaking harshly to the girl. She was young and kind and wished only to serve her, but Dove steeled herself. The time for weakness and sentiment was gone. The God of Death had banished it.

"Then do as he commands."

"Yes, Mistress!" Lily hurried away, and as she did Dove felt the God's attention turn from her.

Moments after His food and drink were brought to the balcony, she heard Iron Fist race into the chamber, going directly to the God's balcony to join Death. Moving with the graceful silence that had kept her invisible to the loathsome Watchers, Dove took a basket of hemp rope that needed to be knotted into fishing nets and went to a shadowy spot near enough to the balcony that her sharp ears could hear while she remained hidden. Her hands worked as she listened with growing dread.

"Who do you see when you look at me, Iron Fist?" Death asked His Reaper.

The man did not hesitate. "My leader. My Champion. My God."

Cloaked by shadow, Dove's hands stilled. She had thought the Death God was still masquerading as Dead Eye, the God's Champion. But she realized she shouldn't have been surprised. The obvious changes in His body, coupled with the arrogance of the God, should have prepared her. For once Dove was glad she had been born eyeless. Had she eyes, Dove would not have been able to keep from dissolving into tears— and those tears would definitely have been noticed by the God. Instead, she tucked her heartache deep inside her. She would bring it out later and mourn Dead Eye's loss properly, but only after she found a way to escape the touch of Death.

"Which of the Hunters and Harvesters I have not yet changed to Reapers is the sickest?"

Death's question to Iron Fist broke the morose spell that had settled over Dove, and she mentally shook herself, listening intently once again.

"That would be Lizard. His skin is very bad," Iron Fist said.

"Is he strong enough to join us on a very important mission near the City in the Trees?" the God asked.

"He has not yet lost all of his strength, but his appearance is loathsome—his skin cracks and sloughs, and he is covered in oozing blisters."

"Excellent! Get Lizard. Bring him here to my chamber. We will paint our skin to camouflage us, and then you and he will join your God on a mission of the utmost import. After you call for Lizard, command all of the People to gather in the courtyard below. I have a question to put to them."

"Yes, my Lord." Dove heard the reverence in Iron Fist's words. Before he could hurry from the chamber Dove moved soundlessly from her shadowy corner, taking her weaving supplies and making her way to the warmth of a firepot. There she sat, appearing busy with her net making, and waited for what terrible thing would happen next.

"Dove! Come to me!"

Smoothing her face into the benign listening expression that had helped her survive the sixteen winters of her life before Dead Eye had freed her from the abuse of the Watchers, Dove walked the familiar path to join Death on the God's balcony.

"I am here, my Lord."

"Excellent. I need you to command your Attendants to ready the body paint. None of the white paint, though. Tell them to mix forest colors—greens, browns, and blacks. And tell them to hurry!"

"Yes, my Lord. Where shall I have them bring the paints?"

"Here, to my balcony. Iron Fist and Lizard will be joining us. The People will be gathering below. It is my desire to speak to them before Iron Fist, Lizard, and I go to the forest."

"It will be as You command, my Lord." Dove bowed low and backed quickly from the balcony. "Lily! Your Champion has orders for you."

The girl was by her side in an instant. "Yes, Mistress?"

"Mix the tubs of body paint for three of our men. Your Champion commands you only use forest colors. Quickly! The People will be gathering to watch."

"Yes, Mistress!" Her bare feet padded against the tile floor as she rushed from the chamber.

While her Attendants did the God's bidding, Dove went to the private space she had shared with Dead Eye. She dressed carefully. She did not know what the God was planning, but she was certain He would somehow put her on display, and her survival depended upon whether or not her appearance and her actions pleased Him. By the time she'd donned her most decorated skirt and brushed her long hair free of tangles, Iron Fist had returned to the God's balcony. Dove knew the badly infected Lizard was with him—she could smell the stench of his rotting flesh and she heard the wheeze in his breath that foretold his end was not far away, that soon he would drown in his own blood and puss and be free of the misery of his diseased body.

"You may join me on my balcony," the Death God called when Iron Fist and Lizard hesitated, waiting for permission to enter the presence of the massive statue that most of the People still believed was their Reaper God. "Dove! Bring your Attendants here when they return with the body paint."

"Yes, my Lord," Dove called.

She was inside the chamber, but Dove could hear the sounds of the gathered People lifting from the courtyard below. She could smell the gamey scent of boar stew that wafted through the open balcony and she knew that the aroma of food and the promise of a full stomach would draw even those of the People who might not come quickly at the command of a Champion they were not certain they needed.

He is wily, this Death God, Dove acknowledged silently. *I must always remember that.*

"Mistress, we have the body paints ready," Lily said.

"Very good. Follow me to the God's balcony."

Inside the Temple, Dove needed no guide. She knew every step of the chamber and the God's balcony, so she lifted her chin and walked gracefully, with the pride her extinct title of Oracle afforded her. She didn't need to be guided to the Death God, either. She could feel Him, just as she had been able to feel Dead Eye's presence—except Dead Eye had drawn her to him with love. Death drew her with loathing.

Dove strode directly to the shell of the man she used to adore. "My Lord, the Attendants have done as You commanded."

"Very good, little bird." He stroked her cheek intimately. Dove forced herself not to flinch away. Then He turned His attention to her Attendants. "You women, I would have you paint my Reaper, Iron Fist, and my Hunter, Lizard, completely with camouflage." The God spoke to the two men. "Stand near the lip of the balcony so that the People below may see you being anointed for our mission."

Then Death surprised Dove. He turned His back to the People and faced her as He spoke in a voice filled with power and authority.

"My People! You have gathered today to witness a miracle and to answer a question. One is no less important than the other. But first, I must be anointed along with my men. Dove! Come, anoint me!"

Dove didn't know what the God was planning. She only knew she was trapped in His waking dream and she must play her part or perish. Lily pressed three pots of sticky dye mixture into her hands. Dove could not hesitate, so she moved with feigned confidence forward until her outstretched hand met with His skin. He was standing near the lip of the balcony, facing Dove. She knew that from below the People could see some of His body but not all of it. Dead Eye had insisted that they address their People from atop the balcony ledge, where they could easily be seen from below. She had no idea why the God chose to hide part of Himself from the People. She didn't care. And Dove didn't allow confusion to slow her hands. The quicker she worked, the sooner she'd be able to stop touching Him. She scooped the muddy paint with her fingers and began slathering it on the God's enormous body. *He's grown so much bigger!* The thought helped her by giving the being before her yet another degree of separation from the man she had loved with all of her heart.

Dove worked quickly. The God had a deerskin cloak hanging from His wide shoulders, but except for that and breeches He was naked. Her hands felt the changes in His body. Dead Eye had been a big man—muscular and powerful—but in the short time the God had possessed him he had grown. His shoulders were wider. His muscles were thicker. He was undeniably taller. When she tried to reach around and spread the dye mixture across His back, Death waved away her hands, but not before she felt the deer pelt that had spread to cover His entire back.

"Just the front of my body, little bird."

Her hands did not tremble, though her spirit did. Dove concentrated on her duty, covering the God quickly and efficiently with the thick paint. He did not allow her to touch His hair, though she did paint His face, and as she did Dove felt that He had fashioned a hood for the cloak, which He kept pulled up over His head.

He hides the horns, she thought. And His hiding of them made her wonder how much they, too, had grown.

"It is finished, my Lord," she finally said, taking a small step away from Him.

"Excellent." Then He ignored her.

First, He spoke to the two men. "Mark me. These next moments will change our People for an eternity."

Dove heard Him whirl around, His cloak making the sound of a bird's wings. She imagined that He must be facing the People who were gathered below, gazing up at Him. She took another step back. Reaching with her hand, seeking, and finding Lily's wrist, Dove pulled the girl another step back with her and whispered, "Describe to me what I cannot see, but quietly so that we do not test His patience."

"Yes, Mistress," Lily said, pitching her voice low for Dove's ears alone. "Your Dead Eye is moving to the edge of the balcony."

Dove's grip on Lily's wrist tightened. "Do not *ever* call Him my Dead Eye again."

"Y-yes, Mistress. What shall I call him?" Lily whispered.

"*My Lord,* or whatever He commands. Just not Dead Eye. Never again my Dead Eye. What is He doing now?"

"He has leaped up on the lip of the balcony."

"My People, today is the first day of your new lives!" The God's voice was swollen with power. In the silence between His words, Dove could hear the susurrus of those gathered below as their attention turned upward to the man they had first called Dead Eye and then Champion.

"Is His head still covered?" Dove whispered.

"Yes, Mistress," Lily said quietly. Then, in a puzzled voice, she added, "Mistress, he is turning around, so that his back is to the people."

"*Behold your awakened God!*" Death spoke, and then a monstrous bellow filled the world around them, more powerful than a stag—more horrible than an army of men. His roar was that of a God, newly awakened after eons of slumber.

"Oh! Oh, Mistress! He has flung off his cloak and . . . and . . . *He is so very changed!*" Through their joined hands, Dove could feel Lily tremble, even though she gripped her Mistress's hand as a lifeline.

"I know, Lily. Speak quickly and quietly. Describe Him to me."

But as Lily's tremulous voice told her everything, Dove realized she already knew—her hands had already informed her mind of what the rest of the People were just now being called to witness.

She already knew what was under the cloak He'd thrown off. She heard the shocked murmurs rise from below as the People saw that the pelt of the stag had merged with the man.

As He bellowed His inhuman roar to the sky, Dove heard the People's murmurs change to gasps. She didn't need Lily to tell her that He had turned to face the watching crowd and revealed the horns growing from the thick fall of mane that had usurped what had once been her beloved's hair.

"Oh, Mistress! The People can see all of him now. His head—there are horns growing there! And . . . and his hair has changed as well. It is—It is—" Her words were broken by her frightened sob.

Dove squeezed her Attendant's hand. "S-s-sh, I know. Control yourself or you will draw His attention." Dove felt Lily's head nod in acknowledgment and her other hand lift to press against her mouth, stifling her terrified sobs.

And then, in a voice amplified by dark, divine forces, the Death God spoke.

"My People! Mark my words, for I shall not repeat them. You worshipped me in one form as the Reaper God, and you were so faithful, so true, that I awoke and claimed the body of my Champion! Now, witness my true form! I am the God of Death, risen from the realm of dreams to the mortal realm to lead you, my chosen People, from this vile, poisoned City to a new life, a new world, a new day! Which of you will be true? Which of you will swear your lives to me?"

There was a terrible, stretching silence. Dove knew she must hesitate no longer. Her will to survive propelled her forward on legs that were so numb she feared they would crumble beneath her. When she reached the lip of the balcony, she raised her arm up and up to touch Him.

In a strong, clear voice, Dove proclaimed, "I will be true, my Lord!" She bowed deeply, gracefully, to Him as the voices of the People below buzzed like frightened flies.

The God touched her chin, lifting Dove from her bow. She stood very still, her sightless face turned up to Him, her back straight and proud, her expression as open and as guileless as it had been when she had fabricated visions to placate the old Watchers who used to hold her life in their hands.

"Ah, faithful Dove. You please me, little bird. I give you my oath that when my Consort awakens within you, you will be able to see my glory through the eyes of a Goddess. Would that make you happy?"

"Yes, my Lord," she lied.

"In return I will be true to you throughout eternity." Instead of helping her up to the lip of the balcony to stand beside Him, as Dead Eye would have, the Death God turned His back to her, once more addressing the People. "Dove is the first to worship me. Who will be next?"

Dove was shoved out of the way as Iron Fist rushed to take her place. She stumbled and would have fallen had Lily not caught her elbow and righted her, pulling her to the side as the Reaper exclaimed, "I will worship and be true to You, my Lord! Always!"

"Iron Fist, I accept you and name you The Blade of the God. Henceforth, let the People know that The Blade speaks with his God's voice."

"Thank You, my Lord!"

Dove knew who moved to speak his oath next. She could smell the rot that followed poor Lizard's every breath.

"I will worship and be true to You, my Lord!" Lizard's voice cracked and was thick with pain, but his shout was loud and traveled easily to the courtyard and the watching People.

"Lizard, I accept you and assure you that soon you will be free of your suffering."

Dove gripped Lily's wrist painfully, whispering urgently, "Pledge yourself to Him. Now! Call for the other Attendants to follow your lead."

"But, Mistress, I—"

"*Do you want to live?*" Dove spoke quickly.

"Yes, Mistress."

"Then do it! *Now!*" Dove freed her Attendant with a small push.

"Come, Attendants! Let us swear ourselves to our God!" Lily said.

Dove heard the soft padding of the bare feet of her Attendants hurrying to follow Lily's lead. There was a rustling of their skirts, like fall leaves blown by winter wind, and Dove knew the Attendants were bowing before the God.

"Excellent! I happily accept the supplication of Dove's Attendants. Stay close to your Mistress, women, and prepare to welcome a Goddess to join her God!"

"Yes, my Lord," they intoned after Lily.

"And now, what of you? What of the rest of my People?" The God's voice blasted from the balcony as Lily hurried back to Dove's side.

"Motion for the rest of the Attendants to go inside the chamber." Dove spoke softly and urgently to Lily.

The girl didn't hesitate. Dove felt her make several small, fast gestures and then heard the sound of the Attendants' bare feet moving past them as they scurried back to the relative safety of the Chamber.

"I will worship You!"

"I will follow You!"

"I will fight for You!"

The shouts began to lift from the courtyard as Lily described to her Mistress what was happening below. "The men He made Reapers—they are all moving forward and falling to their knees to swear allegiance to Him."

"As will I!"

"And I!"

More shouts joined the voices of the Reapers. Dove tried to place each of them in her mind, but there were too many of them and their pledges devolved into a din of noise.

"Are all the People accepting Him?" she asked Lily.

"Not all, Mistress, but most. I can see a group of Hunters who are keeping to themselves and have not spoken."

"Enough!" At the roar of the God, all of the People fell silent. "I am pleased that so many of my People have chosen to remain faithful to their God."

One voice broke free from the silence below. It was strong and sure, and Dove recognized it at once as that of an old Hunter named Fist. "But your form is not that of our Reaper. The God we worship is a woman, and you, though powerful and obviously divine, are a man. So, my question is are you *our* God or simply *a* God?"

"That is easily answered. But first, tell me, are there others who would like to ask this question of me?"

A tremor of fear skittered through Dove's body. The God's voice seemed kind, as if He welcomed the question and would welcome more questions from the People. Dove knew better. She knew one surety beyond any other—Death would not abide being questioned.

"Yes, Champion," another man called from below. "I am River. Like Fist, I would ask this question."

"And I am Slayer. I would ask this question, too," said another man.

"Excellent! And I shall answer your question. Move forward, Fist, River, and Slayer, so that I may see to whom I speak."

Dove heard the crowd moving and murmuring.

"What is happening?" Dove asked Lily.

"The three Hunters have left the others and are standing before the central fire. The one over which the boar was roasted."

Dove bowed her head and waited.

"My answer is thus—*you were wrong*. This statue is not a God. It is dead metal. It matters not at all whether it is an image of a man or a woman, because *it was never a God*. I am Death and I am your God. Not because of this statue. Not for any reason except that I have chosen you as my own. And I thank you for giving me this opportunity to show my divine power to those of my People who are *truly* faithful."

Then there was a horrendous sound of screaming metal that was joined by the hysterical shouts of the People as Dove heard something heavy plummet to the courtyard below.

Lily gasped in horror, hiding her face in Dove's shoulder as she sobbed.

"What is it? What has happened?" Dove shook the girl, forcing her to answer.

"H-he tore the trident from the statue of the God and hurled it into the courtyard. He has killed Fist, River, and Slayer!"

"NEVER QUESTION DEATH!" the God thundered.

"Are the People fleeing?" Dove asked.

"No, Mistress. The People are falling to their knees and bowing to Him. . . ." Lily paused while she sobbed, finally managing to whisper, "What are we to do?"

"We are going to survive." She put her arm around her Attendant and let the girl weep into her shoulder as Dove's sharp, resourceful mind began to make plans. . . .

CHAPTER 22

The day dawned overcast and cool, with the taste of smoke heavy in the air and in Wilkes's throat as well. His eyes felt as if he'd rubbed sand in them, and as he stretched and unwrapped himself and Odin from the cocoon-like hammock he'd fashioned late the night before in the great boughs of an ancient pine left untouched by the fire, Wilkes heard his cough echoed around him by his brother Warriors.

"Wilkes! You up there?"

Wilkes glanced below to see Claudia with her Shepherd, Mariah, peering up into the boughs of the pine, face ashen and expression grim.

He cleared his throat painfully and steeled himself for bad news.

"I'm here. Give us a minute. Odin and I will be right down."

Claudia nodded and sat heavily beside her Shepherd, draping a slender, soot-smudged arm around the big canine as Wilkes quickly reworked his travel cloak into a sling, lowering Odin to the ground before he followed him more slowly, climbing down the broad tree trunk.

"Here, I brought this for you." Claudia handed Wilkes a wooden cup filled with hot, honey-laced tea.

Wilkes nodded gratefully, blew on it, and then took a big gulp, savoring how the herbs soothed his smoke-abused throat. Then he met Claudia's gaze. "Okay. Tell me."

"We found Ethan."

Wilkes's stomach clenched with dread. His mate had been missing since the day before. He hadn't made it to the Channel—Wilkes already knew that—but he'd hoped Ethan was one of the wounded who had lost their way in the smoke and fire and had begun straggling back to the Tribe since the blaze had been extinguished.

"Where is he? Is he hurt badly?"

Claudia stood and rested her hand on Wilkes's shoulder. "I'm sorry. Ethan's dead. We found him not far from where the Council was killed."

Wilkes bowed his head and let the grief wash over him. He and Ethan had been mated for a decade. Wilkes had liked to joke about how much Ethan nagged him, but the truth was that he counted on his partner to keep him grounded. And now—now Ethan was no more and Wilkes felt as if he'd lost his true north.

"What about Ginger? Was she with him?"

Claudia sighed sadly. "His Shepherd died with him. They were found together."

"Where are they? I want to see them."

Claudia's hand tightened on his shoulder. "No, my friend. You do not. Ethan and Ginger were placed with the Council, their canines, and those who died on the way to the Channel. Some of the Hunters are building a pyre for them. It should be done around sunset."

Wilkes wiped tears from his face with the back of his hand as Odin whined and pressed against his leg. "Did you see him?"

Claudia nodded wearily. "I did."

"Do you think he suffered?"

"It happened fast and he wasn't alone. Ginger was wrapped in his arms, and there were several other people beside them as well. Let that be a comfort to you," she said.

Wilkes nodded sadly and dropped his hand to rest on his Shepherd's head, finding comfort in his Companion's nearness. *I can't think about Ethan and Ginger right now. I can't mourn yet. There is too much to do—too many lives that might still be saved.* He cleared his throat again and lifted his head.

"Were any Healers found alive?"

"No. Emma and Liam are the two apprenticed Healers Kathleen sent from the infirmary before the blaze destroyed it and everyone in it. A third trainee, Olivia, did find her way to the meditation platform late last night, but she almost didn't make it through the fire and said the other three apprentices who were following her weren't as lucky."

"So, we have three half-trained Healers. Okay. Well, that's better than none, but we're going to have to get them some help." He cupped his hands around his mouth and shouted up into the boughs of the nearest trees, "Warriors! To me!" Instantly the tree limbs began to sway with the weight of humans and canines awakening from much-needed sleep. "Wait here for the Warriors to get themselves awake, and then bring them to the meditation platform. Have you seen Latrell? I need him to gather his Hunters, too."

"Latrell is dead. Thaddeus has taken on the role of Lead Hunter." Claudia's frown clearly said what she thought of the change of Hunter leadership.

Wilkes ran a hand through his matted hair. "That news could be better."

"Yeah, well, none of the Hunters challenged him. Not that I blame them. He's mean. Almost as mean as that Terrier of his."

"I thought after Odysseus was wounded Thaddeus might focus on his Companion," Wilkes said.

"That's a nice thought, but the wound seems to only have slowed Odysseus down—not Thaddeus," Claudia said.

"Hopefully, when we ordain a new Council they'll appoint someone more appropriate as Lead Hunter." Wilkes shook his head, muttering, "I blame Thaddeus for this mess."

"That bastard! Just the thought of him pisses me off. I don't understand why he's still free, let alone Lead Hunter. I can't stand that he's walking around like he didn't cause—"

Wilkes made an abrupt motion. "Never mind. That was self-indulgent of me. There's no time for blame or what-ifs right now. I'm heading to the platform."

Claudia shook herself. "You're right. Thaddeus can wait. I'll follow you with the Warriors."

Wilkes tried to smile his thanks, but his face felt cracked and broken. At that moment he wondered if he would ever smile again. So he simply nodded and began picking his way through the underbrush that peppered the forest floor around the old pines that were too ancient to hold the Tribe's nests but still sturdy enough not to have been culled for wood and reseeded.

This was the part of the forest closest to Port City, and it had always seemed haunted to Wilkes. When their ancestors first found that they could survive with the help of the Mother Plant by living in the trees, it must have seemed logical to built their new city just outside the old one, but as generation after generation passed, the Tribe had chosen to expand away from the ruined city, moving farther to the north and west. The meditation platform had been the last of the usable relics, and the Tribe rarely went past that old sentinel. Wilkes looked uneasily around him, feeling as if the ghost of those first Tribesmen were watching him . . . judging him.

As the Tribe grew and the trees aged, they shifted the heart of the city into stronger trees that were just reaching their maturity, so the enormous old pines around him stood silent, abandoned, with remnants of nests and lift systems that had been cannibalized for anything of value to the ever-expanding Tribe.

Well, we used to be ever expanding, Wilkes thought morosely. *Now we're just trying to survive.*

His feet felt heavy and he made himself finish the strong tea, hoping the honey it was laced with would give him a boost of energy. His stomach growled, surprising him. He'd been too busy to think about food before he and the Warriors who had taken the late shift with him had finally wrapped themselves in their cloaks and managed to steal a few hours of sleep. Odin whined and Wilkes patted his head.

"Okay, I hear you. We'll eat soon." Which reminded Wilkes to check and see if any of the rabbit warrens had survived. *Damn, I hope so. Don't know how we're going to feed hungry canines with no rabbits.* Wilkes's shoulders slumped. There was just so much to deal with in the aftermath of the blaze. *Sunfire!* How he wished Sol were alive—or, at the very least, he wished Nik and his Healer had stayed. Nik's presence would have given the Tribe a sense of safety, especially as Laru had chosen him. And Mari? Wilkes didn't give a damn what idiots like Thaddeus thought—the girl was a gifted Healer who could wield sunfire. She belonged with the Tribe!

"He'll be back," Wilkes told Odin. "And this time I'll do a better job about convincing him to stay."

Wilkes trudged his way through the forest to the temporary infirmary they'd established on the meditation platform that served as border between the old, uninhabited section of the forest and the outskirts of what was left of their City in the Trees. He heard the sounds of the wounded before he got to the clearing that surrounded the old tree. He tried to prepare himself, but as he stepped from the forest and he took in the sight of the wounded lying in a wheel-like arrangement around the tree, spreading into the clearing and beyond, Wilkes knew nothing could have prepared him for the reality of the losses his Tribe had suffered.

Warriors and Hunters who were finishing their early shifts were staggering from the direction of their still-smoldering city. Wilkes knew they'd been combing the wreckage of the huge, blackened pines and the rubble of graceful nests and platforms that had, for generations, sheltered the Tribe of the Trees, looking for survivors and putting out any hot spots that might begin the blaze anew. One glance at them and he knew they had not found survivors.

"Here. Eat this. You look awful." Wilkes blinked and refocused as Ralina, the Tribe's Storyteller who seemed to have taken up permanent residence with the wounded, pressed into his hand a wooden bowl filled with porridge, almond milk, and more honey.

"Thank you," his scratchy voice said. "I need to feed Odin, too."

Ralina nodded. "The Carpenters built a temporary platform in that gnarled old oak about twenty yards over there." She pointed toward the far side of the meditation platform. "Two of the rabbit warrens survived. We're rationing food for the canines from there."

"Only two warrens left?" Wilkes shook his head. There had been twelve major warrens where rabbits were bred and then distributed to the Tribe for food and pelts.

"Only two," Ralina said. "And that was a close thing. But the Hunters are already setting traps for more breeder rabbits. Maybe they'll manage to bring back a deer, or even a boar." The Storyteller looked up at Wilkes, and he could see a world of misery in her eyes.

"I'm sorry. Two warrens are a lot better than none. And the rabbits can be replaced. Easily. How about you take a seat with me on that log and fill me in on everything else?"

"Okay. Yes." Ralina began to walk with him the short distance to a singed log, but she staggered and almost fell.

Wilkes helped right her and kept a tight hold of her arm, easing her into sitting beside him. He noticed how pale she was and the terrible dark shadows under her eyes.

"Did you sleep at all?"

She shook her head.

"You have to," Wilkes told her gently.

"I tried, but when I closed my eyes I saw nothing but fire and death. I—I don't know if I'll ever sleep again." Her head bowed and her shoulders shook as she cried silently.

Wilkes put his arm around her. "Hey, we'll get through this. Think about The Tale of Endings and Beginnings. Worse has happened to our ancestors and they survived and thrived. We will, too."

"More than anything else I hope you're right about that." Ralina wiped her face with her sleeve as her Shepherd, Bear, padded up to her, whining his concern.

"It's okay, Bear. I'm okay," she murmured as he licked her face and she slipped from the log to sit on the ground beside him. It wasn't long before she crossed her legs and leaned back, looking up at Wilkes. "I'm better now. What is it you need to know?"

"How are the Mother Plants?"

"They're being tended. It's too early to be sure, but Maeve says most will live. She transplanted them into the branches above the meditation platform, though they will soon need to be permanently planted in a new cluster of Mother Trees."

Wilkes closed his eyes briefly in relief. "Maeve made it. How about her new pup? Fortina, right? Is she fine, too?"

"Both are well. And all of her assistants live, too. As soon as the fire broke out, Maeve ordered the Mother Plants moved."

"That was wise of her." He shoveled a couple more bites of porridge into his mouth, asking around it, "Do we have a death count yet?"

"We have an estimate. The count is almost two thousand Companions lost, but it's probably low."

"Sunfire! *More than two thousand* dead! But that's almost half of the Tribe."

Ralina nodded. "There are another five hundred plus wounded. Many of them will die, too. And that doesn't take into account how many of us will perish later from the blight."

The Storyteller looked down at her arms, and Wilkes followed her gaze. Her forearms were riddled with scratches he hadn't noticed before through the sweat and soot that pretty much covered all of them, but now he saw the bloody wounds and he felt a terrible hollowness in his stomach that he knew no amount of porridge would ever fill. Her wounds were minor, but blight could infect any break in the skin, with a survival rate of less than five out of ten. He took quick stock of his own body. He was bruised and sore, though he didn't think his skin had been broken anywhere. *But Ralina's right. How many of us who look healthy right now, who think they've come through this terrible fire safely, will die slowly of the blight because of scratches and cuts?*

"Hey, we will get through this. One day at a time," Wilkes said. "Someday you'll be telling this tale to our rebuilt Tribe with a new generation of youngsters all big eyed over the story while we oldsters cheer and drink too much winter beer."

Ralina was almost smiling when from the ancient, uninhabited forest behind them came the sounds of boisterous Tribesmen approaching. Wilkes thought he might be hearing things—that he might have been driven mad by death and the stress of the past days—because *why would anyone be laughing and joking at a time like this?*

Thaddeus and a small group of his Hunters burst through the underbrush. They were carrying big leather satchels—the kind used to strap supplies on Shepherds' backs if they were on long forage trips with their Companions. And the Hunters were laughing and joking with one another.

The Hunters were laughing and joking with one another.

With Ralina beside him, Wilkes stood and turned slowly to meet the group, trying to keep a hold on his rising temper.

"Wilkes! Ha! There you are. Wait till you see what we found— medical supplies! A lot of them. Can you believe our luck?" Thaddeus said, tossing one of the satchels to Wilkes, who caught it, glanced at its contents, and handed it to a gray-faced Ralina.

"Bandages and salves," Ralina said.

"Yeah! And there's more in the rest of the satchels, as well as a fairly large amount of herbs and tinctures. See? Lucky find! Right, Story-teller? This would make a great tale, don't you think?" Thaddeus's men nodded with their Leader, but Wilkes noticed none of them were as animated as him.

"I'm not sure," Ralina said, her voice hard and flat. "Great tales need heroism and heart."

"Perfect! We have plenty of that!" Thaddeus spoke as if he were on-stage, putting on a show for his men.

Ralina didn't answer but turned her face from him in disgust.

"Of course there are a few supplies missing. I used them to pack Odysseus's wound. He'll be good as new soon! Won't you, boy?" He bent to pat the little Terrier on the head, but the canine wasn't by his side— which Thaddeus seemed to just notice. He stood and whistled sharply.

A yip came from the trees behind the group of Hunters. "Odysseus! Come on! Hurry up!"

Wilkes watched the little Terrier limp into the clearing. He went to his Companion and collapsed by Thaddeus's feet.

"Have you had one of the apprentice Healers check out Odysseus's wound?" Ralina asked. "His limp looks pretty bad."

"Ah, he'll be fine—especially after I doctored him with those medicines."

"Where did you find them? I thought the infirmary burned," Wilkes said.

"It did! But the Healers loaded as much as they could onto their Shepherds, and then sent them out of the infirmary. We found them not far from here."

Wilkes looked behind the group but saw nothing. He glanced at Odin and Bear, who weren't giving any sign that there were Shepherds to greet. Feeling sick, he met Thaddeus's gaze. "Where are the Shepherds now?"

"Back there where we found them. I was going to drop off the supplies at the meditation platform and then find you to see what you wanted to do about them," Thaddeus said.

"But I don't understand. Why didn't they come with you?" Ralina asked.

"Because they are all dead," Wilkes said.

Thaddeus nodded. "Yeah, you guessed it. Strangest thing I've ever seen. The Shepherds were curled up together. Thought they were sleeping at first. But they were already stiff. Been dead since last night, but they weren't burned, and I didn't see any wounds on them, either."

Wilkes forced himself to control his anger. Slowly, he stepped over the log and approached Thaddeus. Wilkes could feel Odin by his side. He could also feel the rage that burned within his Companion, mirroring his own. He stopped a hand span from the Hunter. Wilkes noticed that even before he spoke the other Hunters had moved back and were watching him warily.

"How *dare* you come here laughing and joking. Those Shepherds—those heroes—willed themselves to die because they couldn't bear the horror of the deaths of their Companions. *They felt their Companions suffer and burn!* Can you even imagine the agony of that? And still they brought medicine to us—still they thought of the Tribe, even in the immensity of their grief and pain. What is wrong with you, Thaddeus?" Wilkes said.

"What's wrong with all of you?" Ralina's red-eyed glare took in the group of the Hunters as she hurled words at the men. "*They* are the heroes! Not you! Their sacrifice is the stuff of legends and bittersweet tales, *and you came here laughing and joking after discovering their bodies!*" The Hunters behind Thaddeus looked away, unable to meet Ralina's gaze.

Thaddeus had no such problem. "We found medicine! Things that will *help* our Tribe. That's what we were celebrating. I didn't realize we needed to check with the Tribe's Storyteller or the Leader of the Warriors first!" Thaddeus puffed up his chest and balled his fists by his sides.

Wilkes stared at him in disgust. "You don't get it at all, do you? Sunfire! You were truly not affected by the deaths of those canines."

"They're *dead*. Nothing can bring them back. I choose to focus on the living. So do my Hunters."

"This isn't the way of the Tribe. This is *your* way, Thaddeus," Ralina said.

"And your way is disgusting," Wilkes added.

"It's a new time, Warrior. Get used to it," Thaddeus said with a sneer.

He started to brush past Wilkes, bumping him hard with his shoulder, obviously trying to throw him off balance. In his hand a knife suddenly appeared, and he brandished it at Wilkes.

Ralina cried, "He has a blade!"

Wilkes moved with the instincts of a well-trained Warrior. In an instant he had Thaddeus's arm bent behind his back, twisting it until the knife fell harmlessly to the ground. Then, with one quick kick, he knocked the Hunter's legs out from under him, sending him to sprawl, face-first, on the forest floor.

Odysseus snarled, and as the Hunters gasped in shock the little Terrier launched himself at Wilkes. In a movement so swift that his body blurred, Odin intercepted the canine, knocking him over, rolling him, and then pinning him to the ground, his huge jaws open and ready to rip out the Terrier's exposed underbelly.

"Submit!" Wilkes's abused voice growled along with his Shepherd. "Or I will let Odin kill him."

Wilkes watched Thaddeus's anger-filled gaze flick to his downed Terrier, and for a moment he actually thought the Hunter would refuse and cause his Companion's death—and as Wilkes realized that, he finally understood just how dangerous Thaddeus had become and how very badly he needed to be banished from the Tribe.

"Submit!" Wilkes repeated.

"Do it," Thaddeus told his Terrier. "Submit to him."

Odysseus struggled for a moment longer, and then the Terrier's body relaxed and he stretched his neck back, ritualistically offering it to a canine who was Alpha over him. Odin sniffed at the littler canine's neck and then the big Shepherd lifted his leg and relieved himself on the Terrier's belly before allowing him to get up.

Ralina went to Thaddeus's dropped knife and picked it up, tucking it into her leather belt. She gave the Hunter a disgusted look, saying, "This blade is forfeit because you raised it against a Tribesman. Consider yourself lucky that we have no ruling Council right now, as you would surely be banished, or worse, for what you just tried to do."

Wilkes released Thaddeus. "You may still be banished. Tribal Law is Tribal Law, whether there is a Council or not. No Companion may take up arms against another—on pain of banishment or death. Consider yourself lucky if all you get is banishment. I'm the third Tribesman you've raised a weapon against."

Thaddeus wiped dirt and moss from his clothes as he glared at Wilkes. "Don't be so sure of yourself. In case you're too bound by the past to notice, let me be the first to tell you—*the old Tribe is no more!* I have a feeling things are going to be a lot different in the future—the very near future. Watch yourself, Warrior. You're right. I did raise my weapon against other Tribesmen—traitors—you would do well to remember how that went for them. *One is dead. One is on the run.*" Thaddeus made a sharp gesture to his men. "Let's get these supplies to the wounded. Maybe they'll appreciate them." He turned his back on Wilkes and Ralina and stalked away, with Odysseus limping at his side and the Hunters following as they cast looks that ranged from apologetic to angry at Wilkes.

"That's bad. Really bad," Ralina said when the forest had swallowed the group. "There's something incredibly wrong with that man. And I've never liked Odysseus—he's always been too quick with his teeth—but Thaddeus doesn't seem concerned at all that his Companion is wounded."

"By his own hand," Wilkes said. "But Thaddeus isn't one for taking blame or cleaning up after his mistakes—ever."

"Exactly. . . ." She paused and then added, "He was talking about Sol and Nik, wasn't he? Tell me that bastard didn't just brag about killing our Sun Priest and chasing away his son."

"That's exactly what he was doing." Wilkes stared after the Hunters. "And I think it's even worse than that. I think Thaddeus's hatred has begun to spread to his men."

"And from there, it could easily spread to the Tribe," Ralina finished for Wilkes. "We can't let that happen."

"I'm afraid it already has," Wilkes said. "Come on. Let's gather the Warriors and see what we can do to help the wounded. They're more important than Thaddeus's hate right now. Let's hope if we ignore him Thaddeus will fade into the background of the Tribe."

"I can't believe Companions will actually follow him. He's mean, self-serving, and full of spite. Our people will see the truth about him."

"I hope so, Ralina," Wilkes said sadly.

Slowly, the two Companions began walking back to the meditation platform. Neither of them saw the two men, bodies painted with the camouflaging colors of the forest, rise from the concealment of a mound of forest debris and retreat silently back into the cover of the ancient trees.

Death could hardly contain His glee. It was happening just as He had intended! He tapped into Dead Eye's memories and knew the Tribesman the Others called Thaddeus was the human who had been infected with the skin sloughing disease. Since canine flesh had merged with the human, Thaddeus had obviously grown stronger, angrier, and more discontented. It seemed he was even responsible for the death of a Leader and for the blaze that had decimated his people. And now that the Hunter's Companion canine was wounded Death chuckled low in His throat.

"It is all going even better than I planned," He said, more to Himself than to Iron Fist, who jogged beside Him.

"How so, my Lord?"

"I have divided the Others, and that division is going to be their undoing." The God paused and chuckled again. "Well, that and a little help from Death."

"Are we going to gather our men and attack now that they're weak and wounded?"

Death held on to His patience, reminding Himself that Iron Fist was only a man, and not a very bright man at that. "No. We are not. You are my Blade. You must learn to think beyond your base emotions. Did you not hear the Warrior recount how many of the Others are dead?"

"I surely did, my Lord! Over two thousand. That is why I thought—"

"No!" The curt word silenced the God's Blade instantly. "Did you not hear the rest of it?"

"That there are another five hundred wounded?"

Death stifled a sigh. "Yes, but beyond that the Warrior let it be known that there are still another two thousand of their people alive, many of them Warriors and Hunters. They vastly outnumber us."

"Oh. Oh, I see. Then what are we to do?"

"We?" Death laughed again. "First, *I* am going to use the opening that little canine has provided and use it to draw Thaddeus closer to me."

"My Lord, forgive me, but I do not understand," Iron Fist said.

Because He enjoyed reasoning through His plan aloud, Death decided to enlighten His Blade. "It's quite simple. I've already touched Thaddeus. He is primed to hear my voice. Imagine if he chooses me—even over his bonded Companion. Imagine the chaos he would cause within his Tribe."

"You're going to ask him to join us? To become a Reaper?"

"Not so blatantly, but yes," Death said. "I am going to present him with a choice."

"Do you want me to follow him? Perhaps take him captive again—with his canine—and bring him to You, my Lord?" Iron Fist asked.

"No, I have a better way to reach Thaddeus. His wounded Terrier has provided it for me."

"I still don't understand."

Death blew out a long breath, wishing He had someone to talk with who wasn't a complete dolt. "The creature—the canine—he is wounded. Badly enough that he is susceptible to my touch, even from a distance. And if he is susceptible to me, so his Companion will be. Watch and learn, my Blade. There is much for us to do."

"Give me a task, my Lord! What would You have me do?"

"The next task is not yours. Lizard, though, is going to do *every-thing*."

The God was pleased that Iron Fist asked no further questions, and He increased his speed so that the man would have to strain to keep up with Him. It wasn't long before they came to the place they had left Lizard, hidden far enough from the Tribe that their sharp-nosed canines wouldn't alert on the scent of rot that clung to the diseased man.

"My Lord!" Lizard went to his knees as the God and His Blade approached. "How is it with the Others?"

"It is even better than I hoped. The Tribe of the Trees is very close to self-destructing," said the God. "All they need is a small gift from

Death to complete the process." He walked to the sick man and gently lifted him to his feet. "I need you to do something for me, Lizard."

"Anything, my Lord!" he said without hesitation.

"Anything, even if it is unpleasant?" Death asked.

"Yes, my Lord."

The God rested His hands on the man's shoulders. "Your fidelity pleases me greatly, Lizard." Death turned to Iron Fist and commanded his Blade, "Go. Find evidence of hog scat. We weren't far from here the day the boar crossed the stream. There must be others about. I will wait here with Lizard."

Iron Fist looked surprised but bowed and sprinted off.

"Come, sit." The God gestured beside Him. "This shouldn't take long. The fire has caused the beasts of the forest to be out of sorts."

"And Iron Fist is our best Hunter," Lizard said. With a groan he sat beside the God.

Death studied him. "Is your pain great?"

"It is nothing for You to be concerned about, my Lord," Lizard said quickly.

"And yet I am. Answer my question truthfully."

Lizard's gaze fell to the forest floor. "My pain is great."

"Are you weary of it?"

His eyes found the God. "I am."

"Ah, I can see that. Your suffering will soon be over."

Lizard's pale face lit with hope. "Thank You, my Lord!"

"Rest now. You will need all of your strength for what is to come."

Lizard did as the God commanded. He closed his eyes and slumped to his side, sighing wearily. As he fell into a fitful sleep, Death dismissed him from His thoughts. Instead, He meditated, entering a dreamlike state, searching . . . searching . . .

With little effort, the God found the bitter connection that linked Him to the small, wounded Terrier named Odysseus. He followed the thin thread of pain, feeling with the immortal sixth sense that had connected Him to humanity and the mortal world for countless ages.

The God could not see the creature. He could only feel Odysseus—his pain, his stress, and the heat that was building in his little body as it tried to fight off infection.

Hear me, small one, Death whispered to the wounded canine.

The canine's attention shifted inward as the Terrier suddenly found the thread that connected him with Death.

Yes! That's it! Hear me, small one. Open to me! Your wound has made us close! Now, let us grow even closer. . . .

Death could feel the canine's consciousness retreating fearfully from Him, fleeing to Thaddeus as he sought comfort from his Companion.

And that was when Death struck.

The God followed the canine's deep and mystical connection with his Companion directly to Thaddeus's mind. Once there, Death carefully, gently, probed—and was instantly rewarded by the knowledge that this mortal's mind hungered for one thing beyond all else: power. Which meant Thaddeus was ripe for Harvest.

You can have more, Death whispered to the Hunter. *You deserve more. All you need is power. . . .*

"We need more power!" Thaddeus's sharp voice echoed back to the God as Death listened to Thaddeus lecture the men gathered around him. *"If we're going to build the Tribe back to what it used to be, we need more power."*

"What kind of power do you mean, Thaddeus?" a man asked.

"Leadership! The only kind of power that counts," Thaddeus said.

"That's already happened," said another man. *"You're the Leader of us, your Hunters, now."*

"I'm not talking about just being Lead Hunter," Thaddeus said. *"I'm talking about Leading the Tribe."*

"Sounds good, but it'll never happen," said the first man. *"Not as long as our Companions are Terriers and not Shepherds."*

Death felt the surge of anger that flooded Thaddeus. *Yes, you should be angry,* the God prodded. *Embrace it! Accept it! Use it! And don't let them tell you what you can't do.*

"*Stop telling me what I can't do!*" Thaddeus's anger exploded around him.

Into an uncomfortable silence, another Hunter spoke up.

"Uh, Thaddeus, I heard that some of the people are saying we need to do what that Scratcher girl said—swear that we won't take captives anymore and grant her safe passage so that she can heal our wounded."

"That bitch is the reason the fire started and the reason Odysseus is wounded. If she comes back here it should be at the end of a rope." Thaddeus spit the words at them.

Yes, Death murmured.

"But she can wield sunfire. How do we force her to do anything?"

You can force her if you have more power, Death whispered.

"Let me figure that out—that's what a leader does," Thaddeus said.

That's right, Death said. *All you need is more power.*

"She may have called down sunfire, but she's a Scratcher. And a woman. I'll take care of that bitch."

Yes! Death goaded. *Yes-s-s-s-s-s. . . .*

The God quickly became bored as Thaddeus continued to bluster and pontificate, and His attention shifted, turning inward. Searching . . . searching . . . searching . . .

Always searching for his sleeping Consort.

He found her so swiftly that it surprised Him. She was there, just at the edge of His consciousness. The Great Earth Mother, giver of Life, His eternal lover, reclined on her side in the center of a moss-carpeted grove. Her naked skin was the color of moonlight. Her dark hair was a glistening river of silk that poured past her smooth shoulders to wash around her waist. Her breasts were full and perfect. Her eyes were closed in sleep, and her lips curved up, as if he'd caught her in the middle of a sweet dream.

My Consort! How I have missed you! Death said.

Ah, my love. I hear Your voice outside my mind, but cannot find You in my dreams. You no longer sleep?

No! I have taken a warrior's body and, my Consort, I have found a body fit for you, as well. Soon I will ask you to awaken, to join me in the flesh so that we may rule the world of mortals side by side and be worshipped as we were worshipped too, too long ago!

The sleeping Goddess's full, beautiful lips lost their smiling curve and her brow furrowed in distress.

My love, that cannot be. Do you not remember what happened when last You awakened? The world burned and was almost destroyed by Death.

But that was only because you refused to wake as well. With Life by my side, it will be much different.

No, my love, no. Death and Life cannot exist together except in our dreams. You know this—we know this. The sleeping Goddess stirred and languidly opened her arms. *Leave the warrior's body. Sleep again where we can forever be entwined.*

Death reacted instinctively to Life's invitation. He craved her—He would eternally crave her. She was everything He wasn't. He had to have her. He had to possess her!

He reached for her, but His movement broke His trance and He shouted in grief and frustration as the lush Goddess faded into mist and He was jolted to consciousness.

"My Lord! I found sign of hog—"

Death moved quicker than the human eye could follow. His massive hand closed around Iron Fist's throat and He lifted the man from the ground.

"Never wake me!"

Iron Fist sputtered and tried to speak, but his eyes rolled to show white and his body went limp. Disgusted at human weakness, Death dropped him, growling, "You are my Blade. You do not have permission to die!"

Iron Fist's heart began to beat again. He gulped air and coughed, rubbing his throat with a trembling hand. "F-forgive me, my Lord," he rasped.

"You are forgiven. Rise and report."

Iron Fist staggered to his feet, gasping. "I-I found hogs. As You said, n-near the stream where You killed the boar."

"Excellent! Lizard, your time is here."

The sick man rolled over and then sat, looking blankly around as if he wasn't sure where he was. Then his eyes found the God and he struggled to his feet.

"I am ready, my Lord."

"Iron Fist, take us to the hogs. Remember to stay downwind. They must not scent Lizard."

It didn't take the three of them long to find the hog wallow. It was indeed close to the crossing point in the stream where Dead Eye had killed the enormous boar just the day before. There was a run-off area near a dam of flotsam that had created a muddy pool surrounded by dense brush. As they crept close, they could hear grunting and a few muffled squeals. The God went to His hands and knees, crawling the last few feet with the two men beside Him doing the same.

The God gazed through the brush to see one large red sow wallowing happily in the mud with two piglets at her side. He turned to Lizard and spoke fast and low. "She is exactly what we need. Stay here, but when I call for you, you must come to me with no hesitation. Stand behind me wherever I am—whatever is happening. Can you do that?"

"Yes, my Lord." Lizard's eyes were shining brightly with equal parts fever and excitement. "I cannot wait to be healed by the flesh of the beast, just as You healed my brothers."

The God said nothing to Lizard. Instead, He commanded Iron Fist, "You remain here. No matter what—do not come to the wallow."

"I understand, my Lord."

The God began to crawl, moving with speed and stealth that shouldn't have been possible for such a large man. Soon He was within arm's distance of the wallow. There He paused, waiting in absolute stillness until the piglets wandered close to Him.

Death erupted from the ground, surging forward so quickly that He had no trouble snatching up each piglet. They squealed their terror as He held them aloft by their hind legs.

"Come to me, Lizard!" the God bellowed as the sow turned her massive head toward Him, roaring in anger.

Lizard did not hesitate. The diseased man ran toward his God as if his life depended on it, coming to a halt behind Death as he had been ordered.

The God dangled the piglets, swinging them around in front of Him, causing them to squeal deafeningly.

The sow responded immediately. She bared her teeth, lowered her head, and charged the God, but just before she reached Him Death lunged to the side.

Lizard, too sick—too *human*—to move with the God's speed, could do nothing but scream as the sow rammed him. He fell backward, exposing his belly to the ferocious beast, who began shredding his stomach. His entrails spilled like fat, pink serpents from his body as he screamed over and over and over until the God cried *"Enough!"* and the sow's body was lifted from behind and tossed to the other side of the wallow, where she got slowly to her feet, shaking her massive head, preparing to charge again.

"My Lord! Save me!" Lizard cried.

Death tossed the piglets into the brush behind Him. "Iron Fist! Do not let them get away!" Then He bent and took the Lizard's face between His hands. "Know that you have helped save your People."

"But I want to live!" he gurgled through bloody froth that spewed from his lips.

"Ah, but Death has called you. I honor and accept your sacrifice, your strength, your spirit." The God kissed Lizard's forehead softly. "Behold Death's merciful blow!" In one motion the God twisted Lizard's head, cleanly breaking his neck.

Then the God faced the charging sow, shaking out the rope He'd carried wrapped around His waist. She didn't seem to notice He no longer held her babies. Her eyes were completely red with rage, just as her muzzle and teeth were red with Lizard's diseased blood. She came at the God. Again He sidestepped easily, this time throwing a noose around her head, jerking it tight, and pulling the huge creature off her feet. Placing His knee on her neck, He pinned her to the mud, staring into her eyes.

Death smiled.

"I see myself already within you. The rest will happen quickly. I am sorry for your suffering but know it is not without reason." He raised his voice, calling into the thicket above the squeals of the terrified piglets, "Do you have them, Iron Fist?"

"I do, my Lord!" Iron Fist stood, holding the struggling, squealing piglets tightly.

"Come closer, but only near enough for the sow to see that you have her young."

Iron Fist obeyed. The God turned the sow's head, lifting it so that she could see her screaming babies.

"When I release her, run toward the City in the Trees—lead the sow to the Others!"

Understanding flashed through Iron Fist's eyes. "I will, my Lord."

"Now!" the God shouted as He freed the sow. She surged to her feet. Roaring with rage, she ignored Death. Choosing her young instead of revenge, she charged after Iron Fist, who sprinted away.

Back as they had come.

Back to the hungry, wounded, waiting Tribe of the Trees.

Content, Death stepped over Lizard's body, leaving it to sink into the blood and the mud as He went to the stream, washing Himself while he anticipated the return of Iron Fist and the beginning of His People's new future.

"Four days," He said to Himself. "In four days the disease will have fully infested the Others. Thaddeus will be completely mine. Then will be time to strike. Then I will lead the People from the ruins of the poisoned City and into the trees. And *then* I will awaken my Consort, who will rule beside me for eternity, whether She desires to be awakened or not!"

CHAPTER 23

Mari woke slowly. She had no idea how long she'd slept, but by the cocoon imprint she'd made in her side of the pallet it was obvious she hadn't moved all night.

My side of the pallet . . .

Mari's eyelids went from heavy and sleepy to wide open as she turned her head, expecting to see Nik beside her. Sifting back through her dreams, she thought that he'd cradled her all night in his arms. Laru had been at the foot of the bed, and Rigel had been snuggled close on her other side. Surrounded by love, she'd slept better than she had since her mama's death.

But now she was alone.

Mari sat, rubbing her eyes and trying to tame her wild hair with her fingers.

"Rigel?" she called softly, and just before he came galloping through the woven curtain that separated the main room of the burrow from her sleeping chamber and the well-stocked pantry that stretched behind it, Mari was pretty sure she caught the scent of rabbit stew.

The young Shepherd bounded up on the pallet, grinning his tongue-lolling, puppyish smile and covering her face in licks.

"Okay! Okay! I see you. Good morning to you, too." Mari laughed and hugged the half-grown canine, kissing his muzzle and trying to avoid as much of his slobber as possible.

Laru stuck his head through the curtain and gave a soft *woof* of greeting.

"Hello, handsome!" Mari opened her arms in invitation. The big canine didn't need to be asked twice. Two jumps and he'd joined his son on her pallet, licking her as the Shepherds wagged their tails and wriggled like they were both still puppies.

"I see I have competition."

Three sets of eyes turned to the doorway where Nik was standing with a cup of steaming tea in his hand, grinning at the knot of canines and Moon Woman.

"Good morning," Mari said, trying again to smooth back her hair as she wiped the Shepherd kisses from her cheeks.

"Good morning! I'm glad you're finally awake." Nik came to the bed, offering the mug of tea to Mari. "It was getting tough to keep Rigel from sitting by your pallet and whining like an anxious pup."

"Thank you for the tea and for not letting Rigel wake me." Mari took the tea and loved the way Nik bent and kissed her softly before he sat beside her.

"You taste like Shepherd slobber," he said.

"Is that a good or bad thing?"

"It's my favorite. How are you feeling?"

"Really, really hungry. Ravenous, actually. Is that normal? How long have I been asleep? Oh, Goddess! Don't tell me it's been days! Sora is going to kill me. Literally. Or do you have her bound and gagged in the other room? Not that that's a particularly bad idea sometimes." She finally paused to take a breath and sip the tea, peering up at him over the rim of the ornately carved wooden cup.

"Okay, I'll answer in order. Yes, it's normal to be starving after calling down sunfire. It's normal to feel the effects for a few days yet. Just eat and drink more than you normally would—and sleep—and you'll be fine. You only slept one night, but it is past midday. I don't have Sora bound or gagged in the next room, but now that I know you're not opposed to the idea I'll consider it next time she drives either of us too crazy."

"Past midday!" She swung her legs around, meaning to get out of bed quickly, but then she noticed how very bare they were and how almost naked—except for a thin sleep shirt—she was, and she paused, feeling her cheeks warm.

Nik gave her a long, intimate look. "Don't be embarrassed about showing me your bare legs. They're very beautiful. And did you know you like to sleep with them tangled up with mine?"

"No, I was asleep, so I couldn't know it. Are you making that up?"

"Absolutely not. Ask Rigel."

Mari glanced at her Companion, who gave her an openmouthed canine grin, tongue lolling. "I don't have to. I see the answer in his face. Um, I'm sorry?"

"Sorry about wrapping me in your beautiful leg blanket? Don't ever be sorry about that." He leaned in and kissed her cheek, somehow making an innocent gesture feel intimate, even exciting, as his lingering lips promised more to come. Then he stood. "But I will let you get dressed in peace. You are *dressing*, right? And not considering *undressing* and letting me shoo the Shepherds into the other room?" His moss-colored eyes glinted mischievously.

"I'd like to consider it, but if I'm gone too much longer Sora is going to march through the door with a mixed group of Earth Walkers and Companions in her wake, and that would be . . ." She trailed off trying to find the right word.

"A definite turnoff?" Nik offered.

"Yep. A *definite* turnoff. Um, and is that stew I smell?"

Nik chuckled. "It is, and far be it from me to stand in the way of a Sun Priestess and her breakfast."

Mari's brow furrowed. "I'm not a Sun Priestess. I don't even know what that is."

"Then how do you know you're not one?"

"Because I don't even know what it is?"

"You're answering my question with a question. You definitely need food. I'll ladle up a big bowl of stew for you. Do you want bread and honey, too?"

"I want a whole loaf, please. And an entire comb of honey. I mean it. I'm going to eat a lot."

Nik stopped at the curtain and then turned to look back at her. "I'm not surprised, and I already have the loaf sliced. Oh, and a Sun Priestess is a revered member of the Tribe who has been chosen by a Shepherd as Companion and has the ability to call down sunfire—which tends to make said priestess ravenous. The Tribe hasn't had one for generations, though the appearance of one is considered magickal and auspicious for the future. Laru, Rigel, with me! Let Mari get dressed in peace." The canines bounded after him, leaving Mari alone with her thoughts.

Sun Priestess? Is that what calling down the sun makes me? Wonder how that works with being a Moon Woman? She mentally shrugged. *Since I'm not going to be part of the Tribe of the Trees, I don't think I'm going to have to worry about serving two roles at once.* Mari washed her face in the wooden trough that Nik had somehow refilled while she'd been asleep. *How had he found his way out of the bramble thicket?* As soon as her mind formed the question she realized the answer—*Rigel.* He had to have led Nik. *I probably should feel worried or at the very least a little strange about Rigel helping Nik, but I don't. It makes me feel safe, loved even.*

Mari used a willow twig to clean her teeth, and then she dressed and combed her hair. She liked hearing the sounds of Nik and Laru and Rigel in the other room. It made her feel safe, too. And loved.

She wondered at the changes in her world. In just a few weeks she had gone from being committed to living a solitary life with Rigel as her only companion to having a burrow filled with people and canines—and even a Lynx.

Mari's hand paused mid-brush of her hair as she realized, *I like it. I like having people and their animals around. I like being part of something more than myself.*

But it wasn't the Clan way. Moon Women led their Clans but were supposed to live solitary lives committed to serving, but serving alone—except for an occasional lover and the gray-eyed, female offspring those lovers produced. The thought of going back to that lonely life made her feel hollow.

Nik is right. It is time for all of us to make a change.

Mari stepped through the room-dividing curtain and stopped. Her stomach did a little flip-flop as she took in the pelt Nik had spread on the floor of the burrow before the hearth fire. On it were two bowls of steaming stew. The one that was heaped completely full was also sitting next to an entire loaf of sliced bread and a wooden container brimming with honey. And beside the bowl of stew was a small figure, carved from wood. Rigel and Laru were lounging before the open door of the burrow, and a lovely warm breeze was drifting in with the wan light of an overcast day.

"Moon Woman, your breakfast awaits." With a flourish Nik gestured to her place at the makeshift table.

"Wow, this is wonderful!" Mari hurried to take a cross-legged seat before her bowl of stew. She picked up the wood figure and gasped in pleasure. "Nik! It's Rigel!" Her eyes found Nik's. "You carved this?"

He nodded and shrugged a little uncomfortably as he took his place beside her on the floor. "Yeah, well, I'm not sure my mother would approve. It's not very good. I'll make you a better one when I have more time. I barely finished that before you woke."

"I love it!" Mari studied the little figure, turning it over and over in her hands. It was definitely Rigel. The details of his wide, intelligent brow, his gangly paws and oversized ears—they were completely her Rigel. Mari's eyes swept around the burrow. Nik had made breakfast, tidied up, fed the canines—obviously, as they were snoring contentedly in the doorway instead of begging and slobbering all over Nik and her—and carved a miniature figure of her canine for her. Her eyes found Nik's, and she leaned into him and touched his cheek, drawing him closer to her. "Nik, I am sure your mother would approve. Everything you've done here is perfect. Absolutely perfect." Then she kissed him, long and thoroughly, pulling away only because she couldn't ignore the steaming stew for another moment.

She felt Nik's eyes on her and looked up, mouth full.

"In case I haven't made myself completely clear—Mari, daughter of Leda, I am courting you."

Mari managed to swallow the stew without choking. She took another drink of her half-finished mug of tea and then, with a smile, said, "Oh, you've made yourself clear."

"Good," Nik said.

"Good," Mari said.

"Is it wrong that I wish we could stay here together for a while, just the four of us, and ignore the outside world?" Nik asked.

"If wanting that's wrong, then I suddenly like being wrong," Mari said. "But we—"

"I know we can't," Nik interrupted. "It's just so peaceful here. The world's falling apart out there, but in here . . ." He paused and his gaze swept around the neat little burrow. "In here everything fits perfectly."

"Nik, do you think there's any chance that we'll actually be able to stay? I don't mean just you and me and Rigel and Laru—I mean your new Pack, with the Clan and whoever from your Tribe wants to join us."

Nik chewed his stew thoughtfully before he responded. When he spoke, his voice was heavy, as if the weight of the words made them difficult to speak. "I wish we could. But I don't think we would ever be safe here."

"Thaddeus." Mari said the name as if it tasted rotten.

Nik nodded. "Yes, but not just him. Cyril was with him when he attacked us on the island, and Cyril is Lead Elder of the Council. With Father gone, there is no voice in the Council to stand for us."

"You mean to stand for not enslaving my people," Mari said.

"*Our* people. We're allies—Pack and Clan. If they come against you, they'll be coming against me, too."

Mari was silent, considering how she could form the words she needed to say. She didn't want to hurt Nik, but she had to be clear. "What if we fight?"

"Fight the Tribe?"

"Yes."

Nik drew a long breath and then let it out in a sigh. "You mean go on the offensive. Attack them while they're hurt and trying to recover."

"Would that be the only way?"

He moved his shoulders restlessly. "Not the only way, but probably the best chance we'd have at winning." He met her eyes. "I don't think I could do that, Mari. I would fight to protect you, protect the Pack, and protect the Clan, but I don't think I could go into that wounded Tribe and hurt them even more. I don't think I could add to their suffering."

Mari felt almost dizzy with relief. "Oh, Nik, I'm so glad to hear you say that!"

"Really? You're not upset?"

She gripped his hand. "No! I would have been upset if you'd said yes, if you'd wanted to attack them, which is why I had to ask you—had to be sure. No!" she repeated. "That's something Thaddeus would do. We're not like that. Nik, let's promise to *never* be like that."

"You know that means we'll have to leave the forest and find a new home in a new land."

Mari's stomach clenched nervously, but she nodded. "I know. When do we have to leave?"

"We should have a while. The fire was bad. The Tribe will be focused on healing and surviving. All of the floating cages on Farm Island were destroyed. They have nowhere to put captives until those are rebuilt. Unless something dire happens, we may have weeks, even a month or so."

"In other words, long enough for us to get comfortable and let down our guard."

"Exactly," Nik said.

"We'll have to leave before then."

"I think so, too. . . ." Nik paused, then spoke reluctantly. "I have to go back."

"To get a Mother Plant?"

"Yes. For our children. For the Pack's children. Mari, I had a thought while you were sleeping. You were swaddled in the Mother Plant when you were an infant, right?"

"Yeah, that's what Galen was killed for—stealing the fronds of the Mother Plant for me."

"And the Night Fever all Earth Walkers get—all Earth Walkers except you—do you think if we swaddled *all* babies in the Mother Plant fronds that maybe, just maybe, they would turn out like you, immune to Night Fever?"

Mari straightened, intrigued by the idea. "I've never thought of it! I always thought I was immune to Night Fever because of my father's blood, but if there's even a slight chance that you could be right, oh, Nik! If we could rid Earth Walkers of Night Fever forever, just think what that would mean for our people!"

"*Our people*—I like the sound of that."

"So do I. Let's eat! We need to talk to Sora!"

It had taken until midday, but Sora finally had everyone fed, medicated, and freshly bandaged. She'd made sure O'Bryan, Sheena, and Davis were standing guard—though *standing guard* was too official sounding. Sora had simply asked the three of them if they could keep an eye open for danger. From where she sat braiding feathers and beads into Lydia's hair, Sora could see Sheena throwing a stick for Captain, and he, for reasons Sora absolutely could not understand, continually ran after it and brought it back to her. The same stick. Over and over again.

O'Bryan was over by the stream. He'd found line and lure in the birthing burrow and she thought he'd already caught a basketful of trout. Davis and his silly little Cammy canine had gone off to hunt turkey, which she'd promised to roast to perfection if they managed to bring any home.

She'd had to send the Clanswomen to different tasks, mostly to keep them from being too insistent about going off to find their old burrows.

She'd sent part of them to where the stream widened to dig in the shallows of the bank for wapato roots, another part to hunt mushrooms, and the rest were sitting in peaceful, chattering groups around the clearing either washing bandages or weaving baskets to store supplies.

Jenna, Danita, and Isabel were sitting cross-legged near the stream, separating herbs and following Sora's careful instructions—which were actually Mari's careful instructions—and blending new tonics and salves. Bast was, of course, meticulously grooming herself within sight of Danita. Sora had no idea where Antreas had gotten himself off to. She stifled a snide grin. He probably needed some time alone after she'd explained the Clan's courting traditions. Danita's youthful laugher drifted across the clearing, and Sora glanced at the girl. Danita looked happy and, except for some lingering bruises and the pink lines of healing cuts and scratches, she seemed healthy again. Actually, now that Sora really considered the girl, she was more than healthy. She'd grown into a pretty young woman whose laugh was infectious and whose heart, despite what had happened to her, was still open and kind.

Wonder how open and kind she'll be to Antreas if he does decide to court her. The thought had Sora camouflaging a giggle with a cough.

"Are you feeling okay, Sora?" Rose asked.

"Absolutely!" Sora said. "Just had a tickle in my throat. Would you like me to braid your hair next, Rose?"

"Oh, would you? Yours is so pretty, and what you're doing to Lydia's hair is wonderful."

Sora nodded happily. "Of course! I am running out of beads, though. I saw another basket of beads in the back of the pantry. If you feel up to it, I'd appreciate you getting it for me."

"I'll go look. Fala needs a break from nursing her puppies anyway. Would you mind keeping an eye on them while she comes with me?" Rose asked.

"No problem," Sora said. "All they do after they eat is sleep anyway."

"True, but they waddle faster than you'd expect when they wake. Just be sure none of them get away from you—not that they wouldn't sit their plump bottoms down and scream for Fala as soon as they real-ized they were lost," Rose said, stroking the sleeping ball of pups fondly before she began moving slowly and stiffly toward the burrow, with the mother Terrier by her side.

Sora had situated Rose, with Fala and her pups, Sarah, and Lydia on a thick bed of moss beside an old log near the middle of the clear-ing. The two girls were sore and hadn't wanted to get out of bed, but Sora knew fresh air would be good for them both and Rose had—very nicely—sided with her in encouraging the girls to come outside. As the morning had progressed to midday and Sora had been able to breathe more easily, she'd decided the two wounded girls would feel better if they looked better. So she'd searched the burrow until she found a small basket of hair decorations and managed to talk Lydia into letting her dress her hair.

Sora had been surprised at how readily the girls had agreed to let her coif their hair—she suspected at first their agreement had been out of apathy, but soon after she'd begun to comb through and then braid Lydia's hair Sarah had perked up and begun asking questions about the intricate work Sora was doing. And she was thoroughly enjoying her-self. Lydia's hair was thick and had a beautiful natural wave to it. It fell halfway down her back and was an astonishing blond, so light it was almost white. Sora thought it felt like water between her fingers. She could hardly wait to get her hands on Sarah's hair. It was shorter and the golden color of wheat and so, so very different from the dark hair of Earth Walkers that the novelty of it intrigued the Moon Woman.

As her hands worked familiar braid patterns into unfamiliar hair, Sora's mind wandered. She tried not to obsess about their situation and their vulnerability. But Nik's new—what had he called them? Pack! His new Pack was pretty pathetic. They had a grand total of three males, and one Warrior female, to protect them. And with all the coming and going of Clan and Tribe, Sora was pretty sure it wouldn't take much searching for the Tribe's Hunters to find them and recapture all of them.

I need Mari to get out of bed with that tall Companion and get here so we can decide what we're going to do with this new Pack, Sora thought.

"Ouch!" Lydia squeaked, putting her hand to the side of her head where Sora had yanked too hard.

"Oh, sorry. I'll be more careful," Sora apologized, then she squeaked, too, as a little ball of black fur waddled over to her and began licking her toes. "Sunkissed! You scared me. Are you the only escapee?" Sora glanced at the puppy pile and quickly counted four fat, sleeping pups.

"She really likes you," Lydia said.

"She's less bothersome than I expected," Sora said, moving her foot so the pup could get more comfortable.

"Why do you call her Sunkissed?" asked Sarah.

"She has a little spot on her chest that looks like a splotch of sunlight. O'Bryan told me you call that being sun-kissed."

"What? Did I hear my name?" O'Bryan joined them, holding a basket that smelled of fish.

"I was just telling Sarah about the girl pup being sun-kissed. That is the word, right?" Sora said.

"That's the perfect word!" O'Bryan bent, scooped up the sleepy pup, and turned her over to expose the splotch of color on her chest. "See, sun-kissed."

The pup opened her eyes, and Sora could almost swear the little girl canine was frowning. Then she opened her mouth and began to shriek as if O'Bryan were pinching her.

"What are you doing? Give her to me!" Sora stood abruptly and snatched the pup from the openmouthed Companion. She hugged the fat little creature to her chest and the pup immediately quieted.

"I didn't do anything! I wouldn't hurt a pup—I swear!"

"Torturing puppies, O'Bryan?" Antreas joined the group while he sniffed at the basket by the Companion's feet. "Bast sent me an image of fish. Good! Hey, Sora, I'm great at grilling these. Want some help with dinner?"

"That's very kind, Antreas. Thank you," Sora said absently as she went back to her seat on the log and put the pup down on her feet again, but the fat little thing started whining pitifully. "What's wrong with her?" Sora asked.

"She wants you to pick her up," Rose said, limping up to them, a small wooden cup filled with beads in her hand. "Was that why she was screaming? Fala almost had a heart attack when she heard her." The adult dog had gone to Sora, licking and nosing the girl pup, trying to get her to stop whining.

"O'Bryan was torturing her," Antreas said.

"I was not!"

"Well, it sounded like you were torturing her," Antreas said.

"You know I wouldn't *ever* do that," he said beseechingly to Rose, who simply smiled wryly at him.

"Okay, okay, everyone stop yelling!" Sora said. "Including you, young lady." She picked up the pup, who instantly stopped crying. Sora held her at eye level. "Well, now you're up here. What do you want?"

And then something extraordinary happened. The puppy met her gaze, and suddenly Sora was filled with the most incredible feelings she'd ever experienced. Love, happiness, acceptance, and an indescribable sense of belonging flooded the Moon Woman, and with those emotions came a single name.

"Chloe!" Sora gasped. "Your name isn't Sunkissed; it's Chloe!"

"Sora! What are you saying?" Rose rushed to Sora's side, peering over her shoulder at the puppy.

Sora looked up at Rose and in a voice that shook with the tears that ran unnoticed down her face said, "She just told me her name. It's Chloe."

"Great bloody beetle balls! The pup just chose Sora!" O'Bryan said.

"Stormshaker! How is that possible?" Antreas said.

"I have no idea," Rose said, smiling through tears of her own. "Chloe's too young, and Sora's not even a Companion."

"But it's true!" Sora's voice had become frantic, and she clutched Chloe to her chest. "She told me her name, and she—she's making me feel all sorts of things." Sora pressed her face into the pup's fur, breathing in the intoxicating smell of puppy. "Please, you can't take her away from me!"

"Hey." O'Bryan went to Sora, touching her shoulder gently. "No one will ever take Chloe away from you. You have my word on it."

"And mine," Rose said.

"Mine as well," "And mine," said Sarah and Lydia.

"It's never happened before," O'Bryan said. "But that pup has chosen you, and if you accept her you are bound for life."

"Is there something I have to say, something I have to do, to accept her?" Sora asked.

"Well, there is, but the words aren't important," Rose said. "All you have to do is love her back."

"Then I've already accepted her." Sora smiled up at them through her tears as the pup snuggled against her.

O'Bryan threw his head back and shouted, "The pup has chosen!" Then he turned to Sora and spoke formally. "May the Sun bless your union with Chloe, Moon Woman."

"May the Sun bless your union with Chloe!" Sarah, Lydia, and Rose intoned together.

"What? Did I hear you say—" Sheena and Captain came running up to the group. "Oo-o-oh, I see I did hear you say a pup has chosen. Wow! She chose Sora?"

Sora narrowed her eyes at Sheena. "Yes. She's mine and I'm hers."

Sheena held up her hands in mock surrender and stepped back, laughing softly. "Yep, she's definitely chosen you. What's her name?"

"Chloe!" Sora spoke the word like a prayer.

"May the Sun bless your union with Chloe!" Sheena said.

"Hey, Cammy started acting all weird, and insisted we come back, even though I think I could have bagged at least one more turkey. What's going on?" Davis said as he and his little blond Terrier jogged up.

Cammy went to Sora, looked up at the girl and the pup, sat his butt down on the moss, and lifted his muzzle to the sky, howling with happiness. Beside Sheena, Captain joined in, and then two more Shepherds sounded the celebratory howl as Rigel and Laru galloped down the wide stone stairs, racing into the clearing, with Nik and Mari, looking utterly confused, running behind them.

"What has happened?" Mari gasped the words between panting breaths.

"It's Sora! She's spectacular!" O'Bryan beamed at the Moon Woman cuddling Chloe to her chest.

"Spectacular, huh?" Antreas muttered, sending O'Bryan a knowing look. "Boy, you and I better have a talk."

"What?" asked Sora. She was hardly able to take her eyes from Chloe.

"Nothing," Antreas said quickly.

"No, someone tell me what *really* happened." Mari moved to Sora's side and began checking her for wounds.

Nik took Mari's hand, stilling her. "If I am not mistaken, this lovely little Terrier pup just chose Sora as her Companion."

"Huh?" Mari said.

Sora looked up at her friend, eyes shining with tears and happiness. "He's right. She chose me! Chloe chose me. Oh, Mari! I—I didn't know it was like this. I had no idea. It's . . . it's—" Sora broke off with a sob, unable to find the words.

"It's wondrous," Davis said, bending to hug Cammy.

"It's breathtaking," Sheena said, resting a fond hand on Captain's broad head.

"It's miraculous," Rose said, picking up Fala and kissing her softly on the muzzle.

"It's forever magickal," Mari said, smiling through her own tears as she knelt and hugged Rigel. "Congratulations, Moon Woman. You will never be alone again."

Sora held her Chloe close. *She won't leave me like my parents did. She'll love me for as long as we live.* Chloe lifted her head and met her Companion's gaze, sending waves of love and reassurance to her as Sora sobbed and laughed with joy.

CHAPTER 24

S o, what now?" Mari was finally the one to ask the question they all must have been thinking. The group of them—Mari, Nik, O'Bryan, Antreas, Davis, Sora and her Chloe, Sheena, and Rose—had gathered around the center bonfire area after settling Sarah and Lydia back in the burrow for a much-needed nap.

"What do you mean, *what now*? Chloe's mine. I'm hers. That's it. Nothing to *what now* about," Sora said stubbornly, cradling her pup close.

"Sora, no one is going to take Chloe away from you." Mari sat beside her friend on the soft, mossy ground and leaned against the big log. "But she is very young, and can't be parted from Fala yet." Mari looked to Rose for help. "Right?"

Rose nodded. "Yes, Chloe's only a couple of weeks old. Fala won't wean her until the litter is about six or seven weeks old, and they won't leave her until they are twelve weeks old or more, which is why Chloe choosing you is such a surprise. Actually, I've never heard of a pup this young choosing a Companion. They always make their choice when they're between about four and six months old."

"Oh, I thought everyone was so shocked because I'm an Earth Walker," Sora said.

"Well, that's surprising, too," Nik said. "But a canine's choice can never be manipulated—so little Chloe knew what she was doing when she let her choice be known."

"Yeah, I think you'll find that that little one has a definite mind of her own," said Davis.

"They do tend to have the same personality as their Companions," Nik muttered.

"What did you say?" Sora narrowed her eyes at him.

"Not a thing! Not one thing," Nik said, grinning. "But Mari is right. We do have things that need to be discussed, especially because of Chloe's age."

"All right. Let's discuss," Sora said.

Mari shared a long look with Nik before she began speaking. "O'Bryan, Davis, Rose, Claudia, and Antreas. All of you belonged elsewhere before the fire. Since then you have chosen to find safety and healing here, with us. Some of you—Davis and Antreas—have even sworn to follow Nik and to be part of his new Pack, allied to our Clan. And we welcome you. Others—Rose, Claudia, and O'Bryan—have yet to decide, or at least have yet to tell us their decision."

"What does that have to do with Chloe?" Sora asked.

Rose answered right away, "Well, Chloe should stay close to Fala for about ten more weeks. Which means if I choose to return to the Tribe of the Trees, Chloe will have to return with me until she's old enough to leave Fala and join Sora permanently."

Sora's face had gone white and she hugged Chloe so tightly that the pup yelped in protest, which had Sora loosening her grip and covering Chloe's face with apologetic kisses. When Sora recovered, she stared up at Rose and spoke slowly but emphatically. "If you decide to return to the Tribe, I ask that you let me go with you. I can't be away from Chloe."

Rose sighed with relief. "And that's all I needed to hear—that you love Chloe enough you would risk your freedom, maybe even your life, just to be with her. No, Sora. I've already made my decision. After being here and feeling the peace and acceptance I've found with your people, I've realized I don't want to go back. I want a life that isn't tainted by slavery and laws we've outgrown. And I'll admit that your ability to cure the blight weighed heavily on my decision. So, if you'll have me, I'll swear loyalty to the Pack as well."

"Oh, thank you!" Sora said, taking Rose's hand and squeezing it.

"Of course we'll have you," Mari said.

"Yes, you, Fala, and the pups will be a wonderful addition to our Pack," Nik said.

"I wish to swear to the Pack as well." Sheena spoke up. Mari and Nik turned to her in surprise. She shrugged. "I can't go back there without Crystal. Captain and I need a new beginning, and I like these people, these Earth Walkers. I like that they're ruled by women. It's how it should be."

"We happily accept you," Mari said.

"I go where Nik goes." O'Bryan looked from Nik to Mari. "But I wonder something. Would you accept other Companions if they wanted to leave the Tribe?"

Nik didn't hesitate. "Yes," he said firmly.

"That's right," Mari said. "All who wish to make a change—to live together in peace, without prejudice, without judgment, without enslaving others—are welcome to join us."

"Then I want to join the Pack," O'Bryan said.

"Nik, when are you going back?" Davis asked, causing everyone to turn to him.

"But I didn't think anyone was going back!" Sora said.

"I have to," Nik said. "I have to get a Mother Plant."

"What's a Mother Plant? And why are all of you clustered around Sora?" Isabel asked as she, Danita, and Jenna joined the group, their arms filled with herbs, and baskets and wooden bowls that held the salves and tinctures they'd been working on.

"One of Fala's pups has chosen Sora as her Companion," Rose explained.

"Seriously?" Jenna asked.

"Wow!" Danita said. "Congratulations, I think."

"I didn't even know that could happen," Isabel said. "I mean, Mari's half Companion, so Rigel choosing her made sense. But Sora's one hundred percent Earth Walker. She doesn't even like canines—do you?"

"Well, Chloe is different. She's *my* canine. And I said from when I first met her that puppies are much less horrible than I'd imagined. Um, she's not going to get as big as the Shepherds, right?"

Sora looked beseechingly at Rose, who laughed and said, "Right. She'll only be Fala's size."

"She'll be perfect," Sora said, snuggling Chloe close.

"I think this proves that we're all more alike than different," Isabel said.

"Exactly!" Nik said. "And that's what our Pack is going to be about— we *can* be different. Our differences make us strong. Earth Walkers have skills Companions know nothing about, and Companions can do things, like build a City in the Trees, that Earth Walkers have never done. Together, we can change the world."

"Or build a new one together," Mari added.

"But first Nik has to go back to the Tribe and get a Mother Plant," O'Bryan said. "And I'm going with him."

"No, no, no. I need to go in alone, quietly. Sneak a Mother Plant, and get out of there," Nik said. "If I'm alone, I'll have less chance of getting caught."

"You'll also have less chance of getting out of there if no one's watching your back," Davis said. "Cammy and I will go with you. We're Hunters. We know how to stay on the outskirts without being seen or scented. If you don't return, I'll know you need help. If bad goes to worse and I'm caught, too, Cammy can escape and track his way back here."

"And then we'll come get you out of there," Sheena said.

"Find that Claudia woman," Antreas said. "She seemed like an ally. But stay away from Thaddeus. He's trouble."

"Agreed," Nik said.

"Wait; why is it so important to get a Mother Plant? I've never even seen one; though the Tribe had us farming all of their food, we never once had anything to do with something called a Mother Plant. What's so special about it?" Isabel asked.

"Nik thinks it's why the Tribe doesn't get Night Fever, and he could be right. I was swaddled in a Mother Plant, and I'm immune from it," Mari said.

"But I thought that was because of your father's blood," Jenna said.

"So did Mari," Nik said. "But my gut is telling me there's more to it than that. We *are* more alike than different, and the Mother Plant is what allows us to channel sunlight, to strengthen our bodies and thrive. And we never get Night Fever. Maybe it can do the same for Earth Walkers if you start swaddling your infants in the Mother Plant, too."

"If there's even a chance that the Mother Plant will rid our children of Night Fever, we have to try," Danita said.

"Then we're all in agreement? I return to the Tribe to harvest a Mother Plant," Nik said. "And to see how bad it is there. See how long we have before . . ." His words trailed off, and he looked to Mari.

"Before we have to leave here," Mari finished for him.

O'Bryan nodded somberly. "I knew it would come to this."

"As did I," Davis said. "And you didn't even hear Thaddeus last night. He was filled with hate, especially after that Terrier of his was wounded. He's not going to give up until he's tracked and killed Nik and Mari, and enslaved Earth Walkers again."

"I'll never go back to that," Jenna said.

"Neither will I," Isabel added.

"None of you will have to. We're going to leave before the Tribe comes after us again, and any who are part of the Pack may join us," Mari said.

"Wait; are we all part of a Pack now?" Sora asked. "Or are we Clan Weaver that is allied to Nik's Pack?"

Nik and Mari shared a long look. He said, "I'd like it if we were all one Pack, but that's up to Mari."

"And Sora," Mari said quickly. "She's a Moon Woman, too, so together we make decisions for our Clan. What do you think, Sora?"

"Would the basic rules of the Clan still apply? Would women still rule the daily life, and men be in charge of protection and building?" Sora asked.

Mari turned to Nik. "Well?"

"I like the way the Clan is ruled," Nik said honestly. "You've never enslaved another people, have you?"

Mari's lips twitched up. "No, we have not."

"And you don't intend to?" Nik said.

"Absolutely not," Sora said.

"And you also don't intend to subjugate men in general?" O'Bryan spoke up.

Sora laughed. "How in the world would we do that?"

O'Bryan smiled at the Moon Woman. "I don't think there's much a Moon Woman can't do if she puts her mind to it."

"Well, my mind definitely doesn't want to subjugate anyone—and that includes men," Sora said.

"Good to know. I'm still in," O'Bryan said.

Sora nodded slightly to Mari. "So are we," Mari said. "We'll be a Pack!"

"Um, that's nice. I like the sound of it," Jenna said. "But where is our Pack going if we have to leave our homes?"

There was a long stretch of silence. Mari tried to think of the right answer. Should she recommend they follow the scattered Clan Weaver and go south, or west to the coast? Or even north to the Winterlands or Whale Singer territory? But how would that be any different? Earth Walker Clans would be no more accepting of their mixed Pack than the Tribe of the Trees would be. Sure, none of the Clans would try to enslave them, but the Clans also wouldn't welcome them and very well might try to execute any Companion who trespassed on their territory.

"I know where we should go." Into the silence Antreas spoke the words that would forever change the future of their combined peoples. "The Plains of the Wind Riders."

Nik sat up straight, anticipation animating his handsome face. "Wind Riders! And you know the way!"

"I do, but that doesn't mean once we're there—and keep in mind it's a long, dangerous journey—they'll accept us and let us settle on their plains."

"But you must think we have a chance or you wouldn't have mentioned it," Nik said.

"I do." Bast padded up. She sat beside Antreas and looked up at him as a mixture of purr and her strange coughing meow rolled from her throat. "Bast agrees, and Bast is always right. I can lead us to the plains, but it's up to all of us once we get there to show the Equine Companions that we deserve a place in their land—that our presence will be a benefit to them."

"And if we can do that, they'll let us stay?" Mari asked.

"They will. It's their way. But you should know that if we don't impress them they will force us to leave, and if we don't leave they will execute us," Antreas added.

"That won't happen," Nik said.

"They'll want us to stay," Mari said, nodding her agreement.

"What's an equine?" Danita asked.

"An animal with hooves like a deer, only they aren't split. They're bigger than the largest stag you've ever seen, and their Companions ride them," Antreas told her.

"Are you making that up?" Danita asked, frowning at the cat man.

"No, he's telling you the truth," Nik said. "I've wanted to meet a Wind Rider since my mother told me stories about them when I was a boy. She saw one once, and used to carve little equine figures for me to play with."

"Yeah, I've heard stories, too," Sheena said. "Crystal's grandfather talked about them. He made a trade run decades ago to the plains and was mesmerized by the huge equines and their beautiful riders. He told her they were majestic."

"They're also a strong matriarchy, which is something they have in common with Earth Walkers, and our new Pack," Antreas said.

"So, we're agreed? I get a Mother Plant, and we move our new Pack to the Plains of the Wind Riders," Nik said, eyes shining with excitement.

"We're agreed. Let's announce to the rest of the Clan tonight and see who wants to join us," Mari said. "Antreas, we're going to need to know everything we need to do to get ready to travel—and even though the Tribe is preoccupied right now with recovering from the fire, my intuition tells me the sooner we leave the better."

"Well, your intuition is right, and not just because of the Tribe. We have a small window to cross the Rocky Mountains before snow closes the passes. We're lucky it's still early enough in the spring to make the crossing possible at all. I'll get a list together of what we'll need," Antreas said.

"Nik, when are you going back to the Tribe?" O'Bryan asked.

"And are you taking me with you?" Davis added.

"Yes, he's taking you with him," Mari said, ignoring Nik's frown. "He's right, Nik. You need someone there in case something goes wrong. I'd come, but—"

"No! Thaddeus can't get his hands on you," Nik said. "Davis and Cammy can come."

"But not today," Mari said. "No, you can't argue about this, Nik. You're injured, remember? And if you have to fight to get out of there, and run and hide and race back here, you need to be healthy. How about we say you can go as soon as Sora says you're well enough to go?"

"Me? Why me? You're a better Healer," Sora said.

"I'm also biased when it comes to Nik, and you're not."

"Oh, well, that's true enough. Fine. I'll let you know when his wounds are healed."

"And then our future begins," Nik said. "As we head to the land of the Wind Riders!"

CHAPTER 25

Well, what do you think?" Mari asked, looking over Sora's shoulder while she examined the wound in Nik's back.

"I think the same thing you do—that's he's healing remarkably well for a man who was close to death not long ago and who hasn't given his body time to rest and recoup since," Sora said.

"This one is a lot worse than the laceration on his leg," Mari said, reaching down to prod at the pink edges of the nasty spear wound in his back.

Nik sucked in a sharp breath but didn't make any other sound.

Mari and Sora exchanged a look.

"You can say ouch," Mari said. "You're not going to fool either of us by keeping still. We know it's painful."

"And we can see that you broke this open recently, too," Sora added.

"Yeah, but Mari repacked it last night, and it's feeling a lot better."

"And yet it still broke open. That's not good, Nik," Sora said.

He sighed. "How long before I'm cleared to do what I need to do?" Nik asked.

"This is just a guess, because it could change if you go out and do something stupid and break either wound open *again*," Sora said. "But I think five days of rest and you'll be healthy enough to overdo without killing yourself, though if you want the truth, you should give yourself several weeks before—"

"I like the sound of five days much better!" Nik interrupted.

"And I do mean five *full* days of rest," Sora reiterated.

"So, how about we leave at dawn, six days from today?" Nik asked.

"I wish we had longer," Mari said. "But I really don't think we can chance it. Thaddeus and the Tribe are going to start hunting us again. Soon," Mari said.

From her comfortable spot by the hearth fire in the birthing burrow, Isabel looked up from the salve she'd been mixing for Mari. "Early spring crops will be ready to harvest from Farm Island in another week," she said. "How many generations has it been since the Tribe harvested their own crops?"

"Generations upon generations," Nik said.

"So, I think it's safe to say that no matter how much time Nik's back needs to heal, a few days are all that he has," Isabel said.

"I don't want to agree with you," Mari said. "But I do."

Nik took Mari's hand in his. "I'll be fine, and if I'm not, I know a talented Moon Woman who can heal me. Again."

"Thank you," Sora said.

"I wasn't talking about you," Nik said.

"I'm going to pretend I didn't hear that," Sora said. Then all kidding left her voice. "Nik, do you think any other Tribesmen or women will want to join us?"

"I don't know. I think that will depend on what's happened with the Council and how they've dealt with Thaddeus," Nik said. "Are you against more of the Tribe joining us?"

Sora moved her shoulders restlessly. "Yes and no. In theory, I don't mind. Like Mari, my heart says anyone who wishes to start over—to make the kind of change we've decided to make—should be welcomed. But I'm worried about what Antreas said."

"Which part?" Mari asked.

"The part about the long, dangerous journey. Maybe before we allow anyone else to join us we need to talk with him about whether numbers are good or bad on a trip like the one we're getting ready to take."

"I hear you," Mari said slowly. "But I think we have to do what's right, whether it makes the journey more difficult or not."

"So, getting our Pack to safety in a new land isn't what's right?" Isabel asked.

"It is, but there's more to it than that," Mari said. "If we start picking and choosing who is worth joining us, how does that make us any different from the Tribe or the Clan?"

Isabel blew out a long breath. "I understand. I don't like it, but I do understand." Then she put the wooden bowl down and approached Mari and Sora, bowing formally to them. "Moon Women, Danita, Jenna, and I would like to request an audience with you."

Mari blinked in surprise. "Isabel, you and Danita and Jenna can talk with us anytime. There's no need to be so formal anymore."

"Hey, don't be so fast to throw out all of the old ways. Whatever they want to talk to us about is obviously important, and we should treat it with the same respect they're treating us with in requesting an audience in the traditional way," Sora said.

Mari gave a small, conciliatory nod. "Okay, I get your point. Isabel, Sora and I grant you and Danita and Jenna an audience. When do you want to talk?"

"Now would be good, but we want to talk in private," Danita said, coming out of the storage area in the rear of the burrow with Bast and Jenna close on her heels.

Jenna gave Nik an apologetic smile. "No disrespect intended, Nik, but it's Moon Woman business."

"None taken," Nik said. "As soon as Sora reapplies the bandage to my back, I'm going to take my Moon Woman's advice and plant my butt beside the stream and watch O'Bryan do some more fishing. I may even help him, but not too strenuously."

"How about I find you there when we're done here?" Mari asked.

"You, my beautiful Moon Woman, may find me *anywhere*."

"Okay, okay, enough, you two. There, your bandage is reapplied. Put your shirt on and get out of here," Sora said.

"I love your bedside manner, and by *love* I mean 'dislike pretty intensely,'" Nik said.

"Just kiss her and go." Sora gave him a push toward Mari.

Nik kissed Mari softly. "Hey, anything else you'd like me to carve for you?"

"Yes! How about an equine, so we can all see what they look like?" Mari asked, eyes sparkling with girlish eagerness.

"An equine carving for my Moon Woman it is. Ladies, I will see you by the stream." He bowed rakishly and winked at Sora, who rolled her eyes at his back.

"He's very cocky," Sora said.

"He's courting her," Isabel said.

"Huh?" Sora's head whipped around. "Is he? I mean, formally?"

"Yes, he is," Mari said.

"Great Goddess! I knew it. I told you way back when you wouldn't let me kill him that he had a thing for you. Are you going to accept him as your mate?"

"I do believe I am. Eventually," Mari said, lifting her chin even though she could feel her cheeks blaze with embarrassed heat.

"Seems logical," Sora said. "But torture him for a little while, first."

"Yep. I think it's a good idea," Isabel said.

Mari giggled. "The torturing or the mating?"

"Both!"

"I like him," Danita said. "I mean, he's a man and all, but I try not to hold that against him."

"Danita, maybe we should talk about your dislike of men. They're not all bad, you know," Sora said.

"Really? Then why don't you have one?" Danita asked.

Sora opened and then closed her mouth, cleared her throat, and deftly changed the subject: "What is it the three of you wanted to speak with us about?"

Danita and Jenna sent Isabel pointed looks. Isabel nodded, straightened her shoulders, and then bowed respectfully to her Moon Women, arms spread in openness. Danita and Jenna mimicked her.

"We come with formal petition," Isabel said. "To ask favor of our Moon Woman. Um, I mean Women."

Mari stifled a grin and answered with equal formality, "You may rise. Your Moon Women will hear your petition."

"This Moon Woman, for one, is intrigued," Sora said, and then added hastily, "I didn't mean that with any less formality, but it's the truth."

"We'd like to be allowed to study Moon Woman practices," Isabel said.

Mari felt a start of surprise. "All three of you?"

"Yes," Jenna said. "And I know I wasn't born with the gray eyes that mark a Moon Woman candidate, but Mari, I believe I could be a help to you. I've always wanted to learn more about healing—ever since my mother died so suddenly and so young. You know I used to take care of my dad, even when Night Fever was affecting him. Sometimes it was hard, but I learned a lot about how to care for someone who has a sickness. I won't have the power of the moon to call on, but I could be an assistant to you and to Sora."

"But how much healing can you do without drawing down the power of the moon?" Sora asked, though not unkindly.

Jenna answered her frankly, "More with training than I could with no training at all."

"That's true," Mari said.

"I'm drawn to the healing arts of a Moon Woman as well," Isabel said. "I know Leda chose Sora over Danita and me, and she should have. Sora clearly has been greatly gifted by the Goddess. But that doesn't mean that Danita and I—and even Jenna—can't be helpful."

"I don't want to weave!" Danita blurted. "I used to think I did and I was even relieved when Leda didn't choose me as her apprentice, but recently the way I look at things has changed. A lot. Mari, Sora, I want to try to draw down the moon! Maybe I'll never be good enough to Wash a Clan, or our Pack. But maybe there's some small piece of moon magick I could find that is my very own. I'd use it to help our people and even the Wind Riders once we get to the plains."

"We know this is an unusual request," Isabel said. "But you did say you'd agree to apprentice more than one Moon Woman at a time."

"Actually, it's a request that's never been made before—at least not to my knowledge," Mari said.

Isabel hung her head. "Yes, that's what we thought, too."

"But that doesn't mean it's something that shouldn't be tried," Danita said stubbornly.

"And Mari, you said it yourself. Our new Clan—our Pack—should be a place of acceptance," Jenna said. "Well, for us the new start we want isn't just about accepting different kinds of people into our Pack."

"It's about accepting a new way of living and of learning," Isabel said.

"And of following our dreams," Danita said.

"But we will abide by your decision as our Moon Women," Isabel said, and the other two young women nodded in agreement.

"So, let's get this straight. Isabel and Jenna, you want to study to be Healers?" Mari said.

They nodded.

"And Danita, you want to learn to draw down the moon?" Sora said.

"I want to try," Danita said eagerly, and Bast added a rolling purr to punctuate the girl's words.

Mari met Sora's gaze. Almost imperceptibly, Sora nodded.

"Sora and I need to consider your very important request." Mari tried to sound as wise and formal as Leda would have. "We will make our decision by dinner hour tonight."

"Thank you, Moon Women." Danita, Isabel, and Jenna bowed again and then quietly left the burrow, with Bast trotting after them.

Mari glanced over her shoulder. Lydia and Sarah were sleeping soundly on pallets well across the burrow, and everyone else, even Rigel and Laru, was outside, either resting, like Nik, or hunting and gathering and preparing for dinner. Mari took a seat beside Sora.

"Well?" Sora asked.

"Easiest decision I've made in a long time," Mari said.

"Totally simple," Sora said.

"But they surprised me. How 'bout you?"

Sora shrugged. "Jenna did. I can't say the other two were a shock. They're smart and talented—even if they're not as talented as a Clan would require for a traditional Moon Woman."

"Maybe they are, but in a different way," Mari said.

"It'll be interesting to find out," Sora said.

"I never thought life would be this strange; did you?"

"Nope," Sora said, rearranging Chloe more comfortably on her lap. "All I wanted was to be worshipped and adored as a very fat and very lazy, though still incredibly attractive, Moon Woman," Sora said with a cheeky grin.

"Well, there's still time to get fat."

"At least I have that to look forward to," Sora said, and the two Moon Women's laughter filled the warm burrow.

Dinner didn't take as long to prepare as Mari thought it would—not with Sora commanding an army of Clanswomen who had Davis's turkeys and O'Bryan's trout to cook as main courses and a fresh crop of kale and garlic and onions to add to the fragrant wapato roots that baked to perfection in the coals of the bonfire. Sunset was painting the clouds that had been scudding across the sky all day with blushing colors when Sora finally proclaimed dinner was ready.

Mari called the mixed group of Tribe and Clan and Pack together once again in the little clearing after encircling the space with the oils and salts that would keep out hunting insects. The people waited eagerly for their Moon Women to appear.

"Is my hair really okay?" Mari asked Sora nervously as she tried to keep her fingers from plucking at the blue jay feathers her friend had braided into her short, curly blond hair.

"Yes, but only if you stop messing with them. Sheesh, you'd think you've never had your hair properly dressed before. . . ." Sora paused. "Um, that was inconsiderate of me. You *haven't* had your hair properly dressed before, have you?"

"No. I've spent all of my life until recently hiding my hair, my face, basically everything that was really me." Mari looked down at her bare legs. "And are you sure we shouldn't put on skirts?"

"What did you think last night when you saw me down there in just a tunic?"

"I thought you were beautiful. But you *are* beautiful, Sora."

"Yes, I am. And thank you. So are you. There's nothing wrong with showing our beauty to our Cla—, I mean Pack. And you have Leda's lovely cloak on. That covers you from your head to your toes."

"I'm nervous, but I'm not sure why," Mari said.

"It's because you're used to hiding. Think of it like this—once you get used to *not* hiding, your nerves will go away," Sora said.

"Promise?"

"No, that's up to you, but it makes sense. Hey, if you want another opinion, just look at Nik. I'll bet his teeth will fall out when he sees how gorgeous you are tonight."

"That's not a very appealing image."

"I was trying to be dramatic. You know what I mean. Now come on. They're all hungry and no one will eat until we do."

"Okay, okay. I'm ready." The two Moon Women began to walk slowly down the wide steps that led from the birthing burrow to the clearing beside the stream. Just before they became visible to the people gathered below, Mari touched Sora's shoulder. "We're making history tonight; do you realize that?"

Sora's eyes glinted with excitement. "Yes, I do. We're doing the right thing, Mari. Your mama would be so proud—of the both of us."

"That's exactly what I needed to hear. Thank you."

Sora patted one of Mari's curls back into place. "You're welcome. That's what friends do—say the exact right thing sometimes."

"I'm glad you forced me to be your friend, Moon Woman," Mari said.

"Me, too, Moon Woman," said Sora. "Forward together?"

"Always."

As one, they descended into the Gathering. Following Sora's idea, they were dressed in short tunics that left their legs and arms bare. Freshwater shells had been sewn into the hems of the tunics where they dangled to make music with their every step. Sora had taken special care with their hair. Hers was, as always, a magnificent dark mane that fell well past her waist and was decorated with beads and shells and feathers. Mari's hair, though much shorter, had brilliant blue feathers braided within it so that it appeared as if she were wearing a beautiful headdress. She'd brought her mama's cloak from their burrow—and it was draped across her shoulders. The flickering firelight caught the intricately embroidered fabric so that it seemed the birds and vines and flowers were magickally alive. Together, the two young women were as beautiful as they were powerful.

"Our Moon Women! Our Moon Women are here!" Isabel's voice was the first to take up the cry, but it was followed by a swell of greetings that rolled over Mari like a warm summer rain. All faces turned to them as the canines barked enthusiastically and Rigel, unable to contain himself any longer, sprinted to Mari. She'd expected him to jump up and act like the puppy he still was, but Rigel shared her emotions and he felt her nervousness. Instead of jumping about, he fell in beside her, keeping pace with Mari and Sora and looking regal and very adult.

"Good boy, smart boy. I love you so much!" Mari whispered to him. His tail wagged with happiness, but he maintained his adult demeanor. When she walked he did, too, his shoulder touching the side of her leg. When she paused he did as well, and as he moved with her Rigel flooded his Companion with love and strength and a great sense of unwavering pride in her—and Mari's nerves dissipated like dew before the magnificence of the sun.

Nik was there, with Laru beside him. He stood in the center of the small group of Companions, with O'Bryan on one side and Antreas on the other with his Bast. As she met his gaze, Nik lifted his fingers to his lips, kissed them, and then bowed his head to her.

There was a confusing flurry of activity at the edge of the little group that clustered around Nik, and suddenly Chloe bolted from her littermates who were nestled beside Fala. Chloe half ran, half waddled to

Sora, who bent to scoop her up, but instead of whining and wriggling and begging for kisses, the pup quieted as soon as she was in her Companion's arms. Chloe lifted her head and gazed out at the gathered people, looking as serious as was possible for a fat, adorable puppy.

"She's amazing, isn't she?" Sora whispered to Mari.

Mari stifled her grin and nodded in agreement. Up until today Mari would never, ever have even considered the possibility of Sora being chosen by a canine as a Companion, but already the two of them fit so well together that Mari couldn't imagine them any other way. And it was wonderful to see Sora filled with such happiness.

They approached the center bonfire that blazed high and hot before the reclining image of the Great Mother. As they had practiced when they prepared in the burrow, Mari and Sora lifted their arms together and shouted, "Bright blessings to you all!"

"Bright blessings to you, Moon Women!" the people cried in response.

"Before we eat, Sora and I have two announcements to make, and after that we will ask each of you to make a difficult decision," Mari began.

"Danita, Isabel, and Jenna, please come forward," Sora said.

The crowd stirred, letting the three girls through. Mari thought they looked nervous, and she didn't blame them.

"These three Clanswomen petitioned us earlier today, asking that we apprentice them in the healing arts of being a Moon Woman, as well as the magick of drawing down the moon," Sora said.

Mari waited until the curious whispering of the Clanswomen in the crowd silenced before she spoke. Then she drew herself up as tall as possible and spoke formally to the Gathering. "Sora and I have considered their request, and we are announcing tonight that we have happily accepted the three of them as apprentices."

The joy that lit the three girls' faces made Mari's heart sing.

"But Mari, Jenna does not have gray eyes."

Mari looked through the crowd until she saw that it was an older woman named Adira who had spoken.

"True," Mari said.

"And even though Danita and Isabel are marked by gray Moon Woman eyes, our Leda did not choose either as her apprentice," Sora said.

"But that was another time. Things have changed since my mama chose Sora," Mari said. "The Clan has fragmented. The Tribe of the Trees is in turmoil. Our people have been freed from their captivity."

"And that is just the beginning of our changes," Sora continued. "Mari and I will keep some of the Clan's traditions, but we also intend to create new ones—traditions that work for the new world we want to create."

"Clanswomen, you didn't know who I really was until recently. I had to hide myself from you. That made me miserable. Except for Mama, I was alone. Had Rigel not come into my life I would have had no will to live after Mama died."

"And we would have no Moon Woman at all," Sora said. "We all know the consequences of that. We never want that to happen again."

"I never want anyone to feel as sad, as alone, as I have felt. So, we have decided to encourage each of you to follow your dreams, even if they are secret dreams you think might never be able to come true," Mari said. "And we hereby name Isabel, Danita, and Jenna apprentice Moon Women."

"Do you accept our naming?" Sora asked the three girls.

"Yes!" they shouted in unison.

As the girls smiled and were congratulated, Mari and Sora shared a long look. Sora nodded, and Mari raised her hand. The group fell silent.

"The next change we must announce will be more difficult to hear, but even more necessary. As you know, much of the Tribe of the Trees has been destroyed. Sadly, we do not believe their recent tragedy will change them as a people enough that they will stop hunting and enslaving us."

Sora let the Clanswomen's murmurs die before she began speaking. "There are good people in the Tribe. You see several of them here, with us now. But there are also dangerous, angry people who do not want change. Those people will not let us live in peace."

"They especially won't let Nik and me live in peace," Mari said. "So, I have decided that we must leave and make a new home, a new Clan, far away from here."

"I am in agreement with Mari, and I am going to join her as well," Sora said.

The Clanswomen erupted in frantic shouts and denials. Sora and Mari raised their hands, calling on quiet.

One broken voice lifted from the silenced group. "But what will we do without our Moon Woman?"

"Come with us," Mari said. "Join us, and you will not be without a Moon Woman—you'll have two of us!"

"Are the Companions coming, too?" Another Clanswoman shouted the question.

"Some of them are," Mari said.

"Then what will we be? A Tribe or a Clan?"

"Neither," Mari said.

"We'll be a new group, for a new way of living," Sora said.

"We'll be a Pack," Mari said. She nodded at Nik, who stepped forward.

"I have sworn to be part of this Pack," Nik said, his voice loud and strong. "O'Bryan, Rose, Davis, Sheena, and Antreas have sworn to join me. And I have agreed to follow the Earth Walker tradition of matriarchy." His eyes searched his group until he found the young sisters Sarah and Lydia. "It is your choice," he told them. "You may join our Pack if you want to. If you would rather return to the Tribe, I will make sure you get there safely once the Pack is on its way to a new land."

The two girls clutched hands and put their heads together, whispering. Then Sarah surprised Mari by addressing her, and not Nik, directly. "If we belong to the Pack, does that mean you will cure us if we get the blight?"

"It does," Mari said.

"Then we will join your Pack," Sarah said firmly. "We watched our grandmother and grandfather die of blight. It's a terrible thing. Something we've been afraid of for years. We don't want to fear it anymore."

"And our parents perished in the fire. We have no family to return to," Lydia said. "If you accept us, we will make a new family with you."

"Our Pack accepts you," Mari said. Then her gaze moved around the clustered Clanswomen. "And now the rest of you have a choice. Join our Pack and leave to make a new world with us, or Sora and I will help you collect enough supplies to reach the Clan of your choice."

There was a long, pregnant silence. Then Adira stepped forward. "You want us to leave our burrows where we have lived, loved, and raised our children for generations in this forest we know as well as our own bodies?"

"For your safety, yes," Mari said.

"Mari, I mean no disrespect when I say this, but is it not true that the Tribesmen will be hunting you and Nik specifically?" Adira asked.

"Yes. That's true," Mari said.

"And for the rest of us, it will be as it was before—the Tribe will hunt us, capture some of us, and leave the rest to live our lives in peace."

Adira didn't say it as a question, but Nik spoke up in answer. "They may. They may also hunt you harder than they did before."

"But you don't know for sure," Adira said.

"No, I don't."

Adira turned to Sora. "Then why don't you stay and be our Moon Woman? I understand why Mari must leave and it is right that the Companions go with her, but you are an Earth Walker, fully one of our blood. Why not stay here, where you belong, with your true people?"

Sora answered with no hesitation, "Because I want a different kind of world—the kind where we don't judge each other by Tribe or Clan, the kind where we can be free to be ourselves, the kind of world Mari and Nik want to make together. Adira, for most of my life my only desire was to be Moon Woman for Clan Weaver, but now I want more."

Adira looked beseechingly from Danita to Isabel. "Would one of you stay? Would you be our Moon Woman?"

Danita's eyes went wide with shock and she began to shake her head while Isabel said, "No, Adira. We want more, too."

Adria's shoulders slumped in defeat. "But where will you go?"

Mari met Antreas's gaze and nodded encouragement. His voice rang throughout the clearing. "I will lead our Pack through the mountains to the Plains of the Wind Riders and the new world we will build there!"

CHAPTER 26

I t wasn't a Third Night, but Mari and Sora had decided before they joined the Gathering that the Clanswomen could use an extra boost, especially after they'd just been told they needed to leave the homes to which they had so recently returned. Also, it was an excellent way to begin Danita's Moon Woman apprenticeship, with an added bonus that it would be a very public beginning, leaving no doubt as to the seriousness of the undertaking. After the gasps and whispered chatter caused by Antreas's proclamation about leading the Pack to Wind Rider territory had died down, Mari called, "Danita, please join Sora and me for the Washing of the Clan."

Danita had been standing a little to the side of Antreas and Bast—the Lynx always seemed to be within view of the young Earth Walker—and Mari watched her eyes widen in surprise and her face flush with nerves when she called her name. But Danita didn't hesitate. She moved quickly to Mari and Sora, taking her place between them.

"You're going to hold our hands," Mari explained. "And we're going to do a simple call to the moon. You just join us in saying the last part of the invocation when we squeeze your hands. *By right of blood and birth channel through me / the Goddess gift that is my destiny!* Do you think you can remember that?"

"Yes."

"Okay, then you'll walk through the Clan with us. You only need do one thing—just focus on being a conduit for the moon," Mari said.

"Moon power is cold, so don't let that shock you," Sora added. "Instead of accepting the power for yourself, you have to remember that you're just the means through which it is Washing the Clan."

"It might help to imagine you're like a riverbed, or maybe a pathway, and the moon magick is like water flowing effortlessly through you," Mari said.

"You might feel dizzy and even sick. That's normal," Sora explained.

"Just remember to keep focused. You're going to do well; I just know it," Mari said. "Ready, Sora?"

"Ready!"

"Danita? Ready?"

"Absolutely!" Danita said, doing a good job of covering her nerves with enthusiasm.

Mari and Sora each held one of Danita's hands; then they raised their faces to the darkening sky. Mari nodded briefly in encouragement to Danita when she turned her face upward. She could feel the watching crowd and sent a silent prayer to the Earth Mother: *Please help Danita have a positive first experience.*

Mari drew three deep breaths in and out, relaxing and centering herself. Sora did as well, with Danita mimicking them. Mari began the invocation with a shout.

"Moon Woman I proclaim myself to be!"

Sora continued:

"Greatly gifted, I bare myself to thee.
Earth Mother, aid me with your magick sight.
Lend me strength on this special night."

Mari spoke, feeling the cool silver power of the moon begin to rain into her body:

"Come, silver light—fill us to overflow
So those in our care your healing touch will know."

Together Mari and Sora squeezed Danita's hands, and then the two young Moon Women, joined by Danita's soft-spoken, but earnest voice, finished the invocation.

"By right of blood and birth channel through me
The Goddess gift that is my destiny!"

Mari hadn't known what to expect. She'd channeled moon magick her mama had invoked and had led Sora in drawing down the moon, but she'd never invoked the silvery light with another Moon Woman, and especially not someone as novice as Danita, so she was utterly surprised when a sweet, sparkling beam of energy filtered from above and settled over the three of them. It glistened downward, flowing first into Mari.

Mari felt the jolt as the pure, cold energy passed from her and into Danita.

"It's okay," Mari spoke quietly to Danita. "Relax and release it to Sora."

Danita was chewing her bottom lip, brow furrowed in concentration, and in another heartbeat Sora began to smile. She nodded encouragement. "Yes, Danita! That's it!"

"Ready to walk with us?" Mari asked.

Danita nodded tightly. "Yes. I think so."

Joined by their hands, as well as their intentions, Mari and Sora and Danita began to move among the crowd. Mari and Sora gently touched bowed heads while Danita kept pace with them, her face a study in concentration. The Clanswomen smiled and whispered blessings to their Moon Women, including Danita's name in their thanks, which almost caused the girl to lose concentration, but she caught herself and continued to channel moon magick.

Davis was the first of the Companions to bow his head before them.

Mari didn't hesitate. She placed her hand, cool and shining with the power of the moon, on his head and felt his body startle. He looked up at her, eyes filled with tears.

"I felt it! I felt the touch of the moon!" Davis exclaimed as Cammy barked happily.

O'Bryan moved to stand beside the Hunter. He grinned a little shyly at Sora and said, "I've been healed by Moon Woman magick before, but I don't remember much of it. Would you mind if I felt a little of it again?"

Sounding much older than her years, Sora spoke the traditional Moon Woman blessing: "I Wash you free of all sadness and gift you with the love of our Great Earth Mother." Then she rested her hand on O'Bryan's bowed head.

The Companion sucked in a breath, and when he raised his head Mari thought that his face was almost glowing with pleasure.

"Thank you, Moon Woman," he said in a voice that shook with emotion.

They continued to move among the crowd, touching the people with the most gentle Washing that Mari had ever experienced. When they finally stopped in front of Nik, Mari placed her hand on his bowed head.

"I Wash you free of all sadness and gift you with the love of our Great Earth Mother," Mari spoke the ancient blessing softly and allowed her hand to linger longer than was strictly necessary.

He lifted his face, which beamed with love and pride. "Thank you, my Moon Woman!"

Together, Mari and Sora and Danita returned to the center of the circle before the bonfire that burned steadily, casting flickering shadows around the clearing. Sora and Mari finally let loose Danita's hand. The girl staggered, and Bast was suddenly there, pressing into her side, chirping reassurance.

"Are you okay?" Sora asked.

"My, um, stomach is not so good." Danita looked almost as pale as the moon.

"You should eat. You'll feel better, even if you do throw up," Mari said.

"I'll be sure she gets something to eat and keep an eye on her." Antreas seemed to materialize beside his equally silent Lynx.

Mari half expected Danita to refuse his help, but she nodded shakily and made no protest when he took her elbow and helped her toward the roasting turkeys.

"Clanswomen, you have a difficult choice to make," Sora said when Danita was gone. "We won't ask you to make it right now."

"Think about what we've said. Ask us or Nik or Antreas any questions you might have about our journey," Mari said. "But know that as dawn breaks six days from now our Pack will be leaving this place forever." She paused as emotion threatened to overwhelm her. She felt Rigel's comforting presence at her side and drew strength from her Companion before continuing. "I've lived in a burrow that has sheltered the Moon Women of Clan Weaver for generations. I've never known any other home. My mama is buried there. Sometimes I almost can't bear to even think about going, because it's like I'm leaving her." Mari had to stop then and wipe tears from her face. In the respectful silence around her, she could hear several of the Clanswomen sniffling softly. She lifted her chin and continued in a voice that grew stronger and surer as she spoke. "But I'm not leaving Mama. She'll always be with me—here." Mari placed her hand over her heart. "I'll take her love with me wherever I go. I want you to know I hope you decide to join us. I hope you take the love of generations of Earth Walkers with you, too, and use it to help us build a Pack that is kinder, wiser, and stronger than a Clan or a Tribe."

"I hope you join us, too," Sora said. "Wind Riders allow others to settle in their lands if the settlers can prove that they are worthy. If there's one thing I know for sure it's that the women of Clan Weaver are worthy. Now, let's eat!"

The Clanswomen were subdued during dinner. They clustered in small groups, eating and talking quietly among themselves. Mari and Sora sat on the mossy ground, forming a little circle with Nik, O'Bryan,

Davis, Rose, Isabel, and Jenna. Rigel, Laru, Fala, and Cammy lay on the ground not far from them, busily chomping on turkey necks and bones. Sora's Chloe was tucked inside her tunic, sleeping soundly.

"Where're Sheena and Captain?" Mari asked as she blew on a sizzling piece of turkey meat.

"They're patrolling the circle," Davis said. "Cammy and I will relieve them as soon as we get done eating." He glanced at Mari. "Thank you for Washing me. It was incredible. I'd had a headache—probably from staring at turkey sign all morning—but as soon as that coolness touched me it went away."

"You're welcome," Mari said. "I wondered what someone outside the Clan would feel during a regular Washing. I mean, I know Nik could feel the power of the moon when it healed him."

"So could I, but I didn't remember much of it," O'Bryan said. Then he cleared his throat and turned to Sora. "Thank you for Washing me."

"No problem. It's all part of being a Moon Woman," she said.

"Well, it may be normal for you, but for me it was special. Probably the most special thing that's ever happened to me in my entire life. I—uh—I just wanted you to know that," O'Bryan said.

With increasing curiosity, Mari realized O'Bryan's face was flushing. Sora leaned toward him and touched him gently on the arm. "I'm glad, and it's nice to be appreciated. I didn't mean to pass off your thanks like it was nothing." Then she sat back, rearranging Chloe more securely on her lap while Mari watched O'Bryan's gaze linger on the spot on his arm Sora had touched.

Mari felt Nik's eyes on her and she gave him a look, mouthing, *O'Bryan likes Sora.* Nik's eyes opened wider for an instant; then he shrugged and shook his head a little. Mari couldn't tell if he was baffled or amused, and she made a mental note to ask him what he knew about O'Bryan's intentions when there were fewer ears listening.

"From the outside it seemed to go well with Danita," Jenna said. "How was it for the two of you?"

"She did great," Sora said.

"Better than I did my first time," Mari agreed. "I threw up."

"Me, too," Sora said.

"So, you're not sorry you accepted us as apprentices?" Isabel asked.

"Not at all," Mari said.

"No way!" Sora agreed. "The washing was lovely with Danita. Gentle and effortless."

"I hope we do as well healing," Isabel said.

"I'm sure you will," Mari said.

"There she is!" Isabel jumped up to greet Danita, who looked a lot less pale and was accompanied by the ever-present Bast and, this time, Antreas. Isabel hugged her. "Mari and Sora were just saying what a great job you did tonight."

Danita's pretty gray eyes widened and her gaze jumped from Mari to Sora. "Really? It was so hard! And cold! I thought I was going to have to let go of your hands because I was going to be sick."

"But you didn't let go," Mari said. "And that's impressive."

"Oh, I'm so glad! Um, now do you mind if I go lie down? I'm still feeling a little strange."

"Rest will help," Mari said. "Mama used to be so tired from Washing the Clan that I used to think she was sleepwalking when she got back to our burrow."

"But you and Sora don't seem tired at all," Danita said.

"That's because the Washing was easy tonight," Sora said. "And because you helped."

"Plus, after a while you'll get used to it. The less you fight the power the easier it is to release, and the easier it is for you afterward," Mari said.

"I'll remember that," Danita said. She started to bow a formal goodbye to her Moon Women, but Danita paused and her eyes found Antreas. "Are you and Bast staying here tonight, or returning to Mari's burrow?"

Antreas hesitated, glancing at Bast, who rubbed against Danita's leg, purring loudly.

"We'll stay here. Bast likes the birthing burrow."

Relief flashed across Danita's face. "Oh, good. Do you mind if she lies down with me for a little while? It's night, and I'd, um, just rest so much better if I didn't have to be afraid that males might come back to the burrow."

"We wouldn't let them hurt you. Not ever again," Mari said firmly. "You don't need to be afraid."

"My mind knows that, but the rest of me—not so much," Danita said.

"Bast would love to sleep with you," Antreas said. "And I'll know right away if anyone approaches the burrow. Bast will tell me."

"Thank you."

Danita beamed a true smile at Antreas, and Mari saw a jolt of surprise cross the Companion's face. Apparently Antreas had never experienced the full force of Danita's smile—a smile that turned her from a sweet-faced but rather ordinary girl into a sparkly-eyed beauty. As the Lynx and the girl slowly walked side by side to the stairs leading to the burrow, Antreas's gaze followed them.

"Better keep in mind what I said." Sora spoke sotto voice to Antreas.

"Huh?" Mari asked.

"Nothing!" Antreas and Sora said together.

Mari meant to scowl at them and push harder to know what was going on, but Nik held his hand out to her, palm up. And on his palm was a wood carving of a four-legged animal with an arching neck and a sleek, powerful body.

"This is an equine," Nik said. "And it's for you."

"Oh, Nik! This is beautiful!" Mari turned the figure over in her hands, loving the smooth feel of it, completely intrigued by the majestic-looking creature.

"They call them horses, and it's not an insult," Antreas said.

"So that's a Wind Rider." Sora leaned forward, studying the carving. "And you say they're big enough for a person to ride?"

"People," Antreas corrected. "I've seen three girls, not much younger than Danita, all on one horse's back. "But they do vary in size."

"It's hard to believe," Mari said. "But I'm looking forward to seeing them."

"When they charge across the plains in their herds, they make the ground shake," Antreas said, gaze distant with remembrance.

"Sounds frightening," Jenna said.

"Not if they're your friends," Antreas said. "Then you know that charge is your protection. There's nothing that can stand against them, not even a swarm."

"Great Goddess! Not even a swarm?" Sora asked.

Antreas shook his head. "They can outrun it."

"Impressive," Nik said.

"It's something to look forward to seeing, that's for sure," Davis said. He stood, wiping his hands on his pants. "I'm going to relieve Sheena so she can eat. And I think I'll stay at the birthing burrow again tonight. I like it here, too." He whistled sharply, and Cammy sprinted from the bone-gnawing group to join his Companion, tongue lolling in a doggy grin.

"Is he ever *not* happy?" asked Isabel as she reached a tentative hand out to pet the little blond Terrier, who instantly diverted from his path to Davis to allow the girl to scratch behind his ears.

"Nope, Cammy pretty much chooses to be happy, especially now that he doesn't have to worry about Odysseus bullying him. And feel free to pet him anytime, Isabel. He loves the attention, especially from pretty girls."

Showing off, Cammy huffed and jumped around Isabel as she giggled.

"He's a flirt," Rose said, grinning at the little canine.

"That's part of his charm," Davis said. "But that's enough now. Time for us to go to work, Cammyman!" Davis picked up his empty wooden bowl and tea mug, and with Cammy trotting beside him he headed toward the central bonfire to drop them there before relieving Sheena.

"I have to get more of this wapato," Mari said to Sora. "I don't know what you did different to it tonight, but it's even more delicious than usual."

"I managed to find a stash of salt in the back of the pantry. That with the garlic makes it scrumptious," Sora said.

"Well, *scrumptious* is the right word, and I'm getting more," Mari said. "Be right back!" She leaned down and kissed Nik, not even realizing how oddly natural it had become to kiss Nik—*hello, good-bye, see you soon,* or just because she liked kissing him—until she straightened and felt eyes on her.

Nik smiled and squeezed her hand, pulling her gently down so that he could whisper, "You do you, Mari. Ignore watching eyes."

She squeezed his hand back and stood a little straighter, ignoring the curious stares.

The wapato roots were buried in an ember pit, not far from where the image of the Earth Mother rose from the fertile ground. Mari was crouching to begin the process of plucking a steaming-hot root from the glowing embers without burning her fingers when a motion at the corner of her eye shifted her attention. She glanced to the side and saw a man standing before the Earth Mother, head tilted back, gazing up at her. Beside the man sat a little blond Terrier.

Why's Davis with the Earth Mother? Mari thought, curiosity moving her toward him. When she was just a few feet from him, Davis crouched down and pried a small section of moss from the ground in front of the idol. Then he took something out of his pocket and put it in the hole created by the uprooted moss before pressing the green carpet back into place. He stood again, gazing up into the Goddess's serene face.

Mari made a small sound in her throat and Davis jumped a little. "Oh, Mari. I didn't see you there."

"Hi. I was just getting more wapato root, and I saw you over here with the Goddess. . . ." Her voice trailed off as she realized how intrusive she must sound. "Not that I mind you being over here. That's not what I meant."

Davis nodded. "I know what you meant. You're curious about what I'm doing."

"Well, sure, but I shouldn't intrude. This is your business. Yours and the Goddess's."

"Does she talk to you?" Davis asked, his voice sounding wistful.

"She hasn't yet. But she talked to my mama a lot. And I think she talks to Sora."

"Do you think the Goddess might ever deign to talk to someone who isn't an Earth Walker?"

As Mari answered, she heard Leda in her words and it brought her great comfort, as well as a wave of longing for her mother. "I think the Great Earth Mother belongs to everyone, not just Earth Walkers. So, sure, I do think it is possible. Davis, you don't have to tell me if you'd rather keep it to yourself, but what did you just bury there?" Mari pointed to the spot directly in front of the Goddess.

"I don't mind telling you, but it might be silly," Davis said. "I found a pretty piece of shell years ago and I didn't know why until now, but I've carried it everywhere with me ever since. And when I heard talk about how Earth Walker men court Clanswomen, I realized why I'd never traded away the shell."

When Davis just stood there, staring up at the idol, Mari prompted, "Why didn't you trade away the shell?"

"Because I had to give it to the Great Goddess, of course. Clanswomen always choose their men, but only after their men court them properly. I gave the shell to the Goddess to court her favor. Maybe, if I court her nicely enough, she'll accept and speak to me, too."

Emotion clogged Mari's throat and tears stung her eyes, but before she could tell Davis what a lovely sentiment that was Adira stepped from the shadows on the far side of the idol. She was studying Davis intently, as if secret words might be written on his soul and if she looked hard enough she could read them.

"Who told you to bring the Goddess a gift?" Adira asked, though not in an unkind voice.

Davis moved his shoulders. "No one. It was my idea. I didn't mean to be disrespectful. Forgive me if I—"

Adira brushed away his apology. "You need not ask forgiveness. We often leave the Goddess gifts. I was just surprised to see a stranger, especially a Companion, doing it, too."

Davis's gaze moved back to the Goddess's face. "I don't know why, but she makes me feel like I'm not a stranger."

"Yes, that can happen. It's a great blessing to feel at home in the presence of the Goddess. Listen in the wind for her voice; she's most easily heard there. Brightest blessings to you, Davis." Adria nodded slightly to Davis, then bowed with formal respect to Mari before moving back into the shadows.

"I didn't think she liked any of us Companions," Davis said.

"I don't think she did—until now. Good job, Davis."

"But I didn't do anything."

"I think you just did more than you could ever know," Mari said.

She patted Cammy affectionately on the head before going back to the ember pit, where she quickly plucked two succulent roots, and then returned to her little group, taking her place beside Nik. Rigel, Laru, and Fala had joined them, and Sora had finally surrendered Chloe to her mother, though the young Moon Woman's gaze kept returning to her nursing pup.

"Do you think the Earth Mother speaks to others—I mean, people who aren't Earth Walkers?" Mari asked Sora.

"I don't see why not. We call her *Earth* Mother, not *Earth Walker* Mother," Sora said.

"I guess that makes sense," Mari said, still considering what she'd just witnessed. Adira seemed to be in agreement with Sora. And when Mari really thought about it, she had to agree as well. She was the Great Goddess—Life herself—and not some shallow, limited deity. Leda had raised Mari to believe in her divine compassion, and even though Mari had never heard her voice or felt her presence, through her beloved mama she'd witnessed the strength of the Goddess's love.

"Mari, Sora, may we speak with you for a moment?"

Mari mentally shook herself, refocusing on the now and then to see Adira standing nearby with several other Clanswomen beside her. Mari blinked and realized there weren't just several Clanswomen with Adira—*all* of the Clanswomen except for Danita were with her.

"Yes, Adira? What is it?" Sora said.

"Of course you may speak with us," Mari said.

"Should we leave you in privacy?" Nik started to rise, with O'Bryan and the other Companions following him.

Adira lifted her hand, staying them. "No, what we have to say you should hear, too." Then she addressed her Moon Women, saying, "The Clanswomen have made their decision about joining your new Pack and journeying with you to Wind Rider territory."

As Adira paused, Mari held her breath.

"We would like to join you," Adira said.

"How many of you?" Mari asked.

"All of us," Adira said firmly. "With the very strange help of that Companion named Davis, and the Goddess, we have remembered ourselves. We want to make a new life where we can live in peace without fear of being captured into slavery again, whether just some, or all of us, are captured. We don't want to live like that again."

"We also want more, and we believe the Goddess wants more for us," a younger woman spoke up behind her, and the group nodded in agreement.

"So, we swear our oath to you, our Moon Women." Adira knelt as she spoke, bowing her head and extending her arms, palms facing outward. Each Clanswoman knelt behind her, mirroring her actions. "We are no longer Clan Weaver, but we belong to something bigger now. And now we will call ourselves Pack."

"I swear to the Pack!" came the combined shouts of the women.

"And we accept you!" Sora cried, clapping her hands.

"With great happiness!" Mari added, clapping with her friend.

Then all of the Companions stood. "To our Pack!" Nik cried.

"To our Pack!" the Companions shouted, and then everyone broke into cheers and barks.

Mari felt enfolded by the love and security of the Pack as Nik took her into his arms and, laughing, swung her around with a victory shout.

Maybe, just maybe, we can create a new world, Mari thought. *Thank you, Goddess, for touching Davis, and for reminding the Clanswomen that love is stronger than fear or hate.* When the music began, Nik grabbed her hand and twirled her across the clearing while Mari laughed and, for the first time since her mama had been taken from her, felt as if she belonged to a family.

CHAPTER 27

Dove knew the God had returned even before He bellowed for food and drink. It was like the sensation of someone's breath on the back of her neck just before they spoke. She didn't need to see or hear Him to know He was there.

Her Attendants scrambled to obey his commands as his heavy footsteps sounded closer and closer to where Dove sat, quietly sewing tufts of boar hair around the hemline of one of her skirts.

"Dove! Your God returns victorious!"

She put her sewing down just before He lifted her roughly to her feet and pulled her into His arms, kissing her passionately. She forced herself to go soft and compliant under His touch, though she noticed that now even the taste of Him was different from that of her usurped beloved.

When she was free to speak, she bowed to Him, saying, "Congratulations, my Lord. Would You like to sit with me on the balcony while You eat, and tell me of Your victory?"

"Actually, I am hungry for more than food and drink." He hooked one massive arm around her, lifting her off her feet, while He groped her body.

Dove could hear the shocked gasps of her Attendants and feel their stares on her. She wanted to break away from Him and run to the private area she and Dead Eye had made their bedroom chamber—and then curl up and disappear. But Dove could not. Even if she escaped His unwanted embrace, He would just chase her as if she were an errant child—or, more accurately, a slave. And Dove had no way of gauging what He might do to her if He lost patience. So she submitted, though it humiliated her to know the young women who served her were witnessing the God's rough treatment that was so, so unlike how Dead Eye, her Champion, her beloved, had been with her.

"You are soft and young. That delights me," Death murmured into her ear. "You will make a lovely vessel for my Consort, whether the Great Goddess is ready to awaken or not."

Dove felt a flush of hope. "Does the Goddess not wish to awaken, my Lord?"

"My Consort can sometimes be overly cautious, but I am very persuasive. Do not worry yourself, little bird. She shall awaken within you. I insist she shall."

"Wh-when will that happen, my Lord?"

"Are you eager or afraid?"

"Both," she told a half-truth.

"Four nights from now as darkness falls we will take possession of the City in the Trees. Once the city is ours, I will infect you with the skin sloughing disease. It takes hold quickly, which pleases me. I have waited long enough for my Consort," He said. "Within just a day or two after being infected you will begin to show symptoms. Once you do, I will choose the finest doe in the forest to join with you. When you have merged with this queen of the forest, *then* I will make blood sacrifice and force the Goddess to awaken."

"Blood sacrifice? Whose?" Dove asked, though she felt the answer in the pit of her stomach before He spoke it.

"Yours, of course. Just as Dead Eye awakened me with his blood, so shall you awaken the Great Goddess with yours." He nuzzled her neck and bit her soft flesh painfully. "You will rule for an eternity by my side!"

No, Dove told herself silently as He continued to grope her unresisting body. *I won't be here, just as Dead Eye is no longer here.*

"Kiss me, little bird!"

Dove did as He commanded, though it turned her stomach. As soon as she was able she broke off the kiss. "My Lord, You need to feed Your strength. Shall we go to the balcony? I can smell the food. My Attendants must have it almost ready for You. We can sit, eat, and You can tell me of Your successes today. Then we can retire to our bedchamber."

"I don't need a bedchamber to have my way with you," He said gruffly.

Dove couldn't stop herself from tensing. She resisted Him, pushing against His massive chest until the God put her down.

"My Lord." She spoke softly, for His ears alone. "I know You don't need a bedchamber, but I do. I would be much more comfortable there, and much more able to please You."

"And do you truly care about pleasing me, little bird?"

"I do, my Lord," she said earnestly. *But only because I care whether I live or die,* she added silently.

"And would you have asked your Dead Eye to wait for his pleasure?" The God's voice was low but had a dangerous edge to it.

"I wouldn't have had to, my Lord. He would not have insisted I please him in front of my Attendants. He would show me more respect than that." She held herself very still after she'd spoken the words that seemed to spill from her lips without her volition. *Will He kill me now? Or will He simply just hurt me more than He usually does?*

Many footsteps pounded against the tiled floor, causing the God to turn from her, though He kept one hand clamped tightly around her slim wrist.

"Ah, Iron Fist! You have come and brought the other Reapers more quickly than I anticipated. Good! You may all join me on the balcony to eat and drink as we discuss what is to come." His attention returned to Dove. "Have your Attendants bring more food and drink, and then you may join me, but only if you are truly *with* me." He paused and lowered His face close to hers. "I feel your apathy. Do not imagine you are hiding it from me. I grow weary of it, little bird. Always remember, I *am* a God—fully awakened. I need a vessel for my Consort, but I do not need an Oracle."

Dove swallowed her fear and lifted her chin. "That is only true if there are no other Gods but You, my Lord."

Death laughed, long and heartily. "Your courage is entertaining, little bird. Now do as I command before I become weary of it, too." He loosed her wrist with a shove that had her staggering away from Him.

Lily was by her side in moments. "Mistress?"

"Death commands you bring enough food and drink for His Reapers. Please do so." Then she lowered her voice. "How many Reapers have joined Him?"

"All of them, Mistress," Lily replied in an equally quiet voice. "It is Iron Fist and the eight others."

"Lizard is not with them?"

"Lizard did not return with the God," Lily said.

"Where is our food and drink?" bellowed the God.

"Go!" Dove said. "Quickly."

"Yes, Mistress." Lily hurried away, calling to the other Attendants.

Dove smoothed back her hair and went to the part of the chamber where her Attendants always kept clean freshwater in troughs, wooden bowls, and buckets. She took one of the buckets, dipped it into a trough, and then felt for the dry, clean cloth that hung nearby. Folding it neatly over her arm, she carried the bucket to the God's balcony, pausing at the entrance.

"Little bird, I am pleased you decided to join us," Death said.

"My Lord, if You allow, I would wash Your hands and feet in preparation for Your meal."

"I will indeed allow. And when you have finished with me, you may wash each of my Reapers as well, starting with my Blade, Iron Fist." His voice changed as He addressed His men so that the God sounded almost jovial. "Though do not get accustomed to my Dove serving you. When the Great Goddess resides within her body, she will serve no one except me."

Dove made her face neutral as the Reapers all chuckled along with their God, though her thoughts were whirring. *Life serves Death? That doesn't seem right. Doesn't Death ultimately serve Life? No matter His bravado now, I heard Him say that He was going to force the Goddess to awaken. But can a Goddess be forced to do anything?* Keeping her thoughts to herself, Dove felt her way to Death and knelt before Him, gently washing each of His hands as He ignored her and spoke to His men as if she were deaf as well as blind.

"We take the city of the Others four nights from now," Death said. He paused then, as if waiting for questions. When there were none, He continued, and Dove could hear the smile in His voice. "Very good. Very, very good. And because you show the trust you have in me by not asking, I will gladly explain. Today, Lizard made a noble sacrifice. Tell the Reapers, Iron Fist."

"Lizard died today after infecting a great sow with the skin slough-ing disease. The beast then followed me to the place of the Others. I saw them capture her. I saw them rejoice for the food she brought them."

"Food that is as poisoned as was poor Lizard's body," Death finished for him.

"And that is it." Dove recognized Rebel's voice. "Any of the Others who eat of the sow's meat will be infected. My Lord, there will be no one left to stand against us!"

Dove moved from the God's hands to His feet, washing them care-fully as she listened.

"Their numbers will still be far more than ours, though they will be ill, and much weakened. And they will not expect an army such as ours led by a God."

"Yes! To war! To the City in the Trees!" the Reapers shouted.

Dove felt Death lift His arm and they quieted. Soundless, she moved from the God to the first of the Reapers, the God's Blade, Iron Fist, quickly and efficiently washing his hands and feet and trying not to flinch at the filth and grim that sloughed from his skin.

"We are not yet ready. Over these next days the Others will grow weaker, and more divided, but we must grow stronger. I need each of you to gather any Hunter or Harvester who has not yet begun to cough blood. Take them to the forest, far enough in that the animals are not tainted with mutations and poisons but are pure and disease-free. Then do for them what I have done for you. Flay each creature and join it with a Harvester or Hunter so that they, too, may be changed into a Reaper, a Warrior, a demigod!"

The men surged to their feet, and the bucket was knocked from Dove's hands, spilling its foul water all over her skirt and legs.

"Dove, go inside. Wash yourself. Wait in my bedchamber. You have made a mess here. Begone!" the God snapped at her.

Dove stood. She faced Death. Slowly, gracefully, she sank into a deep bow. "Yes, my Lord."

She held her head high, walking with regal dignity from the God's balcony as her Attendants rushed past her, carrying platters, fragrant with food, to the men. Dove went to her bedchamber, stepped within the veiled area, and crumpled to the floor. She put her face in her hands and her body quaked with misery as she wished she could shed tears and with them maybe shed some of the despair that pooled within her.

"Mistress?" Lily's voice wasn't much more than a whisper. "Are you well?"

"No," Dove moaned. "I am not well. I am broken."

"Oh, Mistress!" Lily stepped through the veil and knelt beside Dove. Hesitantly at first, Lily put her arms around Dove. When she didn't resist, Lily hugged her, rocking slowly as Dove continued to tremble in her embrace. She sang a sweet, wordless melody that Dove recognized as a song young girls sang as they waited to be presented to the statue of the God when first they began to bleed. Somehow it calmed Dove. It also made her wonder at Lily's age.

"How old are you, Lily?" Dove asked, still resting her head against her Attendant's shoulder.

"I have known fourteen winters," Lily said.

"So young and kind," Dove said. "Forgive me for ever speaking harshly to you."

"I knew it was not in your true nature, Mistress. . . ." Lily paused, and Dove could feel a new tension in her slim body.

"Go ahead. Ask," Dove said.

"What are we going to do, Mistress? Is He really our God awakened?" Lily whispered frantically.

"He is *a* God. There are others. He wants to bring one alive inside me, to take me over, just as He took over my Dead Eye."

"You'll be gone? Just as our Champion is no more?"

"Yes," Dove said.

"I—I will still serve you faithfully, Mistress," Lily said with a sob. "Even when you are no more."

"Thank you, Lily. But for right now, I need a friend more than I need a servant," Dove said. "Will you be my friend?"

Lily hugged Dove more tightly. "I already am, Mistress. It just took you until now to know it. And I know it's blasphemous to say, but I do not want a Goddess to take over your body."

"Neither do I, Lily, and after hearing what the God revealed to me today I am beginning to think the Goddess does not want it, either." Dove lifted her head. Her hand found Lily's soft face. Gently, Dove traced the lines of her cheek. "Will you help me, my friend?"

"Yes, Mistress. What is it you would like my help with?"

Suddenly Dove knew what she must do. "Have the other Attendants gathered sacrificial creatures as the God commanded?"

"Of course, Mistress. They try to only capture creatures that do not appear to be sick—just as your Dead Eye commanded before the God silenced him."

"And there are creatures caught right now? Being held for the morning sacrifice?" Dove asked, feeling more and more hopeful.

"Yes, Mistress. They are caged on the floor below us."

"Take me there—quickly and quietly. Draw no attention from the God or His Reapers."

Without another word Lily took Dove's hand. They tiptoed on bare feet from the Chamber of the God to the broken staircase. Lily helped her Mistress pick her way slowly down to the floor below them, which was empty except for several cages, one of them filled with animals waiting to be sacrificed.

"What have they captured?" Dove asked, running her hands over the wooden cages.

"Pigeons," Lily said. "Six of them. They are all in one cage."

Dove lifted her face, feeling for wind from one of the many broken windows. "Help me carry their cage to the opening, there, across from us."

"Yes, Mistress." At the window Lily paused with Dove beside her. "Now what?" she asked.

"Now we pray," Dove said. She bowed her head and spoke the words hesitantly at first and then with growing confidence as she felt the rightness of it within her. "Great Goddess, I am Dove—the vessel your Consort, the God of Death, wishes you to inhabit after He forces you to awaken. But, Goddess, I believe you do not wish to be awakened, just as I do not wish to be possessed. If I am right, I beg your help, Great Goddess! Save me from Death, please. To show my respect and my fidelity to you, I release these creatures that were to be sacrificed to Death, and instead I give them to you, to Life, as I also give myself and my life to you!" Dove felt around until she found the latch that held the cage closed and then opened it. In a flurry of wings the pigeons flew from their jail, rushing through the window and into the night sky.

"Did She speak to you?" Lily asked in a small, tremulous voice.

"I can't tell yet," Dove said. "But I feel the rightness of this within me, and it is enough that I make this offering to the Goddess. Let us hope that She is content to sleep and does not wish to awaken."

Lily's small hand closed over her Mistress's. "I follow you, Mistress, and if you worship this Great Goddess, so will I."

"Then know this: I will never enter the City in the Trees, and I will never be made into a shell for a Goddess to claim, even if it's against Her will."

"But the God just said that we will take the city in four days."

"*He* will. I will not."

Dove felt Lily nod slowly. "I understand."

"And still you will help me?"

"I will."

"No one must know," Dove said.

"What of the other Attendants?" Lily asked.

"Do you trust them completely?"

Lily hesitated, and into the silent pause the sounds of woman's giggles drifted from the God's balcony above, punctuated by deeper murmurs of male voices speaking intimately, coaxingly, teasingly.

"No," Lily whispered sadly. "I do not trust them. They serve you, Mistress. They even like you. But all they can speak of is the City in the Trees and the new life awaiting us there."

"And is that not what you want, too?"

"It was, until *He* took over our Champion." Lily slid even closer to Dove and lowered her voice so that her Mistress had to strain to hear her. "I have watched him. He does not treat you with the respect His Oracle deserves, as Dead Eye treated you. And if He can treat you so roughly, what chance do any of the rest of us have?"

"Thank you, Lily." Dove felt weak with relief.

"Where shall we go, Mistress?"

"Anywhere that is not ruled by Death."

"Odysseus!" Thaddeus looked around, thoroughly annoyed. It was already dark. He'd found the perfect tree to spend the night in—it had a serviceable nest, one that hadn't been discovered and packed with the sick or wounded. There were even blankets left on the sleeping pallet and they didn't reek of smoke—or at least they didn't reek *too much* of smoke. He'd rigged a rope sling and was ready to pull himself and Odysseus up for the first decent night's sleep they'd had since that Scratcher bitch had caused the forest fire—and somehow he'd lost Odysseus. Again.

Thaddeus put his hands on his hips, whistled sharply, and focused his mind on calling the Terrier to him.

He felt Odysseus then and with a small jolt of surprise realized just how weak his connection to his Companion had become. Thaddeus began searching around the base of the tree in earnest, sending more energy to their bond.

He heard the whimper before he saw the canine. Lifting the torch he was holding, Thaddeus moved toward the sound. Finally, Odysseus's eyes caught the torch's firelight.

"There you are!" Thaddeus hurried to the Terrier. "What are you doing over here in the dark? I thought you were right behind me. Come on. I found a habitable nest. Let's get up to it before some do-gooder decides to pack it with people." Thaddeus slapped his thigh, expecting Odysseus to trot up to him, as usual. But the little Terrier only whined again and turned his head, trying to lick at the stained bandage wrapped around his flank.

"Yeah, I know it's sore. But if you don't use it, it'll never get better. Come on, Odysseus!" he commanded.

With a pain-filled yelp, the Terrier staggered forward, dragging his wounded leg.

Thaddeus sighed. "Oh, okay. I'll carry you, but only this once." He went to Odysseus, carefully picking him up—and noticed instantly how warm the Terrier felt. "Hey, I think you might be worse. How about some water?" He carried Odysseus back to the base of the tree, where he'd placed a pack filled with food and a water bladder. Thaddeus put Odysseus down, then poured water into his cupped hand, offering it to the canine.

Odysseus lapped a little of the water before turning his head away.

"Hey, you're going to have to do better than that, but it can wait until we're up there, snugly in bed." Working efficiently, Thaddeus slung the pack over his shoulder, placed the torch in a holding spot built into the tree, and then picked up Odysseus, who felt limp and hot in his arms.

Thaddeus tried not to worry. Instead, he focused on putting one hand over the other as he used the pulley system he'd rigged to lift himself and Odysseus up to the welcoming, familiar, arms of a giant pine.

Then Thaddeus set about lighting a small hearth fire and heating up the rabbit stew he'd confiscated from one of the two remaining warrens while Odysseus lay silently at the end of the pallet.

"Hey, buddy! Food's ready!" Thaddeus called to Odysseus, but the Terrier barely raised his head before closing his eyes, tucking his nose, and going back to sleep. "Are you sure? I'm gonna eat yours if you don't wake your butt up."

This time Odysseus didn't even stir.

Thaddeus frowned at his Companion as he ate his way through the stew. Odysseus was definitely *not* himself. "Because of that bitch. All of this is because of that bitch," Thaddeus muttered softly. It really pissed him off. Odysseus was *always* at his side. *Always* listening to him. *Always* in agreement with his Companion. And now what was he? Tired . . . hurt . . . miserable. "All because of *Mari*." Thaddeus spoke the name as if it tasted bitter. "Well, I'm not going to let her get away with it. She needs to be stopped, and Nik needs to pay for being a traitor."

Odysseus's eyes slitted open and the Terrier sighed heavily, in agreement with his Companion.

"That's right!" Thaddeus bent forward, gently ruffling the dark fur around the Terrier's ears. "*We're* not going to let either of them get away with it."

Thaddeus leaned back, chewing his stew contemplatively. *But how do I stop someone who can call down sunfire?*

You can have more. You deserve more. All you need is power . . .

Unbidden, the words drifted through Thaddeus's mind. He'd had the same thoughts earlier, when he'd confronted that arrogant asshole Wilkes.

Of course he needed more power—enough to defeat sunfire. But how? *How?*

"I'd give anything to get rid of Mari and Nik." Thaddeus ground the words between clenched teeth as he watched his Odysseus sleep fitfully. "Anything . . ."

CHAPTER 28

So, there are twenty-eight of us, not counting our Companions," Antreas said.

"That many? Really?" Sora looked pale.

"You did invite everyone," Antreas said.

"They're our Pack!" Mari almost barked at the cat man.

Antreas held up his hands in surrender. "Okay, okay! I hear you. I didn't mean anything—or at least not anything too bad. We'll make it work, which is why I asked you to call this meeting."

"All right, we're here," Nik said, speaking slowly and reasonably. "We trust you. Tell us what we need to do."

Antreas ran his hand through his hair, making the top of it stand up in spiky tufts. "We need supplies, medications, and travel shelters for twenty-eight people and several animals. We need to go west—through the mountains—and into the Wind Rider Plains. It's a journey of many weeks—months even, depending on the weather. If we don't get through the Middle Pass of the Rockies before snow and ice close it, we all die."

"So, we must get through the pass. We are leaving soon. You said before we had enough time," Nik said.

"Yeah, that was before, when there were only a few of us—young, healthy, strong. You added more." Antreas shook his head. "We're going to need to move and move fast, or it will definitely be too late."

"No," Mari said. "It isn't too late. You said it yourself—before, we had enough time. So all we need is to move quickly. Don't underestimate us. Earth Walkers are tough."

"They are," Antreas said. "But that doesn't change the terrain or the distance. Or the danger. The bigger the group, the more insects you draw."

"And the more people you have to fight them off," Danita said.

Mari sent her an appreciative look, thinking that she liked this young Moon Woman more and more. "Danita's right. We might draw bugs—but we'll kill them, too. Stop telling us about the problems. Help us find solutions."

Antreas sighed. "If you want to take all of these people there is only one viable solution. We must go down the river."

"The Killum?" Nik shook his head. "Bloody beetle balls, I hate that river."

"No, not the Killum. The river north of it—the Umbria, which heads eastward until it empties into Lost Lake. Once we cross the lake, we'll be at the entrance to the Rocky Mountains."

"*More* water travel?" Nik sighed.

"Yes, it'll get us to the pass before snow closes it. It'll also be easier traveling over water than over land—though not without a good amount of danger, but faster, so safer. Here." Antreas moved to the table that sat not far from the central hearth of the birthing burrow. From a satchel he carried slung across his back he unrolled a length of rough mapmaking paper. On it Antreas pointed to waving lines, triangle markings, shaded mounds, and various other indecipherable scrawlings. "See here." He pointed to a thick line that snaked in an east–west direction across part of the paper until it ran into a huge, strangely shaped blob of blue. Backing to the east of the blue spot was a clump of massive triangles with strange geometric markings throughout. "This is the Umbria River, and this is Lost Lake."

O'Bryan spoke up. "I'm not ashamed to admit that the Umbria scares me, and Lost Lake?" He shuddered. "We've all heard stories of it. It's haunted by the ancients. And it's supposed to be bottomless."

"Of course it's haunted and it might be bottomless, so it's a good thing that we're not traveling under it, but over it," Antreas admitted. "Look, that river will get you past Skin Stealers, mutated plants, and a high desert that will make you want to drink your tears. The lake will save us weeks of travel, which means we'll have time to make it through the Middle Pass before it traps us in a frozen world of blinding white with its own special brand of bugs."

"Great. Just what we need. More bugs," Danita said.

"You can handle them," Antreas said. "Bast says you're tough."

Mari watched the smile bloom on Danita's face. "As usual, your Bast is right!" Danita said, meeting and holding the Companion's gaze so frankly that it was Antreas who finally blushed and looked away.

Mari cleared her throat, calling Antreas's attention back. "So, we need to travel down the river and over that giant lake. Which means we need boats." She sighed and looked from Sora to Danita, Isabel, and Jenna. As apprenticed Moon Women, Mari had insisted they attend what Sora was calling their first Pack Council meeting, along with O'Bryan, Nik, and Antreas. "We can make boats, right?"

"Well, rafts, yes," Isabel said. "But they're more for just trading with Clan Carpenter and floating our goods down Crawfish Creek to them."

"Rafts will help carry our supplies, and they can also be used as litters when we do have to travel overland," Antreas said. "But we'll need real boats—though they don't have to be big."

"Clan Fisher could teach us how to build them," Danita said.

"But they're days away on the coast," Jenna said. "And from what Antreas says we definitely don't have time for boatbuilding."

"The Tribe of the Trees has boats," Nik said. Everyone turned to him. "Small ones. A lot of them."

O'Bryan nodded. "They're in the Channel. Dozens of them."

"They'll be guarded," Antreas said.

"Actually, they probably won't be," Nik said. "There is only one lookout post near the bridge to Farm Island, and I would bet no one is manning it. Not so soon after the fire." Nik looked away, pain flashing across his face.

Mari touched his shoulder. "I remember. Like the little boat we rowed away in."

Nik collected himself and nodded. "Yes, and more, smaller boats, too. We call them kayaks. I . . . I don't like to think about stealing from the Tribe, though. There is just no honor in it."

"Then let's not steal the boats. Let's trade for them," Mari said.

"What?" Nik said, though he sat up straighter, his eyes lighting.

"I have an idea." Mari looked to Sora. "When I was in the Tribe, I saw how much the people value beauty and art. Is there any way we could repair the tapestry of the Great Mother over the next few days?"

"We could. I know we could," Sora said. "That's a wonderful idea, Mari!"

"Wait, what?" Nik said.

"I saw the beauty in your City in the Trees," Mari said. "Well, we have beauty here, too. You'll see, Nik. And I assure you, the tapestry our women will leave in place of the boats will make it clear you didn't steal anything."

"I can live with that," Nik said. "So, it's decided. We'll travel down the Umbria River to Lost Lake, and from there we'll go through the Rocky Mountains to the Plains of the Wind Riders."

"Dawn, six days from now," O'Bryan said.

"In six days." Mari nodded her head. She turned to Antreas. "What else do we need to do?"

"Everyone takes only what they, or their canine, can carry. We'll need those cocoons you Tribesmen use when you're traveling. Sometimes we can tie together and stay on the river all night. That'll be a good night. Most times we'll have to beach and find somewhere to sleep. And that somewhere needs to be up, away from bugs."

"Mari, can the women weave large rectangles of strong plant fibers into cloth-sized cloaks?" Nik asked.

"Yes, no problem. Right, Jenna?" Mari said.

"Right. I'm on it, Mari," Jenna said. "Easily done."

"Lydia and Sarah can help braid rope and can show some of the others how to put the cloaks together to make our traveling cocoons," Nik said.

"Good idea," Antreas said.

"We'll need some kind of pack we can use to strap on the canines," O'Bryan said. "That'll increase our supply load substantially."

"We can do that," Jenna said.

"Impressive," O'Bryan said.

"Basically," Sora said with a quirk of her full lips, "if you can describe it, our women can weave it."

"Then weave some floating packs, too!" O'Bryan said. "Those boats are small. It'll help if we can float supplies beside them."

"But we have to be able to carry the supplies. Don't make the mistake of getting bogged down by too much stuff," Antreas said.

The small group nodded and studied the map.

"So, five days to do all this, huh?" Sora said.

"Five days, then we leave," Mari said. "Let's get to work." As everyone started to head to the door, Mari took Nik's hand, holding him back. "Let's talk."

He waited until everyone else had moved outside earshot. "Sounds serious."

Mari raised her brow. "Of course it's serious. Nik, if we're leaving at dawn, six days from now, when do you think you're going back to the Tribe to get the Mother Plant?"

"In four days I'm going to sneak into the Tribe, harvest a young Mother Plant or two, and then return here to you in time to leave at dawn on the sixth day."

"But you know Sora said you wouldn't be healed yet. You promised."

Nik threaded his fingers with hers and she reluctantly came with him to a pallet close to the hearth fire. "Here, sit with me." He waited for her to sit, her face turned from him, and then, still holding her hand, said, "Mari, don't do this. I know you're worried for me. I'm worried, too. I don't want to go back—not to steal a sacred plant, not like a thief in the night! But we must leave this place quickly. What would you have me do? Wait? Tell Antreas to push back our departure? And if that one or two or three days cause us to get trapped in the pass?"

"No, I know you can't do that. I'm just afraid, Nik. Thaddeus will be out to get you. If he catches you there, he's not going to let you leave, no matter what anyone like Wilkes says."

"Then what's my other choice? Not to go at all? Not to get a Mother Plant? I must do it for the future of our Pack and our children, Mari. Can you imagine an Earth Walker who does not get Night Fever? Wouldn't that be amazing?"

"It would—it *will be*. Just promise me you won't get caught."

"I'll do my best," Nik assured her. "I go back to the Tribe. In four days. And then we leave this place. All of us. Together."

Mari drew a deep breath, nodded, and opened her arms to him. "Do what you need to do. I have your back."

"So, did you talk him out of it?" Sora accosted Mari as she was leaving the burrow.

"It?"

"Going back to the Tribe of the Trees. You know it's a suicide mission, don't you?"

"No, it's not! He knows that place like we know our burrows. He's going to sneak in, get the Mother Plants, sneak out, and join us here so that we leave together at dawn. We'll be down the river and well away before the Tribe even knows he's been there."

"Um-hm," Sora said sardonically. "His wounds will actually be almost healed. I added an extra day or so for your stress level. To lower it, I mean. Though I guess it doesn't matter since he's going back early anyway."

"He's going back because he has to. Sora, what if he's right? What if we wrap our babies in the Mother Plant and it makes them immune to Night Fever?"

Sora sighed and put her arm around Mari. "Then it's worth it. Hey, how about you come with me? You need a break and Danita needs training. I told her to meet me a little way downstream. You know, by where the Clan always plants winter kale."

"Yeah, I know where you mean. What are you going to have her do?"

"Practice dancing her name, of course. That's one of the first lessons you taught me."

"What about Isabel and Jenna?"

"I sent them off to harvest more . . ." Sora paused and held up a finger for each plant she ticked off. "Yarrow, goldenseal, dandelion, and cow parsnip."

"Excellent herbal choices, but definitely not as fun as dancing out their names. Are you becoming a mean teacher?" Mari asked, lifting a brow pointedly.

"No! Isabel and Jenna want to be Healers. They can do that without drawing down the moon," Sora said.

"But their skills will only go so far if they don't learn to use moon magick," Mari said.

"Well, yes. Which means Jenna can only go so far—and maybe Isabel, too. I think Danita has shown the greatest aptitude for drawing down the moon."

"Yeah, I think so, too. But that doesn't mean Isabel and Jenna can't be a lot of help. Especially Isabel. She does have gray eyes," Mari said.

"True. But you can understand why I chose to single out Danita, can't you?" Sora said.

"Makes sense. Okay, so you're right. Let's go. It'll be nice to watch you dance your name with Danita," Mari said.

"Me? But you're the real teacher. You taught me. I thought you'd want to show her how to do it," Sora said.

Mari shook her head. "Nope. It's your turn. Pass it along. And someday Danita will be teaching another young girl how to dance her name to the moon."

"It's a lovely ritual, don't you think? I'll always remember the night you taught me how to do it." Sora and Mari shared a smile.

"And I'll always remember that night, too, as well as the night

Mama taught me." Mari blinked hard to keep tears from spilling from her eyes.

"How are you doing? You and I really haven't had time to talk."

"I'm good. Better every day. I still miss Mama, though. A lot. How about you? What are you going to do if Jaxom comes back?" *Or doesn't come back,* Mari added silently to herself.

Sora moved her smooth shoulders restlessly. "I don't know. I thought he was going to be my mate, and now . . ." Her voice trailed off sadly.

"You can't forgive him for what he did?"

"I can forgive him. I already have. But I see him differently now. He's not that young, sweet guy who worked so hard at courting me that it was almost embarrassing." Sora paused and smiled slyly. "Well, no. I wasn't embarrassed. I liked him working that hard. But now he's the guy who attacked and almost raped me."

"He was sick when he did that," Mari said as the two Moon Women walked along the stream, waving occasionally to the groups of women who were already busy repairing the Earth Mother tapestry as they listened to Nik, O'Bryan, and Davis describe what they needed for the traveling cocoons or were harvesting vegetables and herbs from the birthing burrow's garden. Mari noticed that even Lydia and Sarah were moving slowly among the herbs, pulling tender basil leaves.

"My mind knows that. My heart and body don't seem to. Mari, I don't think I could stand to ever be with him again—not as lovers." Sora sounded miserable.

"Well, that just means there's someone else who's meant for you. And for him, too."

"What if he doesn't come back? Are we going to look for him?"

Mari considered her answer carefully before speaking. "Jaxom knows where we are. He should return on Third Night to be Washed. If he doesn't . . ."

"If he doesn't he's chosen to live like a monster."

"Sora, it was the Skin Stealer sickness that made him a monster. You know our Clansmen can be violent during Night Fever, but they don't suddenly turn into rapists and killers. Most of their aggression is turned on themselves, just like our women turn within themselves with depression if they have no Moon Woman. I was thinking that if he doesn't show up he found other Clansmen who were sick, and it was too late to get them to listen to him."

"And they killed him," Sora finished for her.

"Or reinfected him," Mari added.

"Either way, going to look for him doesn't make sense."

"No. But you know what does make sense? Teaching our friend how to introduce herself to the moon." Mari jerked her chin to the right of the stream they'd been following. Danita was there, sitting on a mossy rock, chin in her hand, staring up at the sky as if it held the answers to all of life's mysteries.

"You're right. Would you hold Chloe for me?" Sora pulled the sleeping ball of pup from the front of her tunic and handed the yawning, complaining creature to Mari.

"I had no idea she was down the front of your shirt," Mari said, cradling the baby close to her, shushing Chloe as she started to whine in earnest.

"She's always next to me. Well, unless she's eating." Sora kissed Chloe on her little black nose. "Be good for Mari. I'll be right back." She started to walk toward Danita and then paused. "Hey, where's Rigel?"

"He and Laru went with Davis and Cammy. Seems Rigel wants to learn how to hunt, which surprised Davis, especially when Laru joined in. Apparently Shepherds don't usually *lower* themselves to being Hunters." Mari rolled her eyes.

"Those are Tribe rules. This is a Pack. It's different," Sora said.

"You mean different like a Terrier choosing an Earth Walker as her Companion?" Mari grinned at her friend.

"Exactly!" Sora blew another kiss at Chloe before she went to Danita and began teaching her how to spell out her name for the moon.

Mari looked around and found a comfy-looking spot under a young maple tree. She brushed leaves from the bed of moss beneath it; then with a sigh she sat, leaning against the bark as she rearranged Chloe. The pup was fat and warm, and her breath had a wonderfully distinctive scent Mari already thought of as "puppy breath," and it wasn't long before she had Chloe arranged on her lap, fast asleep again.

Mari tipped her head back, gazing up at the afternoon sky that was the exact shade of diluted blueberry dye. "Looks like it's going to rain again," she murmured to the sleeping pup, mostly just to hear her own voice. "That's good for the harvest . . ." she began, and then trailed off, realizing for the first time in her life she wouldn't be here, in Clan Weaver lands, to harvest summer crops.

The realization had her feeling sad and excited at once. "What's going to become of us, little Chloe? I know we have to leave, but sometimes I feel like I'm leading my people, my Pack, to a path on a moonless night that might end at the edge of a cliff that we might all be hurling ourselves over." Mari sighed. "Know what I mean, little girl?"

"She might not, but I do."

"Great Goddess! Antreas, you scared the breath out of me!" Mari snuggled Chloe close, as the pup had been startled, too, and was whining fretfully. "S-s-sh, it's just Antreas."

"Put her next to Bast. She'll quiet down and sleep." Antreas pointed at his Lynx, who had somehow soundlessly found a spot not more than a couple of feet away from Mari and was grooming herself meticulously.

"Really? She won't, uh, bite Chloe or anything, will she? Sora will be over here in a heartbeat if anything happens to her pup."

"Well, I could repeat myself, but why don't you just ask Bast?"

Mari looked at the big feline, who paused in her grooming and met her gaze.

"Bast, may Chloe lie beside you?" Mari asked the Lynx, feeling slightly foolish.

To Mari's surprise, the feline instantly got up and padded over to her. She sniffed at Chloe, who lifted her head and sniffed Bast right back, wriggling her fat little body along with her wagging tail and licking the Lynx on her nose. She sneezed indignantly, then made her coughing noise before curling up at Mari's feet and looking expectantly at the pup.

"So, I'm thinking that's a yes," Mari said, sending Antreas a look.

"A definite yes," Antreas agreed.

Mari plopped Chloe down close to the Lynx, and Bast set to grooming the little canine as the pup wagged her tail, flopped over on her back, and yawned mightily.

"Thank you," Mari said to the Lynx. "I had no idea you were a good babysitter."

Antreas laughed. "She is—but only when she wants to be. That's how felines are."

"She's really very beautiful," Mari said, taking time to study the Lynx. "I especially like all that fur around her face. And those black things on her ears are pretty."

"Ear tufts," Antreas explained, "actually serve a purpose. They help catch sound. Her hearing is almost as sharp as her eyesight."

"It's interesting. I thought Mama and I knew so much about the world. I was wrong, though."

"Wait till you meet the Wind Riders and their equines. They're unexpectedly beautiful."

Mari heard a change in Antreas's voice, and she shifted her attention from his Lynx to him and saw that he was staring downstream where Sora and Danita were beginning to dance out the letters of their names.

"Unexpectedly beautiful, huh?"

Antreas turned his gaze back to Mari. His smile was wry. "Yes. Unexpectedly."

"You know, I believe Danita has the power to draw down the moon, and not just channel it like she did last night," Mari said.

"Of course she does." Antreas didn't miss a beat.

"Well, you sound pretty certain, especially for a guy who's never drawn down the moon," Mari teased.

"I am." Antreas didn't so much as crack a smile.

"How?"

"Bast told me. And Bast is never wrong."

"Never wrong, huh? What about the fact that she obviously has chosen Danita as your mate?"

There was a long pause, broken only by Bast's rolling purr.

Finally Antreas spoke. "Like I said, Bast is never wrong. Annoying, yes. Wrong, no. Now, if you'll please excuse us, my Lynx and I were on our way for a run. We should get to it." He picked up the complaining Chloe and deposited her on Mari's lap before disappearing into the forest.

Bast stood more slowly. Mari was almost certain she heard the big feline sigh. She padded to Chloe and gave her one more lick, then licked Mari's hand, too. Mari grinned and, tentatively, reached out to stroke the Lynx's head.

"Wow, you're even softer than you look," Mari told her.

Bast chirped happily, licked the pup again, and then silently melted into the forest after her Companion.

Mari resituated Chloe, this time tucking her inside her tunic, like Sora had taken to doing. Almost instantly the pup fell asleep. Mari felt her eyelids get heavy as well as she watched Sora and Danita dance, lifting their arms joyously to the sky.

Oh, Mama, Mari thought sleepily. *I wish you could be here to see this—all of these different kinds of people and animals coming together to make a Pack.* Mari closed her eyes, and as she drifted to sleep the wind blew through the tree boughs above her, whispering, *I am here, sweet girl. . . . I am watching. . . .*

Mari's dreams were usually disjointed snippets of pieces of her life, mixed with bizarre things—like Rigel sprouting wings and flying—that could not exist in the waking world.

This dream was different. From the beginning the entire texture of it was unlike anything Mari had ever experienced. It seemed to Mari that she was watching her dream through a soft, beautiful light from a great distance away. She saw herself then, standing on a high ridge, overlooking the Tribe of the Trees. Half of it was a blackened mess. She could see Companions, who should be working diligently on rebuilding the city in the sky but were instead shuffling about the forest floor as if they were characters in a walking nightmare.

Then there was a terrible darkening of the sky, and like a tidal wave, painted Warriors descended upon the Tribe, overwhelming them, destroying them. Sickened by the slaughter, Mari was trying to wake herself when from the middle of the battle a single dove, as silver-gray as a Moon Woman's eyes, flew frantically away from the carnage—and straight to Mari!

Will you help me? I cannot fly any farther by myself! The little dove's voice was inside Mari's head as the bird fluttered around her, obviously at the end of her strength.

Instinctively, Mari began to lift her arm to give the dove a place to land, but then her mama's voice was inside her head, too.

Help her, but the price of your aid is her vow to be truthful.

Mari met the dove's gray-eyed gaze. *I will help you, but you must promise to always tell me the truth.*

If you ask it of me, I will give you only the truth—but you must ask it of me, Moon Woman.

Then I'll help you. Mari lifted her arm, and the dove landed gracefully on it.

Mari felt pressure on her arm, and her eyes shot open.

"Hey, wake up! You and Chloe are such lazybones!" Sora was shaking Mari's arm.

Mari peered up at her, blinking sleep and confusion from her eyes. "You're not a dove."

"What?"

Mari hesitated and still half asleep said, "If you see a dove, be careful with her. Help her. I think she important, but only if you make her tell you the truth."

"By the smooth thighs of the Goddess, what are you talking about?"

Mari rubbed her eyes and sat up as Chloe whined a sleepy puppy complaint, Sora's tone bringing her full awake. "Sorry, I was dreaming."

Sora's gaze sharpened on her friend. "Dreams can bring omens and signs, especially the dreams of a Moon Woman."

"Okay, yes, I know."

"So, tell me what you saw."

"In my dream a dove flew away from the Tribe of the Trees as it was being destroyed by painted Warriors. She came to me looking for sanctuary. Mama's voice told me to help her, but only if she vows to a Moon Woman to tell the truth as the price of my aid." Mari shrugged. "Does that mean anything to you?"

"Not a thing, but I'll keep an eye out for doves," Sora said.

"And if you find one, help her," Mari said.

"But only if she vows to tell me the truth. Okay, yeah, I heard you."

Feeling strangely relieved, Mari combed her fingers through her hair and looked around. Danita was still over by the stream, carefully dancing the pattern of her name around the mossy clearing. "It's nice that she gets to practice it like this before she dances in front of everyone. She seems to be doing well."

"Yeah, if anything I'm worried that her desire to be perfect will get in the way of the joy she should be feeling when she dances to the moon. And you said joy is a big part of it, right?"

"That's what Mama taught me. How about you and I join her tonight, so she doesn't feel too much like she's on display?" Mari said.

"Nice idea. So, we're Washing the Pack again tonight?"

"Actually, I thought we'd only Wash those who were injured. Third Night is tomorrow. There really isn't any problem with anyone who's healthy waiting until then to be Washed," Mari said.

"Yeah. They don't need to get into a habit of us drawing down the moon every day. It takes a lot out of me. Is it like that for you, too?" Sora asked, sitting beside Mari and taking the still-sleeping Chloe from her friend.

"It can be, but Mama would remind us to keep some of the moon magick for ourselves, even though she usually forgot to take her own advice," Mari said.

"It's hard because I still feel like I only have a limited amount of time I can handle drawing down the moon before it gets to be too much for me. So, I want to give it all to the Pack."

"I think that'll change as we practice. Plus, now there are two of us." Mari jerked her chin in the direction of Danita. "With a very likely third. So, we can start sharing the duties. Did you know Bast told Antreas that Danita does have the power to draw down the moon?"

"That cat knows stuff," Sora said. "It's a little creepy. Canines are much better." She nuzzled Chloe, who made sleepy annoyed puppy noises in response.

"Oh, please. Just a few days ago you were complaining about Rigel and all creatures canine."

"Well, I'll still complain about Rigel, but this little girl is spectacular." Sora kissed Chloe, waking her completely so that the pup started whining in earnest. "Oops, I shouldn't have woken her. She's hungry. Gotta take her back to Fala."

"I'll come with you. I need to check on Lydia's and Sarah's wounds."

"Should we call Danita?"

Both gazes went to the earnest dark-haired girl who was diligently dancing a pattern that spelled out the letters of her name across the soft, waiting earth.

"Nah," Sora said. "Let her practice. It helps her nerves. And she's within calling distance of the rest of the Pack—no harm in leaving her here."

"Okay." The two Moon Women began to follow the stream back to the burrow. "Hey, I'm starting to think Antreas may actually be interested in Danita—as in potential mate interested."

"Well, he did listen when I told him how to court an Earth Walker," Sora said.

"He asked?"

"More like he put his foot directly into his mouth with Danita and then I educated him. But he seemed to listen."

"Life just gets more and more interesting," Mari said, ruffling Chloe's fur.

"I did used to say I never wanted to be bored," Sora said.

"So, all of this is your fault?" Mari teased.

"Probably. And you're welcome."

CHAPTER 29

O kay, one more time," Danita told herself aloud. She spread her arms, tilted back her head, and began to trace a *D* into the earth while she attempted to do as Sora had instructed—be graceful and joyful. Danita had decided to settle, at least for the moment, for not tripping over her own feet. She moved alongside the stream, adding letters to her dance and feeling more and more confident—especially after Sora and Mari had left. Danita liked both Moon Women—very much actually—but she was also extremely self-conscious around them. They always seemed so sure of themselves! Maybe she'd be like that one day in the future. "I hope so," she sighed to herself as she finished the last letter in her name, and then she went to the stream, lifted up the mid-calf-length tunic she was wearing, and waded gratefully into the cool, clear water.

Danita splashed water on her face and arms while her feet found smooth stones. Her toes dug into the mixture of river rock and mud. The feeling was delightful. She kept wading in the stream, not paying much attention to the fact that she was moving with the small current away from the burrow. A sparkle caught her eye and Danita bent to pick up a crystal of a size that fit perfectly into the palm of her hand.

"It's the shape of a heart." She spoke softly. Closing her eyes, she gripped the crystal, holding it close to her breast. "Thank you, Great

Goddess. Thank you for this sign of your favor." Reluctant to leave the stream and the magic moment it helped to create, Danita waded farther downstream, keeping a sharp eye out for any more special signs of the Goddess's favor. Finally, her feet getting cold, she climbed out of the water and onto a gently sloping moss-covered bank. Choosing a wide, flat boulder not far from the stream, Danita lay back on it, staring up at the sky creatures the puffy clouds were creating.

She was drifting off to sleep when a strange sound brought her senses instantly alert. Danita turned, sliding quietly off the boulder to crouch beside it, silently cursing herself, heart hammering in her chest. *I should have never waded so far alone!*

A flash in the trees on the opposite side of the stream caught her eye, and Danita turned so that she could peer across the water and remain concealed by the boulder and the thickly clumped ferns that surrounded it.

At first she didn't realize what she was seeing—it seemed so strange, so impossible. *Could this be real, or am I asleep and dreaming?*

Her breath caught in her throat as she realized she was indeed awake and what she was witnessing was very real.

Antreas and Bast were racing through the forest. But they weren't simply running, or even jumping over fallen logs and other forest debris. Bast and Antreas were leaping from tree to tree! Lynx and man appeared to fly, and they were playing some kind of silly game, where Bast would run up and swat Antreas on the butt (or anywhere a paw could swipe) and then she'd take off and it would be Antreas's turn to race after his Companion until he could tag her and then the game repeated all over again.

Danita stared at Antreas as he shouted at Bast, "Hey, watch those claws! You scratched my butt!"

The Lynx chirped at him, in a voice so filled with sweetness that Danita knew the big feline was making fun of her Companion.

"Oh, you think that's funny, do you? Watch yourself. I'm going to be pulling that black-tipped tail of yours!" And Antreas took off after his Lynx, chasing her around, over, and up trees, logs, and boulders.

Danita was surprised to find herself grinning broadly at the two of them. Of course Bast was spectacular. Danita adored the big feline. What was unexpected was the reaction Danita was having to Antreas. He looked so young and happy that for the first time Danita thought she might consider him handsome. She kept watching him and received a second surprise. *His hands! They're changed!* Danita squinted as the afternoon sunlight caught what should have been a human hand, glinting off dagger-sharp talons that had taken the place of fingernails.

"Wow. That's incredible."

Danita hadn't meant to speak aloud—hadn't even realized she had until Bast's head snapped around and her preternaturally sharp eyesight focused on the rock and then on Danita crouching beside it. With a delighted yowl that turned into a chirping, happy greeting, Bast broke off the game of chase she was playing with her Companion and raced to the stream, leaping it with one flying jump, running directly to Danita. She giggled as the big feline almost knocked her over, rubbing against her, purring loudly.

"It's good to see you, too!" Danita kissed the Lynx on the head between her charcoal-tufted ears.

Danita had been so happy greeting Bast that she'd almost forgotten about Antreas. Then he spoke as he crossed the stream in a more sedate manner and joined them. "What are you doing here?"

"Thinking," Danita said.

"Pretty far from the burrow to be thinking all by yourself."

"Well, part of getting away to think means getting *away*. And I'm not all by myself. You and Bast are here now. What were you two doing? It looked like you were playing a game."

"I'll tell you if you tell me what you were thinking about," Antreas said, sliding up to sit on the flat-topped boulder.

Danita gave a *well, why not?* shrug and climbed up beside him, with Bast jumping up gracefully with her. "I was thinking about being a Moon Woman. And I'm nervous about dancing my name to the moon tonight," she admitted.

"Aren't Isabel and Jenna dancing with you, too? They were also accepted as Moon Woman apprentices."

"No, we're dancing one at a time, and I'm first. It's really a personal thing—an introduction through the Great Mother to the moon as another face of the Goddess. Tradition says it's more intimate, more respectful, to do it one at a time."

"Then that's all you need to remember tonight," Antreas said.

"What is?"

"That it's personal. It's between you and the Goddess. That's all you need to care about—not the watching Pack, not even Mari or Sora. It's just you and the Goddess out there. No one else."

Danita studied him thoughtfully. "That's actually helpful. I'm not nervous about the Goddess; I'm excited. And if she's all I think about, I can pretend like no one else is even there tonight."

"Exactly! And you don't have anything else to be nervous about. You're going to make a great Moon Woman."

Danita's brows hit her hairline. "Why would you say that?"

"Because it's the truth and it's a nice thing to say. Or at least I meant it to be nice. The way you're looking at me right now, I'm not so sure."

"Oh, it was nice to say. I'm just confused about why you said it."

"I thought I covered that in the first part of my answer. Because it's the truth. You're going to be a great Moon Woman."

"How do you know?"

"Bast told me," Antreas admitted.

Danita turned her head to meet the Lynx's yellow-eyed stare that was so much like her Companion's. "You think I'm going to be a great Moon Woman?" she asked the feline.

Bast chirped at her, then coughed, then purred like a storm as she rubbed against the girl.

"I know I don't have to tell you, but for the record that's a yes."

"I get that." Danita blew out a long breath. "And that's a relief."

"So, you believe her?"

"Of course." Danita frowned at him. "Don't you?"

"Yes! I always believe Bast, even when I don't want to," Antreas admitted.

"So, your turn. What were you two doing flying around the forest?"

Antreas chuckled softly. "Flying?"

"That's what it looked like."

"I guess it would," he said. "Bast and I were playing a chase and tag game. It keeps us sharp. Plus, it's fun."

"It looked fun." Danita's gaze slid down to Antreas's very normal-looking hands. "Something happens to your hands when you play the chase game. They change, don't they?"

Antreas's eyes found hers. "Yes. They change. Does that frighten you?"

"No!" Danita said, surprised that he would ask. "Not at all. Um. So, your hands change sometimes. Like when you're flying from tree to tree. Can you make them change whenever you want them to, or does it only happen when you're in the trees?"

"Since Bast chose me and we completed our bonding, my hands have changed, but it's a change I control." There was an awkward pause and then he added, "Other things about me are different, too."

"Oh, you mean like your hair?"

"How did you know that?" Antreas asked as his hand automatically lifted to touch the back of his neck and the Lynx-like pelt that grew there and down his spine.

"Well, it's obvious. Your hair's long, but I can see Bast's fur within it. I figured there's more of it. Is that normal for Lynx Companions? Did you have that fur before you met Bast? What else has changed? Your eyesight? Bast has awesome eyesight. Or maybe your hearing?"

"Slow down! One question at a time!" Antreas's smile was surprised and pleased.

"Oh, sorry. It's just that I've been spending a lot of time with your Lynx—but you know that."

"I do. Bast loves you."

Danita's gray-eyed gaze met Antreas's golden stare. "I love her, too," she said with no hesitation. The silence between them stretched and stretched. Danita wished Bast would say or do something to interrupt—the Lynx was rarely silent—but just then she was curled up between them, appearing to be asleep, though Danita doubted it. She cleared her throat. "Um, that's why I want to know all this stuff. It's fascinating because Bast is fascinating."

"Is that the only reason?"

"Should there be another?" Danita shot back at him with one brow arched.

"Not necessarily. Okay, so, here goes: Yes, I can make my claws come out whenever I want them to. No, I didn't have claws or Bast's fur or enhanced vision or hearing until she chose me and I passed her test."

"Wait; now *you* need to slow down. I want to hear about this test, but first would you mind showing me your claws?" Danita gave him a hesitant smile. Bast's purr heated up.

"I wouldn't mind, as long as you don't scream or anything like that."

"Scream? Why would I do that?" Danita asked.

"Let's just say that women who have never been around a Lynx Chain can sometimes be sensitive to things like claws," Antreas said.

"Well, they must be silly women. I won't scream. I give you my word."

"Okay then." Antreas held out his hand, shook his wrist slightly, and from the beds of his fingernails thick, pointed claws emerged.

Danita sucked in a breath. "Wow! That's fabulous! May I touch them?"

Antreas met her gaze. "Yes."

Danita wasn't hesitant. She reached out and ran a finger down the claw of his pointer finger, pressing it softly against the tip.

"That's really sharp," she said. "So, it's because of these claws that you can fly through the trees like Bast?"

"Yes, that and my enhanced strength. My bond with Bast is deep. When she bit me and I didn't die, it changed who I am at a basic level."

"Bast bit you!" Danita blurted, her eyes going to the Lynx, who still pretended to be napping but whose yellow eyes could be seen slitted through partially closed lids as her purr rolled around them.

"Yep, and it was the best day of my life."

"You're going to have to explain that," Danita said, curling closer to Bast so that she could stroke the Lynx's soft fur as they spoke.

"It's part of the choosing process. When a Lynx picks his or her Companion, she bites her choice. Do you want to see?"

"Yes!" Danita leaned forward eagerly as Antreas rolled up his sleeve, exposing his right arm and the bite scar that was there, surrounded by a tattooed pattern of vines and leaves. "That looks like it hurt."

"It did, but it didn't kill me, and when it didn't kill me that meant Bast and I were bonded for life," Antreas said.

"You mean it could have killed you?" Danita was staring at the bite scar.

"If she'd rejected the den I built for us, yes. But Bast didn't, so the venom in her bite changed me, made me stronger, faster, better— instead of killing me."

"What about these vines and leaves?" Danita reached out and let her finger trace a vine.

"They were added later by an artist who is a priestess of our Great Stormshaker God. It's representative of Bast and me—vines and leaves linking us together."

"Stormshaker God? I don't know about him," Danita said.

"I can tell you, but it's a long story, and it has to do with how Lynxes and humans first started bonding."

"I'd love to hear it." Danita settled more comfortably beside Bast, half leaning against the feline. "And Bast needs a nap. So, why not tell me?"

"Why not indeed?" Antreas muttered.

"What?"

"Nothing. Sure, I'll tell you the story. Just let me know if you get bored."

"Don't be boring and I won't get bored," Danita said with a cheeky glance his way.

"I'll do my best. Okay, so the story goes like this: In ancient times, when the sun storms raged throughout the world, destroying civilization as they knew it, a small group of people escaped into the Rocky Mountains, trying to find respite from the sun and shelter from the storms. This group brought their cats with them."

"Cats? You mean Lynxes, only they called them a different name?"

"No, I mean cats. It's why it can be insulting to call me a cat man, or call Bast a cat." Bast growled low in her throat, though she didn't open her eyes. "Cats were a lot smaller and less powerful than Lynxes, and they lived in cities with their humans, and not in dens like Lynxes. They weren't free, or partners with their Companions. Cats were pets."

"Oh, okay. I understand. Go on."

"So, this group of people fled to the mountains, with their cats."

"Seems like a lot of effort when they're fleeing for their lives, you know—to carry cats along with them. I mean, you said they were smaller, and pets. I'm guessing they couldn't take care of themselves like Bast can."

"You're right, but the ancients loved their cats, just as the ancestors of the Tribe of the Trees refused to leave their dogs behind. So, they brought their cats. A great storm was raging, threatening to wash the group from the mountain trail, and somehow they found the entrance to a den. They ran in to take shelter, only to find a mother Lynx was giving birth to a litter of kittens. The Lynx mother was dehydrated and ill, barely able to give birth to the last of her kittens.

"The humans weren't sure what to do. Most of them huddled near the entrance to the den, staying well away from the Lynx. But one of the women in the group had a mother cat who, not long before, had given birth to a litter of kittens, only to watch each of them die as they fled into the mountains. The woman felt such empathy for the Lynx that we believe the two of them formed the first of the Companion bonds."

"Really? What happened next?"

"The woman helped the Lynx give birth to eight healthy kittens, and then the mother Lynx died."

"No!" Danita said, causing Bast to grumble before relaxing back into sleep.

"Yes, but first the Lynx bit the woman, Marking her as her own, inserting her scent into the woman's blood so that her kittens would know her."

"Yeah, what about the babies?"

"The woman's cat nursed them, raising them as her own," Antreas said.

"That's a sad but nice story," Danita said.

"There's more. The humans, the baby Lynxes, and the cats were trapped in the den—some say for four days, some for fourteen, and some even say for forty full days and nights. Whichever it was, the number four will always be sacred to Lynx people. During this time our God, the Great Stormshaker, pounded the mountains with lightning and sun storms, and something happened within that den— something happened within the Lynx babies, and the humans. When the humans emerged, they were forever changed, as were their children and their children's children. They were bonded on a physical and mental level with the Lynx kittens. That was the first Chain."

"I love that story," Danita said, stroking Bast's soft coat but meeting Antreas's gaze.

"So, you understand now why Bast biting me was the happiest day of my life?"

"I do. Well, actually, I think the happiest day of your life was when you didn't die from her bite," Danita said, smiling at him.

"You're right about that," he said. Antreas paused then. He cleared his throat and drew a deep breath. "Danita, may I ask you something?"

"Yes."

"May we start over? Act like we're just now meeting? I feel like I was a stupid fool when we first met and I—"

"Yes," Danita interrupted.

"Yes?"

"Yes, we may start over. I'd like that," Danita said.

"So would Bast."

"But not you?"

"Sorry, I'm still messing this up. Yes, I would like to start over, too.

Um, Bast and I found something for you." Antreas reached behind him, pulling four long feathers from the satchel he carried strapped across his back.

"Oh! They're raptor feathers! They're beautiful! There are so few raptors left. We almost never find their feathers." She reached for the feathers eagerly but pulled her hand back. "You should keep these. They would make a valuable trade."

Bast coughed and shifted position, laying her head on Danita's lap. "Bast says they're for you. She found them. I just carried them to you. Bast would've gotten them all slobbery."

The big feline slitted her eye at her Companion and sighed dramatically before rolling over and repositioning herself across Danita's lap.

Danita giggled. "I think I got that without your translation."

"Good. I'm not going to repeat what she just said." Antreas offered the feathers again. "Please take them as a gift. From Bast. And from me."

Slowly, Danita took the feathers, taking her time to examine and comment on the beauty of each one before she leaned down and kissed Bast on her nose, saying, "Thank you! I love them." Her gaze lifted to Antreas. "And thank you, too."

"You are very welcome. I'm glad they make you smile. I like your smile. Uh, so does Bast," he added hastily.

Danita cocked her head, studying him. "You know I was attacked not long ago by a group of males, don't you?" Her voice quiet but as steady as her gray-eyed gaze.

"I do. I'm sorry about it. I wish I could have stopped it from happening to you. So does Bast."

"I know she does." Danita blinked quickly as she stroked the sleepy feline. "But no one was there to stop it. The Clansmen. They hurt me. They raped me. I—I'm not sure if I can ever be like a normal girl again."

"Normal is overrated," Antreas said.

Danita looked up at him, her eyes awash in unshed tears.

"I'm not normal, either," he continued. "Lynxes always choose a Companion of their own sex, but Bast chose me. Lynxes are always solitary. They mate and have young, of course, but the male felines don't live with the female felines and the kittens leave the dens, never to return, when they have barely weathered one winter. I've never liked the idea of living such an isolated life, and neither has Bast. So, Bast and I, we're not normal, either."

"I'm glad you're not normal," Danita said.

"For the first time in my life, I'm glad, too," Antreas said.

They stared into each other's eyes for a long time while the feline between them pretended to sleep, even as her rolling purr gave her away.

CHAPTER 30

Nik was standing in the center of a circle of women who were seated cross-legged around him, listening intently as he explained something with great animation. Mari made her way closer, trying to get within hearing distance without interrupting. She settled for sitting, her back to a log, close enough to catch about every fifth word or so.

"He's talking to them about the cloak things he wants them to weave for the traveling cocoons." Jenna came up behind Mari to sit beside her friend.

"I'd just about figured that out. It's funny to see a man teaching Clanswomen, isn't it?" Mari said.

"Well, yeah, it's funny strange. What's seriously funny *bizarre* is the fact that the man is a Companion," Jenna said.

Mari turned her head to meet her friend's gaze. "How are you doing with all of this? Companions killed your father and captured you. It has to be hard, sometimes, to be around them now."

"I had to make a choice. I could either hold on to my anger and allow it to color the rest of my life or I could let it go, start over, join the Pack, and move into the future. I chose to let it go."

"Do you think the other women have chosen that, too?" Mari asked.

Jenna studied the women listening carefully to Nik and nodded. "I think the ones who are content made that choice. The others? We'll know about them soon enough. It's hard to hide hatred."

"I missed you so much while you were gone," Mari said. "And that night—that terrible night your father was killed—I tried to help you. I wanted to help you."

"There's nothing you could have done except what you did—get free and live for another day. Because you did, we're all here right now, starting a new day with a new Pack." Jenna dimpled at her.

Mari returned her smile. "I'm glad you asked to be trained as a Healer. You're really good at it."

"Thank you, Moon Woman!" Jenna said happily. "I did think my best friend was sickly for many years, so I guess you could say I grew up wishing I knew how to cure illnesses." She paused and then added, "It feels so strange to be getting ready to leave here forever. I don't think I've ever been so excited and so frightened at the same time."

"I know what you mean. I'm excited about where we're going, but frightened about leaving our home," Mari said. "I think that's how change is, though."

"It's what your mama would want for us," Jenna said.

"She'd be the first one going through the pass!" Mari laughed softly at the thought of how excited her mama would have been about their upcoming adventure. Then her expression sobered. "I am worried about Nik going back to the Tribe."

"It's dangerous—that's for sure—but if anyone knows what he's doing back there it's Nik. And Davis and Cammy will be with him. If they get into trouble, you'll know about it," Jenna said.

"If I have to go back to that place and get Nik out of there again, I'm not going to be so nice this time."

Jenna's gaze grew hard. Her voice lost its youthful lightness. "I hope you don't have to go back there, either, but if you do, teach them a lesson, Moon Woman."

"Oh, I will, Jenna. I promise."

Wilkes coughed—a terrible, wet sound—and scratched at his elbow. "This is a stupid time to get sick," he muttered to Odin, who was watching him with worry clear in his intelligent amber eyes. With a moan and more effort than it should have taken, Wilkes stood up from the seat he'd taken on the burned ground at the base of what remained of a blackened pine that used to hold nests for an entire family. "Warriors, to me!" he called, and then coughed again.

From the forest around him, Warriors and their Shepherds stood, shaking off leaves and sleep, coughing fitfully. As a group, they were grim faced and quiet. The Shepherds mirrored their Companions' state of mind, staying close to them and lending them strength through their bond. When they were all gathered around him, Wilkes spoke, his voice as dark as his mood.

"We now officially change our mission from a search for survivors to body retrieval. Are we all in agreement?"

Nods and muttered yeses washed through the group.

"Okay, then we begin salvaging everything we can from the ruins. Get all of the metals and mirrors that didn't melt in the fire. Go to each of the lift sites. Let's hope we can salvage at least a few of the pulleys. I don't think many of us are up for making a run to Port City to try to scavenge metal."

"Not with this swarm-be-damned flu that has us all coughing and scratching and thoroughly sick to our stomachs," Claudia said.

"But at least we're alive. Our Companions are alive. The faster we rebuild, the faster we can get the wounded off the ground and back to the safety of the trees," Wilkes said.

"If we have any wounded left," Renard said. "More and more are dying every day. This sickness is taking them more quickly than their burns."

"How is your father?" Wilkes asked the younger man.

Renard rested his hand on his Shepherd Wolf's head. "Not good. He's very ill. I thought he would recover from the burns, but now . . ." He shook his head, unable to continue.

"I'm truly sorry," Wilkes said.

"We are all sorry, but what are we going to do about it?" asked a Warrior named Maxim gruffly.

"We're going to rebuild. We're going to survive," Wilkes said.

"Not without that Scratcher Healer of Nik's," said Maxim.

Wilkes narrowed his eyes at Maxim. "What are you talking about?"

"I'm talking about the same thing Thaddeus and his Hunters have been talking about. That Scratcher bitch has some kind of dark magick that cured O'Bryan and Nik of the blight. It makes sense that if she can cure that she can also cure whatever this sickness is that's spreading through the Tribe, as well as help heal our wounded of their burns."

"I met Mari. She's part Companion—that's obvious by her looks and by the fact that Laru's pup chose her. And she's not a bitch at all," said Claudia.

"She also called down sunfire and saved our Tribe. Is Thaddeus talking about that, too?" Wilkes said.

"That's all the more reason to find her and bring her here," Maxim said.

"Along with Nik," Renard added.

"Nik will return. He said he would, and I believe him," Wilkes said.

"Sure, but when?" Maxim said. "He's snugged away with his Scratcher while we're suffering and barely surviving. If I were him, I sure as bloody beetle balls wouldn't return—or at least not very soon."

"Then your word wouldn't be worth shit," Wilkes said.

"Which is good to know," Claudia said.

"Hey, take your judgment and shove it up a wolf spider's ass!" Maxim told Claudia. "And if you're sweet on Nik, you better remember he has a woman now—a Scratcher woman."

Claudia slowly shook her head. "I'm going to forgive you for that. You're ill and not yourself, although some of us are more ourselves than others."

"I meant everything I just said!" Maxim insisted.

"And I agree with him," Renard said. "If only because we need Nik's woman here as Healer."

Claudia opened her mouth to respond, anger glinting in her eyes, but Wilkes raised his hand, silencing the group.

"There is a point where each of us must make a decision—do we hold true to that which raises us up, or that which is most base about humans? I believe Thaddeus and his ilk have decided to embrace that which is lowest, most base. I don't know if he and his Hunters have done it because that is their way to survive, or whether the darkness, the anger, within them that has been brewing for some time now has an opportunity to overflow. I've chosen differently. And if surviving means I have to lose everything that is good and kind within me to anger, then I would rather not survive. But that is a decision for each man and woman to make. And part of *not* falling into hatred is having the ability to let go. So, how many of you agree with Maxim and Renard?" Wilkes asked. "How many of you believe Nik and Mari should be hunted down and forced to come here as captives?"

"I do," Maxim said quickly. "It's as Thaddeus says. The Tribe has always acted on what is best for the whole, and if that means Nik and a mutant Scratcher woman are inconvenienced to save the rest of us, so be it."

"Inconvenienced? That's what you call captivity and slavery?" Claudia was incredulous.

"Really? You're going to pretend to be above captivity and slavery now?" Maxim sneered. "It didn't bother you when we had an island full of Scratcher slaves tending and harvesting crops for us *for generations*."

"I didn't know better then. I do now," Claudia said. "I met Mari. I listened to Nik. I changed."

Maxim made a disparaging sound and turned his back to her.

"Who else is with Maxim?" Wilkes asked.

"I am," Renard said, only not with the arrogance Maxim showed. "I want my father to live, and Nik's woman is the best chance I have at that."

"Anyone else?" Wilkes prompted again.

Slowly, one by one, each of Wilkes's Warriors, except for Claudia, gave an affirmative. Some reluctantly, sending apologetic looks to their

Leader, but the majority of them responded more like Maxim—angry and ready to do something about it, even as they coughed and looked miserable.

Wilkes blew out a long breath, staring down at the blackened ground beneath him that just days ago had been carpeted by thick, emerald moss. *The world has gone mad,* Wilkes thought before lifting his head and looking around the group.

"Then go to Thaddeus. He is your Leader now, as I cannot in good conscience call you my Warriors if you follow his choices," Wilkes said.

The group stared at Wilkes in disbelief, not moving.

"Go!" he shouted at them. "Go find your new Leader. Plan dark things fueled by anger and fear that will bring you and our people only sadness and suffering. Go!"

Without another word, the Warriors melted away. Except for Claudia and her Companion, Mariah.

"What now?" Claudia asked Wilkes.

"Why are you asking?"

"Because I'm the only Warrior left and I want to know my Leader's plan," Claudia said. "I'm sick, I'm sad, I'm exhausted and afraid, but I have not let sickness and sadness drive me to anger and madness. Neither have you. So, I'll ask again—what's your plan?"

"I'm going to find Nik and warn him and his woman before he walks into a trap," Wilkes said.

"You really think he'll come back?"

"I know he will, and if he does there is no way Thaddeus is going to let him leave, whether Mari is with him or not."

"All right. When are we going?"

"We?"

"Do we really need to go over this again? I'm with you, Wilkes." Claudia coughed, grimaced, and wiped her mouth on her sleeve. "No matter how terrible I feel."

"Okay then. You're with me." Wilkes checked the sky. "It's only about three hours until dusk. To keep Thaddeus from following, we're going to need to leave when he wouldn't expect us to."

"Which means dusk," Claudia said. "I'll put together the travel kits. He doesn't watch me like he does you."

"Be sure you grab torches and tinder. Once we're far enough from the Tribe, we'll light them. They'll keep the wolf spiders away, if nothing else."

"Got it. Where are we meeting?" Claudia asked.

"East of here, at the edge of our city." Wilkes jerked his chin at the ruined forest to his right. "If you get stopped you can always say you're foraging."

Claudia nodded. "The travel packs would look like I thought I might get caught out after dark. Makes sense. At dusk, then?"

"At dusk. Let's go back to camp in different directions. No one should know you're with me."

"Agreed," said Claudia.

They shook hands somberly before separating. Invigorated, Wilkes kicked into a jog, with Odin by his side. The world around Wilkes might have gone mad, but he was determined to hold on to his sanity and to warn Nik—and that determination carried him forward into the unknown.

"Fix him!" Thaddeus spewed spittle into Ralina's face as she turned to look at him over Odysseus's fever-ravaged body.

"I'm sorry. There's nothing I can do. Whether Odysseus lives or dies is up to him." Ralina's voice was filled with pity as she wiped a sleeve across her face.

"That's bullshit! What did the others say? The other Healers?"

Ralina sighed. "Thaddeus, they said the same after they examined him. Odysseus's wound is infected. Badly. It's been packed with herbs and sealed with honey, but he's stopped drinking and eating. If he doesn't fight he's going to die."

"No." Thaddeus scooped up Odysseus, shocked anew at how light his Terrier felt in his arms—as if he was already fading away. "No," he repeated. "You said the fever is killing him?"

"Well, yes. But he only has a fever because of the infection. The knife wound was deep. It got dirty, which isn't surprising in all of this." Ralina gestured around them at the ruined forest. "If he fights off the infection, the fever will break."

"I'll get the sun-be-damned fever to break—no thanks to you or our pathetic Healers." Holding Odysseus close to him, Thaddeus strode away as Ralina stared sadly after him, shaking her head.

Thaddeus walked blindly—not choosing any direction, letting his feet guide him. And as he walked, he kept up a steady stream of words to Odysseus.

"They say you're too hot. Okay. Well. Let's find a stream and cool you off. You'll be good as new in no time. Then you and I will go after that bitch who caused this, and we'll get our payback. Doesn't that sound good, big guy?"

Odysseus opened his eyes. They were rimmed with red and looked brighter than normal. His tail wagged weakly.

"I knew it! Don't you worry. You'll be fine soon, and Nik and Mari will get what they deserve."

And you deserve power! The thought exploded through his mind— foreign, yet familiar, and becoming more and more familiar.

I wonder if I'm going mad, Thaddeus thought.

Does it matter as long as you rule?

I don't have a Shepherd. I can't rule the Tribe of the Trees.

And yet you can, if you have the power to take rather than ask permission!

Thaddeus kept walking—not noticing that the sun was dropping lower and lower in the sky. Not noticing when he entered the edge of Earth Walker territory. All he noticed was the conversation going on within his mind. He didn't come to himself until he heard the sound of water. Thaddeus blinked, as if awaking after a long sleep. He looked around, hardly believing where his feet had taken him.

Thaddeus recognized the clearing instantly.

"This is where that Scratcher bitch's mother died." He glanced down at Odysseus, who barely opened his fever-bright eyes. "See? There's a creek here and those stupid statue things the Scratchers grow. Let's get you some water, big guy."

Gently, Thaddeus crouched beside the edge of the crystal creek, easing Odysseus from his arms and supporting him as he pointed his cracked muzzle toward the water.

"Go on, drink. It'll help you."

Odysseus whined softly and turned his head away.

"Look, you have to try. I know you're not going to like this, but I'm going to hold you in the water." As Thaddeus spoke, he unwrapped the bandage from around the Terrier's flank. The scent of rot lifted from the oozing wound. Thaddeus ignored it. "I'm going to carry you into the water. It'll wash some of that puss and crap out of the wound *and* cool you down."

But as Thaddeus lifted his Companion and began carrying him farther into the creek, the Terrier started whining in earnest and squirming so violently that his wound completely broke open.

"Hey, hey! Stop. Okay, okay. I'll wait a little while."

Feeling hollow, Thaddeus sloughed from the creek with Odysseus in his arms. He made his way to one of the ridiculous statues and collapsed next to it, leaning against it as he placed Odysseus on the soft moss beside him.

Odysseus's eyes were closed tightly, but he was panting and whining softly.

I have to help him! I have to stop his pain! Thaddeus screamed in silent impotence. *I can't lose him!*

Then, miraculously, the words that had been drifting through Thaddeus's mind came to him once again, only this time they felt different— as if they were flowing directly from Odysseus.

You'll never lose Odysseus. Your flesh has joined. Your spirits can now join, too. It is simple. But you must choose. If you choose Life . . . your Companion will be healed and all will eventually go back to how it used to be. You will be a Hunter, but not the Lead Hunter. Your Tribe will be led, but not by you.

If you choose Death . . . your Companion's life will end, but it will fuel a new life for you. Death will lend you power. Death will let you rule. And Odysseus shall always be with you.

Thaddeus went to his knees in front of Odysseus. The little Terrier was lying on his side. His panting was fast and pain filled. Thaddeus framed him with his hands.

"Odysseus, can you hear that?"

The canine opened his eyes and looked directly at his Companion, sending Thaddeus waves of pain and sadness and, finally, acceptance.

"You can hear that! What do I do? What do *we* do?"

Make your choice. Now!

Slowly, Odysseus shifted his body so that he could bare his neck and belly in open submission to his Companion, though his gaze still met and held Thaddeus's.

He wants to die, Thaddeus realized.

You must choose.

Thaddeus's answer exploded from within him. "Death!"

Thaddeus watched as the bright light that had always shined from Odysseus's eyes faded . . . faded . . . and went dark.

He bowed his head and pressed his face against the Terrier's motionless side, and Thaddeus sobbed his grief and rage—not noticing that from Odysseus's body the verdant moss around them began to curl and die, turning the image of the reclining Goddess as wilted, as ruined, as Thaddeus's heart.

And now your true future begins. Listen and learn what you must do to create your followers. . . .

As Thaddeus dug into the mound of ruined moss, dirt, fern, and vines that made up the Goddess idol and at last placed his Terrier to rest, Death continued to whisper dark words to the grieving Hunter, and Thaddeus listened. He listened very well.

CHAPTER 31

As dusk fell on the City, Death stepped out onto the Balcony of the God. He felt good—great actually. That the angry little Tribesman had chosen Death had been a delightful surprise. It had taken only a few whispers to shift the mortal's destiny—to link it with His own and then send him back into the Tribe.

"And they shall continue to rot from the inside out," He murmured to Himself. Then He moved to the lip of the balcony and shouted, "Light the fires!"

Below Him Reapers grabbed torches and held them to the bonfire that blazed in the middle of the courtyard. Then they touched the fire-pots, which roared to life, casting flickering light and shadow around the gathered People who were all staring reverently up at their God.

Death surveyed His army and was pleased. His People stretched, wheel-like, around and beyond the courtyard, and as more and more firepots were lit He could see their bright, eager expressions all upturned to Him. The carcasses of several animals roasted over the central bonfire. Death recognized four rabbits, three turkeys, a small boar, and even a young deer. The People had been busy doing as He'd commanded. His Blade had already reported as much to the God. Groups of the People had scattered into the forest, tracking and capturing creatures untainted by the poisons of the City. Under the watchful eyes of His Reapers, they had flayed the skin from the living creatures and joined that warm, healthy flesh with their own. Then they sacrificed each creature—quickly, with gratitude—and brought the carcasses back to feast upon. Death could already feel the difference in His people. Their energy was stronger. The young males were beginning to visit Dove's Attendants to take their ease in the arms of women blessed by service to the Oracle. He laughed to himself. *Soon her Attendants will know what it is to be in service to a Goddess.*

He spread his arms wide, as if He would embrace them all.

"You have obeyed me, and see what riches you have already begun to receive! Tell me, are you stronger today than you were yesterday?"

"*Yes!*" the People shouted.

"Tomorrow you will be stronger, and the next day stronger yet. And on the fourth day, at dusk, we will take the City in the Trees as I have foretold, as I have commanded, as I have promised my People!"

The cheers lifting from the courtyard sounded like the roar of a great, insatiable beast. The sound thrilled Death. He gazed down at His People and noticed that they completely avoided one area of the courtyard—the place He'd hurled the mighty metal trident, killing the last of His dissenters. Death turned His head.

"Dove!" He shouted.

Instantly He heard the sound of her small, soft feet against the cracked tile of the God's chamber.

"I am here, my Lord."

Her voice pleased Him, though Death knew the truth was that she was terrified of Him—she might even hate Him. Mentally, He shrugged off the thought of her fear and hatred. It mattered little. She had a pleasing body and a gentle voice. She would make an excellent shell for His beloved.

"Little bird, have your Attendants send for Iron Fist. Tell him I want the remains of the traitors cut away from the trident and burned. Not in our courtyard fire, though. Burn them far away from my Temple."

"And the trident, my Lord?"

"What of it?"

"Do you wish Iron Fist and the Reapers to move it? Perhaps return it here to the Balcony of the God?"

Death threw back His head and laughed. Then He faced His People once more. They quieted instantly.

"My little bird asks if I want the trident returned here, to the statue. Do you know my answer?" There was a waiting silence, into which Death spoke. "My answer is no! I do not need a weapon returned to the hand of an empty statue. Your God will take it with Him to the City in the Trees—*our* City in the Trees!"

The roar of the People's worship washed against Death.

"Do you worship an empty statue?"

"*NO!*" the people shouted.

"Who do you worship?"

"*DEATH!*" the people responded with one word.

He glanced at Dove. She was still standing there, head bowed in supplication to Him. Something about the inherent grace of how she held herself rankled. She should be more subservient. It wasn't that she said or did any one thing in particular that annoyed Him. It was more what she *didn't* do.

Dove didn't worship Him.

That was annoying enough in the Great Goddess. She, too, refused to worship Him, but she was the Mother Goddess, Life herself, and not a human spirit housed within a blind, childlike, mortal shell.

"Well, what are you waiting for? I have given a command. Obey!" With His foot, He shoved Dove away from Him and toward the door to the balcony. Caught off guard, Dove stumbled, arms outstretched, and fell heavily to the floor. Within seconds Lily, Dove's favorite Attendant, was at her side, whispering soft words to her and helping her to her feet. The girl was younger than Dove and pretty, if you ignored the pustules just beginning to form at the bends of her elbows and knees.

Death waited, expecting Lily to look up at Him—to bow or at the very least to supplicate herself to Him in some way. She did not—not until she had helped Dove to her feet and the two girls were leaving the balcony. It was only after Dove stopped and whispered something into her ear that Lily paused, turned back to face Him, and bowed.

Impatiently He waved the girl away, and the two of them disappeared inside the chamber. Death would remember. He would remember that Lily was loyal, not to Him, but to Dove.

"Her blood mixed with Dove's will surely awaken the Goddess. I will enjoy sacrificing her," he murmured to himself before facing His people once more and raising His arms to proclaim, "Tonight we feast! And soon, very soon, my beloved People, we will live in a city in the sky!"

Dusk fell quickly in the heart of the forest, even if that heart had been severely wounded by fire. From his elevated position on the last of the platforms intact enough to bear weight, Thaddeus looked back at what was left of the City in the Trees or what he was coming to think of as *his* Tribe.

His clothes were stained with dirt and smudges of blackened moss. His face was ravaged by tracks left by tears. But his eyes were dry. Odysseus's death had changed him irrevocably. He'd tolerated the Tribe's condolences as he'd made his way back through the meditation platform without his Companion beside him for the first time in more than ten winters. He'd nodded and thanked the Hunters and Warriors who had sought him out to share in his grief. Then he had gotten away from them. They didn't understand. None of them understood.

Odysseus wasn't gone. Thaddeus could feel him. If he didn't look directly down at the place by his side the little Terrier had always filled, Thaddeus could even make himself believe Odysseus was still physically there, as well as in spirit.

Thaddeus's city was a mess, but that didn't distress him. Over the past three days little had been done to repair and rebuild. That didn't distress Thaddeus, either.

"It's because they're all sick, right, boy?" He spoke as if Odysseus were still listening attentively at his side. "That's right! We know why."

Thaddeus laughed. It was a relief to laugh about it—to be able to show his true feelings. "So, what's our decision? Do we tell them that this sickness—this poison in their system—can be cured? That the cure will make them stronger, faster, even smarter?"

Thaddeus imagined Odysseus looking up at him, his dark eyes glinting with the same sly intelligence Thaddeus displayed. He could almost hear the Terrier barking sharply, angrily.

"No, of course not! I didn't mean that we tell them *all*. Just the ones we choose. Like our Hunters, and perhaps some of the Warriors who just today finally showed enough sense to turn on Wilkes and make me their Leader. Think of it, Odysseus! I am the acknowledged Leader of the Shepherd-be-damned Warriors! Soon they'll be rolling over and showing *you* their bellies in submission."

Thaddeus imagined Odysseus wagging his tail and barking gleefully.

"Hey, hey, hey—let's not get ahead of ourselves. First we let the Skin Stealer sickness cull the wounded and weak from my Tribe. Thankfully, the fire already got rid of the Council—those relics would never understand about our change. Cyril made that clear before I shut him up for good. But you know who would understand about us? Our Hunters and Warriors who have been the most vocal in their anger toward the traitor Nik and his Scratcher bitch. It's as you and I decided—it's what you made your great sacrifice for. Odysseus, it's time I begin taking them aside and showing them what we know—the cure that changes everything. It works fast—remember? It begins almost immediately. They have canines, and whether they're Terriers or Shepherds isn't important. All they need do is get their canines to agree to share flesh with them." Thaddeus wasn't able to contain his nervous excitement, and he began to pace back and forth, back and forth, across the platform. "They'll have it easy compared to you, my brave one. They won't have to make the choice you did."

Thaddeus bowed his head then as grief momentarily broke through anger. But he waved away his discontent. "It was worth it, and you're not really gone—no matter what those fools think. Even my own Hunters and Warriors, the ones who believe as we do, wouldn't understand what has happened between the three of us—you, me, and Death." Thaddeus shook his head. "No. They will never know, though they will follow me. Oh yes. They *will* follow me. As for the rest of the Tribe, the wounded are dying off daily. Soon, very soon, those who are left, the ones who are simply infected with the skin sloughing disease, will notice the change in those we share our secret with, and if they ask to join us we'll save them. If not, they can live sick and miserable. Well, for as long as they are able to live." He laughed again, a hard, cruel sound. "I never imagined I'd say this, but I'd like to thank those mutant Skin Stealers for what they did to us. Hey, maybe we *will* thank them when I lead my changed Hunters and Warriors into their poisoned city and purge it of their infestation!"

Thaddeus could picture Odysseus jumping around him, barking his agreement.

"That's right, boy! And it all starts tonight. The Hunters most easily led are Andrew, Joshua, and Michael. They're also the three who are most filled with anger about the fire and Nik's abandonment. I'm going to pull aside Maxim as well. That Warrior is mean, and mean is what we need. As soon as it's fully dark, we'll bring them back here where we can have some privacy for what needs to be done. I'll just have to be sure they keep their canines quiet. No one can know about this until it's too late. No one!" Thaddeus shouted, lifting his hands in victory as he heard inside his tainted mind the sound of his dead Companion barking to mirror his glee.

Neither noticed the Warrior and her Shepherd, frozen below them, hidden by the rubble of a fallen nest. Claudia's eyes were huge with shock, and Mariah glared up at the Hunter with the focused intensity of a true Warrior.

Was the man utterly mad? Claudia had heard everything, and she was still reeling from her discovery. For a moment she considered drawing her crossbow and breaking one of the Tribe's basic tenants by killing Thaddeus.

She even reached for her bow, meaning to do it. She sighted carefully. One shot for Thaddeus and it would be over.

But would it be over? Thaddeus said the sickness raging through the Tribe was curable and caused by Skin Stealers! How? Why? What was this strange cure he spoke of? Kill Thaddeus and what were they going to do? Go to the Skin Stealers for help? Not possible.

And where was Odysseus? Thaddeus spoke to his Companion as if he were by his side, but though Claudia's sharp Warrior eyes searched the platform, she could find no sign of the wounded Terrier.

And as she stared up the sight of her crossbow at Thaddeus, Claudia realized something else. Her stomach roiled with more than the sickness that infected her. She couldn't do it. She couldn't murder a Tribesman. Claudia lowered the bow, motioning to Mariah, and the two of them backed silently away from the tree in which Thaddeus was still carrying on a macabre celebration. They made a wide circle before heading east again.

At the edge of the blackened rubble of ruins that used to be a graceful City in the Trees, Claudia found Wilkes waiting patiently, Odin by his side.

"Good, I was beginning to worry about—"

"We have to talk. Not here, though. We're too close. You won't believe what I just overheard from Thaddeus."

Wilkes coughed, cleared his throat, and finally managed, "He should be surrounded by his Hunters in deep mourning. As I was packing to leave, I overheard the news. Odysseus died today."

"Sunfire! I was right. He has gone completely mad." Claudia felt all the blood drain from her face. "Hang on. I think I'm going to be sick—" She staggered a few feet away and vomited the contents of her stomach.

"Hey, are you okay to travel?" Wilkes went to her quickly, holding back her hair and supporting her with a strong arm as she retched miserably.

"No, I'm not okay, but we have to travel. And I'm puking because Thaddeus disgusts me more than because I'm sick."

"All right. Tell me about it while we walk," Wilkes said. "You can walk now, right?"

"Right. Where exactly are we going?"

"Southeast, to Earth Walker territory."

"You know where Nik and Mari are living?" Claudia asked.

"No."

"Then how do you plan on finding them?"

"I don't. I plan on them finding me. Now tell me about the latest poison Thaddeus is spewing."

As dusk softened the light fading over the birthing burrow, Mari and Sora turned to Danita. She stood between them, and Mari thought she looked particularly lovely. Sora had dressed her hair, weaving the feathers of a rare raptor to frame her face, making her look exotic and beautiful.

"Are you ready?" Sora asked.

"I think so," Danita said.

"You're going to do great," Mari said.

"I'm really nervous."

"Everyone is their first time," Sora assured her. "I first danced my name in front of Mari while she scowled at me. I almost cried."

Mari frowned at her. "I was *not* scowling at you! I was—" A look from Sora broke off Mari's words. She looked from her Moon Woman friend to the pale, quiet girl standing between them whose face and shoulders still showed the yellowed and purpled evidence of the violence she so recently survived. "I think the point is, Sora's right. We are all nervous the first time. What Mama told me might make it better for you—it did for me. Remember that you're not dancing for the Clan or for your friends or for any particular male. You're dancing with joy for the Great Goddess, sending an introduction to the moon. Forget everything except that."

"Just dance for the Goddess and the moon," Sora repeated, smiling kindly at Danita.

"I can do that," Danita said. "But do you think the Great Goddess will mind that I'm *broken*?"

Mari took Danita's shoulders in her hands and forced the girl to meet her eyes. "You are not broken. The men who brutalized you— *they* were broken. The Goddess knows that. I promise."

"The Great Mother will strengthen you. Just ask it of her and she will always, always answer her Moon Woman," Sora said.

"But I'm not a Moon Woman yet," Danita said.

"Really? What does your heart say about that?" Sora asked.

"It says I want to be a Moon Woman more than I've ever wanted anything," Danita said.

"Heart is what makes a Moon Woman—heart and spirit and tradition," Mari said. "That's what Mama always told me."

"If Leda said it, then it must be true!" Danita suddenly perked up. "I am ready."

"Okay then. Let's do this," Mari said.

Side by side, the three young Moon Women descended the stone stairs to their Pack, waiting in the clearing beside the stream. As they reached the clearing, Rigel rushed up to them, gently carrying a complaining Chloe by the scruff of her neck.

"Are you eating her?" Sora demanded, snatching Chloe from Rigel, who moved immediately to Mari's side, sending waves of confusion to his Companion.

"Sora, that's how pups are carried around the Tribe. Nik told me. And you know Rigel would never hurt Chloe," Mari said.

Sora instantly stopped her nearly hysterical inspection of Chloe, lifting the whining pup so that she could look into her eyes. "Is that true? Is that the way pups are carried in the Tribe?"

Chloe stopped whining and licked Sora's nose.

Sora sighed and turned to Rigel. "I apologize, Rigel. Chloe was being overly dramatic. I don't know where she gets that."

"It's a mystery to me," Mari muttered sarcastically.

Danita covered her laughter with her hand.

"Well, I thank you, Rigel, for bringing Chloe to me."

"So do I." Mari bent and kissed the half-grown Shepherd on the nose, thinking that this time she didn't have to bend so far to reach him. *Wow! He's growing so fast!*

"Okay, Chloe is situated." Sora patted the front of her tunic where the pup's head poked out, black eyes shining with excitement.

"Perfect. Moon Women, let's go!" Mari said.

They moved ahead together as if they were one—Earth Walkers and their canines. The central bonfire was blazing and the scent of the trout O'Bryan had spent all day catching, as well as roasted garlic, hung heavy and succulent over the hungry people, canines, and feline.

"Moon Women! Our Moon Women are here!"

Mari recognized Jenna's happy shout. She waved and grinned at her friend, pleased to see Sora following her lead and waving and calling hellos to members of the Pack. Danita called one hello—it was to Bast, though when Mari glanced at her she seemed to be smiling at Antreas as well as his feline. Mari even saw the cat man touch his own hair and then give Danita a big smile and a thumbs-up, as if he was commenting on the feathers Sora had dressed her hair with—which made Mari wonder where exactly the feathers had come from. . . .

"Greetings, Pack!" Sora shouted.

"Greetings, Moon Women!" they shouted as one in reply.

"Tonight, as Mari and I call down the moon and Wash those of you who are injured, the first of your new Moon Woman apprentices, Danita, will dance her name into the earth, formally introducing herself to our Great Goddess, as well as the moon," Sora said.

"As tradition dictates, Danita will dance her name by herself, until she has spelled it out once, in its entirety. Then the Pack may join her," Mari said.

"And please do!" Danita blurted. "I'll be nervous enough out there by myself."

Laughter trickled through the Pack as Mari and Sora raised their arms and began the invocation:

> *"Moon Woman I proclaim myself to be.*
> *Greatly gifted, I bare myself to thee."*

Mari faced one side of the loose circle the Pack had naturally formed and Sora the other. While Danita danced her name across the earth, proclaiming herself a Moon Woman apprentice, those who were injured approached either Mari or Sora, kneeling and bowing their heads for the Washing of moon magick.

Nik was there, kneeling before Mari. He smiled at her before bowing his head, and she rested her hand on his soft blond hair. She spoke lovingly, letting her hand linger.

"I wash you free of injury and sadness and gift you with the love of our Great Earth Mother," she murmured the traditional blessing, tweaked slightly because he didn't actually need Washing—he needed healing. But Mari found the feeling was the same. Companion or Earth Walker, when she invoked moon magick she was filled with a cool, silver power that cascaded through her body, engulfing the recipient in the healing embrace of a mother—compassionate, kind, and loving.

"Thank you, Moon Woman." Nik spoke formally, but the expression in his eyes was anything but formal.

Mari moved through the Pack, keeping in time with Sora. They were done quickly, perfectly timed with the last letter in Danita's name. The Moon Woman apprentice grinned at her mentors. "I did it!"

"Yes, you did!" Sora said.

"And now, Pack, please join Danita in dance while we accompany her with music, feasting, and song!" Mari cried. With a whoop of excitement, the Pack descended on the food as drums and flutes began to play.

Nik and Laru finally wove their way through the crowd to her. Nik had two wooden plates in his hands balancing a mug filled with something that smelled suspiciously like spring mead.

"You found the mead again, didn't you?" Mari took her plate from him as the four of them walked to a spot at the edge of the campfire circle that was a little shadowy and less populated than the center of the busy circle.

"Actually, O'Bryan found an Earth Walker named Spencer. Apparently, Sora put her in charge of the mead. He charmed Spencer into digging up another barrel of it. Don't ask me how. I've known him my whole life, so it's hard for me to find him charming."

Mari grinned. "I think he's charming."

"Oh, you do?" Nik pressed his shoulder into hers. "Do I need to be worried?"

Mari's grin turned into laughter. "No! But I do like O'Bryan, and he *is* charming. And considerate. And tall."

"I'm feeling worried."

Mari bumped him with her shoulder. "Is it odd that I want to make it clear that you don't need to be worried about your cousin and yet I'm enjoying the fact that you're worried? I think that's a paradox."

"I think that's a woman," Nik mumbled.

"What was that?"

"Nothing. Not one thing. Your trout's getting cold. Let's eat."

Mari sat, cross-legged, with her back to a log. She expected Rigel to lie down, along with Laru, beside them, but both Shepherds remained standing, tongues lolling, ears pricked, looking around the clearing.

"What's going on? Is something wrong?" Mari asked quickly, though she didn't pick up any warnings from Rigel—just hungry expectation.

"Rigel! Laru! Cammy! Fala! Bast! Come on!" Sheena's voice carried across the clearing as Laru and Rigel stared at their Companions.

"Okay, go!" Nik said, laughing.

Laru sprinted off, but Rigel remained, slobbering and staring at Mari.

"Are you starving him?" Nik asked, bumping her shoulder much as Mari had just bumped his.

She frowned at him. "Of course not. I just don't know what's going on."

"Oh, sorry! Of course you don't. Sheena's calling the canines, and apparently a Lynx, too, to their dinner. She'll have raw rabbit mixed with vegetables, grains, and eggs dished out for them. It's the way of the Tribe—and now the way of our Pack. We all eat together."

Mari looked at Rigel, who was staring at her, drool dripping from his muzzle, but not moving from her side.

"Sweet boy, go!" she told him. He barked joyfully and sprinted after his father. Mari laughed. "I've never been that happy to eat."

"Canines feel things more intensely than we do. It's part of the beauty of being bonded to one. If you concentrate on Rigel while you're eating, your dinner will seem especially delicious."

"Really? That's fabulous!" Mari said. She closed her eyes and thought about Rigel—thought about how much she loved him and how just by pressing against the side of her leg he could make her feel special and protected. Suddenly she was utterly ravenous. "Hand me that trout. I need food," she said.

Nik chuckled. "Far be it from me to stand between a Companion's food and her hunger."

Mari didn't even notice that it took her no time at all to clear her plate. She only knew that everything she tasted was delicious and she was suddenly feeling very full and very, very satisfied.

"He's going to make you sleepy now if you don't separate from him," Nik said.

"Huh?" Mari said around an enormous yawn.

"Stop thinking about Rigel!" Nik said sharply.

Mari blinked, surprised at his tone. She frowned at him. "Why are you yelling at me?"

"I'm not. Are you feeling less sleepy?"

Mari thought about it. "Well, yes, I am."

"It's fun to let his hunger take you through dinner. Your food will always taste better. But you have to stop the connection at the end of the meal. Look at them." Nik gestured to a spot very near the center bonfire.

Mari looked, and the corners of her lips lifted. "They're sleeping. All of them." And they were. Laru, Rigel, Fala, her puppies—minus Chloe—Cammy, Sheena's Captain, and even Bast were sprawled in front of the fire in various stages of sleep. "Oo-oh, I get it. Rigel was making me sleepy!"

"Yep, he sure was, but you're back now." Nik leaned into her and kissed Mari, softly but intimately. Then he sat back and smiled at her. "Danita did a good job of dancing her name. Or, at least, I think she did."

"I'm sure she did. I wasn't able to watch her much, but she practiced over and over."

"You didn't watch her, but I noticed someone who did," Nik said.

"Bast?"

"Of course. But I was talking about Bast's Companion."

"Huh! I knew it. They're going to mate. Just wait and see, and I'm glad of it—very glad of it," Mari said.

"Are you a romantic?" Nik gave her a raised-brow look.

She smacked his arm. "And if I am?"

"Then that makes two of us. My mother died too soon, but she did instill several things in me before she left, and being a romantic was one. You wouldn't think my father would have appreciated it, especially in his only child, but he did. He often said I reminded him of her." Nik smiled sadly, staring down at his hands.

Mari touched his cheek gently, and he turned to her. "It's hard, being without them. I understand."

Nik cupped his hand over hers. "I know you do. That's part of why I fell in love with you. You understand me. But I often wonder why you love me."

"That's easy. It's because you accept me."

"Lots of people accept you. Look around. You have a whole Pack that accepts you."

"I know, but you were the first Companion to accept me. You could have been mean-spirited, especially after you saw that Rigel had chosen me, and not you. But you weren't. Your heart is bigger than that. You accepted me, Sora, Jenna, Rigel, Antreas, and all the rest of us. That's why I fell in love with you."

"Thank you. I don't know what else to say except that. Words aren't enough to tell you how happy I am that we're together—that we're creating a new future, a new world . . . together. But I can show you. If you let me, I'll spend the rest of my life showing you," Nik said.

"I'll let you, Nik." Mari kissed him then. Not one of her chaste kisses. Not a timid kiss. And not a kiss she broke off because she was suddenly embarrassed and unsure of herself. Mari kissed Nik—fully, passionately—pressing herself against him and losing herself in the touch and taste of him.

Nik broke the kiss first. His breath had quickened, and his eyes were hooded, his expression intense. "You can't do that out here."

"Did I do something wrong?" Mari asked, feeling vulnerable and a little confused.

"No! Absolutely nothing!" Nik assured her. "It's just that when you kiss me like that—touch me like that—all I want is to be with you. Alone. In your burrow."

"Oo-oh!" A smile bloomed on Mari's face. "That's good."

"That's good if we're alone and in your burrow. Not so good for sitting in the middle of our Pack with watching eyes everywhere."

Mari glanced around them and saw several people, Companions and Earth Walkers alike, averting their eyes suddenly with knowing smiles. Her face blazed with color and she took a long drink of the winter beer Nik had brought her.

"I'll remember that when we're alone again," she said.

"Sunfire! I hope you do," he said.

They shared another long, intimate look, and as Mari felt herself leaning into him again she straightened and changed the subject.

"So, how's it going with the women? Are they weaving what we need for the trip?" she asked, smoothing her hair as she tried to stop staring at Nik's lips.

"Oh yes!" He brightened instantly. "Mari, they're incredible! You and Sora were right. If I can describe it to them, they can create it."

"Well, I knew that part, but can they create it in just a couple more days?"

"Almost. They have to weave twenty-eight cocoons. They say they can get most of them done before we have to leave. The rest of them, well, they say they can weave as we go down the river."

"If they say they can do it, they can," Mari said.

"So, we're going to need to take some of the rowboats—like the one you and I escaped the island in," Nik said. "The other boats, the kayaks, are smaller, but they'll be helpful if we can rig floating litters behind them. Not much room for passengers with whatever it is the women are weaving the cloaks from. Do you know what it is?"

"Of course. It's hemp. Nik, that reminds me. We're going to have to take several young plants and cuttings with us, as well as seeds and roots and bulbs. It's going to take up a lot of room, but it's part of what Antreas said we needed to do."

"Antreas said you needed to fill a boat with plants and cuttings and such?" Nik looked utterly confused.

"Well, sort of. He said we had to prove our worth to the Wind Riders. Nik, Earth Walkers can grow anything. So, let's show them. Let's show the Wind Riders plants they've probably never seen before, and let's show them that we know how to grow, harvest, and use the plants. Do they know what a wapato root is, and how delicious it can taste if you bake it just right?"

"They probably don't, but I'm with you, Mari. My mouth waters every time I think about wapato baked with garlic and salt." He sat up straighter, obviously excited. "And there's more, right? More plants like wapato and hemp that Earth Walkers know about, but no one else does?"

"I don't know what the Wind Riders know or don't know, but Earth Walkers know plants. And that's a valuable knowledge," Mari said.

"I'll tell Antreas to plan for *two* boats, at least, filled to overflowing with plant things," Nik said enthusiastically.

"Okay, I'm going to need help at my burrow. In the pantry Mama and I have many roots and seeds, as well as dried herbs, fruits, and vegetables. I need help packing it all up after I go through it. The medicines must all come with us, but I'll try to take only the plants that can be eaten on our journey, or replanted once we arrive."

"Good idea. But wait—does that mean we get no alone time tonight?"

Mari smiled at his sweet puppy-eyed expression and kissed his lips softly. "That is exactly what that means."

Nik gave a dramatic, long-suffering sigh. "Is this part of Earth Walker courting?"

"No, silly." Mari kissed him again, this time lingering and whispering against his lips. "This is part of getting ready to travel to a new land."

"Someday we're going to be in our new land, surrounded by our Pack, watching Wind Riders race over the plains, and I'm going to pick you up and carry you into our burrow or nest or den or what-the-bloody-beetle-balls-ever we call it and have my way with you. No matter what anyone says."

"I hope that's a promise, Nikolas," she said, her gray eyes sparkling mischievously.

"Oh yes, my Moon Woman. It's definitely a promise."

CHAPTER 32

"B ut we're breaking with tradition anyway, so I didn't think this would be such a big deal." Isabel was talking earnestly to Sora as Mari and Rigel made their way past clusters of women, busy with everything from weaving travel cocoons to gently packing seeds and roots and pods into woven containers, to the entrance to the birthing burrow. She'd been on a quest to find more storage containers so she and Nik could continue to pack up her burrow.

"Oh, good! Mari can decide," Sora said.

"I can decide what?" she asked, stepping into the relative quiet of the burrow.

"Sora says tonight Isabel is going to dance her name for the moon and then tomorrow it's my turn," Jenna explained, closing the door against the outside noises of a Pack frantically preparing to move. "Well, Isabel says she wants me to dance with her."

"And I said that was breaking with tradition. That it would be traditional for a Moon Woman to dance with her apprentice, so you or I could join her. But for two apprentices to introduce themselves together?" Sora shook her head. "It's not done."

"Isabel, why do you want Jenna to join you?" Mari asked.

"Jenna and I aren't traditional Moon Woman apprentices. Danita wants to draw down the moon. We don't. We just want to be Healers.

445

And since we're different, I thought it would be nice if we introduced ourselves to the Goddess together."

Jenna dimpled. "Isabel and I make a good team. Someday I hope she can draw enough moon magick to help with our healing and I'll be an expert on tinctures and salves."

"And it doesn't bother you that Jenna might be drawing some of the Goddess's attention away from you tonight?" Mari asked Isabel.

The young woman looked honestly surprised. "No! I never even thought of it that way. I just thought that since Jenna and I are a team, it made sense to dance our names as a team. And I think the Goddess has enough attention to split between us, don't you?"

Mari met Sora's gaze. The other Moon Woman shrugged. "You make the decision."

"Then I think it would be lovely if the two of you introduced yourself together as Healer apprentices," Mari said.

"Oh yea!" Jenna clapped her hands as Isabel beamed.

"Okay, go to the clearing downstream. Danita's waiting for you there. She'll help you practice the steps of your naming dance. I'll be by later to check in with you," Sora said.

The girls scampered out of the burrow to meet with Danita, joining the wash of Pack noise that was, thankfully, cut off when the door closed behind them.

"Since when are you a stickler for tradition?" Mari asked Sora.

"I'm not. Not really. But I don't want us to lose everything that made us a Clan."

"Sora, the people made us a Clan, not the traditions. And now we'll make our group a Pack, with a unique mix of new and old traditions, like we're a unique mix of people. But you know that. What's going on with you? What's wrong?"

Sora brushed back a thick length of dark hair and blew at a braided strand of flowers that was flapping in her face. "I'm just not ready to leave!" she blurted. "Are you? We have one more full day, and then the next is the fifth day, and we're supposed to be leaving the very next dawn." Sora gazed around the birthing burrow fondly. "I was just getting settled—just finding my place here. And I love it. I love this women's burrow that's suddenly filled with all sorts of people and creatures. What are we doing leaving all of this?"

"Come on. Let me make you some tea."

"I'll make the tea," Sora grumbled, moving with Mari and Rigel to the rear of the burrow. "I feel bad enough without being subjected to your questionable tea-brewing skills."

"See, you're sounding more like yourself already. Where's Chloe? She'll make you feel better."

"She's eating. Rose said she'd bring her to me when she's done."

"Okay, look, you're scared. I am, too. But leaving is the right thing to do. Are you honestly having second thoughts?" Mari didn't even want to consider what it would be like to leave Sora behind, but she ignored the hollowness in the pit of her stomach and continued. "Stay if you feel you have to. Thaddeus will come after Nik and me. Once he realizes we're gone the Tribe might be satisfied by going back to how things were. They'll capture enough Earth Walkers to tend their crops, and let the rest of you live in peace until they need more of you. Just like they've been doing for generations."

"You don't really believe that, though, do you?"

"No, I don't. I've met Thaddeus. I've seen the attitude of the Leader of their so-called Elder Council. They're narrow-minded men stuck in the mud of their own outdated beliefs. I think they'll come after all Earth Walkers. They blame us for the forest fire."

Sora came to Mari, offering her one of the two steaming mugs of tea. She blew out a long breath. "I'm not going to stay. I know leaving is the right thing to do. I've been excited, happy even, about it. But . . ." Her words faded as she stared into her tea.

"But it is scary, especially the closer we get to leaving," Mari finished for her.

"Yeah, it is."

"Change is scary. I was scared when you first came to live with me."

"Seriously? I would never have guessed that. It just seemed like you were mad at me. A lot."

"I hid my fear in anger. I was afraid of everything! Of living without Mama. Of what you would think of me because I'm part Companion. Of what might happen to Rigel if I couldn't figure out how to take proper care of him. And mostly of what our Clan would do to me when they found out my secret. I wasn't angry; I was terrified."

"Yeah," Sora said softly. "I'm not having second thoughts. I'm terrified."

"But you're not alone. You're part of a Pack. We're in this together. We have your back, Sora."

The sounds of the busy Pack filtered through the burrow again, and Mari looked up to see Nik and Laru standing just inside the entrance. "You two okay in here? I ran into Isabel and Jenna. They said I should check on you."

"We're okay," Mari said. "Sora's just feeling stressed about the move. Nik, would you mind if I—"

"Hey, say no more. Laru and I will make another run back to your burrow. I'll load the rest of your medicines. We should be back here about dusk—just in time for Third Night."

"There are more satchels and medicine carriers just inside the rear pantry. I don't know where Jenna keeps finding them. The girl is a born scavenger," Sora said. "That's what you were looking for when you came in, isn't it, Mari?"

"Yeah, thanks. Hang on just a second, Nik." Mari hurried into the pantry and came back with several satchels slung over her shoulder, which she handed to Nik. "Thanks again." She tiptoed to kiss him, adding quietly, "Sora needs me."

"I get it," Nik said. "Take care of your friend. Want Rigel to come with us? I'll bet he's up for some boy time."

Mari glanced down at Rigel, who was sending her an openmouthed grin, tail wagging manically.

"That would be a big yes from Rigel, and a smaller yes from me." Mari crouched in front of her Shepherd. "Stay close to Laru and listen to Nik. I love you, sweet boy." She kissed him on his nose and he licked her in return. Laughing, she turned to Laru, who was waiting a lot more patiently beside Nik. "Watch our boy. He likes to get into things."

Laru woofed softly, and when she bent to kiss him, too, he flooded her face with licks. Sputtering and laughing, Mari straightened to grin at Nik, who pulled her into his arms and kissed her thoroughly.

"Ugh," she said when he let her go. "I'm covered in Shepherd slobber. I'm sure you got some of it on you."

"You know it's my favorite. Well, besides Moon Woman slobber." He waggled his eyebrows at her before calling, "See ya, Sora."

"Not if I see you first," Sora quipped as the two Shepherds bounded out of the burrow with Nik following close behind.

"There. Now we should have some peace." Mari returned to her spot beside Sora and picked up her tea. "Tell me what I can do to help."

"Really?"

"Really."

"Okay, you asked for it. I don't even have half of the pantry loaded up. And there are so many clothes to go through. What about all of these sleeping pallets? What are we going to do with them? And the weaving supplies? We'll need to impress the Wind Riders, so we need all of the looms and the hemp. The women have been gathering roots and shoots and seeds, but what about live plants? We have to bring some of them. Do Wind Riders have blueberries? Well, they should. What about that? All of that?"

Sora finally took a breath and Mari was able to speak. "First, you need to add some lavender to your tea. Not enough to make you sleepy. Just enough to help you relax a little."

"Enough to make me think things aren't as stressful as they really are," Sora said sardonically.

"Yes and no. You're building up a lot of stress in your mind, Sora. Like the pallets. Each person will pack their own. And I talked with Nik when we were packing my burrow this morning about using litters to carry a lot of these supplies to the boats. He agreed. So, let's start by taking apart the bed frames and using them to make litters. There's nothing wrong with moving the pallets to the floor. We can strap the looms and weaving materials to the litters, as well as live plants, and then transfer them to their own boats. Nik said we can lash boats together. That's what we'll do."

"But what about when we leave the river and have to carry all this stuff?"

"We will have eaten a lot of this stuff by then. And if we have too much to carry, we leave it beside the river. We'll make that decision then. No need to worry about it now."

"I just want to do this right, and that seemed so easy when we were talking about it, but making it happen is a whole other thing," Sora said.

"But you're not alone. I owe you an apology. I've been distracted by packing up my burrow. I should have been here for you," Mari said.

"You don't owe me anything. I should be able to handle this on my own. You're handling it just fine."

Mari laughed. "Oh no, no, no! I'm faking it! I'm just as scared as you are. But I'm used to living day-to-day, afraid of being found out. I've learned to keep my feelings hidden."

"Strangely enough, that's a comfort to me."

"So, you want to add lavender to that tea, and then you and I are going to go through that pantry back there and get it packed up. All of it," Mari said.

"Yes. And thank you," Sora said.

"No problem."

Sora touched her arm. "No, really. Thank you. And thank you for being my friend."

"You didn't give me much choice," Mari said.

"Sure I did. You could have been my friend or let Rigel eat me," Sora said, grinning at Mari.

"Rigel said he was afraid you'd be too fatty to eat, and you know he doesn't like fat."

"He did not say that!" Sora gasped.

Mari giggled. "No, he didn't. But it's funny."

"For whom?"

"Rigel and me, of course. Now, let's get to work. It'll be dusk before you know it, and it's a Third Night."

"Do you think Jaxom will return?" Sora asked.

"For his sake, I hope he does," Mari said.

"I don't know, Mari. For his sake, I hope he doesn't."

"What does that mean?" Mari asked, pausing at the entrance to the back pantry of the large burrow.

"It means I don't think he'll find peace in this lifetime. Not after what he's done. It might be better if he returned to the Goddess and came back around again," Sora said.

"Try to forgive him. If not for him—for yourself," Mari said.

Sora looked surprised. "Mari, I said it before—I've forgiven him. But I know him. I've been his friend, and more, for most of our lives. I don't think he'll ever be able to forgive himself."

The day passed quickly, but Mari and Sora managed to get the birthing burrow's pantries—medical and eatable—completely packed. O'Bryan and Sheena had all of the pallet frames taken apart and moved to the clearing by the stream, where they were being lashed together to form transportable litters. Antreas had even proclaimed that if the women could weave mats or webbing quickly enough the litters could be floated behind the boats and could carry many of their supplies.

Davis and Cammy had been what Davis laughingly called binge hunting. They'd managed to trap several live rabbits to add to the small warren Mari had started for Rigel, as well as a few turkeys and a magnificent young deer. The scent of roasting and smoking meat hung fragrantly over the campsite, lifting everyone's harried spirits. Like Davis often said, *it's hard to be too stressed if there is plenty to eat.*

"Isabel, Jenna, you two look perfect, if I say so myself." Sora stepped back from the girls, walking around them, tucking in a curl here and there.

"It amazes me how fast you can braid decorations into hair," Mari said.

"You think that's a skill Wind Riders will value?" Sora asked.

"Antreas said they're a matriarchy," Isabel said. "So, I think it's a skill they're going to love."

"*We* sure do!" Jenna twirled around, making her long hazelnut-colored hair fly out in an arch around her as the shells and beads Sora had decorated it with made music.

"Isabel, Jenna, you two are gorgeous," Mari said. "Are you ready?"

"Yes!" Jenna said.

"Nervous, but yes," Isabel said.

"Just focus on the joy of the moment and the Goddess," Mari told them. "Forget everything else."

"But know that your Moon Women support you," Sora added.

"That we do," Mari agreed. "Okay, you have an eager Pack waiting in the clearing. Like we talked about earlier, as you begin dancing Sora and I will draw down the moon and Wash the Pack."

Jenna held out her arm, with a small grimace. "The sun's setting. I can feel it."

The smooth skin of Jenna's arm had taken on a sickly gray tinge. Mari glanced at Isabel and Sora. Their skin, too, was beginning to turn, though Mari's wouldn't. Her mixed blood made her immune to the Night Fever that plagued Earth Walkers.

"How about this?" Mari said. "You two will be the first Sora and I Wash; then you can begin your dance and not have to worry about the pain of Night Fever."

"That's a good idea," Sora said. "A break from tradition that I like. There's no need for any of us to suffer from Night Fever, not with more than one Moon Woman in our Pack."

"That's awesome, Mari!" Jenna said.

"We'd appreciate that," Isabel agreed.

"And I also like this new tradition of baring our legs, especially when we dance our names," Sora added, smoothing the side of Isabel's tunic that was embroidered with lovely red flowers.

"The males in our Pack will certainly like it," Jenna said with a cheeky grin.

Mari gave her a sharp look, wondering if there was a particular male she was thinking of—Davis? O'Bryan? Maybe Jaxom, if he returned?

"Mari? Hello? Are you coming?"

Mari blinked and came back to herself. "Oh, sorry. Yeah."

She caught up quickly with the three young women, and together they moved down the wide stone stairs. The evening had been cloudy, and dusk had fallen quickly. The Pack had lit all of the bonfires, and the night was filled with scents of burning pinewood mixed with the aromas of roasting meat and the lavender and salt water that always circled a Gathering. As Danita spotted them and raised the greeting of "Moon Women! Our Moon Women are here!" Mari felt as if her heart might burst with the sense of belonging that rushed through her. *I wish you were here, Mama. I wish you could see that I have a place with these people. I finally belong!* She searched for Nik among the smiling, upturned faces, even though she already knew he hadn't returned from her burrow yet because Rigel wasn't leaping around her, drowning her with slobbery kisses.

"Ready?" Sora asked her.

"Absolutely," Mari said.

The four of them descended into the heart of their Pack.

"Blessed Third Night to our Pack!" Mari called, tweaking her mama's traditional Third Night greeting just a little. "Tonight we have much to celebrate. We have two new apprentices who have chosen to dance their introduction to the moon together. Sora and I have agreed to it because we believe in mixing new traditions with old."

"Like how we've mixed Clan and Tribe to form a new Pack," Sora added.

"Exactly!" Mari agreed. She nodded to Sora, and they moved forward to approach the idol of the Great Earth Mother that seemed to emerge from the center of the clearing. The light of the fires had flickering shadows playing across her beautiful skin of moss. The breeze stirred, brushing through her hair of verdant ferns, giving the impression that she was in motion, rising to greet her people.

Mari and Sora had already decided to open the Third Night by keeping much of it traditional, out of respect for the Great Goddess and for the gathered women who had, for their entire lives until just recently, been part of a Clan steeped in tradition.

Sora had asked Mari if she would begin, and Mari had easily agreed. Sora's connection to the Goddess was strong—maybe even stronger than Mari's. She had never heard the Goddess's voice, but Sora seemed to chat with her frequently.

"I greet you, Great Mother, with the love and gratitude and respect of your newly formed Pack." Sora spoke directly to the image of the Goddess.

Mari watched Sora bow reverently to the living sculpture and was then surprised to see her pull a beautiful bead from her hair and tie it into a frond of the Goddess's hair. Mari heard Sora say, "This is my favorite bead. Keep it here, with you. I know you'll come with us to the Plains of the Wind Riders, as you are everywhere, but part of you will remain here, in our homeland. And I want you to have it." Then Sora brushed away tears that were glistening on her cheeks and rejoined Mari.

It was Mari's turn. She was supposed to announce the ancient call for the men of Clan Weaver to present themselves to be Washed, but as there were no Earth Walker men present, Mari took the opportunity to approach the Goddess.

Mari gazed up into the smooth river stone flecked with sparkles of crystal that had, generations before, been carved into a likeness of the Goddess's face. From her hair Mari disentangled the perfectly blue feather of a jay. She reached up and placed it snugly within the fern that was the Goddess's hair.

"Keep this with you," Mari said softly to the Goddess. "Blue was Mama's favorite color, so I think you'll like it, too." Then Mari stepped back and faced the watching Tribe, pronouncing the words she'd heard her mama speak uncounted times. "Men of Clan Weaver, present yourself to me!"

The silence that filled the clearing was pregnant with anticipation. Mari searched the crowd until she spotted O'Bryan, Sheena, and Davis.

They were turned outward, watching the surrounding forest with the sharp eyes of protectors.

Nothing happened. No one moved.

Mari breathed an almost inaudible sigh of relief and was turning to Sora to begin the invocation of the moon when the night erupted into chaos.

First, Rigel rushed to Mari, flooding her with emotions that ranged from relief to anger and worry.

"It's okay, sweet boy!" Mari crouched beside him, trying to soothe him with her touch. "Where are Laru and Nik?"

Rigel's head swung around, pointing into the darkness outside the cheery fires that encircled the Pack.

"Moon Woman!" Jaxom's voice was tortured as he staggered into the clearing.

"Mari, help us!" Nik shouted at the same time, and Laru burst through the circle, running to stand beside her and Rigel.

The gathered Pack gasped, parting to allow Nik and Jaxom through. Between them, they dragged an Earth Walker male. His hands were bound. His head was lifted; his eyes were completely red. He bared his teeth, sweeping the crowd with his scarlet gaze.

"Moon Woman!" he rasped in a voice that was barely human. "Need Moon Woman!"

"Oh, Goddess!" Sora said, backing into Mari. Her eyes were wide and glassy with panic when she looked at Mari. "I can't! I just can't, Mari!"

"You don't need to. I'll Wash him. Keep Jenna and Isabel behind you." Mari's gaze swept the crowd, quickly finding Danita, whose eyes were wide with fear. Antreas was sprinting to her side, though, and Mari was sure Bast had to be close by, too. *Danita is fine,* she thought with relief. "Rigel! With me!"

It wasn't just Rigel who responded. Laru remained at her side, and then, within a heartbeat or two, Sheena's Captain was there, and Davis's Cammy, as well as the little mama, Fala, and Bast, too. The canines and Lynx surrounded Mari. Each had their ears and hackles raised, growling deep in their chests, their focus poised as one on the red-eyed Earth Walker who was being dragged toward her.

Mari's hand found Rigel's head. As she touched him, she opened herself and a wave of strength flooded into her. Mari felt a jolt of shock as she realized the strength she was being flooded with was coming from *all* of the Companions, not just Rigel!

Focus! Let them help you ground and then call down the moon and Wash that Clansman back to sanity! Her mama's voice was strong and clear within Mari's mind.

Mari moved fast. She stood directly in front of Jaxom and Nik and the struggling Night Fever–filled Clansman. His head was lolling, and Mari could see through the tatters of clothing that remained on his body that his arms and legs were covered with oozing pustules. Then he raised his face again, blinking blindly around him, and Mari got a second shock.

It's Mason! Jaxom's younger brother! He is barely sixteen winters old!

With no more hesitation Mari lifted her arms as if she would cradle the not yet visible moon between the open palms of her hands. She closed her eyes and concentrated with all of her will, sketching within her mind a huge, silver moon and thick ropes of radiant power falling from it down, down, down, to wrap, glowing, around her. When she felt the cold power beginning to flow, she opened her eyes and recited:

> "Moon Woman I proclaim myself to be!
> Greatly gifted, I offer myself to thee.
> By right of blood and birth channel through me
> The Goddess gift that is my destiny!"

Mari reached forward at the same moment she imagined the ropes of silver moonlight power emptying into her, using her as a conduit, and pouring into Mason. She placed both hands on his head and murmured, "Mason, I Wash you free of all anger and sickness and gift you with the love of our Great Earth Mother."

The cold cascaded through Mari's body with such intensity it caused her teeth to chatter and her body to tremble. But she didn't take her hands from Mason's head. She didn't allow her concentration to be broken. She kept the moonlight washing through her and into Mason, illuminating him with a light that made it appear as if his skin had turned silver, until finally the young man lifted his head and met her gaze.

His eyes were a healthy brown, though he looked more than a little confused. He blinked several times, smiled shyly, and in a voice that was raspy and weak replied with the traditional response, "Thank you, Moon Woman."

Mari nodded in acknowledgment of Mason's response and then swallowed several times, refocusing her energy. She turned to Jaxom, who was standing beside his brother, still supporting him, though she could see that Jaxom's eyes were beginning to glow red and his skin was fully flushed with gray. Seeing her attention had shifted, he bowed his head to her. Mari placed her hands on him and focused on channeling more of the lifesaving moonlight.

"I Wash you free of all anger and sickness and gift you with the love of our Great Earth Mother," she said.

Jaxom lifted his head immediately. His smile was radiant. "Thank you, Moon Woman! Thank you!"

Mari turned to Nik then. He was watching her with eyes filled with love. Mason was standing on his own by then, so Nik stepped toward Mari and knelt, bowing his head in the traditional manner of a Clansman waiting to be Washed by his Moon Woman.

Gently, Mari placed her hands on his head, thinking of how much she was coming to love and respect this unique man. She imagined the moon flooding him with health and healing as she intoned, "I Wash you free of all pain and infection and gift you with the love of our Great Earth Mother."

His body glowed silver briefly, and then he lifted his head, his smile beaming up at her. "Thank you, my Moon Woman, my love!"

Mari meant to turn gracefully and move back to stand beside Sora so that they could continue Washing the Pack together, but her legs refused to cooperate. Her graceful turn became a staggering near fall, and she was saved from ending up on her butt and being embarrassed in front of her new Pack by Rigel and Laru. They were there, pressing into her from each side, supporting her, filling her with love and strength. And Fala was there, too, as well as Cammy, lending their love and support. She could even feel Bast's presence. Her feline energy felt completely different from the canines—wilder and more reminiscent of moon power with its cool strength.

Then Sora was in front of Mari, taking her hands and forcing her to look into her eyes. After Mari's gaze focused on her, she said, "Bow your head."

Too exhausted to argue, Mari did as her friend requested.

Sora released Mari's hands and raised her own, cupping the unseen moon in her palms. In a voice strong and sure, she recited Leda's invocation, word for word:

> *"Moon Woman I proclaim myself to be!*
> *Greatly gifted, I bare myself to thee.*
> *Earth Mother, aid me with your magick sight.*
> *Lend me strength on this moonlit night.*
> *Come, silver light—fill me to overflow*
> *So those in my care your healing will know.*
> *By right of blood and birth channel through me*
> *The Goddess gift that is my destiny!"*

Sora placed her hands on her friend's head, and Mari felt a wonderful coolness flow into her body. It wasn't the flood of power that she'd channeled into Mason and Jaxom and Nik. It was sweet and soothing, and it chased away the weakness within her. Mari stopped trembling. Her stomach, which had felt as if it were trying to turn itself inside out, calmed. She drew a deep, thankful breath and lifted her head, grinning at her friend.

"Thank you, Moon Woman!"

Sora touched her cheek gently. "Thank you for doing what I couldn't."

"You didn't have to. There are two of us now," Mari said.

"Three," Danita said, stepping up beside Sora.

"Four," Isabel said, moving to Sora's other side

"Five, if you count a Healer." Jenna dimpled at Mari.

"You count. You all count!" Mari said. "Now Sora will Wash you, and then you can dance your names to the moon."

"Are you not feeling okay now?" Sora asked, studying Mari more closely.

"I am, but Mason has wounds that have to be cleaned and dressed. I thought I'd do that while you Wash the rest of the Pack."

"No, Moon Woman. You stay. Wash your people with Sora. With your permission, I'll take my brother into the burrow and begin cleaning his wounds," Jaxom said. "He's himself again, thanks to you."

"I'll go with him." Rose had stepped from the silently watching crowd. "My wounds are healing well, so I don't need to be Washed, and I've been helping with Lydia's and Sarah's dressing changes. I know where the goldenseal is, and how to clean wounds with it. I'd be happy to help."

Mari opened her mouth to insist that she could handle it—she *should* handle it. She was the Moon Woman. But she was stuck by the realization that this was exactly what she used to complain to Leda about—the fact that she insisted on doing everything herself. She took on the pain and fear, love and losses, of the Clan, and it made her old before her time and, too often, filled her with sadness Mari couldn't touch.

"Thank you, Rose," Mari said. "That would be very helpful."

"I'll come help you after I've danced my name," Jenna said.

"So will I," Isabel added.

Mari wanted to throw her arms around them all and tell them how spectacular they were, but her throat closed with emotion and all she could do was nod and smile at them while blinking tears from her eyes.

When Jaxom and Rose moved off with Mason walking unsteadily, but without being supported, between them, Sora turned to Mari.

"So, Moon Woman. Ready to proceed?"

Mari went to her friend and hugged her, right there in front of the Pack, surprising everyone with her show of affection—including Sora, whose eyes began to fill.

"With my Pack beside me I am ready for anything!"

CHAPTER 33

O kay, tell me everything!" Mari said as soon as the four of them—
Nik, Laru, Rigel, and she—were alone, making their way slowly
back to her burrow with full stomachs and even fuller hearts. "How did
you find Jaxom and Mason?"

"I didn't. Rigel found them."

Mari glanced down at her young Shepherd, who was trotting beside
her carrying a slobbery stick in his mouth. The stick was the size of
one of his legs.

"Now you really have to tell me everything."

"There's not much to tell. I was just finishing up at the burrow. The
door was open—I like the evening breeze."

"Me, too," Mari said, slipping her hand in his.

He grinned at her. "So, the door was open and all of a sudden Rigel
starts air scenting, and he gets agitated."

"Air scenting?"

"It's like the tracking he can do when he sniffs the ground, only he's
sniffing the air."

"Oh, I understand. Okay, go ahead," Mari said.

"Next thing I know, Laru's air scenting, too, and growling. I could tell
that he recognized the scent, and that he didn't trust it. So, I grabbed my
crossbow. . . ." Nik paused and patted the bow that was slung across his

back. "And I told Rigel and Laru to take me to what they were scenting. I found Jaxom struggling with that very sick, very violent kid. I was going to shoot him, but Jaxom called me off, told me Mason is his brother—and that we had to get to you so that you could Wash them both, immediately."

"Jaxom wasn't acting strange?"

"Not at first. It was almost dusk, but the sun hadn't set yet. I had to knock Mason out, but then we tied him up and started half dragging, half carrying him to you."

"Did you mess up your hand?"

"My hand?"

"Yeah, knocking him out." Mari was examining the hand she was holding, finding it uninjured, and reaching for his other hand when Nik stopped her.

"Oh no. I didn't mess up my hand. I used my crossbow to conk him across the head. It's okay, too," he said. "And it was only after the sun set that Jaxom started acting strange. I have to admit that he handled it well, though. He talked to me about what was happening, and told me not to panic when his voice, his skin, and even his eyes started to change. He said he could control it since it was a Third Night and he wasn't infected with the Skin Stealer disease anymore—and he was right. I mean, I wouldn't have wanted to be around him, say, tomorrow night had you not Washed him, but Jaxom basically just stayed Jaxom—only a meaner version."

Mari nodded. "That's usually about what happens to Earth Walker males on a Third Night. As long as they're Washed, they can control themselves."

"And Earth Walker women get sad but not catatonic and mortally depressed if they're not Washed, too?"

"Yes, exactly. Women seem like they can go longer than men without being Washed, but that's only because they don't become violent. Depression is every bit as serious as anger," Mari said.

"Do you know why Earth Walker men become angry and women become depressed?"

"I know what Mama told me. She said that Night Fever strips away who we are and reveals the basest, most negative parts of us. Men focus on the external with anger that can lead to violence, usually against themselves. Women retreat internally, and destroy themselves through sadness and self-hatred."

"But Earth Walker males attacked Danita and Sora—violently," Nik said.

"As far as I know, that's never happened before. Nik, I really believe it's the Skin Stealer disease that caused our males to be so aggressive to others." Mari gave the dark forest around them a nervous glance. "I wonder how many more Earth Walker males there are out there, and how many of them have been infected with that horrible disease?"

"I asked Jaxom the same question. He doesn't think there are many. No, actually, Jaxom said he doesn't think there are *any* left alive at all. He said some began to turn against each other. Others died." Nik closed his lips tightly, obviously not wanting to say more.

"Hey, you're talking to a Healer. Give me the details."

Nik sighed. "Jaxom said he found a small group of Earth Walker males yesterday. They were from your Clan. They were all dead. Their skin had completely sloughed off their bodies. They died in terrible agony, in pools of blood and pus."

"That's horrible." Mari felt her own skin crawl.

"Just another good reason to leave this place. The poison of Port City is spreading," Nik said.

"I'm with you. But leaving is going to be hard. I'm trying not to think about it too much, but—" She broke off, blinking fast and willing her threatening tears to go away.

"It's okay. I understand. It'll be worth it, though. I promise."

"I know. We all do. Change is good, but hard." Mari paused and then continued. "Nik, can you ever feel Rigel?"

"Feel him?"

"Yeah, like you share with Laru, only maybe not as strong, or at least not as intimately. But do you ever pick up emotions he's sending to you?" Mari asked.

"Nope, can't say that I have."

"How about any other canines? Like maybe Laru when he was your father's Companion?"

"No. Well, Laru and I have always been close, but that's how it often is with the children of Companions."

"How about your father? Or anyone else from your Tribe?"

"No. Companions can be very close to other people. For instance, I feel close to Davis's Cammy. He's a good little guy and very friendly. Davis and I are friends, so it's natural that Cammy and I are, too. But I've never picked up any actual emotions from him. Why do you ask?" Nik gave her a perplexed look.

"Tonight when you and Jaxom brought Mason to me and the canines with Bast surrounded me, I could *feel* them. Like Rigel, only not as clear. But I could. Actually, it was really interesting. Bast has a much calmer feel than I would have thought. She reminded me of the touch of moon magick when I draw it down—cool and powerful in a very feminine way."

Nik had come to a halt and was staring at her. "Laru!" he called, and the Shepherd, who had been padding several yards in front of them, checking for wolf spiders, sprinted to his side. Nik squatted beside his Companion. "Could you send Mari a feeling?"

Laru's tail wagged, and suddenly Mari was washed in happiness.

She giggled. "That's really nice, Laru! Thank you."

Nik stared up at her. "You felt it, too?"

"Sure—happiness. Laru's a sweetheart."

Nik stared from Mari to Laru, finally blurting, "Why are we just now finding out Mari can accept emotions from *any* Companion?"

Laru barked twice, sharply. Then Nik and Mari spoke at the same time. "Because no one asked before now!"

Mari laughed again as Nik took her in his arms and kissed her hard and quick. "You are magnificent!"

"Well, thank you, Nikolas."

"As far as I know, and all members of the Tribe of the Trees learn our history—whether we want to or not—never in the history of the

Tribe has there ever been an account of a Companion being able to receive from other canines, let alone a *feline*."

"Huh. I'm glad I didn't know that before. I probably would have been too shocked to focus and draw down the moon."

"I doubt that. Mari, I think you can do anything you set your mind to."

Nik took her hand and Mari was so happy she felt as if her feet hardly touched the ground the rest of the way to her burrow.

"Nik! What did you do?"

Mari had stopped at the entrance to her home. She'd expected it to look different. They'd spent the past days going back and forth from there to the birthing burrow, carrying medicines, cookware, clothes, and supplies—leaving only what was needed for their last night. What she hadn't expected was to step into a fragrant wonderland of color.

Nik had collected flowers, hanging fragrant lavender upside down from the ceiling and placing colored flowers in roughly carved wooden containers. There were brilliant maiden pinks, bursting with color, white star showers in another, with the gorgeous blossoms dripping from clusters of small, emerald stems, orange daylilies that were as fragrant as they were beautiful, a magnificent cluster of hard-to-find purple and yellow irises, and interspersed among all of them were bouquets of honey-scented forget-me-nots.

Mari went to a bouquet of the unforgettable blue flowers. She lifted a shaking hand, touching the velvet petals as she inhaled their familiar honey scent.

"Do you like it?"

Mari turned to Nik, tears washing down her face. "I love it."

"Then don't cry!" He pulled her into his arms. "I wanted to make you happy, not sad."

"These are happy tears—mostly. Did you know these blue flowers are called forget-me-nots?"

"No, but I thought you'd like them because Rigel took me to them.

They cover the little clearing above your burrow, totally surrounding that pretty Goddess image. But you already know that."

"They were Mama's favorite flower. They'd never bloomed there until I buried her beside the Goddess; then all of a sudden the clearing was filled with them." Mari sniffed and wiped her eyes. "The Great Goddess loved Mama. I think that's her way of showing me—though I already knew it." Then Mari noticed what was sitting in the center of her sketching table, and she went to it, picking up the little figurine and exclaiming, "Oh, Nik! This is exquisite!" She turned the figure over and over, studying its graceful lines and its strange beauty.

"It's a better version of the equine you asked for," he said. "I've been working on this one in secret for days."

"The detail is amazing!"

"My mother used to draw them, so I've been intrigued by them since I was a little boy."

"And she said the same thing Antreas has been telling us—that they're big enough to ride?"

"Absolutely."

"It's hard to imagine," Mari said.

"Well, we're going to see for ourselves," he said. "Won't that be something?"

"It will." Mari put the carving back on her desk and turned to Nik. "You're leaving tomorrow."

She didn't ask it, but he answered anyway. "I am. As soon as I help you take the rest of your things to the birthing burrow. I didn't know if you were going to stay here the next two nights."

Mari didn't answer quickly because her initial reaction was to say, *Of course I'm going to stay here—it's my home.* But the more she thought on it, the more she realized that she should be with the Pack on the last nights in Earth Walker territory. They would need all of their Moon Women—and she would need them. Being here would just be too sad, especially if Nik was late getting back and she and Rigel were all alone.

"Tonight will be my last night here. With you and Laru and Rigel. Tomorrow, after you leave, I will, too. I'll join our Pack at the birthing burrow, wait there for you. It's the right thing to do. It's past time Moon Women stop isolating ourselves."

"I'm so glad you said that!" Nik hugged her. "I hated the thought of you being here, alone except for Rigel."

"It's going to be hard enough to leave. I don't want to be alone. I've been alone too much," Mari said. Then she took Nik's hands and looked into his loving moss-colored eyes. "Nikolas, would you take me to bed?"

"Sure! You must be tired after . . ." His words faded away as he understood her shy smile and the excitement in her eyes. "Oh! Bloody beetle balls, yes, I'll take you to bed! I mean, crap! That wasn't very romantic."

Mari giggled. "I think it was. I appreciate your enthusiasm."

He took her hand and they walked together to the soft pallet that had been Mari's for her whole life.

"Would you sit there for a moment?" she asked him.

"Mari, I'd do anything you asked me to. And that includes stopping if anything doesn't feel right to you," Nik said.

"Oh, I wouldn't worry about that. There's something you should know about Earth Walker women." He sat, and she took a small step back. "Once we decide to share ourselves with our mate, we do so fully, joyfully, and without embarrassment. Or at least without much embarrassment."

"That's good to—" Nik began, but when Mari reached up and with a single motion pulled her tunic over her head and then untied her pants and let them pool around her feet his words stopped.

Mari stood before him, naked. She felt the heat of the hearth fire against her back and the heat of Nik's gaze on the rest of her body. She'd thought of this moment often, imagining her nervousness and her excitement. But she'd never imagined the pleasure she felt as Nik's eyes devoured her.

"You are so beautiful—so perfect." His voice had deepened.

"Your turn," she said, but when he started to yank off his tunic she moved close to him, stilling his hands. "I want to do it. Is that okay?"

"Mari, anything you want is okay."

She dimpled. "Be careful with that kind of talk, Nikolas. It could get you into trouble later."

"Well, my beautiful Moon Woman, do you know the trouble with trouble?" He raised her hand to his lips, kissing her wrist and then moving slowly, sensually, up to the inside of her forearm, to the pulse point at the bend of her elbow. There he stopped and looked up at her, a mischievous grin lifting his lips. "It starts out as fun."

"Let's see what kind of fun we can get into." She pulled off his tunic, dropping it to the floor. Then she let her hands explore his naked shoulders and chest. "I like how you're hard where I'm soft. And I like this, too." She pulled playfully on the springy blond hair in the middle of his chest. Her hand drifted lower, caressing his muscular abdomen and finding the waist of his pants, causing Nik to suck in his breath. "Is what I'm doing okay?"

"More okay than you'll ever know."

"Oh, good. Would you stand up?"

He did as she asked, and she slid his pants down; then she stepped back, studying him.

"You look a lot different now than you did last time I saw you naked."

"I was sick and half dead then. I hope you mean different as in better," he said.

"Definitely better." She reached out and touched him, feeling him tremble under her caress. "You're shaking."

"I know. I can't help it. Your touch feels like sunfire."

"Should I stop?"

"No! Never stop touching me."

Nik pulled her into his arms, falling back on the pallet, kissing her deeply, thoroughly, lovingly. And Mari discovered the simple but miraculous truth—they fit together perfectly.

CHAPTER 34

As dawn broke, Death was partying. He and his newly made Reapers had crowded onto the God's balcony and were spilling out into the main chamber as well, filling the Temple with the raucous sounds of half-drunk men and giggling women.

Dove crouched just inside the opening to the private room she and Dead Eye had sectioned off from the rest of the chamber. Dove touched the fragrant curtain woven from dried lavender. The scent used to remind her of love and happiness. Now all it did was make her sad and remind her of all that she'd lost when her lover surrendered himself to the God of Death.

Dove had lost all hope that her Champion would wake again—would come back to consciousness, if only for a few moments. She still craved his protective arms around her, and she wished she could speak with her lover just one more time. But her focus must now be on survival and escape—for the two were one and the same.

Screaming giggles drifted to her from the other side of the God's chamber. Dove didn't need eyes to understand enough of what was happening out there that she wanted to stay hidden. She could hear the sounds of the God's men chasing her Attendants as the women pretended to flee from them—only to be caught and carried to pallets or caught and ravished right there in front of the rest of the men as they cheered their brother Reapers on.

And in the center of it all, Dove could hear Death's booming voice calling encouragement.

She hated the sound of His voice with an intensity that sometimes left her breathless.

She heard the soft footfalls of one of her Attendants approaching and knew before she spoke that it was her only friend and confidante, Lily.

"He demands your presence, Mistress." Lily's voice was filled with regret.

Dove nodded and smoothed her hair. "I've been expecting His call."

"Would you have me tell Him you are ill? Perhaps that it is your monthly moon time?"

"He'd know it was a lie. I'll go to Him." She stood. "How do I look?"

"Lovely, like a Goddess yourself," Lily said.

"I didn't know people thought I was beautiful," Dove said. "And then my Champion turned his eyes to me, and he told me that I was fair of face and body, and I was so, so glad. Now I wish I was an ancient, wrinkled crone, like the Watchers used to be, so that He would leave me alone!" She almost spit the words.

Lily moved closer to her Mistress. "I've heard them talking. They leave this evening for the Others' City in the Trees. They attack after sunset."

Dove squeezed Lily's hand tightly. "Then we must leave today, too! Are we ready?"

Lily nodded, moving closer to her Mistress so that they would not be overheard. "I've done all that you asked."

"Good. I will find a way to be absent without Him suspecting that I am gone. As soon as I do that, we will leave this place, as I will never join that monster in the trees, or anywhere else!"

"Dove! Come to your God!"

Lily flinched at His shout, and Dove squeezed her hand again, before letting it go. "Remember," she whispered to Lily. "Our God is a Goddess—we follow the Great Mother Goddess now, Life herself. Be ready. I am sure She will help us flee Death." In truth, Dove wasn't sure at all, but she kept thinking it, kept praying it, kept believing it, hoping by her will alone she would make it true.

"I've hidden our packs outside the Temple. I wish I'd had more time to prepare," Lily whispered back.

"Dove!" the God roared.

Dove began to walk quickly out to the chamber she knew so well, but Lily caught her up, taking her elbow.

"Don't come with me. I want you out of His sight as much as you can be. I can find my way easily inside the Temple. You know that, Lily."

"Not today you cannot. There are Reapers and your Attendants coupling in places you wouldn't expect." Lily's voice was filled with disgust.

"Oh. I understand. Yes, please guide me."

Together the two girls made their way through the crowded, chaotic chamber. Dove could smell the thick, sour scent of sex mixed with the sweet tang of the fermented apple drink they were all guzzling. She swallowed several times to keep from getting sick.

Dove loathed them all. Each day the God's army of Reapers grew stronger. They also grew more arrogant and more animalistic. Gone were the rites and rituals that used to fill the Temple. Gone were the traditions that kept alive the worship of a metal statue. The God had awakened, and He desired more than quaint traditions and ancient rituals.

Dove had decided that Death desired nothing as much as He desired chaos.

"Ah, there you are, little bird!"

She bowed gracefully to Him. "My Lord, what may I do for You?"

"Nothing from way over there, but come here to my lap! I have something for you that isn't so little."

Dove recognized the sarcastic laughter of Death's Blade, Iron Fist, as well as the chuckles of several of the God's favorite Reapers, and she realized they surrounded Him, which meant the God wanted her to go to Him—and to allow Him to take her there, intimately, in front of all of His men, as well as her Attendants.

She set her jaw and lifted her chin. "My Lord, I would be pleased to welcome You to my bed, but not here." With her hand she beckoned to Him. "Come with me to a more private place."

"I am happy to stay where I am, surrounded by my Reapers. They are making free with your Attendants—and your women have not complained. Have you, my dears?"

A chorus followed of her Attendants insisting, "No, my Lord!" and, "We welcome your Reapers, as we welcome You, my Lord!"

"See, little bird! They freely share themselves. I insist you do the same." The God's voice had gone from the pretense of sweetness to a more truthful hardness.

"Will your Goddess be so free with Herself, my Lord?" Dove spoke in a sharp voice as she held herself straight and strong. The only evidence of her fear was the bloody gouges her fingernails were drawing in her palms as she fisted her hands, stealing herself for whatever might come next.

There was a long pause as the Balcony of the God fell silent. Dove could feel everyone's attention focused on her. Then Death laughed—long and hard and loud.

"What a strange girl you are, little bird," Death said. "You seem timid, childlike even, and yet here you are, evoking the Goddess as if you speak for Her."

"And who should speak for Her?" Dove demanded, holding herself rigid. "Would You? Does that mean You would allow the Goddess to speak for *You*?"

"Careful that you do not go too far, little bird. Don't make me clip your wings."

"Apologies, my Lord." Dove dropped into a deep, graceful bow. But when she stood she struck out verbally against the God again. "Is this not the Temple in which the Great Earth Goddess will reside once you have awakened Her?" Dove made a sweeping gesture that took in all of her young, nubile body.

"It is indeed," the God said.

"Then until She claims what will be Hers, I believe it is my responsibility to keep this Temple sacred for Her, and that means I will not fornicate with You for the entertainment of Your Reapers."

"How *dare*—"

"I dare because I have spent my life as Oracle to the Gods! I know something of what they require from a Temple." Dove's voice silenced His. "If I overstep myself, I assume the Goddess will correct my error once She takes control of my body. Until then, I ask that You respect me as You would Her Temple."

"I may have misjudged you, bird." Death sounded annoyed and dismissive. "Begone. Return to your solitude. My Reapers and I leave this evening. We will take the city of the Others after dark. Then I shall come for you, and begin to awaken my true Consort. Leave my sight and remain gone from my sight until I return to collect you. You make me weary."

"Yes, my Lord." Dove bowed deeply again. She reached out for Lily's arm and the girl began to lead her away, but the God's sharp command halted them.

"Your Attendant can remain in your place," Death said. "I feel the need for the sweet release you deny me. Come here, little flower," He said to Lily.

Dove could feel her friend's body begin to tremble. "Which Attendant would most like to lie with the God?" she whispered quickly to Lily.

"Rabbit—she would give herself willingly to him," Lily whispered back in a tremulous voice.

Dove turned her head, speaking nonchalantly over her shoulder. "I have need of my Lily to guide me back to my solitude. Your Reapers make it difficult for me to find my way safely within the Temple. Rabbit!" Dove called.

"Yes, my Lady!" came the girl's breathless reply from somewhere behind Dove.

"Would you be pleased to see to my Lord's needs while Lily is busy elsewhere?"

"Oh yes, Mistress!" Her answer was immediate and eager.

"Present yourself to Death," Dove commanded.

"Yes, Mistress!"

Dove could hear Rabbit's bare feet padding over the tile floor as she hurried to the God's balcony.

"She is full-bosomed and her skin is almost unmarred." Lily spoke under her breath to her Mistress. "I've overheard several of the men calling her beautiful."

"Disrobe, Rabbit. Show yourself to our God." Even though Dove could feel Rabbit's eagerness and heard her clothes slithering immediately to the ground, still her stomach rolled. "My Lord? Does this Attendant please You?"

Dove heard Death chuckle low, intimately, in a tone she understood all too well. "She will do just fine. Now, as I said, leave me! I tire of you."

"Get us out of here. Forever," Dove told Lily quietly. "Now!"

Against the backdrop of low sighs, girlish giggles, and deep moans of ecstasy, Lily pretended to lead Dove to the rear of the chamber and her private area, but they paused there only long enough for Dove and Lily to pull on the shoes they had hidden under her pallet. Then Lily peered back and announced, "They are all watching Rabbit please the God—even the Reapers who were inside the chamber."

"It is time. Circle around my private area. Then we pause to be quite certain no one is watching before we head out of the Temple."

Lily did as her Mistress and friend asked, pausing to peer across the wide chamber.

"Daisy and Lace have joined Rabbit. They are dancing for the God. The Reapers cannot take their eyes from them," Lily reported. "We can leave without being seen!"

Dove should have rushed out of the Temple to freedom, but she hesitated one last time. "Lily, are you quite sure there are no other Attendants who feel as we do?"

"Mistress, I've told you before—no. The Attendants like the attention of the Reapers. The men are finally strong, healthy, and they have the ear of a God. They want to live the future Death has planned for the

People. They are content to be cared for and to imagine a life lived in the trees, free of disease and death."

"But they won't be free of Death. He will subjugate them all."

"It is a subjugation they welcome," Lily said.

Dove lifted her chin. "Then let us leave this awful place. But slowly. We should walk as if we are doing nothing out of the ordinary."

"I understand."

Holding hands tightly, the two girls walked across the God's chamber, following the narrow path that led through the rubble that was the stairway to the courtyard. There they paused.

"What do you see?" Dove asked.

"The firepots are lit. They're being tended by some of the sick ones. You know, the People who are too old or too ill to be of interest to the God, so He has left them unchanged and given them menial tasks to perform until they die. I've hidden our packs behind the rubble on the far side of the courtyard."

"Then let us go there."

"The old ones will see you, Mistress," Lily said.

"I'm not worried about them. I'm worried about Death."

"Then you have no worries, at least not until much later. For the time being, He is well entertained," Lily said.

"And after that, He will be attacking the Others. I won't worry until tomorrow."

"And by tomorrow, we will be well away from this place," Lily said.

They moved across the courtyard slowly, as if the Oracle and her favorite Attendant were out for a stroll. Several of the old, sick People called greetings to Dove. She smiled and nodded, careful to behave as she would any other day.

Her and Lily's travel packs were where Lily had left them. Behind the concealment of a broken building, the girls strapped the packs across their backs. Lily took her Mistress's hand again.

"Are you ready?"

"I'm trying to be." Dove's breath had gotten short and she felt hot and cold at the same time.

"Mistress, are you well?"

"I've never been outside the courtyard," Dove blurted. "When I was born, I was brought directly to the Watchers to be sacrificed to the God, but one of the crones proclaimed that I was born sightless because the God had gifted me with inner sight so that I could part the veils of the world and see the Divine. I have known sixteen winters since then. I have known fear and anger, love and joy, hate and disgust, but I have never known anything outside the God's Temple and this courtyard."

"Mistress, I believe the Watchers were right. You can peer into the Divine. Have—have you looked through the veil and glimpsed our future?" Lily asked hesitantly.

"I have," Dove said slowly. She hated lying to her friend, but what choice did she have? If Lily knew Dove was just an eyeless girl with whom Death was infatuated, would she help her escape? She couldn't chance Lily changing her mind. So Dove lied with an ease she had been practicing her entire life. "All I see for sure is if we stay, Death will overtake us." She touched Lily's arm gently. "I'm sorry that I will be a burden to you. Out there"—Dove gestured before them—"I will be helpless without you."

"Then you have nothing to fear, Mistress, for I shall not leave your side."

Dove hugged her. "Thank you, Lily. I give you my word that someday you will be rewarded for your fidelity to me."

"Escaping Death is all the reward I need. And now we need to move. The sun has risen and we need to get far from the City before dark."

"You brought the ropes so that we can tie ourselves to the boughs of a mighty tree tonight, didn't you?"

"Of course, Mistress," Lily said. "I followed the Reapers yesterday as you asked. I know the way to the ridge that separates the City from the Others, and the hidden path that takes us to a crossing point. Soon we will be out of our territory and in the concealment of the forest."

The girls began walking. Dove's arm was linked through Lily's and the Attendant's eyes constantly scanned the ground before them so that she could guide her Mistress around clumps of ferns, tree roots, and fallen logs.

"When we reach the ridge and cross it, then we turn south. Dead Eye told me he found sign to the south of a people who live burrowed into the earth," Dove said.

"And your Champion said they were peaceful?"

Although she had already explained this to Lily, Dove understood the girl's need for reassurance. "Yes. He said they tend plants and weave. I asked him if it wouldn't be less trouble to take over their burrows rather than battle with the tree people, but my Champion said he did not wish to burrow into the ground when he could live in the clouds instead." Dove shook her head. "I wish I had found a way to stop him. Maybe he would still be here with me and the God would have remained asleep."

"Mistress, I mean no disrespect, but I believe Dead Eye's fate was sealed when he was chosen to be the God's Champion. You could not have stopped it. You are an Oracle, not a God."

Dove bit her lip, nodded, and kept putting one foot in front of the other. She was frightened and unsure about the future, but that fear was nothing compared to the terror of losing herself, as Dead Eye had lost himself.

"I will survive. It is what I do." She didn't realize she'd spoken aloud until Lily responded.

"And I will be by your side."

"Thank you, my friend. As we walk, let us pray to the Great Goddess for her help," Dove said.

She held tightly to her friend, her guide, her salvation and left Death behind as she fervently prayed to a Goddess she could only hope was listening.

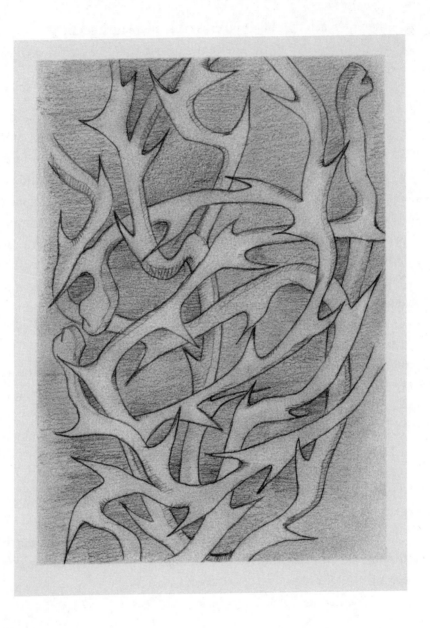

CHAPTER 35

Just before dawn Mari and Nik awoke, slowly, sensually, bodies tangled together with an intimacy Mari couldn't have imagined before loving Nik. Mari didn't want to let him go, but she knew it was like taking a dressing from a wound—better if it happened quickly so that the suffering wasn't prolonged.

"If you take Rigel and Laru out, I'll heat up the last of the rabbit stew for all of us," Mari said.

Nik kissed her nose. "Tea with lots of honey, too?"

"Sora says that's the only way my tea is drinkable."

"Sora is a smart girl."

"Nik!" She smacked his naked butt teasingly as he bent to put on his pants.

He laughed and moved out of range. "But don't tell her I said that."

"Your secret is safe with me. Rigel, sweet boy, go with Nik and Laru." The young Shepherd put his paws up on her pallet, licking her face, before he trotted after the other two males.

Mari washed and had the stew simmering and tea steeping when her males returned. She loved how the proprietary words fit together: *her males.* They did belong to her and she to them. Before Nik and Rigel and Laru, she couldn't have imagined her life so filled with people and animals and love—and now she couldn't imagine her life without them. She'd just tucked a sprig of forget-me-nots behind her ear when her males burst into the little burrow, bringing with them noise and laughter and love.

The canines dug into their much cooler stew while Mari dished up full bowls for herself and Nik—and she added a healthy dose of honey to her questionable tea. Then Nik and Mari sat beside each other, bodies so close they often touched, gazes just as often meeting and holding. Mari loved the fact that she could reach out and touch him—whenever she wanted to—and that the more comfortable she felt with him, the more affectionate Nik was in return.

Mari ate slowly, savoring each moment with Nik, knowing that this was the last they would be alone for a very long time. But inevitably the meal ended and Nik began packing his satchel, preparing to leave.

"Davis should be here any moment." Nik went to the door to the snug little burrow and opened it. "Rigel, Laru, let me know when you scent Cammy." The Shepherds padded to the open doorway and stretched out in the sunlight, eyes deceptively half lidded. He took Mari's hand, sitting beside her. "Let's go over it one more time."

She nodded and gripped his hand tightly. "Okay. You and Davis are going to circle around the Tribe, coming at them from the direction of the Gathering Site by Crawfish Creek."

"Which is the opposite direction from which you and the Pack will make your way to the Channel at dawn, the day after tomorrow, whether we've rejoined you by then or not."

"That makes me nervous, Nik. You say you're not going to let them see you—you're going to sneak in, get a Mother Plant, and get out. Yet you want us to go to the Channel from the opposite direction, whether you and Davis have returned to the birthing burrow or not *in case you get caught.* I don't like it."

"Mari, it's wise to plan for the worst and envision the best. That's all I'm doing. I have every intention of spending our last night in this forest with you and our Pack at the birthing burrow and then leaving at dawn. But if dawn on the sixth day breaks and we haven't returned yet I'll meet you at the Channel." When she started to protest again, he pressed his finger gently against her lips. "Hey, it's going to be okay. There are many reasons we might not make it back to the burrow in time. The Tribe should be very active rebuilding right now. I have no idea where they have moved the Mother Plants, and I may have to stay hidden until well into the night before I am able to take one. If that's the case, it would be better for all of us if Davis and I went directly to the Channel and waited for the Pack. By the time you get there we'll already be with the boats and will have taken care of any lookouts there might be."

"You won't kill them, right?"

"Not unless they're Thaddeus. Then I don't make any promises."

"Agreed. I don't much like Cyril, either, but don't kill that old man."

Nik touched her cheek. "I won't, Mari. I'm not a killer."

"I know. I'm just—"

"Scared? Worried?" he offered.

"Both."

"It's okay. It'd be stupid not to be scared and worried. I am. But I also believe in myself—and Laru, and Davis with his Cammy. And most of all you, Mari, and our Pack."

"I do, too, Nik. So, if you're not back by dawn the day after tomorrow, we'll meet at the Channel at dusk," she said with more confidence.

"Yes. We'll load the boats as quickly as possible and then be off. I hate the idea of being on that swarm-be-damned river at night, but I know Sheena can navigate for us."

"Like Antreas said, leaving at night is our best chance to get away from the Tribe without being seen," Mari said.

"Yeah, the Tribe won't be focused on the Channel at night. There aren't any more captives on Farm Island to guard, and no one with any sense goes down that damn river after dark. We'll be quick and quiet, and we'll get away without any problems, but just in case we are spotted . . ."—Nik paused and reached into his travel satchel, drawing out a stone-topped hammer—"I'm going to break holes in the boats we don't take. The Tribe's filled with excellent Carpenters. They'll be able to repair the boats, but not in time to chase us downriver."

"That's a good idea, Nik. And let's hope the moon is bright. It is close to being full," Mari said.

"Be sure we're taking plenty of torches, though. Just in case."

"We will. Don't worry. The Pack will be ready. We're almost ready now. All you need to focus on is getting the Mother Plants and getting out of there safely," Mari said.

Laru made a low noise in his chest, then Rigel got to his feet, tail wagging as he sniffed the air.

"Cammy's here," Mari said, smiling at the two canines.

"Did you hear that from them both?" Nik asked, grinning incredulously.

"Yep, I did. Loud and clear," she said. Then she added, "And Cammy's not the only one I hear." She and Nik were just making their way to the door when Davis's voice drifted to them, muffled by the briars that protected Mari's home.

"Hello the burrow!"

"Davis! We're coming!" Nik shouted in return as he and Laru followed Mari and Rigel through the labyrinth of thorns.

As Mari held aside the last of the heavy bramble branches so that the four of them could emerge safely, she stopped, smiling in surprise. All of the Companions and their canines were there, standing in the morning sunlight, their smiles as bright as the golden day.

"What's this about?" Nik asked, looking pleased but confused.

"We wanted to see you and Davis off," Sheena said.

"And we wanted to do a little something for Mari," O'Bryan said.

"Me? What?"

"Nik said you still have travel supplies to carry from your burrow," Rose said. "And we're here to help with that."

"And we also thought we'd start a new tradition with you," O'Bryan said.

"I like the sound of that," Mari said. "What's the new tradition?"

"In our City in the Trees we greeted each sunrise with our Sun Priest, absorbing the morning light and giving thanks to the Sun,"

Davis explained. "You share moonlight with us—so we thought it was only right that we all share the morning sunlight with you."

"Not that you need us to call down the sun. Anyone who can call down sunfire doesn't need help with that," O'Bryan said.

"But it's better together," Sheena said. "We wanted to share that with you, and with your permission we'd like to start sharing it with the Earth Walkers, too."

Mari blinked in surprise. "But you know Earth Walkers can't absorb sunlight."

"Well, we didn't know about moon magick until you shared that with us, and even though we can't channel that power like you can, it feels great when you do it," O'Bryan said.

"Yeah, so we were talking about it and we thought that maybe Earth Walkers might be able to feel something if Companions, as a group, call down sunlight," Sheena said.

"And if they can't, maybe they'll find some beauty in it. Like we have found when we watch you draw down the moon," Rose said.

Mari couldn't imagine the sun making her feel any warmer than her Pack was making her feel. "I think that's a wonderful idea! Thank you." She glanced at Nik and saw that he was smiling through eyes that were suspiciously wet.

"I agree with our Moon Woman. That's a wonderful idea," he said.

"Then lead us, Sun Priest," O'Bryan said. "And let us absorb the morning sunlight."

Mari could feel the jolt that went through Nik when his cousin called him Sun Priest, and she squeezed his hand with encouragement, repeating, "Yes, lead us, Sun Priest."

"All right then." Nik met Mari's eyes. "I know the perfect place for this, but I need your permission to go there, and your help."

Perplexed, Mari moved her shoulders. "Okay, where?"

Nik pointed up—to the spot above and behind the little burrow that was a secret clearing where Mari and Leda had spent a lifetime drawing down the moon and dancing their names joyously into the earth.

And where Mari had buried her beloved mama, near the image of the Goddess Leda had cared for her entire life.

Suddenly finding it hard to speak, Mari nodded, picked up her thick walking stick, and headed back into the bramble thicket, counting on Nik to be sure everyone was safely following her.

"Sheena and Captain, Rose and Fala, you haven't been inside the bramble thicket before, so you should stay close behind Mari. She's going to hold the thorny branches aside for you. Davis and Cammy and O'Bryan, you know the drill. I'll bring up the rear." He grabbed two more walking sticks, hidden under branches at the edge of the thicket, tossing one to O'Bryan. "Use this to catch the branches as Mari lets them go."

"Got it," O'Bryan said.

"Ready, Mari," Nik called.

It took longer than usual to wind up and around and get everyone safely and mostly unscratched to the clearing. Mari was the first to step out onto the carpet of fragrant blue flowers. She breathed deeply, savoring the scent that would always remind her of her mama.

"This is spectacular!" Sheena said, stepping out into the clearing.

"How did you get these flowers to bloom up here? Isn't it the wrong time of the year for forget-me-nots?" Rose asked.

"It is," Mari said after swallowing the knot of emotion in her throat. "And I didn't get them to bloom. The Goddess did."

As a group, they turned to the statue of the Earth Mother that seemed to be emerging from the earth, half reclining in the center of a field of flowers. This idol was the largest Mari had ever seen—and rightfully so. It was the idol that had been created and tended by Clan Weaver's Moon Women for generations. Her skin was the softest of mosses, and her hair was fashioned from the most delicate maidenhair ferns in the forest. Her face was a flawless oval of obsidian, carved to appear both serene and watchful.

Mari began automatically to bow to the Goddess when Davis walked right past her, going to stand directly in front of the idol. He gazed up at her for several long moments, with Cammy beside him being uncharacteristically quiet. Then he bowed deeply, placing his hand over his heart.

When he turned to look back at the group, Mari could see tears washing down his face. "I can feel her! Can't you feel her?"

Mari decided right then that she was going to stop being surprised by anything this new Pack did.

"She's beautiful, but I don't feel anything," Sheena said.

"I don't, either," said Nik. "But I love her face—how she looks calm *and* ready to leap up to protect her children."

"None of the rest of you can feel her, either?" Davis asked, looking shocked and a little frightened.

The rest of the group simply shook their heads.

"Mari? You do, though, right? You're an Earth Walker. She's your Goddess. You must feel her, too, don't you?" Davis asked beseechingly.

Mari went to Davis's side. "I've never felt her. I've never heard her voice. But my mama did. Often. And, Davis, the Great Mother isn't just the Goddess of Earth Walkers. She's anyone's Goddess who chooses to follow her—or who *she* chooses. I believe she's chosen you."

Davis's gaze flew to the idol's face. "Really? You really think she's chosen me?"

"Ask her," Mari said.

"How?"

"Follow your heart."

Davis nodded. Then he moved so that he stood even closer to the reclining idol. He went to his knees, though he didn't bow his head. Instead, he gazed up into the face of the Goddess, asking in a voice thick with emotion, "Is it true? Great Earth Mother, have you chosen me? May I call you my Goddess?"

There was a long, silent pause, and then the wall of brambles that encircled the clearing began to sway as if a brisk wind were blowing through them—though no wind so much as whispered past Mari's hair.

"Oh! Thank you! Thank you, *my Goddess*!" Davis exclaimed. When he stood and turned to the group, his face was alight with happiness.

"She spoke to you, didn't she?" Mari asked.

"She did! I heard her. Here." He touched his head. "And here." He touched his heart.

"What did she say?" Sheena asked.

Mari thought Davis's smile could have lit a thousand torches. "She said, *'I have always been your Goddess—it is only now that you know it.'*"

"Wow!" O'Bryan said, gazing up at the image of the Earth Mother. "That's miraculous."

"And it means we're on the right path!" Nik said, hugging Mari and then going to Davis and enveloping him in a hug, too. "What we're doing—the choices we've been making—they brought you to your Goddess. We're doing the right thing, Davis."

"You doubted it, Nik?" Mari asked, feeling suddenly vulnerable.

Nik met Mari's gaze without wavering. "Not for myself and not for you with me. I never doubted that this is the path for us. But for these others?" He moved his shoulders, looking around the small group at his friends. "I wasn't sure. I was trying to do what I believed was best for everyone, but I just wasn't sure." His gaze drifted up to the face of the Goddess. "Now I'm sure—and not just for you and me."

"I'm sure," O'Bryan said. "This is the path I want to be on. None other."

"And I," Sheena said.

"Me, too," Rose said. She grinned and added, "But Fala's little Chloe knew that before I did."

Cammy barked then, as if he, too, had known, and everyone laughed.

Nik looked at Mari. "Ready?"

"I think so," she said. "What do I do?"

"It's simple and completely natural." He took her hand, guiding her to his side. "Just follow along. Your father's blood and the sun will do the rest." Nik turned so that he was facing the east and the fiery yellow ball that had just risen above the wall of thorns. Mari did the same, and the Companions spread out beside them, all facing east, canines close beside them.

Nik paused then, and Mari could see from his expression that he was concentrating—choosing his words carefully. He lifted his face and spread wide his arms, crying, "Behold the wonder of our Pack! And behold the first beams of our lifeline—our salvation—our sun!"

Mari was watching Nik, and as he spoke his eyes changed color, turning from warm, mossy green to blaze a shining gold—a gold that was mirrored in Laru's eyes. Then, laughing joyously, Nik opened his arms even farther, and the sleeves of his tunic fell back to expose the delicate filigreed patterns of fronds that Mari now recognized from the Mother Plant as they lifted to become visible, glowing just beneath the surface of his skin.

With the others, Mari mimicked his actions, tilting back her head and spreading wide her arms. She gasped in pleasure as the sun caught her eyes. Instead of blinding her with its brilliance, the sun flushed through her, gently filling her, warming her, strengthening her. Mari glanced at her own arms, and for the first time in her life she appreciated the delicate fern patterns that were rising to the surface of her skin to greet and absorb the power of the sun. She looked down at Rigel to see that he, too, was staring up at the sun and his eyes were blazing golden. Around her she could feel the joy of the Companions. Some of them laughed; some of them shouted a greeting to the morning; some of them whispered their thanks more intimately into the sky.

The rightness of it settled over Mari as she realized this greeting of the sun wasn't that different from drawing down the moon. Yes, one was cool and one was warm. One ruled day and one night. But the joy was the same, as was the life-sustaining nourishment each gave their people. Content, Mari finally embraced the heritage that was her father's legacy to her.

CHAPTER 36

Mari stood with Nik under the big cedar that marked the entrance of the path that would lead him and Davis to Crawfish Creek and the Gathering spot that had brought so much pain and so much joy to them.

"Cammy and I will give you two some privacy," Davis said. He went to Mari, shyly asking, "May I hug you, Moon Woman?"

"Of course!"

Mari pulled him into a hug, but before he let her go the young Companion whispered into her ear, "The Goddess wants you to take her face with us."

Mari stepped back, blinking in surprise. "What?"

Davis blushed. "I, um, didn't want to say this in front of everyone. It felt too private, like something for you to know alone. But she definitely wants to come with us. Bring her face, Moon Woman. She'll be the first idol we create when we finally get to the Wind Rider Plains."

"But who will watch over Mama if I take her with us?"

"Oh, Mari! Your mama's *with* the Goddess. She'll be coming with us, too. And you do know that the idol up there or any of those other idols they're not *really* the Great Earth Mother, don't you?"

"I know it here." Mari pointed to her head, just as Davis had done not long ago. "But not here." She shifted her hand to her heart.

"Trust your Goddess. She's everywhere. Remember, she found me in the Tribe of the Trees before I even knew her name," Davis said. "Goodbye, Moon Woman. I'll see you, and our Pack, soon."

"Bye, Davis." Mari knelt and Cammy trotted up to her. She hugged the little Terrier as he rubbed his head against her happily. Grinning, she looked up at Davis. "What is he doing?"

"He's giving you what I like to call Terrier lovin'. You're officially part of his Pack now," Davis said.

"Why, thank you, Cammyman," Mari said, taking his face between her hands and kissing him squarely on the top of his nose. With his tail wagging and his tongue lolling with canine joy, he trotted after Davis.

"Is it my turn for hugs and kisses?"

Mari stood and stepped into Nik's arms. She buried her face in his chest, breathing in the scent of him as she held to him tightly.

"I love you," she said.

"And I love you."

"Don't die," Mari said.

He leaned back, lifting her chin with his hand so that she looked into his eyes. "I won't."

"Swear it," she said.

"I swear that I won't die. Not yet. We have a world to build and babies to make," he said.

She smiled through her tears. "Yes, we do. And remember—you belong to an Earth Walker, and we do not let our mates just disappear."

His brows shot up. "Mate?"

"Yes, mate. If that's okay with you," she added.

"It's better than okay. Um. Isn't there a ceremony we should perform, or something?"

"Absolutely, and you're going to love it, which is all I'm going to say right now. Curiosity will give you more incentive to remain not dead."

"This is all the incentive I need." Nik bent and kissed her, filling her world with his touch and taste.

She didn't want to let him go. She didn't ever want to let him go.

Reluctantly, she stepped from his arms. "Tomorrow night—or dawn the day after at the Channel. I'll see you then."

"Tomorrow night—or dawn the day after at the Channel," he repeated. "Not even death could keep me away. You have my oath on it."

"Good. I'll keep your oath." Mari turned to Laru. "Take care of him, and take care of yourself, too." She kissed the big Shepherd on the top of his head. Instead of wagging his tail and licking her, Laru met her gaze, flooding her with love. Mari wiped her eyes, saying, "Thank you, my friend. Thank you."

Rigel went to Nik, jumping up on him and staring into his eyes. Mari was surprised by the young Shepherd's behavior—he rarely jumped on anyone. She was also surprised to see that he'd grown so much that his paws almost reached Nik's shoulders.

"I'll come back. Safe. I give you my oath, too. You be sure Mari stays safe, too," Nik told Rigel. Then, acting more like himself, Rigel licked all over Nik's face.

Rigel went to his sire then. Laru and he touched noses and Rigel bowed his head, exposing his throat to his Alpha. Laru licked him affectionately before he began trotting after Cammy and Davis.

Nik took her in his arms one more time, hugging her so tightly that it took her breath away. Then he was gone, jogging after his Companion, his broad shoulders and muscular back disappearing into the forest.

He didn't look back. Mari was glad. She didn't want him to see her clutching Rigel as she sobbed silent tears into her Companion's soft coat.

They made excellent time and it wasn't even midmorning when Nik and Davis reached Crawfish Creek. They followed the path they'd once believed was a simple deer path but now knew it was a trail made by the feet of generations of Earth Walkers going to Gathering. The trail brought them to the west bank of the creek where it was easy to climb down to water level.

"Let's cross here. This side of the creek gets really steep if we follow it much farther north," Nik said.

"I remember," Davis said. "The current doesn't look bad here, either." He motioned for Cammy to swim across the creek, which he did with Laru joining him.

The water was cold, but it felt good after their walk, which had been mostly uphill. Nik bent and splashed his face, then cupped his hands and drank thirstily—until he heard the sound.

Davis was already on the east bank, laughing at Cammy as he rolled around in the moss, trying to dry himself.

Nik hurried to Davis. "Did you hear that?"

"All I heard was Cammy."

Nik moved closer to the water and faced north. Davis hushed the little Terrier, and they all stood, listening, with Nik.

The all too familiar sound drifted down the creek. Nik and Davis, as well as Laru and Cammy, instantly went on alert.

Davis moved to Nik's side, straining to hear more. The sound came again, accompanied by another—similar yet different.

"Are two people coughing?" Davis whispered to Nik.

Nik nodded. "Sounds like it to me. Could be Earth Walker males who have been infected, like Jaxom and Mason were."

"At least we know how dangerous they are." Davis mirrored Nik's actions as both young men pulled their crossbows from the slings across their backs, notching arrows at the ready.

More wet, nasty coughing drifted to them, followed by a terrible retching sound.

"Definitely that damn Skin Stealer disease," Nik said quietly. "Look at Laru and Cammy. They're focused ahead of us and on this side of the creek. Let's cross again and approach from the west bank. I remember it looks down on the creek and the clearing beside it. If they're Skin Stealers, we can take them out from the cover of the ridge."

"And if they're diseased Earth Walkers?"

Nik sighed. "If they're Earth Walkers and we can get past them without engaging, that's what we do."

"If they see us?"

"Then we protect ourselves," Nik said grimly.

"This is the first time in my life I'm hoping we run into Skin Stealers and not Earth Walkers." Davis touched his friend's shoulder. "You know Mari will understand. She would expect us to protect ourselves."

"I know. I also know she can heal them so that they're like Jaxom and Mason *after* they were Washed—just decent guys who were infected with a terrible disease."

Davis nodded. "I hear you. I don't like it, either, but we don't have much choice."

"Well, let's get across the creek and up that ridge and see what's waiting for us in the clearing. It's probably a good idea if you send a prayer to that Goddess of yours asking for her help," Nik said.

"Good idea." Davis bowed his head and whispered an urgent prayer to the Great Earth Mother: "Please protect us, Great Goddess. It is our choice not to hurt anyone—to get to the Tribe and the Mother Plants without shedding any blood, be it Companion, Earth Walker, or even Skin Stealer. Please help us."

Davis and Cammy followed Nik and Laru—much more quietly this time—back across the creek. Staying as silent as possible, they made their way up the ridge that overlooked Crawfish Creek and the Gathering Site, dropping to their stomachs as they reached the edge of the steep bank.

Nik peered over, hardly believing what he was seeing.

"Bloody beetle balls! That's Wilkes with his Odin, and Claudia with her Mariah," Davis whispered. He started to stand and call to the Companions, but Nik's hand on his arm stayed him.

"They're sick." Nik kept his voice low. "Very sick. Look, Claudia is throwing up over there by that log. And I can see how flushed and feverish Wilkes is from here."

"Oh, Goddess! Do you think they've been infected by the Skin Stealer disease?"

Nik stared at the two Companions. Wilkes was sitting with his back against a tree. Odin lay close beside him. Nik could see that the big Shepherd wasn't taking his gaze from his Companion, which was a bad sign. The canine was obviously worried.

"Looks like it to—" Nik began, but Davis cut him off.

"Bloody beetle balls!" Davis whispered urgently. "Look at the idol of the Great Goddess. It's been completely destroyed."

Nik had to search to find what used to be a lovely idol of the reclining Earth Mother. Her body had been devastated—caved in and then mounded strangely. Most disturbing of all, the moss, ferns, grass, and even ivy had somehow been blighted. In a wide circle around the desecrated image, everything was marred, wilted, blackened.

"Could they have done that?" Davis said.

Nik's eyes shifted to Claudia. The young woman had stopped throwing up and was staggering to the bank of the creek. Mariah was by her side, watching her with the same worried expression Odin kept trained on Wilkes. Claudia dropped heavily to her knees and carefully pushed up the sleeves of her stained tunic, and Nik heard Davis suck in a breath as they both recognized the angry pustules that clustered at the creases of her wrists and elbows.

Wincing in pain, Claudia rinsed off her arms before drinking thirstily. Then she turned to face Wilkes. The wind carried her voice over the water to them.

"Go on without me. If you find Mari, you can come back for me. I'm holding you up," she said.

Wilkes shook his head weakly. "I'm as bad as you. I just haven't started puking. Yet. No, we'll go on together. We have to. Thaddeus will miss us sooner or later, and my best guess is that he'll come after us—out of spite if for no other reason. Out here, away from everyone, he'll kill us without a second thought."

Claudia made a shaky gesture, pointing back to the log she'd been sick by and the bow and quiver of arrows that rested beside it with her travel satchel and cloak. "Then if he tracks us to here, I'll hold him off so that you can get away. Finding Mari is our only chance."

"Doesn't sound like they destroyed the Goddess, and it doesn't look like they had the energy to do it, even if they wanted to," Nik said.

"But a Hunter is tracking Warriors?" Davis's hushed voice was filled with shock. "How can that be?"

"Let's find out." Nik stood and waved his hands above his head, shouting a greeting: "Hello, Companions!"

"Nik?" Wilkes said, and then Davis stood, too, and Wilkes's voice was filled with relief. "Nik! It *is* you! Oh, thank the Sun!"

Nik and Davis hurried down the steep bank with Laru and Cammy bounding down ahead of them. They jumped into the creek, swimming strongly, to be greeted by the Companions' two excited Shepherds.

Not far behind the canines, Nik and Davis sloughed through the creek, fighting the stronger current. When they emerged from the water, Claudia and Wilkes were there, standing beside each other, looking as relieved as the canines and a lot more wobbly.

Wilkes went to Nik and threw his arms around the younger Companion, completely taking him by surprise.

"Damn, boy! I cannot tell you how good it is to see you!" Wilkes said.

"Is Mari with you?" Claudia asked, hugging the equally surprised Davis.

"No, it's just us. Who else is with you?" Nik asked, looking around the clearing with the sharp eyes of a Warrior.

"No one. We left. We had to find you—and Mari," Wilkes said. Then a wrenching cough had him breathless, bending at his waist, unable to continue.

"What has happened? Why are you here, and what happened to the Goddess image?" Nik asked, putting his arm around the Leader of the Warriors and helping him back to sit and lean against a tree as he struggled to catch his breath.

"Goddess image?" Wilkes gasped between coughs.

"She was there. In the middle of that blackened mess," Davis said, pointing.

Wilkes shook his head. "I don't know what happened here. It was like that when we got here."

"The Tribe has been infected with the Skin Stealer disease," Claudia began as Davis helped her to sit beside Wilkes while Laru and Cammy curled up next to the two Shepherds. "We don't know how. All we know is that Thaddeus had something to do with it, or at the very least he knows some kind of cure, which he's not sharing with anyone except his handpicked minions."

"Thaddeus isn't sick, too?" Davis asked.

"No. But he's changed. Has been since he got back from our foraging mission," Wilkes gasped between breaths. "But it's worse now than ever. Odysseus died."

Nik felt a jolt of shock. "Wait, how? Not from that dagger wound?"

"Yes. It festered. Got infected. And Thaddeus has gone completely mad. He talks to Odysseus as if he's still beside him," Claudia said. "And what he says is crazy."

"We had to leave. Had to find you and Mari."

"Where are the other Warriors?" Nik asked.

When Wilkes didn't answer, Claudia spoke for him. "They turned from Wilkes. All of them. All except me."

"What the hell are you talking about? How could *anyone* choose Thaddeus to lead over Wilkes? He's a bully—a terrible leader who threatens and blusters demanding respect instead of earning it. I know! He was my sunfire-be-damned mentor and I hated every moment of it." Davis sounded incredulous.

Wilkes shook his head sadly. "The people who are following him—they're all angry, too."

"Or they believe Thaddeus—that the only way we're going to survive, going to, in his words, *make our Tribe great again,* is to do exactly what he demands—track down Mari, drag her back to the Tribe, and force her to heal everyone," Claudia said, coughing wetly and looking disgusted.

"They'd have to kill me first," Nik said darkly.

"That's Thaddeus's plan," Wilkes said.

"But Cyril and the Council couldn't be in agreement with him," Davis said.

"There is no more Council. They're all dead," Wilkes said.

"All of them were killed in the fire except Cyril. Thaddeus killed him," Claudia said.

"Has the Tribe gone completely mad, too? How could they allow Thaddeus to kill Cyril?" Nik said.

"They don't know Thaddeus killed him," Claudia explained. "They think he died in the fire, too. But I heard him talking to Odysseus, even though his Terrier was dead—*boasting* about ending Cyril's life." Claudia wiped her arm across her sweaty forehead. "You wouldn't recognize the Tribe, Nik. More than half were killed in the fire, with another five hundred or so more wounded. Then this disease—this terrible sickness—struck us. We escaped at dusk last night, and it had already killed more than half of the wounded."

"With the Warriors turning from me, Thaddeus and his thugs have taken over," Wilkes said.

"It makes no sense," Davis said. "I don't understand how our people could allow this to happen. Most Companions don't even *like* Thaddeus, let alone trust or respect him."

"He's stronger than everyone else," Wilkes said. "Especially after the sickness hit us. Anyone who would have stood up to him either became too ill or is so filled with frustration and anger that they're ready to do anything Thaddeus wants them to do—all in the name of making the Tribe great again."

"So, we left," Claudia said. "We came to warn you and Mari. This thing—this disease—it has something to do with Skin Stealers. That's something else I overheard Thaddeus saying. He also said he knows a cure, but it sounded like it's not a complete cure—it's more like a change. And it has something to do with flesh and the canine Companions. I couldn't figure out exactly what he was talking about, but it sounded disturbingly like the Skin Stealers and their need to fillet flesh from people and merge it with their own." Claudia paused to cough, and her whole body shuddered. Finally she finished, "I don't know if Mari can cure us, even if she agrees to help us, but Wilkes and I had to try to find her—find you—and warn you before it's too late. Don't go back there. You can't go back to the Tribe. Not like it is now. Thaddeus will kill you."

"We know this disease," Nik said. "It's affected the Earth Walkers, too. And, you're right, there is more to it than an infection. If we're correct, and you'll have to discuss it with Mari, but from what you're telling me it seems as if we are, the *cure* Thaddeus has taken has more to do with mutating the infection than actually getting rid of it."

"You were right to get away. Right to warn us," Davis said. "And Mari can cure you."

"But will she?" Wilkes asked.

"Not if you try to drag her back to the Tribe," Nik said. "And if you plan on trying that, you're going to have to go through me and an entire Pack of people, canines, and one very tough feline who will fight to protect her."

"Not that she needs our protection. She's fierce all on her own," Davis added.

Wilkes shook his head. "We're not capable of forcing anyone to do anything."

"That's right now. What about when you're healed and well again? What then?" Nik asked pointedly.

"I wouldn't force Mari to go there—back to the Tribe." Claudia looked away, shaking her head sadly. "It's been my home for my entire life, but I don't even want to go back there."

"What about you?" Nik asked Wilkes.

"There is nothing for me back there. Ethan and his Ginger died in the fire. The Warriors have turned from me. I don't recognize my people or my home. My place in the Tribe is no more." Wilkes's eyes were dull—his gaze far away.

"There's a place for you in our Pack," Davis said. "They'll accept you. Both of you, and your Companions."

"What is a Pack?" Claudia asked.

"It's our new version of a Tribe," Davis said, pride obvious in his voice. "We've blended Tribe, Clan, and Chain to form something new. Something where people can be themselves without being banished or judged."

"And we're leaving here. Forever. To build new lives in a new world,"

Nik said. "You're welcome to join us. Or, I'm hesitant to speak for Mari, but I do know her well enough to be able to assure you that she won't let you suffer, whether you choose to join us or not. She'll heal you, but she also won't let you sabotage our Pack, so you may find yourselves healthy, but tied up in a tree somewhere on the edge of Tribal territory."

"She holds that much power over you?" Wilkes said.

Nik laughed. "Yep, over me and everyone in the Pack. But it's not just Mari. There are other women in leadership positions. The Pack is a matriarchy. Everyone's opinions are respected, but women have the final say."

"Sounds intriguing, and a refreshing change from what's happened in the Tribe. This new Pack interests me very much," Claudia said.

"Is there a place for a Leader who has lost his Warriors?" Wilkes asked.

"There's a place for everyone who swears loyalty to the Pack and who wants to build a better life," Nik said.

"I'd like to try," Wilkes said. "I'm not as young as the rest of you, but my experience should count for something."

"It counts for a lot, my friend," Nik said.

"So, where is this Pack and your Mari?" Claudia asked. "Nearby, I hope. I don't know how much farther I can walk—Wilkes and I are getting sicker and sicker."

"They're not close," Nik said. "But Davis can help you get to Mari."

"No! We agreed I'd go with you in case something happened," Davis said.

"That plan has changed now. Wilkes and Claudia will never make it to the birthing burrow without your help, and there isn't time for me to go back with you—or wait here for you to come back. Davis, you know what this means. We need to leave at dusk—*tonight*—instead of dawn the day after tomorrow."

Davis was shaking his head. "The Pack isn't ready."

"But they will be once you get back there and tell Mari what's happened." Nik turned to Wilkes. "How likely is it that Thaddeus will track you when he figures out you've left?"

"Very likely," Wilkes said.

"Which means he could track us straight to Mari," Claudia said.

"And that's why Mari and the Pack have to move. Now," Nik said. "Davis, you and Cammy run ahead of Wilkes and Claudia. Tell Mari everything. She'll send people back down the path to find Wilkes and Claudia and help them to the burrow."

Wilkes nodded. "Odin and Mariah can track Cammy. We'll follow you, Davis."

"Okay, that sounds good," Davis said.

Nik met Wilkes's fever-glazed eyes. "I need to know where the Mother Plants are."

Nik was watching the ex–Leader of the Warriors carefully, gauging his reaction. He saw surprise in the man's eyes and then understanding. "That's why you're here. You're on your way back to the Tribe to get a Mother Plant."

"I am," Nik said.

"If they catch you, they'll kill you," Wilkes said. "And I don't mean just Thaddeus and his Hunters. The Warriors will, too. Thaddeus has convinced almost everyone that you and Mari are responsible for the fire and for Sol's death."

"He was my father! Thaddeus killed him—not me!"

"We know that," Claudia said.

"Hell, Nik, I was there. I saw everything that happened. I know you weren't responsible, but many of the Warriors were there that night, too. They saw what I saw, and somehow they have completely rewritten an alternative past with Thaddeus's words. If they catch you, they'll kill you, Nik," Wilkes repeated.

"No, not right away they won't," Claudia said. "They'll catch you and hold you as bait for Mari."

"Then they won't catch me. Are you going to tell me where I can find the Mother Plants or not?"

Wilkes sighed. "Maeve and her women are tending them in the topmost branches of the old pine that holds the meditation platform. But,

Nik, it's also the temporary infirmary. There are sick people everywhere. It's going to be almost impossible to get in there and get out without being seen."

Nik narrowed his eyes, thinking. Then he sat up straighter and grinned at his friends. "Well, what if I'm seen, but not recognized?"

"What do you mean? Everyone knows who you are—and who Laru is," Claudia said.

Nik nodded. "Yeah, that's true. So, Laru needs to stay hidden, and I just need to blend in with everyone else."

Davis clapped Nik on the back. "I get it! You're going to pretend to be sick."

"Very sick." Nik pulled the hood of his travel cloak low over his face. He hunched his shoulders and bent as if his stomach were paining him. Then he coughed wrenchingly and wiped his mouth with a shaky hand.

"That's good," Claudia said. "But you'll need to cover your arms and wrists so that no one can see you don't have these sores."

"Dirty yourself up, too. The Tribe stopped washing a couple of days ago," Wilkes said.

"I'll do one better," Nik said. "I'll dirty up and cover my arms, but I'll also drag some brambles across my wrists and my face—anywhere that might be seen. I'll make sure I look a mess."

"No, Nik! You can't do that. You'll catch the blight," Claudia said.

Nik smiled gently at her. "And if I do, our Moon Woman will simply heal me. Again."

"If anyone stops you, hide your face and mutter that you just wanted to sit with the Mother Plants. That they comfort you," Wilkes said. "I heard Maeve say that once."

"Maybe I'll get lucky and Maeve will be the only person I run into," Nik said.

"No," Wilkes said firmly. "You don't want to be seen by her. She's changed since she found out about Sol's death."

"Changed so much that she would cause harm to the son of the man she loved?" Davis asked.

Wilkes and Claudia exchanged a worried look before he nodded slowly. "I think you're going to find that much of the Tribe is almost unrecognizable."

"And I think you should not talk to *anyone*. Get in. Stay silent. Get out," Davis said.

"I agree." Nik studied Wilkes and came to a final decision. "I'm going to trust you, but if my trust is misplaced you'll have to deal with Mari and Sora and O'Bryan and Antreas—"

"And Sheena and a whole bunch of Earth Walkers and me," Davis added.

"You can trust me. I give you my word, but I understand that the only way for you to truly believe me is for me to show you," Wilkes said.

"You're right about that, but this is a start. Is anyone guarding the Channel and the boats moored there?"

Wilkes snorted in disgust. "No. Everyone is too sick. We can barely feed ourselves and keep shelter over our heads. Thank the Sun for the sow and her piglets that wandered into the Tribe several days ago. The rabbits are almost gone and—"

"Wait! Did you say 'sow'?" Nik said.

"Yeah. It's all we've had to eat since the sickness hit. Well, that and a few rabbits, but most of the rabbits have to be saved for the canines."

"Did you see the sow?" Nik asked.

"Yeah, it was my arrow that felled her." Wilkes shook his head, remembering. "She was monstrously mad. Her piglets were squealing like something was killing them and she charged into camp trying to find them. When we caught them I said not to kill them—that we should raise them. But who knows what's happened to them since."

"Did you notice anything about the sow that was strange?"

"She was all bloody, like she'd just come through a battle, but the blood wasn't her own. And it smelled terrible."

"That's it," Nik said to Davis. "That's how they infected the Tribe. Same as the deer that infected Thaddeus and the Earth Walkers."

"What are you talking about?" Claudia asked.

"Davis will explain on the way." He turned to the young Hunter.

"You need to get them to the burrow. Fast. Tell Mari everything. Then tell her the leaving has been moved up to tonight at dusk. She'll understand."

"I hope so, because I certainly don't," Wilkes said.

"You will, but I promise that won't make it any better," Nik said. He stood and offered a hand to Wilkes, who took it and allowed Nik to pull him to his feet as Davis did the same for Claudia.

"Tell me truly—Mari can really cure us?" Wilkes said.

"She can. I give you my word on it," Nik said.

"I've seen her do it—three times," Davis said.

"Nik, circle around and approach the meditation platform from the north. Follow the path of the fire from the Channel side. Anyone who has the energy is focused on trying to make the surviving nests habitable, and getting the people back up into the trees," Wilkes said.

"Good to know. Thank you."

"And remember, if they see Laru they'll know it's you," Claudia said. "The entire Tribe knows he chose you after Sol died. There was a lot of talk about how the canines still consider him their Alpha."

Nik rubbed Laru's head and gave him a fond smile. "That's because he *is* their Alpha."

"Alphas don't like to hide," Wilkes said, giving Laru a look.

"Alphas are also extremely smart and they put the good of the Tribe before themselves. My Laru will put the good of the Pack before himself."

Laru barked once, low and rough, as if to punctuate Nik's words.

"Be careful," Wilkes said, shaking Nik's hand.

"Get a Mother Plant and get out of there," Claudia said.

"I will. Tell Mari not to worry."

"Oh, she's going to worry," Davis said grimly. "And she's going to be pissed, too, about you going in on your own."

"But she'll understand. I'll see you and her at the Channel at dusk, my friend. Let's go, Laru!" With the big Shepherd by his side, Nik jogged away, heading once more toward the Tribe of the Trees.

CHAPTER 37

N ik didn't overthink it. He ran, stopping only twice—once at a blackberry thicket where he gritted his teeth against the pain and then dragged his wrists and the backs of his hands against the knife-tipped thorns before slicing off a thick branch and doing the same to his face and neck. His next stop was at a stream that was really little more than a brackish low spot in the forest. He rubbed mud on his face, hands, and clothes. He wished he didn't have to but decided it would be safest if he frayed the ends of his cloak and ripped holes in his pants and shirt—not holes big enough that uninfected skin could be seen through them but big enough for him to not stand out in the grim picture Wilkes and Claudia had painted of the Tribe.

He dug into his travel satchel, pulling out the large square of clean bandage cloth Mari had given him. He dunked it in the water, completely soaking it before he packed it into the woven pouch Sora had given him after he'd explained what he needed to transport a shoot from the Mother Plant.

And then he ran again. Nik was glad Sora and Mari had made him wait and heal—even if he hadn't been able to wait long enough to heal completely. His leg ached, but it stayed strong. His back was sore, but he had no problem lifting and sighting his crossbow. His well-conditioned body wasn't one hundred percent, but it carried him forward, barely breaking a sweat as he jogged relentlessly north.

It seemed like hardly any time at all before Nik started to spot familiar landmarks. He adjusted his route, circling farther to the west than he would have liked, as every second was precious, before heading north again. It was only when he came to the blackened boundary that was the fire line that he slowed and left the path.

From there he focused on stealth instead of speed, but he saw no one. Where he would have expected the Tribe to be clearing the path that led through the burned remains of the forest there was only the smell of smoke, blackened debris, and silence.

"It's like the forest has been abandoned." He spoke softly to Laru, if only to prove to himself that sound could still exist in the barren landscape around them.

There was little breeze, and what there was of it brushed softly against his face. Nik was grateful for that. No canine should be scenting for him or Laru, but there was always the chance that someone—and by someone Nik was specifically thinking of Thaddeus's sharp-nosed Odysseus—would accidentally pick up their scent, and that could be deadly.

And then Nik got even closer to the Tribe, and worry about someone scenting them evaporated. The Tribe reeked. Borne on the gentle breeze, death and disease drifted to Nik, filling his nose with a thick, fetid stench that had him wanting to gag. Beside him, Laru sneezed violently several times and even sprinted off the path and into the surviving forest to rub his face in a patch of moss before he padded back to Nik's side.

"I know. It's bad," Nik said to Laru. "Sunfire! Little wonder they're going mad."

Nik heard coughing before he caught the murmur of voices and he slowed. Moving between concealing rubble and brush piles, Nik and Laru inched ever closer to the settlement. Finally Nik ran out of the blackened landscape left as aftermath of the devastating forest fire. This part of Tribal territory was as familiar to Nik as was his own nest. He had often accompanied his mother to the huge old pine that had once been the heart of the Tribe and after being outgrown still served as sanctuary for artists to work and meditate. After her untimely death, Nik had kept coming to the meditation platform because he felt closest to her there.

Finally he took a knee behind a massive cedar whose low-hanging branches almost touched the mountains of ferns growing beneath it. From there, he was close enough to see the meditation platform and what was left of the Tribe.

Nik's chest constricted with the magnitude of the devastation before him. Tribesmen and women lay on makeshift pallets that circled around the tree. People were tending the wounded and ill, but even from a distance Nik could see that they, too, were coughing and scratching at their arms and legs, as well as moving slowly, painfully. Campfires were lit and he could see pots simmering over them, but the only thing he could smell was decay.

He watched as long as he could, but soon he knelt beside Laru and took his Companion's face between his hands, speaking quietly, earnestly, to him.

"You must stay here. Hide. Don't let anyone see you—no matter what happens. If I'm taken go to the Channel. Wait for Mari and the Pack to get there around dusk. Tell her to get free. Tell her I'll follow you and her—that I *will* escape—but don't let her come here. Don't let her fall into their trap. Do you understand?"

Laru huffed softly, sending a wave of warmth and understanding to Nik. Then he rested his head against his Companion's chest. Nik knew he was trying to hide it, but he could feel Laru's stress and fear. He wrapped his arms around the huge Shepherd's neck, hugging him close.

"Hey, big guy, don't worry. I won't let you lose me, too. I promise. I love you, Laru. Always."

Laru licked his face, but Nik could see tears streaking down the Shepherd's sable-colored fur.

"I promise," he repeated. "You won't lose me."

Then Nik stood and carefully rearranged his cloak so that the hood shielded most of his face. He pulled his dirty sleeves down. Except for the bloody marks on his hands and wrists, his healthy skin was completely covered.

He stared down at himself, seeing a stranger and understanding, if only for a moment, how Mari must have felt having to conceal her true self all those years.

"Never again, Mari," he murmured the promise. "That's why we're building a new world—so that we can all be our truest selves."

Nik hugged Laru once more and then stepped out from behind the concealing cedar, changing his movements and his body language. He hunched his shoulders and bent at the waist, as if his stomach pained him. He tried a few ragged, wet coughs and forced his breathing to be audible. Then, slowly, slowly, he began shuffling forward, heading to the familiar entrance to what used to be a place of serenity and beauty but was now a place transformed into a waking nightmare by death and disease.

Nik had to make his way around the sick and wounded. Most of them didn't even glance up at him. He forced himself not to look at their faces. Forced himself not to see what had become of friends and colleagues. *If I look—if I recognize any of them—I won't be able to leave them to this awful fate. This is for Mari and our Pack. I have to get in and get out, for our Pack.*

He was almost at the tree when laughter drew his attention. At first he thought he might be hearing things, but when he glanced up from under the hood of his cloak Nik saw a small group of Tribesmen and their canines, led by Thaddeus, striding into camp.

"Ralina! You asked and my Hunters and I provided!" Thaddeus crowed.

The Storyteller emerged from an area near the other side of the old tree. She moved slowly and Nik heard her coughing, but she stood straight and went directly to the Hunter.

"What is it, Thaddeus?" she asked, wiping her hands on the bloody apron she'd tied over her dirty tunic.

Nik was pleased to hear disdain in her voice. *Maybe not everyone has bought into what Thaddeus is trying to sell,* he thought.

"Turkeys!" Thaddeus exclaimed. He made a brisk gesture, and the three Hunters behind him whom Nik recognized as Andrew, Joshua, and Michael, reached into their trap bags and pulled out several fat birds, tossing them at Ralina's feet with a nonchalance that boarded on disrespect. Then a fourth Tribesman stepped up with the Hunters, opened his bag, and added two more turkeys to the pile. A familiar Shepherd stood beside the man, and Nik felt a jolt of shock—it was Goliath, a large, mature Shepherd who had bonded to Maxim a decade earlier. Nik felt as if he were dreaming as he watched Maxim with the other Hunters laugh and joke *as if they weren't ill at all!*

Nik studied the men and their canines. Yes, all four of them looked strong, but they weren't completely well. Nik could see bloody bandages wrapped around their elbows, wrists, and even knees, though they rarely coughed. Their eyes weren't glassy with fever. Their faces weren't flushed with unnatural heat. And they obviously had a lot more energy than the rest of the Tribe.

Nik's gaze went from the men to their Companions, and he noticed that the canines didn't look as healthy as the men. The three Terriers and one Shepherd moved slowly, if they moved at all. Each of them lay down gingerly as soon as their Companions entered the clearing, as if there was something wrong with their stomachs. Goliath shifted his body then, stiffly, painfully, and Nik caught sight of his underbelly—and he sucked in a breath. Goliath had bloody wounds on his flesh! Nik's own stomach roiled with nausea as he realized what he had to be seeing. *Someone had flayed strips of flesh from the bellies of the canines! Sunfire! What he and Mari had only guessed at seemed right—Thaddeus was flaying the skin from canines and merging it with Companions, just like Skin Stealers did! And it was transforming them!*

Nik turned away, unable to watch any more of Thaddeus and his gang as they postured and strutted while their canines suffered silently beside them. He slid around the tree, taking advantage of the fact that Thaddeus had everyone's attention, easily finding the wide, sturdy steps that had been built into the tree generations before. He moved quickly up the stairs, only changing his posture again as he reached the main platform. Here, in this place that had been fashioned for beauty and meditation, were the most severely wounded and sick. The stench was almost unbearable, making Nik's cough more authentic than he would have liked it to be.

One person was with the dying. She glanced up from the person she was tending, and Nik barely recognized her defeated eyes and her flushed face as those of Emma, a young Healer apprentice.

"There's no room for you here." Emma spoke softly, as if she barely had the energy for words. "If you wait below, there will be a place open soon."

Nik ducked his head and hunched his shoulders. He coughed again, long and wet, then in a whispery voice that he hoped sounded nothing like his own said, "No, I only want to sit with the Mother Plants. They are a comfort."

Emma nodded wearily and made a weak gesture to the rear of the platform and a second series of stairs that wound upward to another, much smaller landing. "Go on. It'll do the Mother Plants good to have company. Since Maeve was taken ill hardly anyone is tending them—though we're lucky. They seem to be flourishing anyway."

"Thank you," Nik ground out the words, and limped to the stairs. He moved slowly and carefully up them, in case anyone was watching, but as he reached the landing and glanced down he realized no one was paying any attention to him. Everyone was too embroiled in their own private misery.

The landing was empty, so Nik straightened to gaze fondly at the life-giving Mother Plants. Emma had been right. They certainly were flourishing.

The ancient stories said that the Mother Plant had been formed from what used to be called a staghorn fern. The resemblance to a stag's antlers was still apparent, though the ferns had evolved to an enormous size. At maturity, their fronds were easily big enough to engulf an adult Tribesman. Their fantastically large root balls anchored them to the pines, and from that security they grew and reproduced. They had three kinds of fronds—shield fronds, sterile fronds, and fertile fronds. The sterile fronds grew all the time, along with the shield fronds, which looked exactly like their name. They shielded the root balls, allowing them to anchor to the surface of the trees as they also wrapped around the bark, creating a barrier protecting the roots. The fertile fronds budded when Tribeswomen became pregnant, opening to form massive sheets of filigree-patterned green as babies were born. The fertile fronds were soft and pliable and covered with spores. It was these fertile fronds in which the Tribe's newborns were wrapped from birth until they had known one full winter. The spores of the ferns—each in a pattern as individual as each infant— were absorbed through the skin, miraculously allowing the child to begin to absorb sunlight, much like the fern itself.

Nik approached the enormous cluster of plants. He reached out and gently stroked a frond.

"I'm sorry I have to uproot you. I promise the Pack will take good care of you. Earth Walkers can grow anything, so I'm sure you're going to do well with us. And I'll be as careful as possible with you."

Nik studied the fern closest to him, lifting the massive sheets of fronds, both sterile and fertile, so that he could peer beneath them to the underside of the plant. Sure enough, peeking out from the moss that Maeve and her Tribeswomen had packed around the root ball were several small plants the Tribe called pups.

"There you are," Nik said. "The future of our Pack."

Nik took the soaked cloth from its woven container inside his satchel. Ever so gently, Nik used his knife to sever the young fern's roots from the main plant's root ball, placing it in the middle of the cloth. He moved to another plant, not wanting to overtax any of the ferns, and chose another pup, carefully severing it from the root ball. Then he moved to yet another fern, harvesting one more pup.

"That should be enough, especially with the Earth Walker's talent with growing things." Nik wrapped the wet bandage cloth around the three pups and was sliding them back into their woven carrier when he heard a sound behind him and whirled to see Maeve with her young Shepherd, Fortina, beside her.

"Nik! What in the name of the Sun are you doing?"

Nik finished packing the young Mother Plants into his satchel before he responded.

"Hello, Maeve. It's really good to see you." Nik smiled at Maeve, trying to sound calm and normal, as if Clan Law didn't proclaim stealing from the Mother Plants was a crime punishable by death.

"You didn't answer my question." Maeve's voice was as hard as her expression. Her young Companion, Fortina, whined fretfully at her side, and Nik could easily see why the pup was so upset—Maeve looked terrible. Her face was flushed with fever. Her bare arms were covered in sores, and when she wasn't coughing her breath wheezed painfully.

Nik forced himself to respond as if Maeve weren't deathly ill. He turned his attention to the pup, just as he would have if they had been meeting under normal circumstances. "Hey there, Fortina. You're looking well, and you're almost as big as your brother, Rigel."

The pup began wagging her tail, but Maeve's sharp tone had her tucking it between her legs and peering up at her Companion with big, sorrowful eyes.

"You still haven't answered my question."

Nik drew a deep breath and told the truth. "I'm harvesting a few pups from the Mother Plant to take with me. I'm not returning to the Tribe but starting a new group of people who want a change from the past. We're called a Pack. Maeve, if you'd like to join us, we would be happy to welcome you."

"And is this *Pack*," she pronounced the word disdainfully, "made up of Scratchers?"

"Earth Walkers. That's their real name. And, yes, there are some Earth Walkers. There are also some Companions—Hunters and Warriors—who have chosen to join us, as well as Antreas and his Lynx, Bast. You remember him, don't you? He was visiting the Tribe to find a mate."

"I remember him. I also remember your father and the fact that he died because of your Scratcher."

"No, Maeve. I was there. I saw exactly what happened. Father was killed by Thaddeus."

"Only because your father was too kind! He was trying to protect that bitch Scratcher. Thaddeus was right. Had she died that night instead of Sol, none of this nightmare would have happened to us."

"Maeve, Father died protecting Mari because he believed in protecting the innocent and he knew Mari was innocent. Don't you think I miss him more than anyone? *He was my only living parent!* And now he's gone, but not because of Mari. Father is gone because Thaddeus is consumed by hate."

"Maybe that's how it looks from where you stand. You're sleeping with her, aren't you?" When Nik said nothing, Maeve's face twisted into a sneer. "That's what I thought. Young men can be so stupid—led around by their desires. Well, from where I stand it looks like this Scratcher has bewitched you."

"You're ill and not thinking clearly. Come with me. Mari will heal you, and you can tend a whole new generation of Mother Plants. Think of the adventure it will be, Maeve!"

The older woman shook her head disdainfully. "If your father could see you now, he would be disgusted."

Nik's anger began to stir. "You don't know what you're talking about. It was Father's wish that the injustices we committed against the Earth Walkers be remedied. He would be the first to congratulate me on our Pack—and the first to join us, as I cannot imagine him wanting any part of a Tribe led by Thaddeus."

"I see you find it easy to put words in a dead man's mouth," she said.

"That dead man was my father. He gave me those words. I have no need to make them up. Now I'm asking that you stand aside and let me leave. I have only harvested three small Mother Plant pups. I have not injured the ferns in any way. I want nothing from the Tribe except to be allowed to go my own way in peace. This is the life you have chosen, so I will leave you to it. All I ask is that you show me the same respect and leave me to the life I've chosen." Nik began to walk past Maeve, but one of her skeletal hands shot out, snagging his wrist with surprising strength as Fortina whined pitifully.

"Quiet, Fortina!" Maeve snapped at the pup. "I think we should see what the Tribe has to say about Nik stealing Mother Plants."

He wrenched his wrist free from her. "As far as I can see, there is no Tribe left. Step aside, Maeve." As he began to walk around her, Nik reached into his travel satchel, feeling for the length of braided rope he always kept there. *I'll tie her and gag her. That'll give me enough time to get away and—*

Maeve's scream pierced through the sounds of the sick and dying, echoing in the fetid air around them. She shouted, "Help! He's stealing from the Mother Plant! Help me! Help!"

"Bloody beetle balls!" Nik swore.

He rushed past Maeve, launching himself down the stairs, three at a time. On the main platform, Emma looked up from administering to patients, her eyes wide with shock as she recognized him, but Nik didn't hesitate. He ran, leaping over the dying, as he sprinted to the final set of stairs. He reached the forest floor in seconds, and then he ran, weaving between pallets of the wounded and sick as they began to stir. Nik could see Maeve on the top landing. She was leaning over the railing, shouting, "It's Nik! He's stealing Mother Plants for his Scratcher bitch!"

Like they were moving through dark dreams, the fallen Tribesmen and women began to rise, their feverish hands reaching for him, grasping at his cloak, trying to stop him. But Nik was faster and stronger. He dodged around them, picking up speed. At the edge of the clearing, he could just make out Laru's amber eyes from where he'd remained hidden. Nik's Shepherd was utterly focused on him. He could feel Laru's strength and encouragement—and he picked up his pace, moving even faster. He was mere yards away from the forest line, and the relative safety the underbrush would provide, when he was blindsided. Someone hit him, and hit him hard, knocking him off his feet and causing the breath to rush from him.

Nik tried to stand, even before he could draw air again, but a foot in the center of his back kept his face pressed into the earth.

"Why in such a hurry, Nikolas?" Thaddeus's voice sneered. "I'd hate to see you go before you said a proper good-bye—and before that whore of a Scratcher comes to rescue you. Again. Only this time we'll be ready for her."

Nik closed his eyes and focused all his energy into communicating with his Companion. *Go, Laru! Run! Meet Mari at the Channel!*

Instantly Nik was flooded with strength and love and understanding. He allowed himself a moment of relief. Laru would go to Mari. Now all Nik had to do was survive and escape so that he could go to her, too.

CHAPTER 38

A s Mari walked through camp she felt as if her heart would swell and burst with pride. Everyone was busy, and even more important, it was obvious that everyone was working together. Earth Walkers wove cloaks beside Lydia and Sarah, who had picked up the skill so quickly that Danita announced that the sisters had true aptitudes for the task.

Jaxom worked with O'Bryan and Sheena, building the last of the litters from the burrow's deconstructed bed frames. Even Mason, who was recovering with remarkable ease from the Skin Stealer sickness, refused to stay abed and was helping roll dried meat in salt and then packing the meat within supple corn husks for travel.

"It's hard to believe, but we're going to actually be ready to leave," Sora said as she joined Mari in the clearing.

"I know. I'd never have thought it possible just a day or so ago," Mari said. She pointed her chin at the little face that peeked out of a pouch-like sling that held the pup securely against Sora's heart. "That seems to be working."

Sora smiled warmly down at the Terrier pup and kissed her on her head. "It does. But now I understand why canines don't choose their Companions before they're weaned. She wants to be with me all the time and I with her—but she's too little to keep up and she needs to be returned to Fala frequently to be fed."

"But she whines the entire time she's away from you," Mari finished for her friend as she ruffled the soft fur behind the pup's floppy ears. "I know. Everyone does. She's a loud whiner."

"She's absolutely perfect," Sora cooed. Then she met Mari's eyes. "But I hear you. It was pretty obnoxious. So, I came up with this sling. It's really not much different from the carriers used for infants—just smaller."

"You do look surprisingly maternal," Mari said.

Sora narrowed her eyes. "I'm going to take that as a compliment."

Mari grinned. "I meant it as one." She cut her eyes to where Mason was packing the dried meat. "He's healing fast. If we Wash him again tonight, he's going to be as healthy as Jaxom."

"Yeah, for such a nasty disease, it's pretty easy to cure."

Sora snorted. "Please. Are you losing your memory in your cloud of new love?"

"I don't know what you're talking about, and no, I'm not losing my memory," Mari said indignantly. "Mason is healing fast."

"Only after you almost passed out last night from channeling so much moon power into him. Mari, this disease isn't easy to cure. It's deadly. It's only the strength of the moon and the Great Earth Mother that heals it. Take those two things away and Mason would be a raving lunatic again, and would need to be put down like any other diseased animal."

"When did you get so pessimistic?"

"I think it happened right after I was attacked by diseased males," Sora said sardonically. "I keep reminding myself of it—of why we're leaving. It makes it easier."

Mari nodded. "Yeah, I hear you."

"Know what I want to hear?"

Mari raised her brows questioningly.

"I want to hear all about what happened last night with Nik." Sora's eyes glittered with equal parts glee and curiosity.

"How do you know anything happened?" Mari felt her cheeks heating, so she turned her face away, pretending to study the small group that was packing the last of the herbs from the burrow's lush garden.

"Because I'm smart. And because Sheena told me how cozy you two were this morning when they met you at your burrow. So, spill it. I want to know every tiny detail."

"No," Mari said, trying to hide her smile.

"Yes," Sora insisted. "Come with me to check on the rabbit cages. Spencer is almost done making the changes to them that you sketched for her. I really like that idea of yours—to make the litters into rafts that can be tied to the boats. It'll take up a lot less room and—"

"Mari! Get Mari!"

Mari's head snapped around at the shout that came from across the clearing. Little Chloe whined softly, and beside Mari, Rigel barked sharply—not in anger, but more in a surprised greeting.

And then two adult Shepherds rushed into the clearing, followed by little Cammy—and Mari's stomach instantly began to feel sick.

"Rigel! With me!" she called, and sprinted toward the canines, but before she'd reached them she was surrounded—Captain was there, solid and strong, Fala beside him, and out of nowhere the stealthy Bast appeared, eyes slitted dangerously, black-tipped tail twitching. Not far behind them came their Companions and O'Bryan, Jaxom, Mason, and every Earth Walker within calling distance.

"There's no danger!"

Mari looked up to see Davis standing at the top of the stone stairs, his arms wrapped around two very sick Companions.

"Wilkes? Claudia?" O'Bryan called as he jogged up to the group surrounding Mari.

Mari glanced down at the two new Shepherds, recognizing them more easily than she did their Companions. "Odin and Mariah?" she murmured as the two canines filled her with a sense of worry and urgency. Mari ran up the stairs, reaching Davis just as Claudia's legs gave way and she collapsed. "What's happened?"

"Nik and I found them at Crawfish Creek," Davis began, but Wilkes interrupted.

"The Tribe is infected." His knees gave way, too, and Mari knelt beside him. "We escaped," he gasped, and then dissolved into a coughing fit that ended with him spitting out blood and rancid phlegm.

"Oh, Goddess!" Sora said, kneeling beside Mari to hold aside Claudia's hair as she fell to the ground, dry heaving painfully. "It's the Skin Stealer disease."

"Get them into the burrow," Mari said. She looked around, quickly finding Danita, who was standing behind Antreas. "Danita! Start boiling the goldenseal."

"Will do!" Danita sprinted off.

"I'll get the poultice that I used for Jaxom and Mason," Sora said. "And I'll start brewing the poppy tea."

"Make it strong," Davis said. "They're in a lot of pain, and moonrise is half a day away."

Mari nodded in quick agreement before she called out, "O'Bryan, Jaxom, Mason, help Davis get these two into the burrow." Then Mari drew a breath and looked behind Davis.

She didn't see Nik.

She didn't feel Laru.

She turned to Davis. "Where is he?"

"It's bad, Mari, but he said you'd understand. The whole Tribe is infected. The Council is dead. Wilkes has been betrayed by the Warriors. Thaddeus and his thugs are in charge."

"*Where is he?*" Mari grabbed Davis's shoulder, shaking him.

"He went to the Tribe. He had to. And he told me to tell you that we have to leave now—today—not the day after tomorrow."

"What? That's impossible!" Sora cried.

"Why? Why can't we stick to our original plan?" Mari asked.

Claudia raised her head. Her body trembled and her voice shook, but she met Mari's gaze unblinkingly. "It's because of us. When Thaddeus realizes Wilkes and I are gone he's going to come after us, and when he does he'll find you. All of you. Odysseus died, and Thaddeus has gone completely mad." Her red eyes filled with tears. "I'm sorry. We didn't mean to do this to you, but Nik said we could join your Pack. Please don't send us away!"

Mari touched the young woman's feverish face. "Claudia, we won't send you away. And it isn't your fault Thaddeus is filled with hate."

"He's planning on coming after you," Wilkes wheezed. "He blames you for everything from the fire to Odysseus's death."

"We know. That's why we're leaving. We were just planning on—" Mari's words broke off as she was filled with a torrent of emotion.

Fear, worry, anger!

Mari fell to her knees, wrapping her arms around herself as she tried to sift through the panic that barraged her mind, her heart, and her soul. Immediately she recognized the touch of Laru's emotions. She drew several long breaths, trying to calm the panic that raced through her, threatening to break her concentration and, in doing so, break her connection to Laru.

Easy, Laru . . . easy. Slow down. I'm here. I'm here.

"Mari! What is it?" Sora was shaking her—trying to get her to speak.

Mari shook her head and met her friend's gaze. "Have to concentrate. It's Laru."

"Oh, Goddess, no!" Sora breathed.

Mari squeezed her eyes shut, blocking out everything except her connection to Nik's Companion. *Laru! Tell me what has happened! Is Nik safe?*

Her only answer was another deluge of emotions: *Fear! Fear! Anger! Worry! Worry! Fear!*

Laru, I don't understand. Where are you? Where is Nik? Please, Laru! Try harder! Tell me!

More emotions inundated her—predominate among them *FEAR.*

"I don't understand!" Mari spoke aloud this time, her voice choked with tears. "Tell me where you are!"

Still, Mari could feel Laru's emotions as if they had originated within her own body, but the Shepherd's thoughts were getting more and more jumbled—more and more chaotic. She was losing him—Mari knew beyond any doubt she was swiftly losing her connection to the panicked canine.

Oh, Laru, please, please! Help me understand!

And then she felt the warmth of Rigel's body beside her and his sense of security—his sense of serenity—cloaked her like a warm blanket on a winter's night. In her mind's eye, there was suddenly an image of Nik—of exactly how he had looked earlier that morning when he was jogging away from Rigel and her. And Mari's eyelids flew open. She stared at her Shepherd.

"Pictures! He can tell me in pictures!" She closed her eyes again and imagined herself sketching a picture of the scene around her—sick Companions, Gathered Earth Walkers, and upset canines. With every ounce of her concentration, Mari imagined sending that picture to Laru.

The flood of emotions ceased. There was nothing left except emptiness.

Mari opened her eyes. Tears poured down her cheeks. She felt dizzy with fear.

"Mari, how can we help?" Sora asked, still holding tightly to her friend's shoulder—supporting her.

"It's Laru," Mari sobbed. "He's suddenly gone and—"

She gasped as a picture filled her mind so fully that it was as if the image were projected before her. Nik was there. His hands were bound behind his back and he was on his knees in a place Mari recognized instantly as the old meditation platform he'd taken her to when they were waiting for Sol to signal that it was safe to approach the Tribe. Nik's face was bloody with scratches and his lip was split as if he'd been beaten.

Standing behind Nik was Thaddeus. He held a rope that was tied around Nik's neck and he was laughing.

I understand, Laru! Hide! I'm coming! She sent an image to the big Shepherd of him hiding as she and Rigel ran through the forest on their way to the Tribe. Then she opened her eyes and got to her feet. Mari wiped her face and turned to Sora. "The Pack has to leave. Now. Do your best to make Claudia and Wilkes comfortable. They can come with us. O'Bryan, lead the Pack to the Channel." She looked at Wilkes. "You know exactly where those boats are, don't you?"

"I do. I'll show you."

"Show *them*." Mari pointed to Sora and O'Bryan as she started moving away from the group.

"Mari! Where are you going?" Sora called.

"I'm going to save Nik," she said.

"No!" Wilkes shouted, causing Mari to pause and look back at him. "You're headed into a trap. Thaddeus has spoken often about luring you into camp and then capturing and keeping you, forcing you to heal the Tribe."

"He will try, and he will fail. Moon Women are not so easily taken, and we can't be *forced* to do anything." She turned and, with Rigel at her side, sprinted up the stairs to the burrow, running for her satchel and the slingshot she wielded with deadly accuracy.

"Thaddeus underestimates us," she told Rigel. "That and his arrogance will be his undoing." Rigel growled deep in his throat. "So, let's go show him what a pissed-off Moon Woman who can also call down sunfire can do when you mess with her mate, shall we?"

Rigel barked in agreement, and the two of them raced into the forest.

"Davis!" Sora's voice echoed across the empty clearing.

Davis patted Cammy on the head, sighed, and turned, calling over his shoulder, "I'm here, Sora!"

The Moon Woman rushed into the clearing with her usual no-nonsense confidence, joining Davis before the Goddess idol. When Sora reached her, she stretched out her hand, gently touching the moss that made up the idol's verdant skin.

"The offerings the Pack left are lovely," Sora said, her gaze sweeping to take in the feathers, beads, and baubles that had been lovingly placed all around the Goddess's image.

"She appreciates them," Davis said.

Sora glanced sharply at him. "You really can hear her, can't you?"

Davis nodded. "I know she's coming with us, but it breaks my heart to leave her here—all alone."

"She isn't alone," Sora said. "She's surrounded by the plants she nurtures and the animals she watches over. And there's a very good chance that Earth Walkers from another Clan will find our burrows once we're gone. Not today or tomorrow, but in winters to come. They will tend her and revere her." She rested her hand on his shoulder. "But we have to leave. Now."

Davis nodded, bowed one more time to the Goddess, and then he and Sora left the abandoned clearing and joined the Pack. They'd waited patiently when Sora had realized Davis and his Cammy were missing, but now they looked restless—restless and sad.

"This isn't really a good-bye," Sora said, wishing Mari were there to help her through the leave-taking. "It's hello to a new life, a new world, and a new adventure. Pack, are we ready?"

"Yes!" they called.

Sora strode the length of the Pack—counting her people to be sure no one was being left behind. When she got to the litters that were carrying Wilkes and Claudia, she paused, surprised to see that Jaxom and Mason were in place to carry one of them while O'Bryan and Sheena were in charge of the other. She met Jaxom's gaze, but as usual now, the young Earth Walker turned his eyes from her.

"Who told you to carry Claudia's litter?" Sora asked.

"No one," Jaxom answered with his gaze lowered from hers to rest on Chloe's small face, which peeked out from the sling that held her close to Sora's heart. "Mason and I volunteered."

Sora studied Jaxom's brother. "Mason, are you sure you're strong enough?"

"With Jaxom's help I am," Mason said.

Sora looked at Jaxom again, waiting for him to give her some reassurance he was ready, willing, and able to help his brother, but he kept his eyes lowered, head bowed respectfully. She sighed in irritation.

"Well, Jaxom, are you okay with helping your brother, even if it means you have to carry more than your share of weight?"

Eyes still on Chloe, Jaxom nodded. "Yes, I am."

Irritation merged with nerves, and Sora snapped, "Jaxom, I'm trying to have a conversation with you, and the closest you'll come to looking at me is staring at Chloe. It's disconcerting and annoying."

Jaxom raised his warm, familiar brown eyes to meet hers. "Forgive me, Moon Woman, but your Chloe is the *second* most beautiful thing I have ever seen."

Sora stared at him. His tone, his eyes, everything about him was the sweet, friendly Jaxom she'd known and been a little in love with for most of her life. But the instant she thought about him touching her—something that used to bring them both so much pleasure—her blood went cold and her mouth filled with bile.

It was her turn to look away. "Good." She spoke briskly. "Rose will be glad to hear it."

"Rose?" he asked.

"Yes, Rose." Then Sora raised her voice, shouting across the column to where the Companion had taken her place between her friends Sarah and Lydia, "Rose! Add Jaxom to your puppy carry list."

"Will do, Moon Woman!" Rose called back.

"Puppy carry list?" Jaxom asked.

"Yes. You said Chloe is beautiful, so I thought you'd be good at helping Rose carry the other four pups. They're too small to be able to keep up with the Pack, so we've rigged slings like the one I made for Chloe and we're passing them around to people willing to help. Let Rose know if I was wrong to volunteer you."

"Sora, is there a problem?" O'Bryan approached Sora, sending Jaxom a suspicious glance.

"No problem at all," Sora said, leaving Jaxom to stare after her as she continued to walk up the column beside the tall Companion.

When she reached the head of the Pack, Sora faced her people. She raised her voice so that the whole Pack could hear her. "We're going to have to move fast to get to the Channel by dusk. If someone weakens, let a Pack Member know. You won't help us by keeping silent and then falling on your face when we most need you to move and move quickly."

"What if we can't make it?"

Sora looked around until she saw Sarah, who still wasn't able to put much weight on her ankle. O'Bryan had fashioned a walking stick for her, and Sora had wrapped Sarah's ankle, trying to provide as much support as possible for the wound. Sora had given her tea for the pain, but not too much—the girl did have to be conscious to walk.

"We won't leave anyone behind, if that's what you're asking," Sora told her.

"I'll take turns with her," Claudia said, and then struggled through a coughing fit.

"As will I," Wilkes called, his voice sounding unnaturally high and weak.

"Thank you," Sora said.

Both Claudia and Wilkes were very ill. They were also full of poppy tea and had numbing poultices wrapped around the oozing sores that wept from the creases of their elbows, wrists, knees, and ankles. But neither Companion would die. Sora would see to that as soon as it was moonrise, so they both could walk for a ways and let Sarah rest her ankle. Sora looked around the Pack, taking pride in what she saw. From the chaos of the morning, the Pack had pulled together to be ready for this moment, and Sora had watched her people go from being hesitant and sometimes even uneasy around one another to truly joining together in a common cause—a cause that should have been impossible.

Yet here they were, ready to leave what they had believed would be their forever homes.

Sora raised her arms, high and wide, and in a strong voice, filled with the pride she felt for her Pack, she prayed.

"May the Great Mother Goddess bless our journey, and watch over us, as well as Mari and Nik, Laru and Rigel, and may we be reunited with them soon and safely!" Sora said.

"Blessed Earth Mother!" the Pack intoned.

Then Sora, with O'Bryan close on her heels, strode to the front of the column, where Antreas waited with Bast beside him—and Danita, as always, beside the big feline.

"Show us the way, Antreas!"

"Yes, Moon Woman!" he shouted, bowing to her. Antreas stepped out confidently, heading north.

They made better time than Sora had expected, mostly because Antreas—or, rather, Bast—was a genius in picking out the fastest, easiest paths.

Sora glanced up at the sky. The story the Sun told said that it had moved from afternoon to evening. She looked back down the column. Claudia had switched with Sarah, allowing the girl to ride in the litter, foot elevated. The Companion walked beside the litter, hand resting rather heavily on the frame, her big female Shepherd, Mariah, staying close beside her.

Wilkes looked to be asleep, and Sora wasn't surprised. He'd allowed Lydia to take a long turn resting on the litter while he staggered beside it—so long that Sora had insisted he get off his feet straightaway. The Warrior had protested until Sora had reminded him that he was the only one of them who knew for sure exactly where the Tribe's boats had been banked, which meant he had to save enough of his strength to lead them when they reached the Channel.

Her gaze went from the sleeping Wilkes to Jaxom and Mason. Jaxom was sweating, but he appeared to be strong. Mason didn't look as healthy as his brother, but neither of the young men had stumbled or asked for a break.

"The Pack is moving well," O'Bryan said, coming up beside her and ruffling the fur on Chloe's head. The pup licked his hand and wriggled a greeting.

"Yes, they are. But are they moving well enough? Will we make it to the Channel by dusk?"

"Antreas says yes, as long as nothing gets in our way. And I don't see that happening. I've never known the forest to be so quiet. It's like the fire has caused a mass desertion."

Sora nodded. "Seems like it to me, too. It's creepy, really. I can't say that I'm looking forward to traveling on the river, but I am looking forward to leaving this part of the forest. The closer we get to Tribe territory, the stranger things seem."

"It's a sign," Davis said, joining them. "I can feel it. It's as if the forest is holding its breath, waiting."

"Waiting for what?" Sora asked. She'd already come to respect this young Companion's unique bond with the Goddess, and it only made sense to listen to what he was feeling.

"I'm not sure. There's something here, though. Something that is out of place," Davis said.

Sora snorted. "We are. We're a group of mostly Earth Walkers decidedly outside our territory."

"I don't think that's it. It feels more—"

"Sora! Sora!" Danita ran up to them, gulping air.

"I'm here! What is it?"

"Antreas has found two people. He needs you—and O'Bryan and Davis and Sheena. He said bring the canines and come armed. He thinks they're Skin Stealers."

"Sheena!" O'Bryan called, and the young Companion stepped out of her place near the end of the column and with Captain beside her jogged to them.

The Pack members closest to Sora began whispering nervously, but one sharp look from her silenced them. "We can certainly handle two Skin Stealers, but not if your whispers cause the Pack to panic!" The Earth Walkers nearby ducked their heads, calling apologies to their Moon Woman. Then Sora shouted down the column, "We halt here for a short rest!" She turned to Danita. "Find Isabel and Jenna. Have them pass the water bladders among the Pack. Give the wounded a few sips of the cannabis tincture—but not too much."

"Understood," Danita said.

"Where is Antreas?" O'Bryan asked.

Danita pointed ahead of them. "Up ahead the path bends toward the ravine. Antreas is there, near the edge. That's where he found the women."

"Women?" Sheena asked as she joined them.

Danita nodded. "Skin Stealer women. You'll see."

Feeling more curious than afraid, Sora pulled Chloe from her comfortable sling, kissed her on the head, and then gently passed the pup to Danita. "Give her to Rose. I don't know what I'm walking into."

"Let's go," Sora said. Flanked by Companions, she jogged up the path, which quickly curved to the right so that it ran along the lip of the deep ravine that separated the territory of the Tribe of the Trees from the ruined City of the Skin Stealers.

Sora spotted Antreas. Bast was beside him. They both were staring at two girls who sat near the edge of the ravine. They were dressed oddly, in hide skirts and roughly hewn, midriff-baring tunics, with coarsely woven travel packs strapped across their backs. Their skin was very pale and decorated with intricate triple designs painted black and red and white. One of the girls had hair so blond it appeared almost silver. The other's was a deep, shining chestnut. At the sound of their approach, the girls turned to face Sora and the Companions and Sora's breath hitched with shock.

The girl with the shining chestnut hair had no eyes.

"Bloody beetle balls!" O'Bryan spoke the curse under his breath. "I've never seen anything like that."

"Neither have I," Sheena said.

When Davis said nothing, Sora shot him a look. "Davis? What is it?"

Cammy whined, and Davis shook himself, reaching down to pet his Terrier reassuringly. "I can't tell. There is something about her, though."

"You mean besides the fact she has no eyes?" O'Bryan said.

"Oh, I think she can see—just not like we do," Davis said cryptically.

"What does that mean?" Sora asked.

"I don't know. Yet. But as soon as I do, you will," Davis said.

They joined Antreas. The younger of the two girls watched them with big, frightened eyes while she clutched the eyeless girl's hand in both of hers.

"This is one of our two Leaders, the Moon Woman named Sora," Antreas said, gesturing to Sora. "Sora, this is Lily and her—"

"You are led by a woman?" The eyeless girl spoke up. Her voice was steady, calm, and curious.

"They are led by two women," Sora said, approaching the girls. "I am one of them. Who are you?"

"I am Lily," the sighted girl said, bowing her head. Sora could see that she was trembling. "And this is my—"

"I am Dove," the blind girl interrupted. "Oracle to the Gods."

"Which Gods?" Davis asked.

Dove opened her mouth to respond, but Sora cut her off.

"Did you say your name is Dove?"

The sightless girl nodded. "Yes. I am Dove."

Sora felt a rush of dizziness as Mari's words lifted from her memory: *In my dream a dove flew away from the Tribe of the Trees as it was being destroyed by painted Warriors. She came to me looking for sanctuary. Mama's voice told me to help her, but only if she vows to a Moon Woman to tell the truth as the price of my aid.*

"Dove, are you and Lily Skin Stealers?" O'Bryan asked sharply.

Dove's eyeless face tilted in O'Bryan's direction. Instead of answering, she asked a question of her own: "Are you earth dwellers? The people who burrow to make their homes?"

"You didn't answer my question," O'Bryan said.

"And you did not answer mine," Dove responded.

"We don't have time for this," Antreas said. "I say tie them loosely, so that they can get free in time to return to their City before dark and let's be on our way."

"You may tie us, of course. You may do anything you like with us." Dove spoke in a perfectly calm voice. "We cannot stop you. But Lily and I will not return to the City. We are searching for peaceful sanctuary with the earth dwellers."

Sora stepped forward and crouched directly in front of Dove. "You say you seek peaceful sanctuary. Why? From whom are you running?"

"No one is following us. Of that you may be sure," Dove said.

"Again, she didn't answer the question," O'Bryan said. "I'm with Antreas. Tie them and leave them here."

Sora was watching Dove closely when O'Bryan spoke, and she saw the flash of raw fear that swept across her unusual face.

"Dove, do you know what a Moon Woman is?"

"I do not," Dove said.

"A Moon Woman is one gifted by the Great Earth Mother with the ability to draw down the power of the moon."

Dove's pale face blanched almost colorless. She let loose Lily's hand and reached out toward Sora, who automatically took the girl's hand within her own.

"You know the Great Goddess?"

"I do."

"And you are under Her protection?" Dove's voice was breathless with excitement.

"I am—and so are our people."

Dove's hand began to tremble within Sora's, and Lily put her face in her hands and began to weep.

"I don't understand. Are you fearful of the Great Goddess?" Sora asked.

Dove's smile was so brilliant that it made Sora's breath catch. "Oh, Moon Woman, no! We are happy, so very happy, to hear that you know the Goddess. We have been praying for Her help, and She has answered with you!"

With Mari's dream echoing in her mind, Sora followed her gut and made her decision. "Dove, I will grant you and Lily sanctuary, but on one condition only."

Dove didn't hesitate. "Name your condition, Moon Woman."

"I want your vow that you will only tell me the truth. Know that your vow to me will be heard by the Great Goddess. She is kind and compassionate, but she does not abide oath breakers."

Dove reached into the travel sack that hung from her shoulder and pulled out a small knife.

Instantly the canines were at Sora's side, growling a warning low in their throats.

Dove froze. "I do not intend you any harm." Dove spoke quickly. "I only wish to seal my vow with blood, as a proper oath should be sealed."

"It's okay," Sora told the canines and their Companions, who each held drawn weapons ready, aimed at Dove. "Let her make her vow."

"Thank you, Moon Woman," Dove said. Then, with a swift motion, she sliced the blade across her palm. She held her wounded hand aloft, squeezing until blood began to pool in her palm and trickle into the ground. "I offer my blood to the Great Goddess who protects these people. I vow to tell this Moon Woman only the truth. As long as blood flows in my veins."

"And you believe her?" O'Bryan said.

"I believe Mari," Sora said.

"What does that mean?" Sheena asked.

"Just yesterday Mari had a dream, and in it a dove came to her asking for sanctuary." Sora spoke to her Pack members but kept her eyes trained on Dove. "Leda's voice told her to give the dove sanctuary, but only if she vowed to a Moon Woman to tell the truth."

"It is a sign from the Goddess," Davis said softly. "You did right to grant her sanctuary."

"Sure, if she actually answers any questions," O'Bryan said.

"Skin Stealers—that is what the Others call us." Dove spoke up immediately, her voice clear and pleasing. "We call ourselves the People."

"And now I ask you again, from whom are you running?" Sora said.

"We are running from the newly awakened God of Death," Dove said.

Sora felt a terrible chill cascade down her spine. "Dove, you say you're running from Death. What are you to Him?"

Dove's lips pressed into a line and Sora could see her fisting her hand around the bloody slash in it. Her shoulders slumped and her head bowed, but her voice was steady when she answered the Moon Woman.

"I was His lover."

"And you're important to Him?" Sora prodded.

"My body is. I am not," Dove answered with a frankness that none of them could deny.

"Please don't send my Mistress back there!" Lily suddenly spoke, pressing her hands nervously to her throat. "The God is loathsome! He forces Himself on her!"

"I won't send her back—not as long as she stays true to her oath," Sora said. "Dove, you are the lover of the God of Death, and you have run from Him, yet you say no one is following you? Explain," Sora said.

Dove didn't hesitate. "Death does not follow Lily and me. He doesn't even know we have escaped Him. He is far too busy readying his Reapers to invade the City in the Trees."

The Companions who surrounded Sora looked physically ill, staring at Dove with expressions of shock and horror.

"When are they invading?" Sora asked.

"Today, after night has fallen," Dove said. "Death will lead the People across the ravine and into the City in the Trees while the sick and wounded sleep."

"Sick and wounded? How does He know the Tribe is sick?" O'Bryan asked.

Dove turned her face to him. "He poisoned them, of course. It started with just one of the Others—the one the People captured several weeks ago. Since then Death made sure the poison spread."

"Bloody beetle balls! Thaddeus!" O'Bryan had gone pale. "It's as Mari and Nik suspected. I have to warn the Tribe!"

"Whoever is with the Others tonight in the City in the Trees will be either killed or captured." Dove's pleasing voice was disconcerting. It almost sounded disembodied in its emotionlessness. "You may warn them, but you will not stop their fate; you will join them in it."

"I must—" O'Bryan began, but Sora's hand on his arm stilled him.

"She's telling the truth. I think this is why Mari was sent the dream of the dove—so that we were warned about what was coming."

"Someone has to warn the Tribe, too," Davis said.

"There have to be good people left," Sheena said, her voice choked with tears. "We can't just let them be invaded."

"You mean like what they were going to do to us?" Antreas broke in. "I know they *were* your people, but they aren't anymore. We all are fleeing because of them—because of what they are going to do to you, and you, and all of us if we remain here."

"If we don't warn them, how are we any better than them?" Davis asked.

"O'Bryan, Sheena, Davis, I won't forbid any of you to go to the Tribe, to warn them. All I ask is that you consider carefully what you're risking. Wilkes and Claudia have told us that Thaddeus and his men have taken control. The Tribe you knew no longer exists. Are you willing to risk your life to warn a people who would most probably take yours if they caught you?" Sora said.

"If Nik and Mari don't get away before nightfall, they will be trapped there as the Skin Stealers attack," O'Bryan said.

"Nik and Mari know they have to get to the Channel by dusk or we leave without them," Sora said. "They will *not* be trapped there."

"Wait! I know how we can warn the Tribe!" Davis said. "We just need to get to the lookout tower at the Channel."

"The warning bell! Sunfire, where is my mind? I'd completely forgotten about it," O'Bryan said.

"It's perfect." Sheena was nodding in agreement. "One of us can sound it as the rest of us are casting off on the river."

"What is this warning you speak of?" Sora asked.

"There are ancient bells, foraged from Port City generations ago—we have them placed throughout the Tribe on lookout platforms, and the loudest of them is on the platform that overlooks the Channel. If we sound it, the Tribe will know danger is coming," O'Bryan said.

"Yeah, but won't they also know we're stealing their boats?" Sora said.

"They might, but if Dove is telling the truth they'll be busy battling Skin Stealers and their God of Death," O'Bryan said.

Sora sighed, running her hand through her hair, staring at the sightless girl as the Companions watched her, waiting for her to lead them. For the first time, Sora truly understood the magnitude of her Moon

Woman status. If she chose wisely, they would make it to the Channel and escape—and they would warn the Tribe of impending doom.

If she chose unwisely, they would all either be killed or be captured and enslaved.

Sora met Davis's gaze. "I believe Mari's dream. Dove is telling us the truth. When we get to the Channel take the lookout platform. Warn the Tribe and then get your butt into a boat. It is my command as your Moon Woman that you will *not* get trapped there. You will join us on the water."

"Yes, Moon Woman," Davis said, bowing formally to her.

"Sheena, I'm putting you in charge of Dove and Lily," Sora said.

The young Companion's brows rose, but she nodded her head in acquiescence. "Should I bind them?"

"No. They aren't our captives, and I have chosen to trust Dove's oath. But I'm also not a naïve fool."

"Understood," Sheena said, moving to stand beside Dove and Lily.

To the rest of them Sora said, "Now we move and move quickly and quietly. Pass the word down the column about what Dove has told us." She shifted her gaze to the girls. "Dove, Lily, if you can't keep up with us, Sheena will leave you behind."

"Yes, Moon Woman," Dove said as Lily nodded, eyes wide in her pale, pale face.

"What about Nik and Mari?" Antreas asked.

"Nothing's changed." Sora spoke calmly, though inside she felt sick with fear. "We have to trust that Mari will get Nik out. O'Bryan, tell the Companions to pray to the Sun to help Nik." She met Davis's eyes. "The rest of us will pray to the Earth Goddess to give Mari strength. Quickly, now! We've lost all the time we can spare. Get the Pack moving!"

CHAPTER 39

As she and Rigel raced northward, Mari made her decision. She wasn't sure if it was fueled by anger or intuition gifted to her by the Great Goddess—Mari hoped it was a little of both—but she knew one thing with every ounce of her being. Mari was done hiding. She would not sneak into the Tribe like a frightened thief. She would demand Nik's release, and woe to anyone who tried to stop her.

Earth Walkers were not warlike—they nurtured the earth and preferred to live lives filled with peace and tranquility. Even males sick with Night Fever were rarely dangerous to anyone but themselves.

But Mari was only half Earth Walker. The other half was Tribal. As she retraced the path she and Nik had taken less than a week ago, Mari's resolve strengthened.

Thaddeus had taken her mother from her.

Thaddeus had taken Nik's father from him.

Men like Thaddeus had taken Mari's father from her and her mother.

Thaddeus was done taking.

So Mari ran with Rigel racing at her side. When she felt her energy wane, she began to panic—she didn't have time to stop and rest or even to slow to a walk! Her breath was coming in heaving gasps and Mari was clutching her side that radiated pain when Rigel suddenly stopped in front of her, forcing her to halt, too.

"Rigel!" Mari shouted between gulping air. "Get out of the way! You know we have no time to play."

But even though the young Shepherd was panting and clearly exhausted, he stood his ground, staring into Mari's eyes, and suddenly the sunlight around them seemed to glitter with an otherworldly glow and she realized what her Companion was trying to tell her.

"Sorry, Rigel. I understand now!" Mari yanked off her tunic, so that she was dressed only in simple hemp-woven pants. She staggered to a spot where the late-afternoon sunshine had found a way through the boughs of the increasingly large pines. Mari threw out her arms and stared up at the fiery orb. "I welcome the power that my blood craves!" Heat rushed into her body. She glanced down at Rigel. Beside her the pup's eyes were glowing sunlit amber and he'd already stopped panting.

The stitch in her side was gone. In another second her breathing had steadied. And in another the exhaustion that running for half of the day had caused evaporated completely.

Her body was filled with heat and strength.

Her mind was completely clear.

She shoved her tunic in her satchel. No way was she going to cover her skin as long as the Sun was still in the sky—still providing Rigel and her with life-saving energy.

"Now, Rigel, we *really* run!"

Moon Woman and Shepherd almost flew through the forest. As they sped forward, Mari's mind was busy thinking of and then discarding plans.

Oh, Mama! I wish you were here. I wish you could tell me the smartest way to do this.

Then, whether it was actually Leda's voice or just an echo from the past, Mari heard her words inside her head as clearly as if her beloved mama ran alongside her.

Often the simplest plan is the best. Just like when you're confronted by a person with a terrible wound. Don't overthink. Don't panic. Act, sweet girl—act!

"Thank you, Mama. That's exactly what I'm going to do."

As Rigel and Mari drew closer and closer to the meditation platform and what remained of the proud Tribe of the Trees, they slowed to a walk. Mari glanced at the sky. There was little of the sun left, and she could feel the moon waiting expectantly for her turn to take charge of the sky. Mari tested the wind and then altered their course so that the breeze was against her face. She wasn't going to sneak into camp, but she also didn't want Thaddeus to be warned ahead of time that she was coming.

The stench of disease came to her before she heard the raucous shouts of men. It seemed as if they were at play, which caused Mari's blood to pound through her veins as her anger built. *They have Nik. And they're enjoying hurting him.*

Mari used her Earth Walker skills. Utterly silent, she and Rigel crept forward until they came within sight of the meditation platform. Mari's stomach boiled with anger.

She needn't have worried about Thaddeus and his men scenting her. They were too busy with their cruel game to take notice of anything except Nik.

As in the image Laru had sent her, they had Nik on the meditation platform. Only now his shirt had been ripped from him. He was bound with his arms tied behind him. The rope around his neck had been looped up over a branch above him. It was taut, and Mari could see that he had to stand almost on his tiptoes to keep from choking. Below them, in the midst of sick and wounded Tribesmen and women lying mutely on pallets around the tree, stood a small group of men—Mari quickly counted four of them, plus Thaddeus. They all had crossbows and full quivers of arrows.

They were taking turns shooting at Nik.

Horrified, Mari watched a man aim and fire. The arrow whizzed past Nik, brushing his right shoulder and ripping a bloody furrow in it before embedding itself in the bark of the pine. Nik made no sound. He didn't even flinch. He just stood there, straining to remain on his tiptoes, his gaze focused on the forest.

Mari heard a whine, and her attention was pulled briefly from Nik to the Shepherd who lay by the feet of the Warrior who had just shot. While he laughed and hooted and was congratulated by Thaddeus, his Shepherd lay disconsolate, whining constantly, his amber eyes focused on his Companion's face. The Shepherd shifted his body, as if he was in pain, and Mari sucked in a shocked breath.

His belly had been wrapped in a bloody bandage!

Her gaze went quickly to the three Terriers lying beside Companions who were laughing and taking aim at Nik. They, too, were bandaged just like the Shepherd.

It has to be true. They've done with their canines what we saw the Skin Stealers doing with that wild boar!

Another whine caught her attention and Mari's gaze shifted to a woman who was seated not far from Thaddeus. Unlike the rest of the people, she was paying close attention to what was going on, and for a moment Mari felt some relief as she thought there might be at least one member of the Tribe who still cared about Nik. Then she saw what had drawn her attention. A young Shepherd was pacing around the woman, whining pitifully. Mari could see no wound on the young canine. With a jolt of shock, she recognized the pup as Fortina, Rigel's littermate! At that moment the woman, who Mari now realized must be Maeve, backhanded the pup.

"I told you to lie down and be quite!" Maeve shouted. Fortina's tail went between her legs and her ears fell back as she took to her belly. Resting her nose on her front feet, the pup continued to stare pitifully from Maeve to Nik.

Bile lifted in Mari's throat, almost gagging her. *Oh, sweet Fortina! I'm so sorry!*

Mari watched as the pup's ears suddenly went up and her sharp eyes began searching the shadows within the forest around Mari's hiding place. She swallowed hard and steadied herself. *I have to keep my thoughts to myself. The pup could give me away, even if she doesn't mean to.* There would be time to feel sick for those poor canines later. Now Mari's focus had to be on Nik.

Mari closed her eyes. Reaching out with her mind, she concentrated on Laru, sketching a picture of herself, with Rigel beside her, where they crouched in hiding near the meditation platform. She added Laru to the image. It took longer than she would have liked, but finally she felt the jolt of warmth that meant Laru was nearby, and within just a few breaths the Alpha Shepherd padded silently up to them.

Mari was so relieved to see him, beside her and unharmed, that she threw her arms around his wide neck, kissing him and holding him close—sharing her love with him. The big canine's body had been trembling, but surrounded by Mari and Rigel he settled. Mari could feel him calming and regaining hope.

"It's okay," she whispered to him, flooding him with love and reassurance. "We're going to save him. I promise."

Mari glanced up at the sky. It was painted with orange and pink and turquoise. She couldn't see the sun, but she could feel its power fading as the cool majesty of the moon was beginning to grow.

Resolutely, Mari reached into her satchel, pulling out her slingshot and the pouch of perfect stones she kept it filled with. She looked at her tunic and decided against putting it on. Mari shook back her hair, still dressed with jay feathers; she loved that it had gotten long enough that it framed her face in a riotous mess of curls and braids. Then, on impulse, she poured a little of the water from her travel bladder onto a patch of dirt at the base of the concealing pine they crouched behind, quickly working it into sticky mud. Using her fingers, she painted an image of the sun in the middle of her chest. Below it, on her smooth, flat stomach, Mari then painted the image of a moon.

Satisfied, she turned her focus to the two canines as she sketched in her mind a picture of herself striding into the Tribe's camp. Rigel and Laru flanked her. Their heads, ears, and tails were up. Their massive teeth were bared. Waves of power radiated from the three of them.

"Understand?" she whispered.

Immediately Rigel moved to her right and Laru to her left. Mari stood. Her slingshot was in one of her hands. She tied the pouch of rocks around her bare waist.

With the two Shepherds beside her, Mari stepped from behind the pine tree and strode directly into what was left of the Tribe of the Trees.

"Hey, Nikolas! All you need to do is beg us to stop and we will!" Thaddeus taunted.

"Yeah, ask pretty please—you know, like you asked your Scratcher whore for a piece of her ass!" the young Hunter named Andrew shouted, causing the other men—those Thaddeus had already healed—to laugh sarcastically and add their own nasty jibes about Mari.

Nik gave no response at all. When Thaddeus had tied the rope around his neck and hung it from the branch above him, being sure that Nik had to stretch to keep from being choked, he'd chosen a spot in the distance—off in the forest that was still filled with green and life—and he focused on that spot, refusing to look away. Nik filled his mind with thoughts of everything he loved—of Laru and Mari and Rigel, O'Bryan and Davis and little Cammyman, of the Pack he longed to rejoin. He kept his thoughts on them—on the people and canines who were his family, his friends, his future. And Nik waited.

Thaddeus was impetuous and filled with anger. His men—especially the four who surrounded him and who had obviously gone through the same "cure" as had Thaddeus—were likewise so filled with rage that Nik barely recognized them. These were men he'd grown up with, men who had followed his father willingly, men who were now dangerous strangers.

But Nik knew anger did odd things to people. It clouded judgment, requiring actions that fed on chaos and fear—and chaos and fear opened the door to mistakes.

So Nik waited for Thaddeus's mistake, keeping his mind clear and present as he meditated on his loved ones and refused to play the Hunter's cruel game.

An arrow whizzed past, slicing through the meaty part of Nik's shoulder. He didn't so much as flinch, but it did draw his mind out of the dream it had been reliving where Mari's head rested on his shoulder while Laru and Rigel curled at their feet, sleeping contentedly.

Damn, that stings! Nik struggled to remain expressionless. He could feel the heat of the arrow slices and was surprised to realize that while his mind had been daydreaming with Mari his body had been nicked by so many arrows that his blood covered his chest like a liquid tunic.

"Ah, come on, Nik! If you won't beg for us to stop, how 'bout you do a little dance?" Another arrow twanged loose from its crossbow, and Nik sucked in a breath as it grazed his side, tunneling another bloody furrow across his naked skin.

A small whimper had his gaze focusing on the canines below him. Mostly, they were quiet. Except for the canines who were Companions to Thaddeus's group, and Maeve's pup, Fortina, they lay beside their sick and wounded Companions, trying to absorb the suffering of their humans as they lent love and strength and hope to them.

Thaddeus's group was different. Their canines were wounded—sick even. They were lethargic and in obvious pain—a pain their Companions completely ignored. It was difficult for Nik to comprehend it. He could no more allow Laru to suffer than he could allow Mari to feel pain. But the Companions who were closest to Thaddeus, the only Tribesmen who seemed to be getting stronger with each moment, paid no attention to their suffering canines. And Thaddeus—the Hunter who had lost his beloved Terrier just the day before—showed no sign of mourning. No sign of grief. Nik had even heard him speaking to Odysseus, as if the canine was still by his side.

The whimper sounded again. Nik's gaze swept the crowded clearing. It wasn't coming from any of the adult canines. It was coming from Fortina, the pup who had chosen Maeve not so long ago. That poor little girl Shepherd was unwounded in body, but Nik suspected she was utterly broken in spirit.

Maeve backhanded the pup and Nik had to use every bit of his self-control not to strain against his bonds and demand she leave the young Shepherd alone. He did let his gaze focus briefly on Fortina, wishing he had Mari's ability to communicate with other Companions. He'd tell the pup, *Run for the Channel! Find the Pack! They'll help you!*

Then a truly odd thing happened. As he watched Fortina, the defeated pup raised her head. Her eyes brightened as her ears went up and she searched the forest behind them.

Oh, sunfire, no! Don't let it be Laru! Nik closed his eyes, concentrating on his connection with the Alpha Shepherd. *Laru! Run! Meet Mari at the Channel!* he repeated.

In return Nik felt a delicious wash of reassurance and hope so strong that he wished he could collapse with relief. Laru's response left no doubt in his mind. His Shepherd had found Mari. Now all Nik had to do was find a way to escape.

Thawp! Nik's eyes shot open as another arrow ripped across the outside of his left thigh, not far from the wound that was already aching. Warmth washed his thigh as scarlet spread down his leg.

"Isn't that about enough, Thaddeus?"

Nik blinked to clear his vision. He looked down to see Ralina, the Tribe's talented Storyteller, struggling to lift herself to a sitting position as her big Shepherd licked her face encouragingly.

"Enough?" Thaddeus turned on her. "Enough?" Spittle flew from his lips as he yelled his rage. "All of this is because of him and his Scratcher whore!"

"Yes, so you keep insisting," Ralina said. She had to pause as she coughed. Then she wiped her mouth and continued. "But if you want to use Nik to lure his Scratcher here, you're going to need to keep him alive. Keep shooting arrows at him and, sooner rather than later, one of you is going to hit something critical. He'll do you no good as bait if he bleeds to death."

"Why the hell do I care if he bleeds to death?" Thaddeus smirked. "As soon as he doesn't meet his Scratcher with the stolen Mother Plants, she'll come looking for him—whether he's dead or alive."

"I told you," Nik rasped, baring his teeth at Thaddeus. "Mari and her Clan have gone west, to Clan Fisher. I was supposed to join them on the coast. She won't expect me for days."

"And I told you—I don't believe you!" Thaddeus shouted. "I don't think that bitch would go anywhere too far without you. I believe she's a lot closer than you let on."

"For once, Thaddeus, you speak the truth!" Mari's voice was a clarion call, blasting throughout the clearing.

Every Tribesman and woman turned as one. But Nik didn't need to turn. Nik had a perfect view, and he would never forget the sight.

Mari strode into the Tribe with Laru and Rigel pressed against her sides. The big Shepherds had their teeth bared and were growling a warning to every canine in the Tribe: *Stay back—stay clear—she is Alpha protected!*

Her feather-dressed hair flew wild around her shoulders. She was bare breasted, covered only by a sun and a moon that were painted on her skin and by the glowing filigreed pattern of fern fronds that glistened as they captured the last rays of the setting sun.

"Get her! But don't kill her—yet!" Thaddeus shrieked.

The Hunter named Andrew was the first to move. He lunged toward Mari. With blinding speed Mari took a rock from the bag strapped around her waist, fitted it in her slingshot, and with a flick of her wrist the rock flew at Andrew, smashing into his nose and sending him staggering backward to fall in a heap to the ground.

With a feral snarl, Thaddeus raised his crossbow, sighting at Mari. Nik shouted, *"No!,"* but before Thaddeus could fire he was shoved to the side so that he lost his aim and the arrow twanged harmlessly into the forest well over Mari's head.

As the Tribe exploded into shouts and cries, Thaddeus rounded on the Storyteller, who had managed to climb to her feet and tackle the Hunter, foiling his shot.

"You bitch! What's wrong with you?"

"What's wrong with you, Thaddeus? You'd kill the one person we know can heal us? Really? Even though your sick and dying Tribe is strewn about you, weak and hopeless?"

"You don't know she can heal you!"

"Of course I can." Mari spoke with a calm authority that silenced the Tribe. "Let Nik go, and I give you my word that I will heal anyone who wishes to be cured."

"Your word? What good is the word of a Scratcher whore?" Thaddeus taunted.

Mari cocked her head to the side, as if considering his question. "Well, Thaddeus, I'd say my word is better than some of your Tribe's." She looked from him to his Hunters and the one Warrior who stood with them and then directly at Maeve before she continued. "Don't you swear to your canines when they choose you that you will honor and love and care for them for their entire lives?" Mari didn't pause but kept speaking, her voice rich with disdain. "And yet I see canines here, suffering at the hands of their Companions."

"You don't know what you're talking about!" Thaddeus snapped.

"See, that's the problem, Thaddeus. I know *exactly* what I'm talking about. I know more than these poor, sick men and women you have duped. I know about the Skin Stealer disease that has infested you—and how you have been flaying the flesh from your Companions as a cure."

"What is she talking about?" Ralina said, looking wide-eyed from Mari to Thaddeus.

"She lies," Thaddeus said.

Mari turned to Ralina. "If you weren't so sick you'd have already realized it, but look at his men—those men who seem to be healing. Then look at their canines—their poor, wounded canines—and tell me what you see."

"You don't need to kill her to shut her up," said the Warrior who moved to Thaddeus's side.

"But if she is lying, why shut her up?" Ralina asked, and Mari noticed that several Tribesmen and women had managed to shake themselves out of painful stupors and were struggling to sit.

"If she can heal us let her!" said a young Warrior whose Shepherd was whining by his side as he pulled himself to his feet.

"Shut up, Renard!" Thaddeus shouted.

"I will not." The Warrior moved slowly, stiffly, to confront Thaddeus.

He pointed back at an older man who lay unconscious on a pallet nearby. "Father is dying. I've already lost Mother. I'll do anything to save the rest of my family—even follow you, Thaddeus!"

Thaddeus's mean eyes narrowed at the Warrior, but before he could respond several people began clamoring to be heard.

"If there is even a small chance she can heal us do not harm her!" called another Tribesman.

"Let the Scratcher heal us!"

"Give her a chance!"

"Fine!" Thaddeus shouted over the noise of the crowd, so that they began to quiet. He turned his malicious gaze on Mari. "Then do it. Heal them."

"Not until you let Nik go."

Thaddeus laughed. "And once I let him go, what then? What if you *can't* heal anyone? No, that's not happening."

"I should have been more specific. Untie Nik. Let him join me. Then I will heal any of the Tribe who wish to be Washed free of disease. If I do as I promise I can, only then will I leave with Nik."

Thaddeus's eyes glittered with victory. "Why not? I don't think you can do it anyway—and then we'll truss you up beside your lover and get back to target practice. Emma!" he shouted up at the platform where Nik was bound. "Cut Nik free—for now."

A young woman who was obviously ill moved slowly, painfully, to Nik. She sawed through the ropes at his wrists first so that Nik was able to loosen and then slide the noose over his head. Then, with a litheness that had Mari feeling much better about his wounds, Nik bent to grab his travel satchel, but Maeve's spiteful voice cut across the clearing.

"No! That satchel has stolen Mother Plant pups in it! Don't let him take them!"

Mari rounded on the older woman. "If Nik doesn't take the plants. I don't heal you. *Ever.* It's as simple as that."

"Let him take the plants. The Scratcher bitch can't possible heal everyone, so they won't be going anywhere."

Maeve started to say something, but Thaddeus turned his back to her, ignoring her completely.

Nik slung his satchel across his bleeding shoulder and hurried to her.

She wanted to run into his arms and sob her relief. But not yet. They weren't safe yet.

He stopped in front of her, bending to greet Laru. When Nik straightened, their eyes met.

"How badly did they hurt you?" she asked.

"Scratches," he said.

"I'll make them pay for every one of them."

"I love it when you read my mind," Nik said.

"That's enough!" Mari and Nik turned to see that Thaddeus and his men had crossbows trained on them. "Get to healing, or I don't care what the rest of the Tribe says—I'm more than ready to put you out of my misery."

Mari saw Nik's gaze flick to the sky that still blushed with the colors of sunset.

"Remember." She spoke her mama's words softly to Nik. "Whether you can see it or not, the moon is always present." Mari raised her voice, saying, "All who wish to be Washed of the sickness that has infested this Tribe, bow your heads and place your hands over your hearts."

"Wait! What of people like my father, who aren't conscious?" asked the young Warrior Renard.

Mari met his eyes, finding compassion as her answer. "I've lost both of my parents," she told the Warrior, being sure her words carried throughout the clearing. "I will not ignore those who are so gravely ill that they cannot accept the Washing willingly, though I do believe that some of this Tribe are pleased with their sicknesses. It is to those people I speak."

"Some of us aren't sick—we're better, stronger, faster!" Thaddeus shouted at her defensively.

"Really?" Mari took a turn at laughing humorlessly. "You seem very sick to me, Thaddeus. But as you and your men don't want to be free of what you have done to yourselves, I will not heal you. Those of you loyal to Thaddeus, move to stand with him and my moon magick will not touch you."

The four men whose canines bore flaying wounds moved quickly to stand behind Thaddeus. Then, more slowly, several Hunters who were still sick—still coughing and weak—shuffled to him as well. Several Warriors, with Shepherds moving slowly, hesitantly, at their sides, joined Thaddeus's group until by Nik's count about fifty people and almost as many canines stood with the Hunter.

Mari nodded. "So be it. Let what happens to you and your people as a result of choosing anger and hatred be on your conscience, Thaddeus, not mine."

Mari took one step away from Nik. She drew a deep breath, grounding herself. Then she reached from within the center of herself and found the moon. Turning to face northeast—the darkest part of the gloaming sky—Mari lifted her arms.

There was no time for nerves. No time for regret that she didn't know more—was perhaps not as strong as she could or should be—she focused her entire being on the moon and began the drawing-down invocation.

> *"Moon Woman I forever will be*
> *Greatly gifted, your power fills me!*
> *Earth Mother, aid me this somber night*
> *So that those who wish it may feel your healing might!"*

Mari didn't need to glance at her arms to know her body had begun to glow with the cold, silver power of the moon. The shocked expression of the Tribe and the gasps that surrounded her told her what she already knew—the moon, although still invisible in the dusk sky, had found her.

> *"By right of blood and birth channel through me*
> *The Goddess gift I embrace as my destiny!"*

Within her mind, Mari sketched a simple picture. She drew the clearing, with the meditation platform and the sick, dying Tribe in it and surrounding it. In the sketch, she created an enormous bubble, like the frothy ones formed at the base of a waterfall, around Thaddeus and his loyal followers, including Maeve, who had stood and joined his hateful group. Then Mari painted the sky with a moon, fat and full. From it poured a silver wave of liquid power. The wave cascaded into Mari, and from her open palms it rained all around her, covering the meditation platform and all of the sick and wounded who were not enclosed in Thaddeus's bubble.

On and on the silver light flowed into Mari to be dispersed out to the Tribe. Mari gritted her teeth to keep them from chattering. Her knees felt weak, but still she kept the connection open. *I am the conduit for the healing—the magick washes through me and into the Tribe. I am the conduit for the healing—the magick washes through me and into the Tribe. . . .*

The litany played over and over through Mari's mind until she became aware of Nik's strong hand on her shoulder and his voice in her ear.

"Stop now, Mari. You've done it. The Tribe is healed!"

Mari drew a long, shaky breath and then released the image to which she'd held so tightly, and the silver light snuffed like a doused torch. She blinked and gazed around her.

Members of the Tribe were stirring. Some of them were laughing in relief. Some of them wept. The young Warrior Renard had rushed to his father's side, and the two men were embracing.

"It worked." Mari smiled her relief to Nik.

"Did you doubt that it would?" Nik asked.

She moved her shoulders. "Well, Rigel and Laru never doubted it."

"Thank you. Thank you so much."

Mari looked over Nik's shoulder to see the woman named Ralina approaching them, an adult Shepherd bouncing around like a puppy at her side. The woman grasped Mari's hands, saying, "You saved us!"

"No," Mari told her softly. "As long as you follow Thaddeus, your Tribe is still infested with disease."

"That's not a very nice thing to say, Scratcher bitch."

Thaddeus and the men surrounding him raised their crossbows and took aim—not at Mari but at Nik.

"What are you doing, Thaddeus?" Ralina asked, moving so that her body shielded Mari's. "She did exactly what she said she would. Now you need to let Mari and Nik go as you agreed."

Thaddeus scoffed, "I didn't agree to let them go. I agreed to let Nik join her. And now he has."

"What do you mean to do, Thaddeus?" Nik asked.

"I mean to keep your Scratcher whore prisoner and kill you. I was going to kill her, too, but after her little exhibition tonight I realize she could actually be of use to the Tribe."

Thaddeus raised his crossbow, aiming at Nik.

As easily as breathing, Mari released the anger the soothing moon magick had been keeping at bay. She stepped around Ralina, drawing the dying sun's rays to her, and lifted her hands, opening them so the Tribe could see the sunfire that flared with her righteous indignation dancing in golden flames on her palms.

"If you hurt Nik, I will kill you with sunfire."

Thaddeus paused, his gaze flicking from her palms to her face. Then a slow, sly smile lifted his thin lips. "You won't do it. You're a Healer. I know your type. You're sworn to help and not harm. You won't kill me, or any of us, because of your Healer oath."

Mari let loose of more of her anger, and the flames in her palms grew, leaping hot and hungry, so that Nik and Ralina were forced to step behind her, shielding their eyes with their hands. When Mari spoke she hardly recognized her own voice, as it was filled with the hot might of the Sun.

"Thaddeus, you're partially right. The only thing that stops me from killing you and your twisted group of followers is the fact that I am a Moon Woman, gifted to heal, and not to kill. I do not wish to poison my soul with your blood."

"You just proved my point, you stupid bitch!"

"You didn't let me finish. Right now I don't want to poison my soul with killing, but if you harm Nik or Laru or Rigel I won't respond as a Moon Woman. I'll be an enraged mate, Leader of my Pack, and I'll respond with my father's blood—the fiery blood that allows me to call down sunfire—but I won't be your tame Sun Priestess. I will be a Sun Warrior, and I will fry your ass dead. On that you have my eternal oath. Now, back off or die. The choice is yours!"

Thaddeus's eyes narrowed with a spiteful intelligence, and his evil smile spread across his face. "Really? What if I told you I know who killed your father, Galen?"

Mari felt Nik's body jerk with shock beside her.

"I know who killed my father. My mother told me. She saw the whole thing. It was someone from your Tribe—filled with hate like you."

"You're partially right. He was from our Tribe, but he was a lot weaker than me, which is why he's dead. But ask his son. He's standing beside you."

Mari's gaze flew to Nik, who was looking sad and pale. "I'm so sorry, Mari," he said.

"Sol killed my father?"

Nik nodded wearily. "And it ate at him for the rest of his life. He would have done anything to make it right—including giving his life for you."

"Oh, Goddess! And that's exactly what he did," Mari said.

"Forgive him, if you can," Nik said. "And forgive me for wishing you'd never found out."

Mari didn't answer Nik. Instead, she faced Thaddeus again. "You actually thought I'd hold Nik to blame for something his father did." She shook her head, lifting her lip in her own version of a canine's snarl. "But that doesn't make any sense at all—at least not to anyone who isn't lost to rage and hatred it doesn't. What Sol did all those years ago has *nothing* to do with Nik, you pathetic, evil little man."

"Die, bitch!" With a growl that was more animal than man, Thaddeus shifted his aim to Mari and loosed an arrow.

Mari heard Nik's panicked shout. She even felt Ralina begin to move forward, as if she meant to shield Mari from the arrow, but they both would be too late. Neither was near enough to save Mari—so Mari saved herself.

Instead of lunging away, Mari strode forward to meet the arrow, and with a flick of her fingers the sunfire at her command engulfed it, burning it to ash.

"Nik, Laru, Rigel! Get behind me!" Mari shouted. She turned her head and met Ralina's wide-eyed look. "Unless you want to leave with us, and we would gladly accept you, you must get back," she told the kind woman.

"I can't leave my people. They need me," said the Storyteller.

"Then move out of my way! Now!"

Ralina grabbed her Shepherd around the neck and lunged back, away from Mari and Nik and their two canines.

Using the same vivid imagination and the concentration her mama had made her practice since she'd been old enough to speak, Mari painted a picture all in gold around the four of them. Sunfire flared hot and high, encircling them with heat as the flames licked hungrily, searching to be fed.

Mari's concentration slipped. This was nothing at all like Moon Magick! How had she thought she could control such an alien power? Mari smelled her hair beginning to singe as her control began to slide from her. It was going to burn her! Burn all of them!

Then from behind her Nik's strong hands were on her shoulders and his calm voice spoke into her ear.

"It's okay. You've got this. *We've* got this. Don't imagine it burning. Imagine it shielding."

"But it's so hot! It's so angry!" Mari panted, struggling not to scream that they needed to run! They all needed to run from the sunfire!

"It's not, Mari. *You're* angry. And if it's you then you can control it, right?"

The logic of Nik's words penetrated through her panic and Mari blinked in surprise. *It is my anger! I let it loose on purpose. I knew that was how I call sunfire.*

Mari forced her shoulders to relax under Nik's hands. She focused on her breathing—in and out smoothly, deeply. She didn't need to be blinded by anger. She didn't need to destroy these people. She simply needed to be free of them.

And suddenly the dome of flame that had been threatening to devour them calmed. Mari could actually see through it to the Tribe. The people were milling around, crying out in fear and panic. Even Thaddeus and his group had backed away from her, though their weapons were still aimed her way.

"That's it!" Nik said, squeezing her shoulders reassuringly. "That's perfect. Now walk forward. Head into the ruins of the Tribe."

Slowly, at first, Mari began walking. The shield of flame stayed with her, surrounding the four of them and making the Tribe cringe away from her as she passed them. And as she walked, Mari's control grew. Her anger simmered low—easily controlled—and the sunfire, made malleable by the gift that was her father's blood, protected them.

She didn't turn and look, but she could feel Thaddeus following. She could also feel the Sun setting.

"Nik, the Sun's going. I don't know how much longer I can keep the shield around us."

"That's okay. We don't need it much longer. Move faster, Mari. Keep some of the sunfire for yourself, like you'd keep Moon Magick to heal yourself. Once we're through the ruins of the City, we'll be within sight of the Channel and we're going to have to run for it."

Mari gritted her teeth and nodded. She tapped into a shaft of sunfire, and like a true weaver she imagined threading that warm power into her veins. Hot strength blasted through her and Mari sprinted forward, with Nik close behind, Rigel and Laru on either side of them. They leaped over blackened logs and the debris of the once beautiful City until Nik's hand closed around her shoulder again.

"That's it. We're here."

Mari staggered to a stop. They were on the edge of the ridge. Before them it sloped down to the Channel, which looked like a shining ribbon of green in the last of the daylight. To their right, the ridge grew to become a wide ravine that separated Tribal territory from the edge of Port City. Mari reached out with a questioning mind and was instantly rewarded by images of the Pack silently entering many small boats that rushed to fill her mind from Cammy and Captain, Fala, and even the precocious flash of an image of Sora, slipping and almost falling headfirst into the water, which she was certain came from little Chloe.

"The Pack made it!" Mari told Nik. "They're down there right now!"

"Then let's join them and get the hell out of here!"

Mari heard a sound behind them and she turned—and was shocked to see that instead of Thaddeus and his goons, just outside the shield of flame stood a Shepherd pup. She was panting with panic, so close to the fire that Mari could see her fur beginning to singe.

"It's Fortina!" Mari cried. "What is she doing?"

Nik shook his head. "I've never seen any canine do this, but I think she's left her Companion."

"There they are! Shoot them! The fire's banking! The Sun's setting!"

From farther behind them, Thaddeus's voice drifted through the crackling of the hungry flames. Mari had one choice. She didn't like it, but she also didn't see any other way to be free. Mari imagined a half-grown-Shepherd-sized hole in the dome of flames, and the shield parted.

"Come on, Fortina!" she called to the pup. The young canine didn't hesitate. She sprinted through the opening in the flames, running straight to Rigel.

"Shoot! Now! They're stealing my Fortina!" It was Maeve's shrill voice, filled with anger and hate that acted like a goad on Mari.

Mari gathered the sunfire to her so that it sizzled in a flame-shaped pillar in front of her, and then she allowed herself to really think about Thaddeus—about all he'd taken from her and from Nik, about all he still wished to take from them.

"*IT WILL NEVER HAPPEN!*" Mari shrieked as she tossed her anger, and the column of flame, into the heart of the ruined City, cutting off Thaddeus and his group and forcing them to retreat.

"Hurry!" Nik said, grabbing her hand. "There's not much left for it to burn. It'll be out soon."

They half ran, half slid down the ridge. The broken road was in sight when the first of the arrows began to rain around them.

"Run, Mari! Run!" Nik shouted.

They sprinted forward, but the arrows were too fast. They were getting closer and closer—and then from the darkened lookout tower that stood as silent sentinel beside the Channel the tolling of a bell split the night, crying danger to the Tribe.

Mari struggled not to collapse in defeat. They were so close that they could see their Pack in small boats, spreading out across the Channel. Mari looked up at the tower. She saw a man, with a small canine beside him, rushing down the wooden stairs. Mari steeled herself, expecting the man to sight with his crossbow and rain deadly arrows down on them, pinning them between the Tribe and the safety of the water.

Instead, the man paused long enough to drape over the railing of the stairs a large, familiar tapestry of the Great Goddess, circled by her Clan. Then he cupped his hands around his mouth and shouted, "Nik, Mari! What are you waiting for? Get to the boats!"

"Davis!" Nik laughed, shouting his relief. "It's Davis!"

"But why was he alerting the Tribe about us?" Mari could hardly believe that Davis would do such a thing, but there he was, climbing down from the tower after ringing the clarion bell.

"Oh, sunfire! He wasn't alerting them about us. Look!"

Mari's gaze followed Nik's pointing finger, and there, swarming down the far side of the ravine, came an army of bare-chested painted men, wielding triple-tipped spears as they closed on the Tribe of the Trees.

There was a shout from behind Nik and Mari, and suddenly the arrows changed direction and began falling on the invading army.

"Go! Now!" Davis shouted as he sprinted past them.

Mari and Nik didn't hesitate. They ran with Davis to the two boats that had been left for them. Mari blinked in surprise as she recognized the single person who had remained and was still smashing holes in the last of the other boats.

"Jaxom! That's enough! Get in the boat with me!" Davis told him.

Jaxom sprinted to Davis as Nik almost tossed Mari into another boat. Rigel leaped onto one of the ballasts made for holding canines, and in a single bound Laru landed on the other one.

"Come on, girl!" Mari shouted to the pup, who paused, shivering at the edge of the water.

Nik gave their boat a huge push and jumped in. Grabbing the oars, he began fighting against the current while Sora and the rest of the Pack called encouragement.

"Wait, Nik! The pup's still on the bank," Mari said.

"Too late. She might have changed her mind anyway. I've never known a canine to leave a living Companion."

"But she did leave Maeve!" Mari cried.

"It's okay; I'll get her!" Jaxom said. He jumped out of the boat, sloughing through the shallow water to the bank as Davis shouted at him to get his ass back there.

Jaxom stopped a yard or so before the young Shepherd. His voice carried easily over the water: "If you want to be free, come with me. I'll make sure you're safe. I promise."

The pup started at him, unmoving.

"Jaxom! I can't wait for you if you don't move and move now!" Davis shouted.

And then Jaxom's body language changed. He suddenly stood straighter, and in a voice amplified by joy he called, "Fortina! Your name is Fortina! Come to me, little girl!"

The pup barked happily before launching herself into the young Earth Walker's arms, and Jaxom used all the power in his muscular legs to fight the current. He reached the boat and tossed the pup in; then he grasped Davis's outstretched hand and toppled face-first into the boat, causing Cammy to yip in concern.

The instant Jaxom was safely in the boat, he crawled to the pup, picking her up and cuddling her close to him as he felt all over her for wounds.

Mari watched him, incredulous, feeling everything the young sister to Rigel was feeling. *Great Goddess! That pup just Chose Jaxom!*

"Go! Go! Go!" Sora's voice shouted from far up the Channel. "Hurry! The Skin Stealers are attacking!"

Each of them grabbed oars and paddles and fought the current that threatened to push them back to the bank. Then Mari felt a catch in the little boat, and it suddenly shot forward.

"That's it!" Nik said between heaving breaths. "The center current has us. We're free!"

Mari's hands began shaking so badly that she dropped her paddle. She wrapped her arms around her chest as if she was trying to hold herself together.

Through the fog of exhaustion that followed calling down sunfire, Mari heard her Pack cheering in celebration, but she couldn't take her eyes off the ridge. There, silhouetted by the wall of fire that was already beginning to smoke and dissipate, Mari's eyes were drawn to an enormous figure. She thought she might have been hallucinating, but she was quite sure the figure had huge horns growing from his head.

And then slowly, purposefully, the figure turned to face her. He lifted a hand that was fisted around an impossibly large triple-pointed spear in what was obviously a bizarre salute to Mari, before he roared a terrible battle cry and turned to join his army against the Tribe.

A shiver of dread skittered down Mari's spine, and she leaned over the side of the boat, vomiting fear into the dark water.

"What is it, Mari?" Nik asked, still pulling on the oars to catch them up to the Pack. "Are you okay?"

Mari wiped her mouth with the back of her hand and said the words that lifted, unbidden, from the recesses of her mind.

"I'm okay for now, but whatever that was—whatever is back there— he is not okay. And he saw me, Nik. He looked right at me. I felt it— like someone had just walked over my grave."

"Whoever he is, we're leaving him behind," Nik assured her.

"No." The words flowed unbidden: "He's going to follow us."

"Then we'll face him. Together. You're not alone. You'll never be alone again. Show her, Laru and Rigel!"

First, from their two Companions, Mari was flooded with warmth and strength—and then she felt Cammy's touch, and Fortina's; then Fala, Captain, Mariah, Odin, Bast, and even little Chloe reached out to her in solidarity until she was bathed in such intense love and strength and hope that it drowned her fear.

She met Nik's gaze as her lover and mate smiled and said softly, "Hey, don't ever forget—we've got your back."

Mari knew Nik was right. Whatever was before them, they would face it—and defeat it. Together.

THE END . . . for now.